CLOUDS OVER RAVENSLEA

The Sequel to 'Ravenslea'

An Historical Novel by

Pamela M. Parry

Order this book online at www.trafford.com
or email orders@trafford.com

Most Trafford titles are also available at major online book retailers.

Note for Librarians: A cataloguing record for this book is available from Library and Archives Canada at www.collectionscanada.ca/amicus/index-e.html

Printed in Victoria, BC, Canada.

ISBN: 978-1-4269-1651-9 (sc)

Our mission is to efficiently provide the world's finest, most comprehensive book publishing service, enabling every author to experience success. To find out how to publish your book, your way, and have it available worldwide, visit us online at www.trafford.com

Trafford rev. 12/15/2009

www.trafford.com

North America & international
toll-free: 1 888 232 4444 (USA & Canada)
phone: 250 383 6864 ♦ fax: 812 355 4082

To my Husband

Robert

With Love

CHAPTER 1

AUGUST 1919 – ENGLAND

WITH the War to end all wars now fodder for the history buffs, it was time for military personnel, war correspondents, medical teams, along with arms and equipment to return home.

That wet August afternoon, Bristol's Temple Meads Station was crowded with almost every denomination of the military, looking anxiously around for the familiar, beloved face to appear among the throngs of people who were jostling for platform space. Emotions ran deep, as could be seen by the tears as family members converged on their military loved ones with hugs and kisses; relieved that they'd survived the dreadful conflict. After four long years of fierce fighting under deplorable conditions, this ghastly war had now officially ended in June with the signing of the Treaty of Versailles at Compeigne. Thousands of young men and women from both sides had lost their lives; not to mention others that had returned home with devastating injuries. The intervention of the United States in April of 1917 had sped up the end of the war, culminating in the capitulation of German oppression to the Allies.

James Thorncroft, who'd worked his way through university and military school to become a Captain in the Royal Engineers, stood apart from the hordes on the platform waiting for the train that would take him to Branton Station and his beautiful home of Ravenslea Manor. He cut a fine figure in his khaki uniform and well fitting peaked cap. Those who noticed him couldn't help but take a second look at this striking man standing unobtrusively alone.

Unaware of his enigmatic persona, James' thoughts turned to the last confrontation with the enemy on a particularly muddy battlefield near Verdun. He'd spent much of the time alongside inexperienced young British soldiers and the deaths of so many had sickened and appalled him. He recalled those difficult moments spent trying to keep his balance in makeshift trenches trudging through squelching mud and tripping over dead bodies of fallen soldiers. Then casting a weary eye across the muddy flat terrain, he knew he'd never forget the repulsion he felt when viewing the vacant, terrified eyes of dead horses along with their dead riders; the unspeakable smell and the absolute desolation. He shuddered at the atrocious events he and his men had experienced.

That dreadful moment when his brother-in-law, Arthur Ellison, who'd only been with James' regiment two months, had, on a wet, miserable afternoon, resisted the cautions of the rest of his unit to remain within the relative safety of the trench. James, noticing Arthur climbing out of the trench, had reached for his rifle in order to cover him should he be attacked. Arthur, after taking a quick glance around the area, ran blindly across a small portion of muddy battleground to reach an injured soldier. He dragged him awkwardly back to the trench, but as he lowered the man over the edge, for some reason that James would never know, Arthur turned to look behind him. Perhaps it was to see if there were more injured men he could reach. It was at that moment James saw the familiar headgear of a German soldier appear from behind a small crest in the landscape just a few yards away. As the German raised his rifle, so did James raise his. To James' dismay, the bullet jammed in the breach. Fortunately, the rifle had not exploded, but the delay allowed the enemy to take aim and shoot Arthur in the head. James shuddered at the recollection. He was sure he would never be able to erase that appalling moment from his memory.

His world was full of 'ifs'. If he had only checked his rifle earlier; if he'd seen Arthur a few moments before he'd decided to venture out into the open; if James had only given him a direct order to return to the trench. As there were so many 'ifs', James couldn't help but feel a certain responsibility for the manner in which Arthur had died.

He'd agonized over this from that moment on; he'd wake up at night sweating and moaning. Some of the other men had mentioned he'd talked in his sleep, though none of what he said made any sense to them. James began taking sedatives before retiring at night in an effort to stop the torment fermenting inside and he stubbornly refused to mention anything about it in letters to Catherine. What good would it do for her to know that he felt technically responsible for her brother's death? No, it was better that she hear from Colonel Cummings that Arthur had died a hero in order to save a friend.

A woman rushing along the platform jostled him out of his musings. James straightened and stared about. He drew his pipe to his lips and lit it abstractedly. It was ironic that the only wound he'd received in the war, which had resulted in a scar down the side of his right cheek, had been caused entirely by his own carelessness, yet Arthur and millions of others had made the supreme sacrifice.

Forcing the image of Arthur's death from his mind, he thought of his commanding officer, Colonel Colin Cummings. Despite all the activity at Temple Meads Station, James could see, in his mind's eye, Cummings back at headquarters striding up and down, his hands behind his back, his head bent in worried speculation. Provisions for his men as well as ammunition and medical supplies were quickly running out. If this part of France was to be saved, their only hope was that their communication system would continue working and other divisions would join the conflict. If that didn't happen, the continual bombardment would eventually annihilate the whole unit. James could only give an educated guess at his commanding officer's torment. Fortunately their lives had been saved by the intervention of two Canadian battalions. During that time, James' division had been able to move further north, but during the hasty evacuation, more men had become victims of enemy bullets.

Now, as he waited for the train, he relaxed, forcing the destructive thoughts away from the war with Germany and the devastation of the French landscape, to his lovely wife, Catherine and their three children, his eldest son, thirteen-year-old Eden; Rebecca who turned ten in July and Luke who would be eight in November. He wondered how the children had grown as he'd not been home on leave since he'd left England for France in 1914.

His daydream was suddenly interrupted by the arrival of a tall, slim woman approaching, her short fair hair slightly windblown. She seemed a little out of breath; the smile she offered to James one of warmth. A girl of around ten clutched her hand and as they drew near, she stared up at James, a look of wonder in her bright eyes.

"James!" The woman cried, letting go of the child's hand so she could draw him to her in a warm embrace. "How wonderful to see you again and to know you've survived this ghastly business. Catherine mentioned you'd probably be catching this train to Branton. I thought it would be nice if we could find you, so we could share a carriage. I'm glad you're so tall and commanding—I'm not sure if I'd have been able to find you otherwise amongst all these crowds."

He smiled at her and touched her cheek in a kiss. "Penelope! What a pleasant surprise! I would have thought you'd have avoided Temple Meads as much as possible these days, to stay with your injured husband."

"I had to visit one of my aunts—she had an accident a few days ago and as she lives alone, needed some help. My cousin has now arrived and I can return. Fletcher was amply cared for while I was away." She paused, her face clouding. She leaned down to clasp the child's hand in hers again. "As far as he is concerned, James, he's not as you remember him, but you will see him soon and can decide for yourself how much my husband has changed." She glanced down at the girl by her side. "This, by the way, is Stephanie—grown up a bit since you two last met."

James Thorncroft smiled down at the little girl. "Hello, Stephanie. I do remember you, my dear. You've certainly grown. You were only a wee little thing when I saw you last."

"Say hello to Uncle James, dear." Penelope Rhodes said, giving her a slight prod.

"Hello Uncle James." The girl said. She had big dark eyes, freckles were sprinkled across a small slightly up-tilted nose and her smile was shy as she looked up at the tall man in front of her. "I'm . . . glad you're home safe. I . . . I hear a lot about you from Rebecca, you know."

"Ah yes," James pushed his hat slightly further back on his dark hair. "She mentions you each time she writes. You've had a lot of adventures since I left, haven't you?"

She nodded. "Oh yes. William—you remember William my brother?" He nodded. "Well, he and Eden are always picking on Rebecca and me. They keep getting us into trouble . . . and . . ."

"I'm sure Uncle James won't wish to hear about that right now, dear." Penelope intervened quickly. She didn't wish her daughter to present James with details of some of the outlandish pranks those two boys would sometimes play on Rebecca and Stephanie. "Perhaps another time when he's nicely settled, you can tell him all about your adventures."

Stephanie grinned. "Well, Rebecca and I are the very best of friends and we don't intend to let William and Eden bully us as we grow older. We may be girls, you know, but we can fight back just as good as they can if we choose to. It's just that, well, we don't really choose to, not yet anyway." She straightened her back a little.

"Indeed I'm sure you and Rebecca will be quite able to put those boys in their place one of these days, Stephanie." James said, throwing a smile in Penelope's direction.

The three of them walked towards the edge of the platform together, trying to find a space that would accommodate them, without much success. They stood behind a group of young women who were giggling and pushing against each other girlishly. James noticed four army privates standing a few yards away and smothered a grin. Young people had been acting in that manner ever since time began. It would never change!

"Rebecca was quite upset, you know Uncle James, when you weren't able to be here for her birthday in July." Stephanie broke into his thoughts.

"I'm sure you must understand, Stephanie that I really couldn't do too much about that. I tried, but it was impossible." James replied.

"Are you going straight back to Ravenslea?" Penelope changed the subject, gazing openly into his bewitching violet eyes. She remembered those days long ago when she'd thought James would one day marry her. Now as she looked at him, she realized she still loved him and the knowledge gave her no comfort. She had lost him fair and square to her best friend, Catherine almost fifteen years earlier and had instead married Fletcher Rhodes who'd swept her off her feet, pushing her feelings for James temporarily to one side.

"I can't wait to get back, Pen." He said. "I've missed those years when my children changed from childhood. Oh, I know Rebecca and Luke are still young enough for me to enjoy them and to be able to take them on my knee and tell them tales. I would have liked to have done it with Eden, but I don't imagine he'd be too receptive at thirteen-years-old." He laughed at the comical look both Penelope and Stephanie threw him. "I wanted to be around while they were learning the rudiments of life" he continued, more sombrely, ". . . teach them things that only a father can; play their baby games with them." James sighed. "Well, I suppose I'll have to wait until I get some grandchildren before I'll be able to do that."

The noisy arrival of a steam engine prohibited more conversation as it entered the railway station, chugging slowly along the shiny track, belching ghostly wisps of steam between its wheels and the side of the platform. Everyone instinctively pulled back and once the engine had stopped, porters began opening doors for passengers to alight, and for new passengers to embark.

Together they moved towards an empty carriage and Stephanie jumped inside in an effort to secure the carriage just for the three of them. James handed Penelope into the carriage and joined them. After stowing all the baggage onto the compartment above the seats he promptly seated himself. Moments later, the whistle sounded, more doors slammed shut; luckily, no-one else entered the carriage. Puffs of grey steam swirled and billowed around the platform outside the grimy window, sending slivers of oily vapours through the slightly open window. James leaned over and pulled the window tightly shut against the offending odour.

"I know Catherine wanted to come and meet you, James. We would be delighted for you to share our vehicle should Percy not turn up." Penelope looked over at him expectantly.

"I'm sure Percy will be here; he's very astute and reliable. Thank you anyway."

"Well, we must make sure we all get together for dinner one night once you're settled in of course. I know Fletcher is longing to meet you and talk military strategy and the like to you. I'm not happy about him discussing such things that will bring back his grief, but knowing him, I'm sure he won't be able to stop himself." She managed a smile and glanced down at her hands.

"Is he cognizant of his surroundings, Pen?" James asked, softly.

She nodded. "He knows where he is and is sometimes coherent, but there are times when he becomes quite difficult. He needs constant nursing." She said, catching her lip anxiously. "I tried to tend him myself, but it . . . it became too difficult, so the doctor thought it best for us to have a nurse take care of him. She lives with us and is very competent. I know Fletcher is happy to allow her to fuss around him—in fact, I think he secretly likes the attention she gives him."

"Well, at least you have help, my dear. I must make a concerted effort to come over in a few days to visit with him, if he's rested enough to have visitors."

"Oh, I'm sure daddy would love you to come over, Uncle James," Stephanie said quickly. "He often mentions you and wonders how you're doing."

For the rest of the journey, James and his companions talked amiably and by the time the train whistled and steamed noisily into Branton's small station, they'd come up to date on a number of interesting facts.

"Well, James, do say hello to Catherine and the children for us." Penelope said, leaning up and kissing him gently on the cheek. "We will arrange a dinner party for you once you've settled in."

"I look forward to that, thanks Pen." He glanced down at Stephanie and grinned. "You'll have to tell me all about your adventures one of these days, Stephanie. I feel I have missed so much of all your lives being so far away and for so long."

"Oh, there are lots of things to tell you, Uncle James, but we'll wait until later for that." Stephanie laughed. She pulled away from her mother, skipping happily ahead as they left the station together.

James watched the little girl with amusement. What a delightful child. She seemed full of fun and life and as he wandered out of the station onto the damp road, he hoped he'd find his daughter with the same, enigmatic spirit.

The rain that had been bouncing off the streets in Bristol, had subsided as he moved from Branton station onto the narrow road that would eventually lead him home. Now a layer of heavy mist encompassed the area. He took a deep breath. The pure, fresh fragrance of the Devonshire countryside re-vitalized him and he felt a contented warmth invade his senses.

As he stood outside, he watched as Penelope and Stephanie passed him in their black Armstrong Siddely with their chauffeur, Barnaby at the wheel. The older man touched his cap to him and gave him a smile as he passed.

At the same time another vehicle came into view. As it pulled up alongside James, the long bonnet with the silver emblem gracing the front, reflected the dullness of the afternoon in its smooth mirror finish. The door opened and a short stocky man of about fifty stepped out.

"Captain Thorncroft? Percy Plummer, Sir. John's uncle. I was available when your family needed a chauffeur since my nephew sadly went missing at sea, so your dear wife hired me."

"I'm pleased to meet you Percy. I did hear about John and am extremely sad for your whole family. Please give my condolences to his parents when you next see them."

Percy opened the passenger door of the shining Rolls Sedanca and moved aside. "I will, Captain and I'm pleased to know you survived this dreadful business." He stowed James' gear into the boot of the car and smiled at him as he slipped behind the steering wheel. "They all wanted to come to meet you, but as the car will not hold that many, they all stayed behind."

James raised an eyebrow and returned the smile. " I can imagine, especially Eden and Luke. When did we get this vehicle?"

"Oh, Mr. Martin decided to buy it the moment he knew you'd be coming home. It's a surprise and we all hope you like it."

James grinned, allowing his hand to caress the fine brown leather interior gently. "It's a beautiful vehicle and certainly looks expensive; but that's my brother all over. He must always have the best." He closed the door and sat back against the leather upholstery with content. "Fire away, Percy—I need to get home as fast as I can."

The ride was swift. Despite his growing years, Percy's prowess behind the wheel reminded James very much of the young John, though he confessed to himself that John took just a little more risks than did his uncle. However, meeting no traffic except a man on a bicycle, they arrived unscathed at the gates to Ravenslea Manor. Percy slowed the vehicle, knowing his passenger would want to have some time to view the property he'd not seen for so many years.

James surveyed the large impressive house handed down from his great, great Grandfather in the 18th Century. The devastating fire of 1904 had made it necessary to carry out extensive renovations. The Music Room had been the only room that had not fallen victim to damage and as such, it had been decided to extend it to incorporate a ballroom. Once that ballroom had been built, Catherine, her sister Sophie and James' stepmother, Elizabeth, had travelled throughout Britain in search of appropriate antiques that would grace the beautiful room. They had done a marvellous job and he could hardly wait for the moment when they'd be able to once again invite friends and relatives to festive occasions.

All these thoughts took seconds to filter through his mind as Percy stopped half way down the driveway. James was jolted back to the present as Ravenslea's tall oak door was suddenly flung open. There in the middle of the top step came his darling wife, Catherine, a slight wind blowing tendrils of dark hair over her forehead. She waved to him and as she did so, he saw his father, Jonathon and stepmother standing close beside her. A moment later, his children appeared, waving frantically. Luke ran helter-skelter down the steps down the wide pathway to meet him. James wound down the window.

"Hop in, Luke!" He cried, turning the handle to allow his youngest inside the vehicle.

The boy happily jumped onto his father's lap, enveloping him in hugs and cries of delight. He was talking so fast, James laughed and tweaked his nose affectionately.

"Whoa there, son! I can't understand a word you're saying."

The car pulled up at the bottom of the steps where, by now, the whole family had convened. James picked up his son and planted him firmly on the ground, then stepped out of the car, straight to where Catherine, with tears in her eyes, held out her arms for him.

"Oh, my darling James!" She kissed him long and hard on his lips. "How I've longed for this moment. You'll never know just how much …" She suddenly noticed the scar down the side of his face and traced it gently with her fingers. "You are hurt, my love. You didn't mention anything in your letters?"

"It is nothing to be concerned about, my love." James said, smiling down at her. "I'll tell you about it later." He kissed her on the forehead. "You said you missed me . . . you just don't know how much I've missed you . . ." He hugged her closer.

When they drew away from each other, he caught a whiff of the familiar fragrance she was wearing and despite all the other odours he'd encountered over the past few years, he recognized it as the perfume he'd bought for her the day he'd left England. "I hope and pray there'll never be another war like this one."

More conversation was impossible, as Rebecca and Eden joined them. Rebecca's eyes were bright from unshed tears; Eden's face a picture of relief. In between the happy tears, laughs and constant embraces, James suddenly felt more loved than he'd ever been before! His father drew him into his arms, thankful at last to have his son back home again; while his stepmother gently pulled him away to hug her stepson possessively.

"Welcome home, James." Jonathon looked into his son's eyes, thinking how very much he resembled his own father, Leighton Thorncroft. The violet eyes had been handed down to the Thorncroft men throughout the generations in the most unusual manner and today James' eyes were glistening with love and relief. There were tiny lines of endured hardship etched at the corners of his eyes and a deep scar to the side of his mouth, but other than that, James Thorncroft looked as elegant and handsome as he'd ever looked. "How was the journey home?" Jonathon wanted to talk about the war, but knew this was not the time. James had to forget, at least for now, what he'd experienced. Jonathon would not be the one to bring it back to him.

"Apart from constant rain and hot sweaty soldiers on the train from London, it was remarkably good." James grinned. "Anything . . . anything at all has to be far more wonderful than anything I've just been through."

Jonathon nodded. "Yes, James, I quite understand. But we must not bring all that back to you right now. There's food on the table and a warm, cosy bed for you tonight." He glanced impishly at his daughter-in-law. She smiled back with not a trace of embarrassment.

James grinned. "All very acceptable."

They all trudged into the large house where someone, Elspeth the house-keeper James thought, slipped his damp raincoat off him and disappeared into the Kitchen with it.

"Was there lots of killing, Daddy?" Luke said, pressing close to him, his light eyes looking up into his father's handsome face with wonder.

Catherine broke in hurriedly. "Luke, dear, we don't wish to discuss this now. Daddy's home and we want to tell him all our news."

"But . . . I want to know if . . ."

"No Luke. Not now!" Her voice was firm and Luke's face fell, knowing he'd have to wait until later to hear about the horrors that had befallen his father.

Once the children had gone to bed after supper that evening, Catherine, not knowing that Arthur had been in her husband's regiment, told him that her brother had been killed.

"So, dear, Martin has taken Allison, as well as Meg and the children to Scotland for a week. He thought that if Meg were to see you so soon after Arthur's death, it would bring it all back; that under different circumstances she too would be welcoming Arthur home. She's completely devastated as is Faith. Little David didn't ever get to know his father, but Faith did and she adored him."

"I'm so sorry, Catherine." James reached over and caught her trembling hand in his. Mentioning Catherine's brother brought the dreadful business back, but he pushed it to one side. For now, he'd carry on as if he knew nothing about it. Arthur Ellison had been one of the most honest, kindest men he'd ever known. There had never been a time in his life when Catherine's brother had not come through at times when illness or worry had incapacitated any member of the Thorncroft family. His wife, Meg loved him unconditionally and Faith now nine years old had followed his pursuits relentlessly while he was away. Now that she knew he would never return, she had become unnaturally withdrawn and uncommunicative. This situation had not helped Meg who'd tried to keep her youngest, David free of this unhappy situation, and feeling as if she'd failed miserably.

"Going away had been the best thing for them all, James," Catherine broke into his thoughts.

"That's characteristic of Martin to take Meg under his wing. I know he's always liked her."

As James thought of his brother, he winced. He knew Martin had wanted to join the army, but a couple of months before war broke out, Martin had been injured. A horse he'd been attending had shied. Martin had lost his balance and slipped between its prancing hooves. Unfortunately he'd not moved quickly enough to stop the horse's hooves from trampling his left foot. He lost three toes. As walking was impossible at that time, his injury eliminated him from any involvement in the conflict. He'd applied to work with the Home Guard, but that had been turned down as well. So he promised James he would care for Ravenslea until his return. Martin was always optimistic his effervescent brother would not die on a French battlefield. He utterly refused to allow anyone to think or speak otherwise.

That night, when the sun had gone down and a bright crescent moon hung in a dark sky overhead, James joined his wife in their bedroom. He could sense her vulnerability and overt shyness as they undressed silently in the room lit only by a single lamp at the side of the bed. It was almost a replica of their wedding night all those years ago and he felt a twinge of excitement at the prospect of once more holding his beloved wife to him again.

She leaned up on one elbow in the bed to watch as one garment after another fell to the floor. The moonlight filtering through the window, cast a glow on the side of his face.

"You were going to tell me what caused the scar, darling?" She asked.

"My own fault, Cath. You couldn't possibly know how dreadful the trenches were over there. They were muddy and abominably slippery. I did just that—slipped and scraped the side of my face against the tip of a bayonet laying beside a sleeping enlisted man. I was lucky it missed my eye." He looked down at her, loving the way her forehead crinkled in concern for him. "The blade cut the side of my cheek which bled profusely, but I managed to get to the medics who stemmed the blood. Unfortunately, I was told I will always have that scar to remind me of less pleasanter days."

"So long as it doesn't worry you, James, it makes not the slightest difference to me. You're still the same man I fell in love with and married—nothing will ever change that." She leaned forward and caught his hand in hers. She patted the empty side for him to join her. As they slowly began to rekindle their love, the last five years melted away as if it had never really transpired at all.

CHAPTER 2

THE first few days of James' arrival at Ravenslea were full of contentment and peace. Even the sun appeared to shine with more intensity and warmth. With the war now over, it only remained for James to pick up the pieces of life at Ravenslea again. He slept contentedly for the first couple of nights, wrapped in the warm comfort of his wife's arms, her kisses sweet as he remembered them and his heart was full with love for her.

Doris, the upstairs maid introduced James to the scullery maid, Edna. Small in stature with a round face and delightful smile, she immediately made a good impression on him. He was glad Doris had someone to help her at Ravenslea. The reason for Catherine hiring young Edna was because Doris was finding it increasingly difficult now to cover every area each day. She needed some help. Catherine was only too willing to engage the easy-going young woman and told James she was quite a treasure.

"Doris has her changing sheets, doing the laundry among other lesser chores. The arrangement is working out very well. Agnes is happy with her and even Elspeth hasn't had any altercations with her."

Instead of the 'iffy' kinds of food James was served on the front, his meals at Ravenslea were plentiful and tasty and the laughter that emanated around him during mealtimes was like nectar. He'd take frequent jaunts around the gardens he loved, re-familiarized himself with the tenants and became once more involved in the affairs of Ravenslea. He began to relax, aware that all this activity had, for the moment, shelved the horrors of the war.

Eden, Rebecca and Luke were his constant companions. Rebecca, her dark hair loose and flyaway, catching hold of his hand at every opportunity they were together. He was glad to see she'd grown up much in the same way as her good friend Stephanie—obviously that intelligent child had had a positive effect on his daughter. Eden was happy to have him home and one day took him to the stables to see the new pony they'd bought for Luke. Luke was in his element— he'd named the pony Shadow because whenever he was in the paddock, the animal followed in his wake, whinnying crossly when Luke left him to move back into the stables. Luke, loving animals the way he did, couldn't get enough of that devotion. He danced around with energy and glee delighted to show his father how proficient he was at riding it.

James' twin brother, Martin was ecstatic that his brother had returned home as he'd predicted. His foot remained troublesome, although it was less pronounced than when James had left. He still walked with a limp and required the use of a wooden cane with a silver head of a phoenix at the top of the handle to keep him mobile.

Martin's 20 year old daughter Allison was overjoyed that her beloved Uncle James had returned virtually unharmed from the bitter conflict. She loved her uncle and aunt, having shared a mutually disagreeable time when her mother had been alive. Her Aunt Catherine had proved her worth in a hundred ways since Martin Thorncroft's wife, Amelia's unfortunate death in 1904 and Allison still had no inkling as to why her mother had been so hurtful to her sister-in-law during the time they lived at Ravenslea together. Martin's only daughter had blossomed into a beautiful young woman with red-gold hair and amazingly blue-green eyes that crinkled when she laughed.

Arthur's attractive widow, Meg and her children along with Nora, Catherine's mother, visited for an afternoon, but they didn't stay long. As Catherine had predicted, Meg's grief was transparent and whenever she looked at James, tears were near the surface. Although James had discarded the uniform, the knowledge that he'd survived when her husband hadn't was difficult for Meg to accept although she tried desperately not to let her grief show.

However, these wonderful days recouping the joys of his life at Ravenslea, were shadowed when one early morning he awoke with Arthur's name on his lips. He had been tossing and turning in mental torment as he'd done at camp and awakened Catherine.

"James! James . . . you're having a nightmare!" She jostled him lightly and he groggily stopped crying out to turn sleep-induced eyes towards her.

"Oh, Cath. What did I say? Was it terrible?" He imagined he'd revealed some of the atrocities he'd seen and couldn't bear for her to hear what he'd actually witnessed on the battlefield. All the bloody bodies, the cries of pain, the deplorable conditions . . .

"Darling," she murmured, kissing him lightly on his damp forehead. "You . . . you mentioned Arthur. Are you still thinking of what I told you?"

He was silent for a moment, caught his teeth against his lower lip and pulled himself up against the pillow encircling Catherine to him.

"I do have something to say to you." He said, trying not to yawn. "Something I should have told you the moment I set foot in the house."

"Go on, dear." She said, softly.

"I didn't tell you that Arthur was in my regiment." She didn't speak, but he heard her intake of breath. "I'm sorry, but . . . he was transferred from another unit and had been with us for only a short while . . ." He relayed to her as delicately as he could the circumstances surrounding her brother's untimely death, feeling the tension building up in him with every word he spoke. He felt her stiffen beside him. "I feel dreadfully responsible, Catherine. I should have checked my rifle before even moving into the trench. I'm so sorry, my love, I feel I could have saved his life had I only . . ."

She looked up at him, his face ashen in the moonlit room. She placed a finger against his lips.

"No one is blaming you, my dear. There were other soldiers in the trench . . .

they could have done exactly the same as you. There's no blame to be attached to anyone." She sighed. "Arthur was a wonderful man, a loving brother, son and husband, but he did things on the spur of the moment—sometimes without thought for his own safety. The only good thing that came out of this act was that he'd saved a man's life. If he can see us, James, I know he would not put any guilt on you. Please . . . please, my dear, nothing can come of you fretting this way; you will always remember it, I'm sure, but you must let it go. You must not let it ruin the rest of your life—Arthur, especially, would not wish that to happen." She leaned up and kissed him. "Now, please try and get some sleep."

He kissed her long and hard, hugging her so close to him he could feel her heart beating rapidly beneath her thin nightgown. Having finally told Catherine the truth, James relaxed and managed to sleep all through that night.

CHAPTER 3

ONE day at the beginning of September, James' half-sister, Fern and her husband, Simon Danby, arrived at Ravenslea. Fern, a sprightly forty year old, had worked diligently as a nurse in a London hospital during most of the war. She'd applied many times for a transfer to the front, but although she was well qualified, it appeared they needed her expertise more readily in Britain taking care of the many thousands of military injured. She'd been disappointed, but soon realized that nurses were in short demand and those that stayed in Britain were subjected to working anything up to sixteen hours a day. Fern, luckily, had a strong constitution and had thrown herself into the disorderly turmoil with feverish activity.

Simon returned to his regiment in India later that month, so Catherine asked her sister-in-law if she'd like to stay at Ravenslea for a while. Fern, not actively employed at the moment, jumped at the chance. She loved Ravenslea with a passion and to stay here again would be a Heaven sent opportunity for her. Her children, Emily at nineteen and Constance, fifteen, joined her and the three of them became integral parts of the household. Emily, an image of her sparkling mother, brought joy and laughter to the household, while Constance lived up to her name, being more cautious and conservative in her approach to life. The two girls complemented each other most favourably.

That same month James and Catherine along with their three children and Allison, were able to finally take the family over to Cavendish Hall. It was close to four o'clock on a fresh, cool afternoon when they eventually left to make the short, pleasant drive. An unusual layer of frost crackled on little puddles in the road. What a difference to the mud and slime James remembered enduring in France. This land, this beautiful England, was a delight to his senses and he stared enraptured at every passing tree and bush on his way, wondering why he'd ever taken such things for granted in the past.

Percy, happy behind the wheel, began whistling a tune that James recognized immediately and began to sing along with him, his true baritone voice filling the car with melody. "It's a Long Way to Tipperary" was one of the most popular songs that were sung during lulls in the fighting. James remembered the men laughing and singing to the tops of their voices whenever someone would pull a harmonica from his pocket to play the familiar and riveting songs. It was good to see the relief on the war-torn faces, if only for a short time.

As they approached Cavendish Hall, Percy drew the car to a stop outside the gates. He turned to James sitting beside him.

"Do you wish to walk down the driveway, Sir? I was told that you do like the walk whenever you visit."

This time James shook his head. "No, Percy, we'll drive down today."

"Very well."

Penelope greeted them with great enthusiasm. She ushered them into the Drawing Room where they found her husband in a burgundy robe sitting in a high-backed chair near a small fire. His feet were encased in slippers and rested lightly on a tapestry pouffe. Fletcher was delighted to see his friend again and they talked animatedly together for almost an hour. When Penelope called them to dinner, James helped Fletcher into the Dining Room appalled to see how frail his friend had become. He remembered Penelope's husband as being a robust, healthy man, full of energy and fun. The war had reduced him to a shadow of his former self.

Fletcher glanced at him. "I can make it." He said, as James helped him settle in a dining chair at the head of the table. "I'm not going to be like this forever, my friend. I intend to beat this thing—my nurse has told me I'm improving every day. I hold onto that and think positively all the time."

"That's the only way to think, Fletcher." James grinned down at him as he pulled out the chair on his left and seated himself. "You just need rest, nourishment for your mind and body. It's going to take a while, but you must stick with it."

"I intend to. I definitely intend to. I don't want to spend the rest of my life . . . like this and for my lovely Penelope's sake I must make an effort to regain my health." He paused as a woman in her late twenties came into the room wearing a white hat stuck jauntily on her fluffy fair head; a smart, starched apron covered her light blue gown.

"Good evening. You must be Captain Thorncroft." She said, addressing James as she neared her patient. "It is good to see you safe home. My name is Ida Munroe—Major Rhodes' nurse."

James pushed back his chair, stood up and grasped her small hand warmly. "I'm pleased to meet you, Nurse Munroe. From the look of your patient, you seem to be doing something right."

She laughed and glanced over at Penelope who was smiling at her. "Thank you. Major Rhodes is a wonderful patient; he never complains when I give him the occasional order or two and although he grimaces when I sometimes have to give him an injection, he gives me no trouble. I have to thank Mrs. Rhodes for a lot of my success. Without her help, it might not have been quite so easy."

"Nonsense, Ida dear." Penelope said. "You are a dedicated young woman and I know it's your encouraging and cheerful outlook as well as your expertise as a nurse that is slowly bringing my husband back to me."

As Ida Munroe fixed a white dinner napkin under Fletcher's chin and pushed his chair nearer the table, James took the moment to look around the group. His daughter, Rebecca was in deep conversation with Stephanie, while Eden chatted amiably with Stephanie's brother, William. Luke was playing with his napkin and listening half-heartedly to something his mother was saying. On the other side of the table Allison, never a person for trivial conversation, surveyed everything with contentment. It was a pleasant scene, warm and congenial.

Later, James singled out Ida Munroe and guided her into the Music Room, sitting her down near the small lit fire. He'd mentioned his intentions to Catherine earlier that he wanted to have a chat to the nurse, so when the opportunity arose, he grabbed it. He had to know just how damaging Fletcher's injuries were; he had an idea everything wasn't quite as it was being conveyed to them that evening.

"Tell me straight, Nurse Munroe," he came straight to the point, "what are Fletcher's chances of a complete recovery?"

She hesitated and glanced down at the small hands in her lap. "I am not a doctor, you understand, Captain, but I do know that Major Rhodes is a long way from being as he was before he was wounded." She paused and stared ahead. "Shrapnel shattered his left leg making walking almost impossible for him. This was taken out in the medical tent on the battlefield to enable him to make his journey home, but his leg is extremely sore and we're having a difficult job treating the infection. He also sustained a serious head wound. With the two afflictions, it was touch and go for a while, but he's a fighter with a strong heart, thank goodness. However, he occasionally sinks into melancholia; when he gets overtired, he gets extremely agitated. This often results in rather violent mood swings. It's then that I have to administer an injection. It calms him down immediately, and usually he slips into a deep sleep."

"Do you believe his leg will heal enough to enable him to walk properly again?"

She turned her head slightly. "I can't say at the moment, but I have every confidence that the treatment we're giving him will eventually stop any infection from spreading to other parts of his body."

"What about the melancholia? Is there a cure for that?" James frowned, worrying now about how Penelope would be able to cope in the future if Ida Munroe could no longer care for Fletcher.

She shrugged. "There is always ongoing research for these kinds of maladies. Many of our young soldiers have returned with similar disabilities and have recovered, so there is a good chance for Major Rhodes. At the moment, though, his prognosis is not good."

"Does Mrs. Rhodes know?"

"Oh yes. She insisted on knowing everything about her husband's injuries and the doctor has told me to make sure she's kept aware of his progress on a daily basis." She paused and looked into James' warm violet eyes. "He's a strong man if anyone can overcome this, I know he will do his very best."

James nodded abstractedly. "If Mrs. Rhodes needs our help in any way, please be sure to contact us. We're not that far away."

"I certainly will, thank you." Ida said. "I'll ask Barnaby to ride over if necessary."

"Thanks. We want to make sure Mrs. Rhodes is coping all right. I know my wife would want to come over to be with her, no matter what. They were inseparable as children and have been very close over the years." James suddenly stood up.

Ida arose and straightened her uniform. "Well, if there's nothing more, Captain, I must return. My patient may be requiring my attention."

"Thank you, Nurse Munroe. I appreciate your frankness."

James watched her small, slight figure move out of the Music Room. So, apart from his obvious leg infliction, Fletcher was having mental difficulties. Well, it was to be expected. James knew that Fletcher's regiment had been stationed on the Somme. It was common knowledge that there had been terrible losses there, but some of those who had not succumbed to their wounds, had returned to Britain with mind altering stress, not to mention loss of body parts.

He shuddered. It had been a Hellish War and as he wandered back to the rest of the family, he wondered what the future held for them all. It would take a while for both Germany and the Allies to return to a normal existence again; he had a premonition that life was going to take some unusual twists and turns as the decades ebbed and waned into the future.

CHAPTER 4

JUNE 1930 – THE DESDEMONA

THE Desdemona gently swayed against the side of the dock, its sails tightly bound to their booms. In the gathering dusk, seagulls swooped screaming, circling around its empty decks. The beautiful ketch that many years ago, had made its one and only voyage to the United States, now lay in melancholy repose as it had done for the past eight months. Barnacles grew freely on its hull and keel.

Eden Thorncroft leaned against a fence post looking down from a sharp incline, his slim face in shadow from the setting sun, his dark features sombre, bright violet eyes transfixed with sadness on the long sleek vessel before him. After a while, he began the slow descent towards the deserted wharf, relishing the exhilarating aroma of fresh seaweed and kelp that wafted up to greet him. As he drew nearer, a sudden rush of wind pushed the Desdemona away from the dock, its rigging jarring melodiously against the mast poles. To him, it sounded like a cry from the heart to make use of her.

The thrill of the sea was stamped in his soul as it was in his father's, but although James had taken her out on short trips around the coast, everyone could tell he'd lost the desire to sail since his Aunt Deanna and her brilliant lawyer husband, David Hallett had drowned five years previously. It'd been one of those spooky moments when in a matter of seconds, a sudden squall had sent the couple over the ship's rail. Deanna's gallant husband had tried desperately to save his frantic wife, but though a strong swimmer himself, had failed, losing his own life in the attempt. Eden, who was nineteen at the time, had jumped into the choppy, icy waters along with his father and Uncle Simon, but it had taken them considerable time to locate and bring the bodies back to the surface.

Eden shivered as he vividly recalled the tragedy. He'd been fond of his great aunt and uncle and even after all this time, still missed their vitality and warmth. He knew that by dwelling on a situation that he could not change, would only bring heartbreak to himself and to those around him. He shook himself thrusting the bad memory behind, bringing himself back to the present. He cast his eyes again to the gently rocking boat, pushing a wisp of windswept dark hair from his brow.

Jumping nimbly onto the dock towards the bobbing vessel, he laid a tawny hand on the sturdy brass rail, loving its smooth coolness which warmed almost instantly to his touch. The breeze again ruffled his hair, teasing dark tendrils across his forehead as his eyes skimmed past the edge of the dock to where the Bristol Channel joined the Atlantic Ocean.

His father had decided to auction off the Desdemona. Eden was sad to think that someone else would be walking her decks and was certain that the lovely vessel would never be treated as well as the Thorncrofts had treated her. Lovingly keeping her royal blue paintwork gleaming; polishing the oak inside and out as well as keeping the upholstery inside the small compact cabins spotlessly clean. He despised the idea, but it was father's craft and he could do with it as he wished. Eden, now 24 years of age had taken over the helm on the last two occasions they took the ship out to sea. James had congratulated him on the way he'd handled the voyage, advising him to attend nautical college to study navigation in an endeavour to finally receive his ticket.

"Once you've got that, my son," Eden remembered his father saying, "I'll have no real worries that you can't handle her."

Learning navigational skills had been, at first, a little harrowing, but after a great deal of encouragement from his father and Uncle Martin, Eden had soon mastered it. He only had a few more months to go before getting his Master's ticket. He could hardly wait for that.

Now, as he stood there, his thoughts turned to his mother. Perhaps the remembrance of her unpleasant voyage to the United States on their honeymoon all those years ago had helped influence his father in selling the Desdemona. Eden remembered them telling him, that his mother had suffered abominably with sea-sickness, as the voyage had been plagued by rough seas. At that time, James and Martin, along with their older cousin, George Thorncroft, Fern's husband, Simon and David Hallett, their brother in law together with two young men they'd hired, made up the crew. Luckily no-one had been hurt and the boat arrived in New York Harbour safely. Its return to Bristol had been beset with much the same problems. Shortly after their return, James had installed more efficient navigational instruments on the Desdemona.

Despite imploring his lovely wife to take another chance when he told her he was contemplating sailing to the Irish Coast, Catherine had adamantly refused never to set foot on the Desdemona again, so the trip was abandoned. She rarely spoke of it, but a year ago Eden and Luke had heard their parents discussing possibly taking the same trip. His father had implored her to accompany them. She again refused, trying desperately to discourage him. Her argument being that if a squall could take the lives of Deanna and David, it could also take the lives of others on the ship. Anything could happen while at sea and Eden remembered her calling his father 'foolhardy and reckless' but no matter what she'd said, he'd summoned up his regular crew and made the short trip to Ireland's Wexford Harbour on the mouth of the River Slaney.

The young man pursed his mouth in thought. If his mother was the reason behind his father's desire to sell the Desdemona, then perhaps he should be talking to her? He had a good rapport with his mother—it might be a solution. If Eden could convince her that his father should not allow the tragedy to impact the lives of the crew, perhaps he would change his mind. It was worth a try and no harm would be done if she had no luck convincing him.

Despite his rising spirits, he soon felt deflated again. Somehow, he didn't think he'd have much success talking to his mother, feeling the way she did about the ship, but at least it was a try. The Desdemona had been in the family all his life—selling her would cause a lot of resentment with those who had loved to sail on her, not the least, his Aunt Fern. He brightened. If he had no luck with his mother, then surely Fern would be the next best to talk to James.

As he stood there, pondering how to approach this problem, he suddenly decided he needed someone with whom to share his despondency. Luke. Yes, he'd discuss this with Luke who also loved the ship, especially now as he invariably came, not as a crew-member but as a photographer to chronologically categorize the ship's journey in photographs. That, along with James' log, told a more thorough story of each trip. The Desdemona was as much an enjoyable part of his life as it was Eden's and the brothers were as adept at handling her as were their father. One of Luke's great talents was his wonderful charisma and enviable talent of being able to influence people into seeing his way of thinking. This ability often caused unrest between the brothers, but perhaps this time it would work in their favour.

Eden drew away from the dock, quickening his step back up the rest of the ramp towards the Lagonda he'd been given by his parents for his 21st birthday a few years ago.

He knew Luke was home in his Studio developing negatives. Luke's expertise as a photographer had become quite well-known in the immediate vicinity of Branton and district. Although only eighteen years old, he'd built up quite a clientele in the village. As a result, his parents had decided to re-vamp one of the upstairs bedrooms to incorporate a dark room for him. Here he worked with dogged persistence in perfecting the best photographs he could with the more recent equipment he'd had installed. His parents had given him a little Brownie camera on his 12th birthday. It had been the best present he'd ever received as he'd found a tremendous achievement when challenged with the occasional difficult shot. Although he'd now purchased a more sophisticated model of camera, he would never completely abandon his Brownie. Now he had it encased in glass on a shelf in his Studio—he knew he'd never dispose of it! He'd grown to love creating photographs, two of which were proudly displayed on the walls of his mother's favourite restaurant in Branton.

A ribbon of pale orange light beamed down the steps from the open front door as he drew the vehicle towards Ravenslea Manor. Elspeth stood there, an uncharacteristic smile on her thin face. Of all the people in this house, Eden knew that he was her favourite. While she'd give wooden, sometimes surly, expressions to everyone else, she always afforded him a smile. When he was little he remembered that all he had to do was give her one of his all-encompassing angelic smiles and she would reward him with little treats from the Kitchen! Rebecca and Luke had never received such special treatment from the austere housekeeper.

"Your father's in the Sitting Room, Master Eden. He has a surprise for you."

She said.

He raised an eyebrow. Now what was he up to . . . he'd been so secretive lately, as if he had something to impart that would shock everyone.

"Thanks, Elspeth. Is Luke in?"

"I believe so—in his Studio."

He ran lightly up the steps in through the front door, closing it gently behind him. Quickly slipping off his brown boots, he hurried into the Sitting Room, anxious to know what surprise his father had for him. Perhaps he'd decided at last to forego the sale of the Desdemona, yet even as he thought it, he discarded it. Opening the door, he glanced inside and saw his father talking to a man who had his back to the door. Puzzled, Eden stopped, caught his lip and slowly walked towards them. They both turned at his approach and the stranger, after first hesitating, afforded him a wide smile, stood up and held out a slim hand.

"Eden! Eden, my boy! How nice to see you again?"

Eden's face broke into a grin as he took the man's hand shaking it warmly. "Uncle Martin! What are you doing in England? I thought New York was your home now?"

The slim man, who was a shade shorter than Eden's father, laughed happily. "Didn't anyone tell you?" He glanced at his twin brother quickly. "Shame on you, James!" James Thorncroft pursed his lips and shook his head, but made no comment. "That was remiss of you." Martin moved away from James and slipped an arm across Eden's shoulders. "You know I got married—he told you that, didn't he?"

Eden nodded. "Actually, mother told us. She received a letter some time back saying you'd met this widow—a fairy tale romance, she said, and that you and she instantly fell in love." He paused, a mischievous smile playing around his sensuous mouth. "I, personally, don't believe anyone could do that, but she was adamant that was what you told her in the letter. Who am I to disbelieve it?"

"Believe it, Eden—it's as true as the fact that your parents did the very same thing!" He laughed. "You have to meet her, Eden, she's adorable. I'd like to introduce you to her and her children. Though, as they are both older than you I can't technically call them children." Martin Thorncroft's eyes twinkled as he surveyed his handsome nephew, knowing his stepdaughter would be quite taken with him. "So, dear boy, you must meet your new Aunt and step cousins. I think your mother has taken them for a tour of the house."

At that moment, the door burst open and four people wandered in, laughing amiably. The three men turned as Catherine walked towards them, smiling.

"Ah, so you've returned, Eden. Just in time to meet your new aunt and step cousins." Catherine turned and motioned for Martin's petite wife to venture further into the room, followed by a tall man with neatly trimmed moustache and light brown curly hair. He appeared to be in his late twenties or early thirties. The young woman at his side was extraordinarily attractive. Eden couldn't help but be fascinated by her sexuality as she looked at him with interest.

Martin's wife held out her hand, grasping Eden's warmly. "Hello, Eden. I am Louise. It's wonderful to finally meet you. Martin has spoken so favourably of you, your brother and sister that we've all been longing to actually see you in person. We met Luke earlier—a fine young man with a wonderful talent." She turned to her family. "This is my daughter Christiana and Adam my son."

Christiana smiled. "Pleased to meet you Eden." She said, her voice unusually low.

Eden pressed his lips together. He glanced quickly at the young woman. She leaned forward grabbing his hand with fervour. An annoying flush tinged his cheeks. Why did he always do that when faced with women?

"Hello, Christiana." He said, politely, catching hold of the small hand and letting it go rapidly as if it had stung him.

Adam moved forward. He was considerably taller than Eden, slimmer in build with close-cropped light brown hair. He held out his hand which Eden gripped firmly. "Great to see you, Eden. I echo Mother's comments—it's good to put a face to the name and hope we'll become good friends."

"I see no reason why not, Adam." Eden smiled gripping the older man's extended hand. He turned to Martin's new wife. "Are you staying here in England now, or is this just a short visit?"

"Oh, I'm not intending to return to the States, dear. I want to stay in England indefinitely." Aunt Louise said in her attractive New England accent. She joined Martin on the couch, catching his hand in hers affectionately. "I would so much like to be living here at Ravenslea Manor with you all. Of course, we would not wish to be an encumbrance—but also, I would not like to vacate the beautiful bedrooms you have so kindly assigned to us, Catherine."

Catherine smiled. "We are only too happy you decided to come to England, Louise. We missed Martin and it's only right and fitting that we all be together. Ravenslea is large enough to accommodate you with no difficulty at all." She glanced at Adam and Christiana who were sitting apart from each other on the adjacent sofa. "Are you happy with your rooms?"

Christiana threw her a wide, toothy smile. "I am indeed, Aunt Catherine. I love looking out the window and seeing those beautiful trees not so very far away and to hear the noises of the black birds in the woods."

"They are ravens, my dear." James said. "There used to be an abundance of ravens so I'm told when this house was built; that was why our ancestor named the house 'Ravenslea'. I don't believe there are quite as many now."

"Well, whatever the names of the birds are, I love to hear them." Christiana said.

Adam grinned. "I feel the same—there's nothing like this in Connecticut. It's funny, but I was born in the States, have only been here a short while, yet I feel really at home in this wonderful house."

Louise smiled at her son. "You feel at home almost everywhere, Adam. So long as you're housed, fed and are comfortable, I think you'd be happy living in a barn!"

Everyone laughed just as the door opened and Doris appeared with a loaded trolley.

"Agnes has included a few biscuits she and Edna made this morning and asked to tell you that dinner will be ready in about an hour and a half."

"Thank you, Doris." Catherine said.

Eden sighed, resigning himself to the fact that the last thing his father would want to do now, was discuss the fate of the Desdemona, when the brother he'd not seen since Martin had left to make the trip to the New World was back in the home in which they were born.

James and Martin had grown even closer after Martin's first wife, Amelia, had died in the fire that had ravaged Ravenslea. Between them, they'd built up the beautiful mansion that was now even more splendid than before. Apart from adding an extension to the Music Room, they'd also added a couple more rooms to the lower level. After modernizing the vast Kitchen, new plumbing was installed in the three Bathrooms. The roof had been resurfaced and the cellar had been gutted, cleared, rebuilt and restocked.

After a while of listening to the hubbub of conversation, Eden found the room suddenly becoming cloying and stuffy. He was acutely aware of Christiana's bold looks whenever he happened to catch her eye. He had to leave, much as he wished to partake in the delicious looking cakes Agnes, the cook, had made. He had to be honest with himself; the main reason for his hasty departure from the cosy family get-together was the fact that he was finding it difficult to think clearly when it was obvious Christiana Whitney found him challengingly attainable. He was not married; she must have found out that he didn't have a young lady waiting in the wings, so perhaps she was thinking this was a chance she could not miss. With her long, silky blonde hair hanging to one side of her face like an actress he recalled, yet couldn't remember the name, she seemed to be studying him unabashedly. He'd never felt so uncomfortable in his life.

"If you'll excuse me, I have to find Luke . . . I have to discuss a matter of urgency with him."

"But, Eden . . . surely that can wait for a moment or two. Your Uncle and Aunt have only just arrived." His mother frowned at him. "It's very rude of you to not even stay for a few minutes."

"I apologize, but I'll be back as quickly as I can. I . . . I am interested to hear all their news and get to know them better, of course." His smile encompassed everyone as he quickly hurried out the door before they had chance to hold him there.

When he pushed the door open to Luke's studio, he was relieved to see that his brother hadn't locked himself away in the little room that seemed not much bigger than a closet, he used as a dark room. Instead, Luke was standing near the latticed window of his Studio holding a negative up to the light. He had his back to the door when Eden entered.

"How's it going?" Eden closed the door firmly.

Luke turned. "I've developed four rolls of film today. This is one of the negatives. I think it's a bit blurred and I think I know what I did, but I'll have to develop it before I can be sure. What's up? You look a bit peeved."

"You're right. I'm really troubled about father's desire to sell the Desdemona."

Luke shrugged. "I don't know what I can do that you haven't already done, Eden. Dad's pretty decided about selling her."

Eden perched himself on the side of a chair and pursed his lips, a furrow appearing between his dark eyebrows. He picked up a photograph of a man standing beside a farm vehicle. "I know. But, I don't know why? He has never told me the reasons behind it. There has to be something other than the fact that Deanna and David lost their lives on her." He sighed and pushed a hand through his hair.

"I agree." Luke glanced out the window. "I wonder . . . I wonder if Uncle Martin would be able to convince him. I know Dad values his ideas." He turned back to Eden. "Why don't you talk to Uncle Martin—it couldn't hurt?"

Eden shrugged. "Maybe—at least I could try. You should too—between us, perhaps we could convince both of them that we must keep the Desdemona. I was thinking that perhaps you could also mention it, casually, to mama. I don't think an auction has actually been arranged yet, so we have some time to our advantage."

Luke nodded. "I'll talk to mother, if you'll try and get Uncle Martin on his own, which might be a little difficult."

So it was agreed and the following morning, Eden luckily found his uncle alone in the Music Room.

Once Eden had related the reason for his concerns about the selling of the Desdemona, Martin leaned back in the high-backed leather armchair and for a few moments was silent; his mind absorbing the information. Finally, he pulled himself forward, absently knocking ash from his pipe into the fire-grate.

"The Desdemona," he said, evenly, "belongs also to me, Eden. What my brother seems to have forgotten is that I have a say in what happens to her. I am not a good sailor and only sailed on the Desdemona once which caused me much grief—sick stomach . . ." he grinned at his nephew wryly, "but I do not wish the vessel to leave our hands. It's a part of Ravenslea as we all are. Also, I believe Adam would like very much to learn the ropes. He had a kayak in the States, but he always said he wished he had a sailboat."

Eden's face lit up. "Then you have a strong reason to make Dad change his mind?" Hope flared in Eden's dark eyes.

Martin shrugged. "I think, as everyone else does, that James lost interest in the Desdemona when our Aunt Deanna and Uncle David drowned, but I believe if we talk to him and make him see that we really do not wish to have it auctioned off, we might just be able to reawaken the love he always had for her." He paused, "I can talk to him—let him know that I disapprove of the idea. It may be that your father will decide to pay me out despite what I might say to him. It remains to be seen just what kind of mood he'll be in when I approach him."

"I'm worried that he will just go ahead with the auction before anyone's had a chance to convince him to change his mind. If we can stop that happening then you have to talk to him as soon as possible, Uncle Martin."

Martin nodded. "I understand, indeed I do so I'll talk to him tonight." He pushed against the chair arms, bringing himself to a stand. Straightening his narrow back, he smiled at his nephew. "Now, I think we should join the family."

Elizabeth Thorncroft, still magnificently statuesque at 78 years of age, smiled at her stepson and grandson as they entered the conservatory. After her adored husband, Jonathon, suddenly passed away three years ago from a massive stroke, she'd sunk into acute depression. She'd lost weight and for a long while wouldn't join in any of the family activities. Now, she had strengthened, although the occasional melancholia would engulf her, she'd basically returned to normal. She waved them to sit beside her.

"Louise and Christiana have gone into Bristol for the day. I think they wanted to see one of England's big cities." She grinned. "Better them than me—give me the glorious Devonshire countryside any day."

"You're too spoilt, mama," Martin teased, dropping an affectionate kiss on Elizabeth's brow. "But I feel much the same—the teeming busy city life is not for me."

"But Branton has little going for it." Eden said, seating himself beside his grandmother. "Everything's too expensive and there's not much competition or variety of goods. It's no wonder that most folk travel all the way to Bristol or Glastonbury when they want to do any serious buying."

"That's true enough, dear, but—" Elizabeth said, then paused as the French door swung open. Her granddaughter, Rebecca stood there, cheeks aglow from the effort of exercise. Her warm blue eyes surveyed the group amiably. "Oh there you are, dear. I was wondering where you'd got to. Do have some tea—I'm sure it'll still be warm enough for you. Did you enjoy your ride?"

"It was wonderful, Gran." Rebecca hurried over to her adoring grandmother and dropped a light kiss on her forehead. "I could do with something stronger than a cup of tea though."

"It's a bit early for that surely, dear. It'll be lunchtime soon; it's not good to be imbibing during the morning hours, you know."

Rebecca shrugged. "I suppose you're right, Gran." She pulled off her brown riding cap and tossed her shining dark hair free, allowing it to fall in a cascade of curls down her back. "I've just been talking to Josh. He says there's blight on the roses near the summerhouse. He'll have to get rid of them or the pest will devour the others."

"Oh dear—and I did so love them. Are you sure he can't do anything to save them?" Elizabeth implored.

Rebecca shook her head. "Not a thing. Anyway, we can get more—he went into a load of detail about splitting some at the west end of the garden and re-rooting them. I know next to nothing about such things, but I do know he's a good gardener."

Elizabeth agreed. The rest of the afternoon was spent in quiet discussion over tea and cakes.

James didn't take much coaxing to keep the Desdemona. He'd known for a long time that his reason for auctioning her off was completely irrational, yet he couldn't erase from his mind the manner in which his Aunt and Uncle had died. Despite his talk of letting the Desdemona go, he knew that if someone had a good reason to keep her, he would reverse his decision. If Adam Whitney wished to learn to sail, then James and, perhaps his older cousin, George would show him the rudiments.

"Doesn't Eden get his ticket in about seven months, James?" Martin asked. James nodded. "Then I suggest we have him train Adam, it would give them something in common to talk about."

"That's a good point, Martin. I'll see what Eden thinks about the idea." James paused, then stood up and began to pace the room. "On another subject, we have to talk about our stocks, Martin. As you know, the depression last year cost us quite a bit on the stock exchange. I'm not at all sure I want to spend money on the upkeep of the Desdemona, at least not right now."

"Nonsense!" Martin interrupted hotly. "Why only yesterday I checked our stocks and bonds. The dividends from the South African diamond mines have declined a little, as has the tin mine in Cornwall, but you have to agree they're still producing if at a lesser level." He paused. "It's the new decade, James, and I feel things are going to change for the better. This recession will ease. Don't do anything rash."

"You may have noticed, Martin that the Yorkshire colliery is floundering again. We're having unrest with the employees and despite the recession, I have a feeling they are on the verge of striking."

"But that's ridiculous." Martin cried. "What on earth would possess them to even think of striking when jobs are so hard to come by at the moment?"

James shrugged. "I'll have to make a trip up there and find out what their problem is. I can only speculate that something is seriously wrong—much like it was before in 1896."

"I agree. I'll come with you when you decide to go."

"I'd appreciate it if you would, Martin. Two heads in cases like this are always better than one and we all know what the young Keeley is like. A chip off the old block, I'd say." He moved towards the window. "If we can't resolve their issues amicably, then it might be prudent to sell out."

"I also agree, James." Martin said, thoughtfully. "It's something we should discuss before venturing up there and in the meantime, it may resolve itself. On another tack—what about the Desdemona?"

James raised his eyebrows. "Despite her being an old ship which has seen much use over the years, she's in great shape." He paused. "Someone, somewhere would get a bargain if they purchased her."

"I'm a partner in the welfare of Ravenslea which also includes the Desdemona and I think we should abandon the idea of selling her."

James gave a slight incline of his head. "You have every right to contest me on this Martin, and if you feel we should keep her, then I'll concede to your wishes. We'll keep her, at least for the time being. Perhaps we should let Adam take advantage of our knowledge of the sea to train him; who knows he may make something of himself, or he may hate it. At least we can give him the choice."

"I'm glad you agree, James. I believe it's the right solution." Martin smiled at his brother. "I don't wish to be a party to selling anything we have here; we have many valuable assets in one way or another, handed down from generation to generation and it should remain with us."

CHAPTER 5

THE INVITATION TO RAVENSLEA

Penelope Rhodes looked across the table to her daughter a thoughtful smile crossing her still handsome face. She scanned the letter in front of her.

"We've all been invited to Ravenslea, Stephanie, for a dinner get-together. You are coming aren't you? I know Rebecca would love to see you again—it's been a long time."

Stephanie looked at her mother, at the same time trying to quell the rise in her temperature and the fluttering of her heart. Having returned from four years in Finishing School in Switzerland recently, she'd not seen Rebecca or any of the Thorncrofts since her return. She wondered what Eden would be like. Would he be the same? For some unaccountable reason, her thoughts suddenly swung to Nigel Whitfield, a young man she'd struck up an acquaintance with during the journey from Geneva to Calais, France. As they were travelling alone, it seemed natural for them to continue their journey to England together. Nigel was nice, she enjoyed his company, but she knew the friendship would have to end once they'd reached England. Her heart had always been with Eden Thorncroft—ever since they were children together. She had enjoyed his teasing—anything to have him near her for no matter what reason. So when the boat had docked, she told Nigel it would not be in his best interests to pursue her any further. Despite his protestations, she was adamant, telling him she would not change her mind about him, because there was another man in her life. Nigel was obviously very disappointed, but they parted company in friendship.

Her mother nudged her shoulder suddenly.

"Is there a special reason, Mummy?" She asked, bringing herself back to the present.

Penelope grinned. "Of course—isn't there always? Martin has returned from the States—for good it seems, and he's brought his wife and family with him. Ostensibly, it's to meet them." She glanced over at her husband. "I hope you'll feel well enough to attend too, dear. You seem so much better these days—I think Ida's excellent nursing has definitely bucked you up. It's about time you got out of the house and began visiting again."

Fletcher smiled. "I will, Penelope. I would like to meet Martin's new family; it'll be good to hear of their lives in America. I understand they're from Connecticut, which I've heard is a beautiful State."

"I don't know much about it," Penelope said. "But I'd like to know something of America. We're hearing more and more about its ups and downs these days, especially since the dreadful Wall Street collapse last year."

"When is the dinner, Mother?" Stephanie glanced at her brother. "You are coming too, aren't you, William?"

Stephanie's twenty-five-year-old brother shrugged raising a dark eyebrow nonchalantly.

"I'm easy." He said, airily.

Stephanie stood up, stretching her arms above her head. "I understand they have a daughter around your age, William—who knows she could be some competition for Rebecca to worry about." She looked at him mischievously.

"Stephanie!" Penelope reprimanded harshly. "I think that's most uncalled for. You apologize to your brother this minute."

William grinned. "Don't bother, Mother; she said nothing offensive and as I think you all know, nothing will change my feelings for Rebecca!"

"Well said, dear." Penelope smiled fondly at her son. "Now to your other question—it's taking place next Saturday. I think you'll find Martin's new family quite enchanting and I'm sure you'll get along well with them." She patted her daughter's cheek gently. "I met Louise briefly in Branton the other day and though we didn't speak for long, she seemed quite the nicest person."

"And her family?" William asked. "What did you think of them? Do you think they'd get along with us?"

"I can't really answer that, dear, as I didn't actually meet them. Now, if you don't mind, I must reply to Catherine this afternoon."

The day of the Ravenslea dinner party dawned bright and sunny, though a skittish breeze sent leaves fluttering to the ground. The air smelled sweet with late blossoms and the warm afternoon sun enveloped the Rhodes family as they stepped from their black Armstrong Siddely at the foot of the steps to the front entrance of the breathtaking façade of Ravenslea Manor. William and Barnaby, the chauffeur, helped Fletcher from the car. He had decided today to abandon his wheelchair and try walking with a cane. His only difficulty now was when he moved from a sitting position to a standing one which apparently gave him quite a bit of pain, although the painkillers he was taking did help.

Ida Munroe remained with them because Fletcher suffered occasional blackouts. The melancholia had lessened dramatically over the past ten years but it would surface spasmodically. Penelope was optimistic that Fletcher's head injuries would heal one day—it needed time and patience for that to take place. Penelope knew she'd always find time in her life to care for the man she loved so dearly, especially with the expertise of the dedicated Ida to help her.

They walked up the steps to the front door, just as it opened. James and Catherine emerged, their faces wreathed in welcoming smiles. Catherine ran lightly down the steps and embraced her best friend.

"I don't really see enough of you, Pen." She exclaimed.

Penelope laughed. "We saw each other in Branton last Saturday, Cath—have you forgotten so soon?"

"Of course not, but it was only for a moment—we never seem to be able to spend long periods of time together any more."

"Well, we'll have to remedy that, won't we?" Penelope turned to Stephanie standing behind her. "Why don't you seek out Rebecca, dear. I'm sure she's dying to see you again You haven't seen her in such a long time."

"Yes I will, Mummy. Hello Aunt Catherine." Stephanie smiled up at Catherine. "Is Rebecca at home?"

"In the garden, dear. A litter of pups were born recently at one of our tenants' cottages. Rebecca fell in love with one of them and is at this very moment trying to teach the little tyke some tricks. You'll find her on the far lawn. She'll be so happy to see you, Stephanie."

"Thank you." Stephanie hurried around the house. As she disappeared, Catherine suddenly found herself caught in one of Fletcher's bear-hug embraces. She laughed, kissing him lightly on the cheek.

"How are you, Fletcher?" She asked.

"I'm coming along nicely thank you, dear." He let her go, smiling warmly. "I have my moments, of course, as I'm sure my dear wife will tell you, but on the whole I know I'm on the mend."

"That's excellent, Fletcher." This came from James. "Come on in."

Half an hour later, James and Catherine coaxed everyone outside. The sun was shining over the neatly trimmed lawn at the front of the house. Elizabeth along with her daughter-in-law, Louise Whitney-Thorncroft, turned her head as the visitors walked towards the summerhouse. A wide smile crossed her face and she put the delicate teapot back on the table before rising to her feet with outstretched hands.

"Hello Penelope, Fletcher. We're so glad you were able to come. Please make yourself comfortable—we've put some chairs aside just for you." Elizabeth stood at the top of the summerhouse steps. She kissed Fletcher and Penelope gently on their foreheads and introduced each one to Louise, who, in turn, introduced her daughter, Christiana and son, Adam, who had also risen with outstretched hands to the newcomers.

"Christiana," Louise began as everyone seated themselves, "is the most energetic young woman. I wish I had even half of the energy she uses when riding."

Christiana chimed in quickly. "Riding is my favourite pastime. I had a wonderful mare in Connecticut and once I'm settled in here, I wish to purchase a foal; I intend to bring her up exactly as I did Trudy in the States and work towards entering equestrian events in England."

Penelope grinned widely. "Indeed, that would be wonderful, Christiana. You'd have plenty of scope in the West Country; gymkhanas are very popular here over the summer months. If you take pleasure in horse-riding as you say you do, I'm sure you'd find great enjoyment in competing in some of those." She glanced at Stephanie. "Stephanie too is quite into horse riding and we do have another horse at Cavendish Hall that I'm sure we could loan you until you get one of your own."

Stephanie eyed Christiana Whitney critically. She had to admit she was an extremely lovely young woman. Her extraordinarily light blue eyes seemed to bore right through her, so much so that Stephanie found it most unnerving. She had to turn away.

"Rosie's the one for you, Christiana." She said. "I guarantee you'll love her. She'll match your mood; if you like spirit, she can definitely give you that, and somehow she seems to sense when you need a little easier gait, so one day soon you must come over and we'll go riding together, how does that sound?"

Christiana looked at her, her expression unfathomable. "Thank you, Stephanie, I believe Ravenslea will have a mount for me. Of course, as we ride Western style in the States, I'll have to get used to an English saddle, but that'll be all part of the fun of riding. Anyway, . . ." she quickly added, ". . . it will be nice to take advantage of your offer."

The rest of the afternoon went smoothly. During the time spent with Louise, Adam and Christiana, the Rhodes learned much of their lives in Connecticut.

CHAPTER 6

JULY 1930

CAPTAIN James Thorncroft stood on the upper deck as the Desdemona cut smoothly through the waters of the Bristol Channel. He realized just how much he would have missed this solid old vessel had he not adhered to his brother's pleas to keep her. He shook himself irritably. He had learned through the years to weigh situations carefully before making rash decisions. His head had been ruling his heart, which is something he always believed in, but deep down he knew that to auction off this magnificent ship would have been the worst mistake he'd ever made. Now he knew he'd keep the Desdemona until she was no longer seaworthy.

He turned now to scan the deck and the feverish activity of his competent crew as they made way for pulling into the picturesque harbour. His brother's stepson, Adam, appeared eager to learn the intricacies of tying knots, even of swabbing the decks without so much as a complaint. James felt he would one day be a dedicated sailor, with as rough humour as his counterparts.

On the bow of the ship stood William Rhodes. Today he wore the usual clothing of a regular seaman, but normally he would be in the regalia of the Royal Navy, kitted out in the neat, clean uniform that set him apart from others. James liked Penelope and Fletcher's only son. He knew that William had wished to be in the Army as had his father, but when Fletcher disapproved, undaunted the young man decided to join the Navy instead. Fletcher knew he wouldn't be able to make him change his mind, so gave him his blessing. He was a fine young man, full of spirit and good fun and James also knew that Rebecca was very much enamoured of him. He smiled. He and Catherine talked about it many times on seeing the two young people together and both hoped the warm friendship that had developed over the years of knowing each other, would blossom into something more lasting. To have William for a son-in-law would, he thought, be the best thing for Rebecca and for the Thorncrofts; the young man was intelligent, interesting to talk to and highly amusing.

James shifted his position as William disappeared into the galley. Dark clouds had altered slightly from a while ago, opening up an area to illuminate the turbulent waters with a wide shaft of sunlight. He shielded his eyes against the sudden glare, breathing easier as land hazily formed before him. Although the run to and from the Hebrides had not been the longest trip he'd made with the Desdemona, it'd been a difficult voyage both up and down the passage, especially through the northern part of the Irish Sea. Here it joined the North Atlantic where violent storms erupted from seemingly out of nowhere. Many of his crew members had suffered sea-sickness at one point or another and the last hundred or so nautical miles had been especially thwarted by gigantic swells.

One of the most amazing members of his crew was his 51 year old stepsister Fern. In all the years he'd been sailing, the only times that she had preferred to stay at home were on the two occasions of her confinement. At all other times, she had balked at the idea of being restricted to staying indoors with only the womenfolk for company, with their constant chattering, crocheting or needle-work. He had to hand it to her, with her slight figure and amazing strength of character, she'd been as stalwart and reliable a sailor as any of the men in the crew.

His stepmother Elizabeth, of course, had been appalled to think that her only daughter seemed to prefer the rough and tumble life on the high seas, where danger lurked unbidden every minute of the voyage. She'd long since refrained from trying to tame her into the more gentile kind of lifestyle more suited to a wealthy young lady. Elizabeth as well as Catherine still protested hotly about taking such risks when he was using the Desdemona for pleasurable trips, mainly around the coastline of the British Isles.

His thoughts drifted again to Fern. Her two girls, Emily and Constance, were now married with children of their own. With Fern's husband, Simon, still in Karachi, the family rarely saw him. As he wasn't due home again now for many months, Fern had diligently learned the skills of sailing with help from James and Emily's husband, Paul Saunders, proving herself an integral member of the Desdemona's crew.

James turned again looking aft to watch the steady activities of his crew. His slim, wiry, thirteen year old nephew, David Ellison, was keen and energetic, often telling James he wanted to make the Navy his career. James, happy to oblige with helping him understand the rudiments, had willingly allowed him to be his personal cabin boy. He was a quick learner and had an insatiable appetite to learn as much as he could about the art of sailing; James was sure, when the young man was ready, he'd find his niche in the service without any trouble. James smiled as he watched him now, helping another sailor secure the mizzen. Many a time, David could be seen talking very seriously to William Rhodes and James knew that the boy had no illusions as to what was required of him should he decide to join the Navy.

James turned his attention to two other men, standing together seemingly discussing something in earnest. His cousin, fifty year old Corwin Chandler, was scratching and shaking his head while the other younger man, Hal Grimm, who James had hired for the last two voyages, was arguing with him. It was soon resolved however, and both men eventually moved aft to disappear behind the mast.

A few moments later, Hal reappeared. On seeing James, he waved and hurried towards him.

"I think you'd better come aft." He said, cupping his hand around his mouth against the roar of the wind. "Bettger and Ames are scrapping again!"

James gritted his teeth. "To Hell with those two." He barked, following close behind as Hal Grimm retraced his steps. "I sometimes curse the moment I agreed to hire them. They'll definitely not be on my next run!"

"Aye! Aye! Sir." Hal said, raising his black eyebrows in agreement. "They've bin nothin' but trouble from the day we set out!"

Randy Bettger, a twenty-five-year-old native of Newcastle was kneeling over a prostrate man on the deck, mouthing obscenities that James had difficulty understanding from the broad Geordie brogue. James strode masterfully over. With the help of another sailor, the large man was dragged off the skinny, smaller Pete Ames struggling beneath him. Ames immediately sprang to his feet fists raised, eyes blazing, ready, indeed, for more altercation.

"I'll see you in Hell, Bettger!" He yelled, wildly as two more sailors leapt forward securely restraining his thin arms.

"Yeah? But you'll be there long a'fore me—!"

"Enough!" James roared. "You'll both be off this ship the moment we reach dock! For now, get back doing the jobs to which you were assigned. Now!!!"

James' voice carried across to the men, who first stared with hatred at each other then realizing their differences would have to be solved at some other time, mumbled incoherently and strode angrily away in opposite directions.

Another fifteen minutes or so passed before the Desdemona had her fore and aft lines fast to the dock; she was now sheltered by the harbour wall. James had no time to watch the two errant sailors, so while the crew fastened down the hatches and eventually disembark, he moved back into his cabin to finish writing up the Log.

After a while, a knock came on the cabin door. It swung open and Fern stood there, a delighted grin on her face.

"Oh James! That was an exciting trip; I wouldn't have missed it for anything!"

He smiled at her. "I don't think everyone thought that, dear." He said. "There were a lot of very sick men on board. I noticed you didn't suffer any."

She laughed. "I'm a tough ol' bird, James. It'd take much more than a few big swells and shaking and bucking of the Desdemona before I'd feel any ill effects!"

"I could see that! I'm very proud of you. You should have been a man, you'd probably be owning your own vessel by now!"

"Very likely! Anyway, I enjoy sailing with you, James. You're a good, fair Captain and definitely know how to handle the Desdemona!"

"I should by now. I've had her a long time and have been many places with her. I know her almost as well as I know Ravenslea!" He stood up, stretching his long arms above his head. He pursed his lips. "I never thought I'd ever say this to a woman working on board ship, Fern, but you have pulled your weight and in doing so, helped considerably in making this voyage a success." He kissed the tip of her nose.

"I've learned a lot by having sailed with you. I'm pretty sure some women, not all mind you, could do it equally as well as men." Fern raised her eyebrows. "Most women wouldn't want to do it . . . but as I don't really have anything else I'd rather do, I take great pleasure in coming on board with you and the excellent crew. Except, of course, when we get sailors like the argumentative Bettger and Ames."

"They're a trial, to be sure. I honestly don't know why they fight so much— I've never yet had the occasion to hear them agree about anything. The trouble is, individually they're excellent seamen—they know the ropes as well as anyone else on board. However, I *will* hire new men next time—I can't afford to allow their feuding to jeopardize all on board." He paused, looking at her intently. "What did you think of Adam?"

"He did very well, James. I was amazed at how quickly he learned the fundamentals of sailing. He'll be a great asset to you."

James nodded. "I felt the same. Every time I saw him, he seemed to be diligently working and I don't think he suffered any dire maladies during the rough weather we experienced off the Hebrides, did you?"

She shook her head. "No, he was sure footed and as oblivious of the raging waters as I was!" She grinned. "We are obviously built of the same, tough stuff!"

He turned back to his desk. "Look, dear, I'll be a while yet on board so why don't you find Corwin or Adam to take you back to the house. I know they're expecting all the family who are aboard to go back to Ravenslea. You can't keep your mother in suspense any longer, knowing how much she worries about you out on the vast unpredictable ocean with a group of unruly men!"

"Aye, aye, Cap'n." Fern grinned, giving him a saucy salute. "I'll find someone. See you later."

Fern happily left him sitting there shaking his head and smiling. Sighing with a resigned sense of contentment, James returned to the task of finishing off the Log.

When Fern, Adam and Corwin Chandler arrived at Ravenslea, the two men immediately disappeared into the Kitchen for a snack while Fern put her head around the Drawing Room door, said a quick hello to everyone. She then ran up the stairs to clean up and change into something more appropriate. Glancing quickly through her wardrobe, she chose her favourite turquoise gown that complimented her colouring. She glanced in the mirror. Frowning she saw how the sea and high winds she'd just endured on the Desdemona had whipped up the high colour on her face. Knowing that over time, her delicate skin could turn leathery if she continued to sail in rough seas, she reached into a drawer and pulled out a large bottle of cold cream. Liberally rubbing it in around her face and neck, she patted a little face powder over it, drew a pale pink lipstick over her full lips and sprinkled lavender cologne at strategic points in order to neutralize the pungent smell of the sea that had not only been on her clothes, but also on her body.

Half an hour later, she returned downstairs, looking as if she'd never been away. Her thick-set cousin, Corwin, was sitting on the arm of her mother's chair, chatting amiably, but Adam was not in sight. They all looked up as she came into the room and Elizabeth proudly smiled up at her.

"Corwin has been telling us a bit about the voyage, dear." She said, making to stand up, but abandoned the idea when Fern shook her head and came to sit beside her on the sofa. "We're so relieved to see you back home safe and sound and actually resembling a lady."

"Oh, mama, I don't know about being a lady. I don't think anyone who knows me could accuse me of being that—but sometimes in the right circumstances, I like to try and look like one, once in a while. You know, of course, that I should have been born a boy, because I'm much happier in slacks than in skirts!"

Everyone laughed merrily, though Elizabeth frowned in mock dismay.

"I'm so glad you're not, Fern." Catherine said when the laughter had died down. "Anyway, was it really bad on the seas?"

"It was wonderfully exhilarating, Catherine." She paused. "Corwin probably told you, we hit the tail end of some really strong north-westerly gales when we approached the Inner Hebrides. This was by no means easy for us, as the winds were terribly cold, but the Desdemona handled it courageously, although some of the crew did seem destined to sea-sickness, we all came through practically unscathed." She grinned. "I'll never complain of the cold again, Mother, because nothing on land could closely compare to the cold biting winds of the North Atlantic!"

"I can quite believe that, my dear." Elizabeth said, squeezing Fern's hand gently. "I do hope you'll be staying awhile now. I'd like you to be here for your niece's birthday in a couple of weeks."

"I wouldn't miss that for the worlds, Mama." Fern glanced around. "Where is she, by the way?"

Catherine waved a hand airily. "Oh, out with Faith, I think. They spend a lot of time together. It's good, because Faith has never really got over her father's death and Rebecca seems so good for her."

Fern frowned. "I don't think any of us have got over Uncle Arthur's dreadful death, Catherine. I still can't believe he'll not walk through that door, even now!"

The door suddenly opened, giving them all a start. Rebecca bounced through the room, smiles all over her face. Her young cousin followed close behind, her dark hair tousled.

"Aunt Fern!" Rebecca cried, hurrying forward and drawing Fern to her in a quick embrace. "When did you get back? You must tell me everything. We've missed you, you know." She glanced at Faith hovering in the doorway. "Come on Faith, say something to Aunt Fern!"

Faith, shy by nature, walked slowly forward. "Nice to see you again, Mrs. Danby." She said.

"Good to see you too, Faith. Please give my regards to your mother when you get home. I think of her often. Come, sit beside me." Fern patted the seat.

Faith smiled and sat down on the comfortable Chesterfield beside Fern.

"Oh Aunt Fern guess what?" Rebecca cried jubilantly.

"I haven't the foggiest, dear!" Fern said, dryly, grinning at her niece's animated features. "Have you come into a fortune, or had someone wonderful propose to you?"

Rebecca giggled. "No, nothing like that. We had a letter from Uncle Simon—he's coming home. So what do you think about that?"

Fern stared at her. "Coming home? I wasn't expecting him until Christmas. How marvellous! Did he say when?"

"No," Catherine said, "and in case you're wondering why he sent the communiqué to us, it was just a courtesy—he included a sealed envelope for you, dear. We're all so happy and looking forward to him being with us. He's always away so much, we miss him at Ravenslea."

Fern was astounded by the news. Simon was coming home! Her happy, warm smile encompassed everyone in the room. "That's wonderful. I have so much to tell him."

"I'll get the letter, Mummy." Rebecca said, turning towards the door. "It's on your dressing table isn't it?" When Catherine nodded, Rebecca left to return moments later complete with an envelope which she thrust into her Aunt's hands.

Fern read the opened letter then slipped her thumb nail along the flap of the unopened one. Reading it quietly to herself, she felt a wonderful sensation of warmth at Simon's beautiful words to her. She couldn't remember him being quite so poetic and it gave her a warm feeling. It wasn't a long letter; Simon wasn't the best at writing, but she was so glad he'd written one specifically for her. He'd missed her terribly, he'd said, and longed for the time when they could once more be together. She felt the same. Spending as much time as she could at activities that took her away from Ravenslea, she'd not had time to think of him, but now, at home again, she longed to be in his arms once more. She tucked the private letter back in its envelope and faced the family.

"Just a little note, that's all. He's looking forward to coming back to Ravenslea and should be arriving sometime in October. He said he'd send us word of the actual date later."

"It'll be so nice for you to have him back again, Fern dear." Catherine said. "Especially as it's your birthday at the end of October. It seems dear that Simon has over the past couple of years been away for that celebration—it'll be wonderful that you can be together this year. You'll have to think of something really special to do on that day."

Fern grinned, bringing a sparkle to her face. "Indeed you're right, Catherine. Oh, it'll be so wonderful to have him home. I'll gladly give up my sailing for him."

"I was sure you'd say that." Corwin said, standing up. "Now if you don't mind, I really must be returning home, my daughter will be wondering where I am."

As Corwin left, the women stared at one another.

"I do wish Corwin would marry again." Elizabeth said. "Since Violet died all those years ago, he's devoted so much of his time to Anita. Now she's 17 years old, I'm sure she'll be leaving to get married before too long. I hate to think he'd have to live alone for the rest of his years."

Fern grinned. "He'll not be alone, Gran. I know for a fact, he'll dedicate the rest of his life to the sea. He loves it as much as I do. I know Corwin well; he'll not sit back and get old. No, have no fear once Anita has moved out, we'll probably see more and more of him here at Ravenslea."

CHAPTER 7

REBECCA'S 21ST BIRTHDAY

T HREE days later, Allison Thorncroft arrived in the neighbourhood. She'd taken considerable time before deciding to accept the Thorncroft's invitation to attend Rebecca's 21st birthday party; the only reason she did, was because she adored her Aunt Catherine who she hadn't seen for a long time.

She wriggled in her seat, feeling anxious. Absently, she stared out the window as the train from Tavistock buffeted along the railway line towards Branton, before ending its journey at Temple Meads Station in Bristol. She knew Catherine would welcome her, but Allison worried as to how anyone else would greet her at Ravenslea as for the past eight years she had chosen to live away from the family and take a small cottage on the edge of Tavistock. Living there with her two feline companions and Edith Pruett, an elderly housekeeper, Allison had been content. The last time she'd been with her cousins, was last Christmas. She'd been so busy with her new business she'd not found time to visit them. Now, to be meeting her stepmother, Louise Whitney-Thorncroft and her new step siblings for the first time was filling her with apprehension.

As she gazed out the window at the passing rural scenes, she brought to mind the reasons for leaving Ravenslea. Though she loved the house and its beautiful grounds, she knew she didn't wish to stay there indefinitely. She had a burning desire to venture out on her own. Her father helped by financing a small cottage in Tavistock and from there, Allison made horticulture her career.

She'd taken lessons at a nearby college and easily learned the basics of growing flowers and vegetables. With a greenhouse at the back of her garden, she'd tried experimenting with cross-pollination. Her efforts had proved rewarding as she had cultured some unique species of flowers that she'd sold at local markets every year along with punnets of vegetables and berries, thereby making a decent living. She'd also dabbled a little in the medicinal value of herbs and could often be seen in her greenhouse concocting yet another remedy for something.

Edith Pruett, a widow in her sixties became her live-in housekeeper and the young woman could not have asked for a better, more amiable arrangement. Edith was a nice enough woman in her own way, but she had no time for the activities Allison performed in the greenhouse. She had no reason to believe that medications prescribed by fully qualified doctors were harmful to anybody— they were all tested and proved to be true and beneficial. The plants and flowers should be used only for decorative purposes; or fodder for the animal kingdom. Allison was aware her housekeeper disapproved though had tried to convince her that as God had put fruits and vegetables on this earth for human consumption, why not other plants for curing us all of our ills. After all, she argued, the earth was created long before scientists and doctors came on the scene; but she may as well have saved her breath for Edith could not be budged.

Allison leaned back against the seat listening to the lulling clackety-clack of the wheels speeding along the tracks and closed her eyes.

Although Allison was ten years older than Rebecca, she'd always felt a warm kinship with her cousin. She wished, in some ways, that she had moved closer to Ravenslea as she would have liked to have kept in touch with Rebecca, particularly as she had never associated with any of her own mother's family. Not that she really wanted to, as she'd only ever heard disparaging remarks about her mother's side of the family. She'd often wondered about that, but had never followed up, feeling it was too far in the past to be concerned about.

Thirty-one-year-old Allison had never married—having learned that her mother's demented life had disintegrated some time after she'd married her father. She couldn't really remember her mother, but though people did try to shield her from learning the truth about her, she had found out quite by accident that her mother had deliberately set fire to Ravenslea Manor in a mad fit of jealousy. Allison was deathly afraid the madness that was evident in Amelia Thorncroft could be laying dormant within herself and she, too, would resort to something just as terrifying in a few years.

She shivered, suddenly wondering if she'd wasted her life now by not marrying. She leaned back in the seat, remembering Oliver Howard. They had both been seventeen when they'd met. The casual friendship blossomed into something more lasting as the weeks and months went by. She liked him immensely and as she closed her eyes, a blurry mental image came to mind. The smiling brown eyes, the slightly parted lips when he'd bend to kiss her and the way he made her laugh. Feeling she was becoming more involved with him, she suddenly became fearful and rashly told him she didn't want to see him any more. He'd been puzzled and distressed, obviously believing they would have a future together. At first, he'd been angry, but when he realized she was serious, he told her that he'd loved her from the first moment they'd met and would never love another. In 1916 he'd joined the army. Two years later, he lost his life to an enemy bullet on Flanders fields.

She shifted restlessly on the seat. No other man had affected her as much as Oliver and she vowed no-one would. With her vocation settled, Allison had no regrets about not marrying; she was quite happy to spend the rest of her life as a spinster.

She glanced out the window again, finding enjoyment in the train journey that bright summer morning. She had never had occasion to travel much, content to spend most of her days tending her garden or caring for her tabby cats, Ossie and Posie. She was also thankful that her housekeeper loved the cats as much as she did and knew she'd take good care of them until her return in a couple of weeks.

Leaning back against the cushions, she fished in her large shopping bag for a book she'd picked up at the station and thumbed through it, finding the place where she'd left off. It was just one of those easy-reading mysteries that always relaxed and fascinated her.

Before long, the train slowed and chugged into the small Branton station. Once stopped, she gathered her case, her shopping bag and handbag and stepped onto the platform, feeling the damp steam hissing and billowing around her.

It was as she waited for the steam to clear that she saw a young woman hurrying towards her.

"Allison?" The young woman cried, smiling broadly and opening her arms in welcome. "I'm so happy you were able to come. Did you have a good trip?"

"Indeed I did." Allison replied, cheerfully.

Rebecca enclosed Allison in her arms in a quick hug. "It's certainly nice to see you again. How's the business been doing over the last six months? One of these days, I'd like to take a trip your way for a visit. I've haven't been to Tavistock in a long time."

"Oh, I'm so happy to be doing the thing I really love, Rebecca. I'm finding great enjoyment in working among plants; the business is actually doing very well. Each few months I seem to increase my orders. Though it's not for the money I do it, you understand, but it's nice to get paid for doing something I so love." She grinned at her cousin. "I'd love to have you stay with me for as long as you'd like, Rebecca. Tavistock hasn't changed much. It's as lovely as most of the villages in Devon and Cornwall; I'm sure you'd like to explore the areas surrounding it. Perhaps we could arrange that sometime before I leave." Allison lifted her suitcase and followed the high-spirited young woman along the platform, out of the station into the sunlit street where the familiar Rolls Sedanca stood. When, Percy saw them, he opened the door and showed them into the back. After packing Allison's suitcase in the boot, he climbed back into the driver's seat and pulled away.

On the way to Ravenslea, the two women talked. Rebecca had much to say to her cousin, but Allison did manage to say a few words. She told Rebecca about her home, Mrs. Pruett, and her two adored cats. When Rebecca asked her why she'd never married, Allison was candidly truthful. By the time they reached the front door of the old mansion, Allison felt decidedly more comfortable when she stepped inside the house.

Catherine greeted her warmly. "Did you have a good journey, Allison dear?" She asked, as Percy put the suitcase on the floor and returned outside.

"Oh, indeed I did, Aunt Catherine. It was a wonderful ride and the weather was next to perfect." Allison glanced at Rebecca. "Rebecca and I have chatted non-stop all the way."

Catherine laughed throwing a special grin at her jubilant daughter. "Oh, yes, Rebecca can talk. When she starts, as you'll find out, I doubt if you'll get a word in edgewise! By the way, do you have any other luggage coming?"

Allison nodded. "Yes, a larger case that I couldn't carry. It's coming separately by train and should be here tomorrow morning." She glanced at Rebecca. "I packed a gown that I'll wear to your party, Rebecca—I could hardly attend in what I'm wearing right now."

"You look fine. The colour suits you to a 'T'." Rebecca said, glancing quickly at her cousin with her olive green pant suit and light green blouse; a single string of pearls adorning her slim neck.

Amiably the three women climbed the stairs.

"Now, my dear, I presume you'd like the same room you used at Christmas?"

"Oh yes thank you, Aunt Catherine. The other room . . . well . . ." Allison broke off.

"I quite understand, dear. That room is not good for you. It could bring back unhappy memories, so it's best to leave it. One of these days, we intend to clear it out, redecorate it and change all the furniture, but for the moment, we're just keeping it closed for the time being." Catherine had never mentioned to her niece the reason why Allison felt uncomfortable, as it was the room where she'd almost died that dreadful night her mother had tried to destroy Ravenslea. The room had suffered a great deal of damage during the fire; it had since been restored, but Catherine knew Allison would not rest easy there.

She shuddered slightly then turned the other way. The two girls followed.

The room that Allison always used on her infrequent visits to Ravenslea was situated at the other side of the house. Decorated in shades of pink with a rose damask counterpane and matching curtains, Catherine knew her niece loved it. A washstand with a shining white ewer and basin stood under the mirror, which reflected the small dainty dressing table at the opposite side of the room. A single wardrobe took up the corner and the hardwood floor was covered in a light tan and red Indian carpet.

"Here we are, dear. Edna, our new maid, has aired the room specially for you and one of my children . . ." she glanced at Rebecca who shook her head, ". . . I think it was Eden, put some roses in a vase for you on the dressing table."

"Oh, how very thoughtful of him." Allison murmured, moving towards the beautiful yellow blooms and sniffing their glorious perfume. "This is lovely, Aunt Catherine."

After Allison had settled into the room, the three women moved downstairs. Catherine couldn't help but think how good Allison looked. Despite her circumstances, the fact that she lived alone and didn't have anyone particularly to impress, she obviously took pride in her appearance. Today, her olive green suit matched her short tawny coloured hair. She wore a very small amount of lipstick, and her pale ivory skin had a healthy glow. She was wearing high heeled shoes in a slightly darker green than her suit and the handbag matched them perfectly. She obviously had good fashion sense.

She recalled the first time she'd met Allison in 1903. She'd been around four years old at that time, the child had been reticent, moody and unfriendly. Despite concerted efforts from Catherine, Allison had not wanted to play with her younger cousin, Emily Danby, but Catherine believed that had undoubtedly been her mother's influence, keeping her cooped up in the house and giving the child no opportunity to meet and play with other children. When her mother had so tragically died, Allison began to form an attachment with Catherine. After a good deal of coaxing on Catherine's part, the child had eventually opened up. Her true personality blossomed and she became a happy child, good at academics and although it took a long time, her association with children her own age became more comfortable. As she grew older, Allison formed a sincere friendship with her cousin Emily and Catherine remembered sighing with relief to see the two little girls playing so amiably.

Allison had been ten years old when Rebecca was born in 1909. As little Rebecca was the daughter of her Aunt Catherine, Allison suddenly wanted to take care of her. Later, as Rebecca grew up they drew closer together; a warm, sincere friendship blossomed between them, despite the difference in age.

Today, as they descended the stairs, Catherine wondered how Allison would react to her father's new wife. Louise was good-natured, but even though Allison must have some inkling of what her mother was like, there could be a shade of resentment there, as Allison's association with Martin was very close.

Outside, the sound of happy voices greeted the three of them as they pushed the door open to the Drawing Room. From the elongated windows that looked out onto the large expanse of lawn, a group of people drew near to the house, laughing and fooling around.

"Ah," Catherine said, following Allison's gaze. "You are about to meet your father again and this time with his new wife and her family. I do hope you'll like them. Your stepmother is really quite charming."

Allison kept quiet. She wasn't sure how she'd be able to greet her father's new American wife. Being a shade prim, she wondered if the difference in their backgrounds would form a wedge between them. As she didn't answer, Catherine kept her counsel. She was sure once Allison got to know Louise Whitney-Thorncroft she'd find her a pleasant person, full of life and gaiety.

Luke was the first one to enter the room, pushing the French windows open with a flourish. He stared at the newcomer for a moment, then patting down his windswept tousled fair hair, came over to her, hand outstretched.

"Allison! So glad you've arrived. It seems ages since Christmas."

She smiled up at him, liking the way his mouth creased at the corners and the merry twinkle in his eyes.

"I've missed being in this lovely house, Luke and seeing you all again."

Eden stepped forward, laying a crumpled hat on a side table. To her astonishment, he leaned forward and kissed her on the cheek. She felt her face flush with colour, not expecting such familiarity.

"You had a good trip, cousin?" He asked, his dark eyes flashing. "You certainly picked a fine day to come. I hope you'll be staying for a while."

"Just a couple of weeks, Eden, then I must return. I do have commitments at home, you know."

A middle-aged woman moved forward, holding out two hands, grabbing Allison's and drawing her to her bosom in a friendly hug.

"So you are the lovely daughter my husband has been talking about so much. You are just as he described, Honey." She paused, holding Allison away from her for a moment. "I'm so pleased to finally be able to meet you. I insist you call me 'Louise' from now on."

Allison managed a small smile. "I'm . . . pleased to meet you too . . . Louise." She found that difficult . . . too familiar . . . it didn't sound quite 'proper'. "I . . . hope you and my father will be happy together."

Louise laughed and drew away from her gently. "I can't speak for Martin, of course, but I'm very happy, he's the most wonderful person I've ever met."

Martin drew his wife to him, kissing her lightly on the cheek. Letting go he pulled his daughter to him in a warm embrace. "I have missed you, dear," he said. "Let me see now, you were in your early twenties when I left to go to the States, weren't you. Now you've become independent with a life of your own." He pushed her gently away to look her over admiringly. "I feel now that you're here, we will be seeing more of you at Ravenslea in the future."

"A lot has happened since we were last together." Allison said, softly. "I was twenty-three when you left to go to America, Daddy. I missed not seeing you and your new wife when you visited a few years later, so . . . Oh Daddy . . .!" She suddenly clung to him, feeling tears of love forming for the father she adored. "I wish I lived closer to you . . . I've missed you so much."

He enclosed her in his arms, kissing the top of her curly red head affectionately. "And, my sweet child, I've missed you too. Who knows one day perhaps you can live closer—it remains to be seen what the future holds for us. Now, we must treasure the moments we have together—we have much to discuss and I intend to be with you as often as I can from now on."

CHAPTER 8

Two days before Rebecca's birthday, Catherine moved into the Kitchen where Agnes was busy rolling dough on the countertop. The cook turned.

"Good morning, Ma'am." Agnes said, sweeping a floured hand across her brow.

"Good morning, Agnes." Catherine replied. "I don't wish to disturb you as I can see you are busy, but I was wondering if you'd arranged for some help for the 24th?"

"Oh yes, Mrs. Thorncroft. You don't need to worry—I contacted the agency in Barnstable last week and they have arranged for three young women, along with three men who will be able to help make sure there are no hitches during Miss Rebecca's party."

"That's good, Agnes. I certainly couldn't allow Doris and Edna to be laden with all the work involved. Thank you very much." Catherine smiled at the red-faced woman, warmly. "Have you arranged supplies for the menu I left with you?"

"Oh yes, Ma'am. The grocer and butcher are arriving promptly around seven o'clock in the morning of the 24th with all the supplies. You have no need to worry about everything not being done in time; with the hired help arriving as well, everything, I know, will go perfectly."

"That's wonderful. Now I must let you continue with what you were doing."

"Thank you, Mrs. Thorncroft." Agnes threw her a smile and returned to her task.

A few minutes later, Catherine opened the door to the Dining Room. The long redwood table in the centre of the room had a flawless deep shine and as she studied it, she began to visualize warm candlelight mirrored on its finely polished surface, delightfully flickering over the guests and silverware. She smiled with satisfaction at the pleasant odour of beeswax that permeated the room. She loved to adorn this spacious Dining Room when the occasion arose for special events. Rebecca's twenty-first birthday was one of those special occasions and Catherine intended to make it one that her daughter would remember with fondness.

Catherine decided to go to St. John's Church in Branton that morning with the express purpose of discussing music for the party with the Rev. Oscar Finley. At the last Church Council meeting, of which she was a member, she'd taken the corpulent vicar aside along with the organist, Sally Watkins and her fiancé, Derek Kenyon whose true bass-baritone voice enraptured all who listened to him. Sally and Derek were members of the Bath Operatic Society and Catherine was well aware the two talented musicians were familiar with the music of Cole Porter and the Gershwin Brothers, of whom Rebecca was particularly fond. The purpose was to see if Sally and Derek would be available to sing at Rebecca's party. Catherine and James had discussed this earlier, thinking that it would be a grand way to round off the evening. Sally and Derek had shown great enthusiasm. Unfortunately, they said they'd be in Bath up until the 23rd. Sally asked if Catherine could let the Rev. Finley know what songs they'd like, so they could get their music together. Catherine had since made a short list, which she'd put in the pocket of her tartan skirt.

As she was about to leave the room, she heard low voices emanating from the Sitting Room adjacent to the Dining Room. Catherine had just spoken to Agnes; Edna was ironing in the scullery and Doris had gone to visit her mother. Apart from Eden and Luke who'd mentioned they were going out on a 'secret mission' that Catherine was sure was a last minute attempt at finding something for their sister's birthday, the rest of the family had gone to Barnstable.

So, it had to be Elspeth in the Sitting Room as she was the only person unaccounted for.

She moved quietly to the slightly open door and glanced inside. Two people were talking in low tones standing close together. Catherine was right. Elspeth was talking to a young woman who was slightly in shadow. They were discussing something most earnestly together. For some reason, Catherine felt a pang of anxiety.

She wondered if she should intervene, but foresight told her not to, so she quietly retreated past the long table and out through the door that led into the Hallway. She felt her heart hammering unnaturally and in trying to steady it began to think more logically. What on earth was she afraid of? True, if there was a stranger in the house, Elspeth should have announced her, but perhaps she didn't know Catherine was at home. It was probably quite innocent and nothing about which to become alarmed.

Treading lightly up the stairs to her room, Catherine closed the door and changed from her day dress to a lightweight suit, picked up a handbag and shoes.

Outside, Percy waved to her as she opened the front door. "I've cleaned the car, Mrs. Thorncroft. It's ready to leave whenever you are." His pleasant face was a wreath of smiles.

"Then I may as well go now, Percy. Thank you."

At that moment, she heard a sound behind her. Elspeth, astride her trusty bicycle, complete with large wicker basket in front and a rectangular matching wicker basket perched behind the seat, was wobbling unsteadily on the two large wheels towards her. A black felt hat perched precariously on top of the housekeeper's greying hair and the long black cloak and boots reminded Catherine suddenly of a witch. She drew her lips together in an effort to cover up her sudden desire to laugh.

"Good morning, Elspeth." Catherine said. "Are you going far?"

"Just to town, Madam." Elspeth said, slowing her gait.

"It looks like it might rain." Catherine responded pleasantly, looking at the ominous clouds rolling overhead. "You'll get drenched on your bicycle. I am quite happy for you to ride with me in the car."

Elspeth shook her head, managing a tight smile at her employer. "No, thank you, Mrs. Thorncroft, that's very kind, but a little bit of rain never did anyone any 'arm, and I need the exercise. Besides, if I were to ride with you, then you might feel obliged to bring me back and I wouldn't want you to be inconvenienced."

"It is no inconvenience to me, Elspeth, but the choice is yours."

"Then, no thank you, Madam. I have some errands to do. Thank you again. Good day."

Catherine watched, raising her eyebrows in amusement. What an odd woman Elspeth was. She was quiet, unassuming and rarely made any waves in the Ravenslea household, yet what did anyone really know about her? Years ago, not long after she and James had been married, she'd appeared on the doorstep looking for work. James, being the kindly soul he generally was, had given her a job in the Kitchen to help Esther, the cook they'd had at that time. Elspeth obviously had aspirations of becoming more than just a mere Kitchen maid for her manner suggested she was far more adept at handling more responsible duties. When James announced he'd let Elspeth take the place of their housekeeper, Harriet, who had given in her notice, Esther seemed happy to have her there. Later, however, Catherine believed the aging cook was relieved when Elspeth spent less time in the Kitchen. Esther and Doris worked very well together but there seemed some contention on Elspeth's part as she tended to become uncooperative and surly when things went wrong. Later, Esther retired and their present cook, the rotund, motherly Agnes Ingham took her place.

Agnes soon realized the disagreeable manner that Elspeth portrayed to her Kitchen staff and one day, so Catherine heard, took the housekeeper to one side and discussed with a certain amount of diplomacy that she, Agnes, had come to Ravenslea to help run a contented ship. As Elspeth was part of that ship's crew, she would have to change her attitude towards the Kitchen staff if she wished to be content at Ravenslea. At first, Elspeth had been angry that a mere cook would talk to her thus, but after a while she appeared to understand the rationale behind Agnes's words. There had been no major upheavals since. In fact, Elspeth proved a very capable housekeeper.

Catherine often wondered about the woman's family. Elspeth had never mentioned she had any kin anywhere, so not wishing to encroach on the woman's private affairs, she had to believe that Elspeth had no family.

Shrugging, she turned her attention to the car where Percy helped her into the seat. By the time they'd reached Branton, the rain had ceased. Catherine actually didn't mind the rain, but she was glad she'd brought her hat as the clouds looked ready to provide more rain before the afternoon was finished. After all, she'd come for a purpose and no amount of rain would hamper her—she had to agree with Elspeth on that—a little drop of rain never hurt anyone! Anyway, didn't someone say once that it was good for the complexion? Not that she needed anything to beautify her own complexion—she had been blessed with very clear, healthy skin and had not even had a blemish when a teenager.

The vicarage was only a few blocks from the centre of town, so it didn't take long for Percy to take her there.

"Wait for me, Percy." She said, as she opened the little wooden gate, "I won't be long."

"Very well, Mrs. Thorncroft."

As she walked down the little path towards the front door, she revelled in the picturesquely landscaped garden along with the aroma of a multitude of colourful flowers on each side of her. On reaching the neat front door with its rose-covered porch, she gave the brass door knocker a resounding rap. The door was opened immediately, as if she had been expected.

"Good morning, Mrs. Thorncroft, nice to see you." Rev. Finley's face was alight with smiles. "At least it's stopped raining for a little."

"Indeed yes."

"Do come in." He opened the door wider, allowing her entrance into his small, but neat Sitting Room. "I was hoping my wife would be here to greet you, but she had to go into Bristol on a personal errand."

Catherine smiled at him as she chose to seat herself in an overstuffed chair near a square paned window. "I am sorry to miss her, but perhaps she'll be at the next Council meeting?"

He nodded. "Oh yes, Myrtle rarely misses one of those. She really likes to keep her eye on things going on with the church, as you well know."

She grinned. "She keeps us in order, Reverend. That's something committee meetings need once in a while." She paused. "I expect you know why I'm here?"

"Oh indeed yes, dear lady. It's about the music for your dear daughter's birthday?"

She nodded. "I have a modest list here that I know Rebecca would enjoy hearing. As I understand Sally and Derek are well acquainted with Cole Porter and George Gershwin numbers, I don't think they'll have any difficulty in executing them in their usual wonderful fashion."

He took the list she offered, placed spectacles on the end of his nose to scan the selection quickly. He nodded. "These are excellent choices, Mrs. Thorncroft. I will make sure Sally and Derek receive them safely tomorrow evening when they get home." He put the list on a table nearby. "Would you care to take in a cup of tea? I have the kettle on the boil as I speak."

She shook her head. "That's very kind of you, but no, I really must be getting along." She stood up. "You and Myrtle will be able to attend the party, won't you?"

He shook his head. "Sadly, no. I have to go to a Diocesan meeting on the 24th and I don't think Myrtle will be back by then. We're sorry we're going to miss it, but please wish Rebecca a very happy birthday from us won't you."

"I will, Reverend Finley." She moved to the door, pulling the handle to open it. "I'll see you next Sunday?"

He nodded. "Of course. Goodbye, Mrs. Thorncroft."

Although Catherine had resisted the offer of a beverage at the vicarage, she was actually ready for a cup of tea. When Percy opened the car door for her, she stepped inside, making herself comfortable against the rich warm leather seat. A few minutes later, they pulled up outside a restaurant on the corner of High Street and the quaint Puddlecum Square with its war memorial in the centre. Percy assisted Catherine out of the Sedanca and Catherine entered Maria's Restaurant with a spring in her step. She was feeling particularly good today—it was nice sometimes to have the day to herself. Not to be laden with Ravenslea responsibilities was a luxury she rarely enjoyed. Oh, she liked going to the Church Council meetings, though that could be tedious on times; she enjoyed the Branton Garden Club which met once a month. Meeting different people always appealed to her, as it did Rebecca.

One of the highlights of coming into Branton, however, was the little teas that she enjoyed at Maria's Restaurant. Today, the restaurant was tastily decorated with dainty white lace curtains in the windows along with blue and white gingham tablecloths on the small square tables. Once inside, she asked to sit at a window seat, where she settled down to watch the occasional automobile or horse-drawn carriage pass by. Pedestrians strolled around the sparse assortment of shops. There were only two eating places in Branton; one was the local public house; the other was Maria's Restaurant which she definitely preferred. Always good home-cooked meals were served there and Catherine had become a firm favourite with the owners and staff alike.

"Hello, Mrs. Thorncroft," a friendly voice cut into her thoughts, "it's so nice to see you again, but quite surprising to see you'd venture out in such inclement weather."

"Good morning, Herbert. It's good to see the sun of course, but the rain is really quite refreshing."

"Yes indeed." He poised with pencil and pad in hand. "And what may I get you?"

"A nice strong pot of tea please and some of those delicious little cakes that Maria makes. Not too creamy though, I do have to watch my waist-line."

He grinned. "Not by much, Mrs. Thorncroft." He said tactfully. He pencilled in the order and pocketed the pad.

After he'd left, Catherine gazed out the window. She loved this little town. It was large enough to be able to get the staples of life; a few newer stores had opened up in the last year offering a variety of choices, thereby keeping the smaller ones on their toes.

A few moments later, Herbert appeared with a small silver teapot, sugar basin, milk jug, a bone china cup and saucer. An array of freshly baked tea cakes made Catherine open her eyes in delight.

"Thank you, Herbert. I don't know how Maria has time to make these wonderful concoctions; she's such a treasure."

"Oh, she always finds the time, Mrs. Thorncroft. She loves baking and even hires herself out sometimes as a caterer for a large gathering."

"Really?" Catherine's eyes widened. She'd never thought to ask Maria if she'd be able to help with Rebecca's birthday, however, it didn't matter now that Agnes had already arranged help. "I didn't realize that. Umm. Well, that's wonderful, but you must see very little of her when she becomes involved in those kinds of activities."

He laughed. "I usually help her. We get along fine in the Kitchen, much to everyone's amusement. I enjoy it almost as much as she does."

It was while Catherine was enjoying Maria's delicacies and tea that she happened to glance out the window. To her surprise she saw Elspeth leaning on her bicycle across the street from the restaurant, talking to a thickset man partially hidden by a bushy tree planted in a wooden tub on the path. She frowned. Every now and again, Elspeth furtively glanced around the area and back to the man again. Catherine felt a tremor of unease. What was going on with the woman? First the surreptitious meeting with the young woman in the Sitting Room earlier and now this?

Catherine continued keeping her eye on the pair, moving a little quicker through her snack. When she'd finished, she paid the bill and hurried out onto the street. Elspeth, now alone, had turned her bicycle around to return in the direction of Ravenslea. Catherine stood there for a moment watching her housekeeper peddling quickly away. At that moment, Percy drew the car up beside her.

"Home, Percy, before it begins to rain again." She said, after he'd opened the door and she'd settled in the back seat. As they were about to move, she leaned forward. "Oh, just stop off at the post-office, I need to get some stamps."

Percy turned. "Of course, Madam." He said, pulling gently away from the curb.

CHAPTER 9

THE BIRTHDAY PARTY

THE morning of Thursday, July 24th saw much activity at Ravenslea. The first up, even before the effervescent Catherine, was Rebecca. A normal occurrence on her birthday, when Rebecca knew the day belonged to her. She was turning twenty-one—a milestone in anyone's life and she intended to live this day to its hilt! She'd found out about the upcoming party yesterday, purely by accident, overhearing Agnes, Doris and Edna discussing icing on a cake and the general feverishness in the Kitchen that always preceded festivities at Ravenslea.

After tying a tangerine dressing gown around her slim waist, she hurried into the Kitchen. Elspeth looked up from a book she was thumbing through when Rebecca swung the Kitchen door open happily. Agnes, busy washing some dishes smiled at her from the sink.

"Happy birthday, Miss Rebecca." She said. "You're up with the lark!"

"Thank you, Agnes." Rebecca said, grinning happily. "I couldn't sleep any more. It's a beautiful day; the birds awakened me and I'm just about ready for anything! Hello Elspeth . . ." She acknowledged the housekeeper, warmly, refusing to let the woman's dour expression dampen her spirits. Rebecca often wondered why Elspeth always seemed to have something bothering her—she couldn't remember ever seeing her smile. Always that severe, thin-lipped look stamped across her face. Rebecca shrugged—well, if the housekeeper wished to be miserable all her life Rebecca had no wish for her to spoil her birthday with her downcast expression. "Are we having anything special for breakfast this morning?"

"Just the usual, Miss Rebecca." Elspeth said, snapping the book shut and turning away from her. "I must check on the table settings. Please excuse me." The thin woman in her drab grey dress walked quickly passed Rebecca and out through the door, closing it sharply behind her.

Agnes raised her eyebrows, but made no comment on the housekeeper's coolness. "I just saw your brother, Miss Rebecca. I think he went into the Conservatory."

"Eden?"

Agnes nodded. "Of course. It takes a little longer for Master Luke to rouse himself in the mornings as you well know." She turned to the stove, picked up a large copper kettle and filled it with water from a dripping tap over the sink. "Now, if you don't mind, Miss, we do have to prepare breakfast, you know, and

Elspeth was right—there's nothing special this morning."

"Of course." Rebecca grinned and skipped out of the room as if this was her tenth birthday, not her twenty-first!

By the time everyone had surfaced from their slumber, the morning had aged by a couple more hours. The Thorncrofts were in good spirits and Rebecca endured the gentle teasing of her brothers remarkably well. She refused to allow anything to mar her happiness today!

After the normal hearty breakfasts, which lasted until almost ten o'clock, Rebecca took her little puppy, Phoebe for a long walk over the moors with her mother. Rebecca always enjoyed these times with her little dog and having her mother with her today was an added joy. Mother and daughter rarely spent time alone together, but when they did it was time precious spent. Occasionally, they'd go riding, but usually Eden or James would accompany them. Then again Louise and Christiana might decide to tag along as well. Martin rarely indulged in riding, not being keen on it since the incident with one of the Ravenslea mares some years ago.

By noon, Catherine and Rebecca had covered a wide terrain of undulating moorland with its purple heather, Roman stone bridges and quaint bubbling streams. Phoebe was in her element, running free, jumping joyously through long grass, becoming enmeshed a few times in brambles and bracken and having to be gently released by one or other of the women. The weather was wonderfully warm—the air sweet with clover and birdsong.

As they neared the raw beauty of Piper's Head that overlooked the ceaseless motion of the Bristol Channel, the women relaxed, sitting beside each other on a smooth wooden bench. For a while neither spoke, just content to be together and to gaze in awe at the ocean surfing against the shoreline, sending seabirds whirling and screaming with every updraught.

"I never tire of looking out over this bluff, it's so beautiful!" Rebecca said at last. She linked arms with her mother affectionately. "I'm so very, very lucky to have been born a Thorncroft and to be able to enjoy the comforts of home and the beauty of everything around me."

Catherine ruffled her daughter's dishevelled raven hair. "Dear, dear Rebecca. How many more times in your young life are you going to tell us that? Of all my children, you seem so appreciative of your heritage and life here."

"No, not just me," Rebecca glanced up at her mother, "I know Eden and Luke feel the same way. They've often told me so."

Catherine smiled into her daughter's animated eyes. "Well, they never tell us—your father or I—we only ever hear it from you." She dropped a kiss on Rebecca's brow. "All I can say is that we are relieved you feel that way. Some of our acquaintances and indeed one or two relatives have children who firmly believe they are the only ones that matter in life. Their selfish regard to their own lives is often an embarrassment to their parents."

"Do you refer to Uncle Martin's new wife?"

"Good gracious no, dear. Your Aunt Louise is nothing like that—!"

"But Aunt Louise's life was so different before she and Uncle Martin were married."

Catherine sighed, remembering vividly the first time she and James had met their new sister-in-law. Martin had enticed Louise to London for a brief honeymoon in 1924. It had been a whirlwind visit as they had to return home within a fortnight, but Catherine and James had taken an immediate liking to her. Martin had brought them to Ravenslea to stay for a few days and it was plain to see that Louise Whitney-Thorncroft was much in awe of Ravenslea's beautiful house and the exquisite well-kept grounds.

Now six years later, Louise and her children had decided to make Britain their permanent home. Martin had taken great delight in introducing her to some of his favourite neighbourhood haunts. They appeared to have settled into Ravenslea very comfortably and secretly Catherine was glad she had someone else in the house in which to share its upkeep, for Louise was a keen organizer, invaluable to Catherine.

Yet, in retrospect, could Rebecca have seen something in them that Catherine had not immediately detected, for over the past year, there'd been a subtle change in Louise. She had become louder, more demanding, but Catherine still enjoyed her happy-go-lucky manner and open mindedness. Louise had never, as far as she knew, crossed swords with anyone; always smiling openly at everyone she met.

"Mummy! Did you hear what I said?" Rebecca broke into her thoughts sharply bringing Catherine down to earth. "I said . . ."

"I know what you said, dear." Catherine said, carefully, "but her life was so different in the States. Before her husband tragically passed away, he'd provided well for his family. Your Uncle Martin mentioned many times the Whitney family had enjoyed a fine home, living in a good neighbourhood and had many influential friends. Louise herself has a sister who has found favour on Broadway—that's no mean feat, Rebecca. It takes a lot of courage and ambition to get that far in the entertainment world these days."

"She's just an actress." Rebecca declared a trifle cynically. "We all know what they're like."

"Don't act the snob," Catherine's warm hazel eyes narrowed. "It's most unladylike and quite unlike you."

"But it's true! Her sister's an actress—she mixes with odd people who pretend to be what they're not all the time—!"

"But Louise wasn't. Her disposition was very different."

"But, Mummy, you've never met her sister. How do you know what she's really like? You can only go by what Louise tells you."

"I agree, dear, but I don't think she would lie to me. What would be the point? From what I understand her sister is a very good entertainer and is purported to have a natural talent."

Rebecca raised an eyebrow significantly. "If that's so, then surely it would be in all of them?"

Catherine smiled, tolerantly. "That's a possibility, dear, but not always the rule, you know."

"Well, I don't know . . . I still tend to want to substantiate all Louise tells us—despite what you think, I'm never too certain she always tells the truth." Then, at her mother's expression, she decided to change the subject. "Anyway, I'm not sure about Christiana either. How come she's in her mid twenties and has never married? From what I can see, she's the type that would attract a man."

Catherine was silent for a moment. "She was married once. She and her husband are divorced, Rebecca." She sighed. "It's good they found out they couldn't live with their differences before children arrived to complicate matters. They were both very young and obviously had made a gross mistake." Catherine turned, brushing a wisp of fine hair off Rebecca's brow gently. "Let's not discuss this now. You know, of course, about this evening."

Rebecca's manner changed and she grinned happily. "How anyone could possibly think they'd be able to keep the preparation of a party from me. Though, I have to admit, I only really sensed something in the last couple of days. I felt sure there'd be some kind of get-together, after all, turning twenty-one is a milestone in everyone's life, so I've heard." She smiled up at her mother. "When I knew Allison was coming, I was sure it wasn't just because her father had returned; it wasn't until I heard Agnes and Doris in the Kitchen discussing a cake that I knew for certain. Thank you, Mummy—I'm so lucky to have you!"

"I'm the lucky one, darling." Catherine squeezed her arm and stood up. "Come, we should return."

By seven thirty that night, Ravenslea's lovely grounds were bright with coloured illuminations and noisily alive with people and laughter. Sally and Derek arrived just as a small quartet of musicians began tuning their instruments ready to provide most of the music for the dance.

Rebecca preened in front of the oval mirror next to her dressing table in the beautiful lilac gown that her grandmother had given to her that morning, stopping only when she heard Sally playing a lively melody on the piano.

When she arrived downstairs, her gown was an instant success and everyone agreed the colour brought out the young woman's raven colouring to perfection. Her brothers whistled their admiration, much to her surprise and delight and her father looked her over with parental love.

Rebecca moved towards her grandmother and drew her into her arms, kissing her lightly on her surprisingly clear cheek. "Thank you so much . . ." she said. "I have this lovely lady to thank for choosing the colour and, somehow, knowing my measurements." She squeezed Elizabeth's arm affectionately.

"You look adorable, dear." Elizabeth returned, kissing her granddaughter warmly.

"I fear my dear, your Mother and I could lose you soon, if you continue to look so utterly charming." James came over to her and imprisoned her hand in both of his.

"It'll take someone very special to lure me away from my wonderful family, Daddy and . . ." she gave a cursory glance around the room, stars in her eyes, " . . . there's not a single man here who even comes close to unseating me from Ravenslea!"

James laughed then glanced at Catherine. Both knew there was possibly one man who'd definitely unseat her from Ravenslea. "You will, of course, have at least one waltz with me?"

"I'm sure there'll be many a jig I'll be sharing with you. I might even have you dance the Charleston with me—how do you feel about that?"

He held up his hands in mock denial. "Heavens, Rebecca—I'd do myself an injury if I attempted that!"

"Oh, I don't know. I've been told by quite a reliable source that you're a wonderful dancer—and you seem fit enough for that." She kissed him lightly on the cheek and glanced over at Catherine who grinned at her.

"He's a good dancer now, dear, but in the early days he gave me quite a few stubs on my toes!" She and James laughed conspiratorially. "The Charleston, however, might be his undoing!"

Rebecca left them to saunter through the many guests who'd arrived complete with an assortment of packages. As she wandered around, she was suddenly aware that the Rhodes family had not arrived. She knew her parents would definitely have invited them—well, perhaps they'd arrive later. She couldn't fully enjoy her birthday if Stephanie and William were not there to share in her special day. In the meantime, she greeted each one with a kiss and welcoming comment until the moment came for her to open the gifts. Colourful parcels of all shapes and sizes were arranged on a long table, with balloons, ribbons and candles spluttering in their holders separating them.

Rebecca walked around the table, viewing each one, picking one up now and again until her curiosity overcame her and she began opening them. From Aunt Fern and Uncle Simon, a French inlaid jewellery box; Uncle Martin and Aunt Louise gave her a sparkling ruby pendant bought in New York all those years ago when Uncle Martin had first visited the States to bring his new wife to England.

"We had you in mind even then, dear." Martin said, kissing his niece gently on the brow.

"It's beautiful. Thank you so very much." She beamed at Fern who was standing next to Elizabeth. "Just the right thing to place in your lovely jewellery box."

Cousin Emily and her husband, Gary, gave her a warm boa wrap for the cool days ahead. Emily's sister Constance and her husband Paul, presented her with a compendium of phonograph records of the music of Ruth Etting, one of Rebecca's favourite singers. Allison gave her a hand-crafted necklace and earring set.

All at once the door opened. Rebecca looked up to see the smiling faces of Aunt Penelope and Uncle Fletcher followed with the petite form of Stephanie and her handsome tall brother, William. Rebecca's heart leapt. They were here. She waved and the four of them hurried to the table complete with gaily wrapped packages. Rebecca leaned over and kissed each one of them, lingering slightly on William, though pulled away quickly when she realized everyone was watching her.

She opened the presents slowly. Penelope and Fletcher gave her a silk scarf and brooch to secure it with. William gave a book of poems and stories by Louisa May Alcott. Stephanie gave her a beautiful, delicate Swiss clock with a little Swiss girl swinging as the pendulum beneath it.

"Oh, Stephanie. Where on earth did you get this?" Rebecca cried. "It's beautiful."

"I brought it back from Zurich when I returned from Finishing School. I've had it tucked away in one of my drawers since then." Stephanie shrugged, a twinkle appearing in her eye. "I thought this would be an ideal present—now you have no excuse to be late for appointments, especially when we arrange to go riding together. You have yet to be on time for that!"

The evening sped along far quicker than Rebecca really wished. She danced almost every dance with William Rhodes. She insisted, however, that she would draw her father onto the floor for a waltz. He agreed wholeheartedly, but refused with a grin, the Charleston she'd warned him about earlier and Rebecca understood. She didn't really believe her father would be able to embark on such a strenuous dance, though she tried it herself with William.

Sally and Derek were a wonderful addition to the gathering. They were applauded time and again for their virtuoso performance. Rebecca marvelled at the strength and vitality in Derek's strident bass-baritone voice. The songs were exactly as she'd wished.

After the dancing had stopped to give everyone including the musicians a break, there was a lull in the hubbub of conversation. It was at that moment that the sound of a vehicle pulling up and sounding its horn, caught everyone's attention. Guests, puzzled and some a little alarmed, converged on the terrace and the windows craning their necks to see who'd arrived so late.

Rebecca rushed towards the front door, as puzzled as everyone else. Before she had a chance to open the door, it was suddenly opened and her heart missed a few beats. A man appeared, a huge smile lighting up his tawny features. It was only Mike. She breathed in relief and was about to say something, when she felt someone move up behind her.

"Our present to you, darling." James whispered, catching her hand in his and squeezing it affectionately. He glanced at Catherine at his side as the three of them moved to the top of the steps.

By now the rest of the guests had joined them as they converged into the shadows of a clear night, the only light coming from a partially concealed moon along with the warm yellow glow from inside the house.

There at the bottom of the steps stood a light coloured sportscar. Rebecca squealed with delight and was about to run down the steps when her father pressed something in her hands.

"You'll need this, my dear." He said, softly. A key was placed in her trembling hand she paused, then flung her arms around first her father, then her mother, tears of happiness in her eyes.

"Oh Daddy! Mummy! Thank you so much . . . it's so beautiful . . . where did you hide this?" She glanced at Mike standing nearby. "You knew all along didn't you . . . and you didn't reveal the secret!" Rebecca's voice broke.

"Go on dear," Catherine gently pushed her forward. "Sit in it. Feel the seats. In the morning, perhaps we'll get Eden to teach you how to drive it."

Rebecca needed no more encouragement. Hitching up the skirt of her gown, she hurried down the steps, opened the door and took up her position behind the wheel. Eden drew alongside her and showed her where to put the key before starting the vehicle.

When that night she finally managed to calm herself down to go to bed, she lay back against her pillow reliving every single moment. Agnes, along with her team of waiters and waitresses, including Doris, Edna and even Elspeth, had done a magnificent job with the pheasant, wines and special mouth-watering desserts.

That beautiful car! Although the gifts were excellent choices, Rebecca's heart was full of love for her wonderful family and friends. She couldn't have asked for a better birthday.

CHAPTER 10

SEPTEMBER 1930

S TEPHANIE threw her gloves, black felt riding hat and matching scarf on the hall table. She ran a hand through her tousled curls. Glancing in the hall mirror, she noticed how her face showed signs of exertion. Pouting, she kicked off her riding boots and black jacket. The invigorating ride over the moors had been a joy for her. She only wished she could have shared it with Eden—being alone was good enough, but with Eden beside her, she'd have been ecstatic.

She walked through the deserted Hallway towards the slightly open Drawing Room door.

"Hello darling." Penelope turned, smiling at her daughter's entrance. "Enjoy your ride?"

"It was terrific!" Stephanie walked quickly towards the bar. "I could do with a drink though. You know how much I love riding, but Kedar was especially spirited today—I had a difficult job holding him back on a few occasions. I don't know what's got into him these days; it's almost as if he doesn't know me any more."

"Arabs are powerful animals, my dear. They should only be ridden by men who are physically able to control them." This came from her father who'd just entered the room behind her, taking off his gloves and laying them on the table. "I told you not to ride him—he can be quite a handful when he takes a mind to be tetchy. You should have chosen to ride Sandy."

"Well, although you've warned me about Kedar's fiery nature, you know how much I like a challenge. Sandy's a sweetheart, there's no doubt about it, but she's timid and shies at everything. I wonder sometimes how she manages to trot around the paddock without having an anxiety attack and throwing me."

"Even so, Stephanie, you chose, as usual, to disregard my warnings." Fletcher's eyes bore into hers accusingly.

Stephanie shrugged. She moved towards the small cocktail cabinet and poured herself a Martini. Plopping into a nearby armchair, she set the drink on the small table beside it.

"I know I disobeyed you and I'm sorry, but I just couldn't resist." She said, glancing up at her father as she took her first sip. "It's just that he was in the paddock, looking ready for a romp and I just had to. He definitely needed some exercise, he . . ."

"Well, I'm not impressed, Stephanie." Her father interrupted. "You could easily have been badly hurt, especially as you were alone. With the recent rains, who knows what could have happened."

"I know. I know." Stephanie's voice rose slightly, showing signs of impatience, "but I'm sure you'd do the same, Daddy, had you been in my shoes."

"Well, so long as you're safe that's all that really matters, isn't it, Fletcher?" Penelope said, turning her head back to the sewing resting on her knee.

"I came to no harm, Mummy; surely that's all that matters." Stephanie stood up. "I'm going upstairs to change; I'll be down for dinner in a jiffy."

About an hour later, when the Rhodes were convened in the Drawing Room, Nancy, their petite young maid, knocked on the door and stepped inside.

"Excuse me," she murmured, "but there's a gentleman in the Hallway wishing to speak to Miss Stephanie. Shall I show him into the Library?"

Stephanie frowned. "How odd, I didn't hear the doorbell? Do you recognize him, Nancy?"

Nancy shook her head. "No, Miss. He said his name was Nigel and that you'd know who I meant."

Stephanie's heart thumped painfully. Nigel! What was Nigel doing here? How on earth did he find her?

"All right, Nancy. Show him into the Library. I'll be with him in a minute. Perhaps you could get him a drink while he waits."

"Yes, Miss." Nancy said, gently closing the door behind her.

Both her parents looked at her, puzzled. "Well, who is Nigel, Stephanie? I've never heard you speak of him before." Penelope frowned at her daughter.

Stephanie hesitated. "Well . . . I did get to know a man called Nigel Whitfield on my trip from Switzerland. I can only presume it's him. I certainly had no idea he'd be calling on me." She stood up. "I suppose I'd better see what he wants."

"Well, when you've become re-acquainted, perhaps you could bring him in here and make the customary introductions." Fletcher tapped the side of the mantlepiece with his pipe, allowing the spent ash to trickle down to oblivion into the fire.

"Of course." Stephanie put down her drink and hurried from the Drawing Room.

The tall, rigid form of Nigel Whitfield was glancing through a row of books at eye-level when she entered the library. A shaft of sunlight fell on his coppery coloured hair as he bent forward to study the book spines, bringing out the golden tints. He turned at her entrance, smiling warmly.

"Stephanie!" He caught her hands in his. "I'm so delighted to have finally found you. It took me all this time, my dear, to find Cavendish Hall and you." He made to lean forward and kiss her, but she pulled away gently.

"Why did you come, Nigel?" She asked, simply, pulling her hands free. She turned away from him and moved towards the window to view the garden.

"You ask me such a thing? I told you I'd find you one day, didn't I? Don't tell me you've forgotten all ready?"

"No, I didn't forget. I honestly didn't think you were serious . . ."

He laughed. Putting his hands on her shoulders, he turned her to face him. She reluctantly turned. He smiled down at her and the times they had shared on their return journey to England came rushing back. She remembered his warm, sultry brown eyes and slightly off-centre smile as he'd asked if he may join her at her breakfast table one morning while they were traveling from Zurich. He'd apologized at having to break in on her solitude, but as there was no other table available, would she mind sharing with him. At the time, Stephanie had been feeling in need of companionship, so had willingly let him join her. His pleasant, light-hearted banter refreshed her and before the journey had ended, they had become good friends.

"Oh, my dear, dear, Stephanie." He broke into her thoughts abruptly. "I'm mortified to think you considered our time together was just friendship without anything more blossoming."

"I . . . I didn't want anything to 'blossom' as you put it, Nigel. I thought I'd made it quite clear that nothing further could come from our friendship once we'd reached England."

"I know you said that, but . . . I tried to put you out of my mind, I really did." He pulled away from her, looking down at his shiny black shoes and twisting his hands in front of him. "I travelled north, tried to get myself occupied at the mill. I tried to sound convincing when my father and brother talked of financial matters, day to day problems, et cetera, but all the time, Stephanie, my thoughts returned to you." He paused. "You see, you must have done something magical to me . . ."

"Stop!" She said, rougher than she intended. "You've said enough, Nigel. I don't know how I can explain any better than I have, that there will never be a future for us together. My heart lies elsewhere." There, now she'd said it. She'd said what she knew she couldn't deny; for the first time in her life she'd actually admitted to herself that her feelings for Eden Thorncroft went far further than just mere friendship.

She glanced up at him. The look of reproach that had replaced the warm smile of a moment ago, moved her to shame. She touched his arm gently.

"I'm sorry, Nigel, I didn't mean to be so horrid to you after you journeyed all that distance. I'm treating you badly. Please forgive me."

He looked at her, a ghost of a smile hovering around his sensuous mouth. "I'll forgive you anything, Stephanie. You mean everything to me and, oddly enough, I understand you don't feel for me what I feel for you, but . . ." he paused, "at least tell me this; are you betrothed?"

"No, but, Nigel, it would make no difference. I couldn't give you what you want when I feel this way. You must understand."

His face brightened. "Well, my dear, so long as no other man has asked for your hand in marriage, perhaps there is hope for me?"

She shook her head. "Sorry, Nigel. I am really flattered that you feel so strongly about me."

"Look, dear." He said, grabbing her hands before she had time to draw them away. "I'm staying at the Cottage Arms in the village—why don't you show me the best places to visit. We could have a drink and a meal somewhere—get to know each other again. That way, perhaps I'll be able to persuade you to turn your desires in my direction."

Talking about turning her desires toward him was certainly not something she wished to discuss. "I'm sorry Nigel, I really don't wish to discuss this now." She breathed heavily and pulled gently away. "How long are you staying in the area?"

He shrugged. "I have no real plans to return just yet, but I shouldn't be away too long. I'm sure my family will need me at some point, so I've tentatively booked in at the Cottage Arms for five days." He paused. "I'd like to make it longer; it all depends on you as I want to be with you all the time I'm here, if you'll have me."

She thought for a moment. Treacherously, giving no thought to Nigel's feelings, she wondered if, perhaps, this was what she needed to take her mind off Eden. Another man in her life would surely broaden her horizons. She had to admit Nigel was attractive; she'd thought him good company on the ship, perhaps by being with him would take Eden's image away, at least for a short while.

"All right Nigel. We'll arrange to use the days you're here to spend together. I'll take you around the area. We have some quite fascinating sights, I'm sure you'd appreciate." She smiled up at him. "Now, my parents have asked to meet you, so we'd better not disappoint them."

"Yes. Yes, of course. I'd be honoured to meet them." Nigel followed her out of the library and into the Hallway.

The Drawing Room door was still ajar as they walked steadily towards it. Penelope glanced up, setting her sewing on a nearby table. Fletcher placed his pipe on the mantlepiece and held out a hand to the newcomer, a welcoming smile on his rugged face.

Stephanie preceded Nigel. "Daddy, Mummy, this is Mr. Nigel Whitfield, the young man I was telling you about earlier." She turned to the man by her side. "Nigel, meet my parents, Fletcher and Penelope Rhodes."

After the formalities were dispensed with, Nigel was shown to a seat. Stephanie's father offered him a glass of wine which the young man accepted. Nigel was then invited to stay for dinner. Later, when the night had drawn in and the cold wind had, miraculously, died down, the two young people donned warm coats and ventured into the Cavendish grounds. Nigel held her arm as they walked along the paved pathway that curved around the house; Stephanie made sure their conversation remained commonplace. She had no desire to encourage him to discuss their relationship, for her generally kind nature did not wish to distress him further. There would be time enough for that when the moment arrived for his departure.

Nigel stayed until the grandfather clock in the Hallway chimed eleven-thirty. Stephanie's parents had retired to bed more than an hour ago; now she was eager to see Nigel leave. At that moment, they were sitting close together on the comfortable sofa, Nigel's arm resting nonchalantly along the back of the seat. He touched her chin with his other hand, twisting her around to face him. Gently he laid his warm, soft lips against hers. To her horror, she felt an unbidden response deep inside her. She had to stifle that or he would regard it as encouragement on her part, which, in turn, would arouse him to a point where it might be difficult to free herself. She gently moved away from him. Smiling, she placed a light kiss on the tip of his nose affectionately.

"Nigel, it's late. I have to get up in the morning even if you don't. I think you should return to the Cottage Arms. We can arrange to go somewhere tomorrow, if you'd like?" She stood up quickly, aware that he was about to draw her back down onto the sofa.

"Oh, my dearest Stephanie," he moaned, leaning back to stare at her as she walked towards the Drawing Room door. "Just a little longer…"

She grinned. "No, Nigel. You really must go now."

He pressed his lips together and slowly rose to his feet, brushing his slightly rumpled clothes. At the front door, he caught her to him again, enveloping her in a demanding embrace.

"It's a start, my darling." He murmured against her hair. "I still have a few days to win you around."

She smiled at him. On opening the front door, a gust of cool air encircled them bringing with it a few newly fallen leaves which landed softly at their feet. She brushed them aside with her foot and ushered the ardent young man out into the night.

"I'll see you tomorrow, then, Stephanie?" Nigel said regretfully. "Around 9 o'clock?"

She nodded. "Of course. I'll be ready."

After she'd watched him leave the house, she leaned against the back of the front door thoughtfully. Eden had never looked at her the way Nigel did. Perhaps her future didn't lie with the handsome young heir to Ravenslea; maybe it would be best if she did pay more attention to Nigel Whitfield. As she steadily climbed the winding staircase to her bedroom, she thought about the difference between the two men. She would always love Eden, she was certain of that, but if she couldn't have him, perhaps she would be able to turn her affection towards the ardent Nigel. It was a thought, and one she pondered on as she bathed and slipped between the warm sheets that night.

The next morning she awoke to odd muted sounds coming from beneath her window. Slipping a dressing gown over her cotton nightdress, she hurried to the window and partially drew the curtains aside. Her eyes widened in astonishment. Nigel was sitting on the bottom step, holding his ankle, while talking animatedly to Eden Thorncroft. Eden had one foot on the step while holding onto Jake's reins. She leaned against the panelling beside the window pane, conscious that her face was suffused with heat and redness. Her heart hammered painfully against her robe; her breath came in ragged disorder. After a moment, the odd panicky feeling abated long enough to allow her to turn back to look through the window.

Eden was laughing! And she could see by the movement of Nigel's shoulders, he was laughing too! She frowned. How very peculiar! She had to find out what was going on. Quickly changing into warm corduroy trousers, dark green sweater and shoes, she hurried down the stairs. When she opened the door, Eden looked up.

"Hi Steph. Look, I found this gentleman by the side of the road. He's hurt his ankle. He mentioned that he knew you, so would you mind looking after him if I help you get him into the house; then perhaps you'd better call the doctor to check him over."

"Don't bother with the doctor." Nigel said. "I think I'll be all right if I just rest it for a while. Thank you so much for being there for me. Don't know where I'd be if you hadn't."

Eden grinned. "Think nothing of it. Can you put him up for the night, Steph? I'll come by tomorrow morning to see how you're doing."

Stephanie hurried down the steps as Eden was attempting to help Nigel to his feet. Between them, they managed to half carry him up the remainder of the steps into Cavendish Hall. Almost immediately they were inside, Eden hurried back out, ran down the steps and straddled his stallion.

"See you later." He thundered out of the grounds in a flurry of hoof beats, sending turf and loose stones flying.

Stephanie took Nigel into the Sitting Room. He leaned back against a sofa with his foot resting on a cushion. "Thanks, Stephanie. I suppose we did make quite a noise—no wonder you were disturbed."

"Well, I heard the horse arrive. When I looked out the window and saw you sitting on the steps, I was concerned. How did you hurt yourself?"

"I don't feel a lot of pain at the moment, my dear, but it was deuced painful on the back of Eden's horse, as you can imagine." He smiled up at her. "I awoke early and couldn't settle, so decided to leave the Cottage Inn for a leisurely stroll through the village. On my way, I thought as the morning was just made for walking, I'd come and see you again. I'd only gone about a mile or so when I caught my foot in a hole in the road, twisting my ankle. I'm glad you weren't there, my dear," he said, smiling down at her, "because I'm afraid I used quite a few choice words as it damned well hurt when I put my foot to the ground. However, I was extremely lucky when a few minutes later, Mr. Thorncroft appeared on his magnificent beast. He heaved me up onto his horse. As Cavendish Hall is closer than his residence, he said he'd bring me here."

"Well, that was very kind of him." She paused, sitting down on the sofa beside him. "I'm a little puzzled, Nigel."

"Oh?" He raised an eyebrow quizzically.

"You ... you and ... Mr. Thorncroft ... sounded so companionable, laughing together as if you were old friends. I was under the impression you'd never met each other before?"

"And you'd be quite right, Stephanie." He grinned, grimacing slightly as he shifted his position. "He seems a decent chap and while we talked, we both realized we have much in common. I have to also admit that Mr. Thorncroft is quite a wit. He was regaling me with some of his juvenile adventures which oddly quite resembled mine in some cases."

Stephanie stared at him. "Did he ... did he mention anything about me at all in all this talk of his past?"

"Not at all, my dear. Why? Do you have some deep dark secret only known to you and Mr. Thorncroft?" His eyes smiled merrily at her.

"Of course not . . . but my brother and I did once in a while play with the Thorncroft children. I'm sure we got up to a lot of mischief as children do, much of which I have completely forgotten. I was thinking that perhaps Mr. Thorncroft may have remembered things that had slipped my mind. That's all."

"He only mentioned some of the adventures he and his brother . . . Luke, is it?" She nodded, "used to have when they were children. Apparently, along with some other boys in the neighbourhood, they often got into mischief at some farmer's field hereabouts. He didn't mention you, Stephanie, so perhaps he, too, has forgotten anything you all got up to." He suddenly winced as he moved his foot.

"Oh dear," Stephanie glanced at his injured leg. "I think we ought to get our chauffeur to get the doctor. I'm at a loss as to know what to do in a case like this."

"I don't think a doctor is required, Stephanie. If you and your family wouldn't mind, I'd like to just rest it up a little, perhaps put a cold compress on it to bring the swelling down as it certainly feels like it's beginning to swell now."

When Fletcher and Penelope saw Nigel's predicament, they insisted on getting him upstairs to the spare bedroom to rest for a while. If, on placing a cold compress on his ankle did nothing to relieve the pain, then it might be prudent to get Barnaby to fetch the doctor. Stephanie was not prepared for this, but could hardly argue with her parents. She would have been happier if Nigel had been driven back to the Inn. When night came, he said he was feeling better, but still had a little trouble putting weight on his foot. That was when they suggested he stay the night; they'd get the doctor the next day if the ankle hadn't healed. To help him sleep, Penelope gave him a couple of painkillers.

As she didn't hear anything more from Nigel that night, Stephanie relaxed. Knowing how potent the painkillers were that her mother had given him, she was certain they had calmed him enough to allow him to sleep.

The next morning, Barnaby took him back to the Inn.

Apparently, while he'd been at Cavendish Hall Nigel's brother, Richard, had telephoned the Inn late last night. The Innkeeper had written a note to inform him that his father had suddenly been taken ill. Nigel immediately telephoned Cavendish Hall and told Stephanie he would have to forego a visit to the doctor as well as their plans for a day together, as he had to leave Branton immediately to travel up to Northern England.

CHAPTER 11

DARTMOOR PRISON
OCTOBER 1930

Tʜᴇ high iron door of the formidable Dartmoor Prison, with its heavy circular rivets embedded within its framework, closed with a loud metallic thud. Outside, shivering in the biting cold wind that permeated the vast open moors, Bernard Webb waited for his conveyance. The moors were always raw and unyielding and even though the past summer had been unusually warm, the oppressive aura emitted by Dartmoor Prison sent a chill of unease through him. He drew the collar of the trench-coat around his long thin neck and over his ears, a trace of impatience in the action.

He dropped a tattered brown case onto the uneven ground and looked around. Although he was relieved to be out of prison, at least he had had three squares a day and a reasonably-sized cell to live in during the ten years he'd been there. Live? He wasn't sure that was the right term for what he'd endured in that little square room. It had been noisy in his cell block. Other inmates, less complacent, had incessantly yelled to one another during the night. Even at 'Lights-Out' it had sometimes been almost impossible to get anything resembling sleep.

But he didn't complain—he'd overcome the annoyance by stuffing cotton wool in his ears. Bernard Webb wasn't a mixer, being content to be left alone. His brother, Ralph, had come in occasionally to visit him which was as much company as he needed. Those were the times when Ralph would bring him in a magazine, or a book which kept Bernard occupied.

He exhaled; his breath vapourizing in the cold air. Now, he had to fend for himself and with little money, he wasn't sure how he was going to go about doing this as he'd more or less forgotten what life was like on the outside, especially for an unskilled man like himself. He'd been away from the workforce too long.

He stamped his feet, blowing warm air into his cold hands and rubbing them together. Where the Hell was Ralph? He'd told him to meet him outside the Prison gate at exactly 9 o'clock and it was already ten minutes past.

He moved forward slightly, looked up and down the road then turned back into the shelter of the Prison Gate. Glancing up he noticed the sign over the large iron door—"Parce subjectis". He'd learned from one of the wardens that it meant—Spare the Vanquished.

Well, he'd not really felt vanquished; it was true he and his fool of a lawyer had lost his case, but after all he'd been guilty of the crime of attempted murder of a juvenile. The child had survived which made Bernard realize that if he hadn't, he probably wouldn't be standing here at this minute. At best he'd have been incarcerated for life; at worst, he would have been hanged!

He ran a hand through his close-cropped red hair. He hadn't wanted it cut, but apparently the rules of the Prison dictated that it had to be done—something to do with hygiene and head-lice. Strangely enough, they'd allowed him to keep his beard, so his worst feature, his almost non-existent chin, was disguised. As he waited, he reminisced on his life inside those formidable gates. He'd become accustomed to the wardens, even loosely befriending a few and he knew his way around the prison like it was his own home. It was strangely shaped, not like any other prison of which he'd heard. The outside walls were shaped in a circle with inner walls spreading like the spokes of a bicycle wheel finally meeting to an irregular point in the centre courtyard. The inside of the outer wall with its metallic walkway was used as a platform for the guards who paraded it day and night. He'd heard of inmates escaping the formidable building in the past, but nowadays renovations had been made to make it far more difficult for those imprisoned inside to leave other than through the front entrance. Despite wanting to leave the institution, Bernard had had no desire to jeopardize his final release by attempting himself, plus he was wise enough to know it was foolhardy to attempt escape as the terrain outside the prison was bleak and treacherous. Pursued by guards and their hounds, many men were recaptured sick with hunger and cold; those that weren't, often perished on the merciless Devonshire moors.

The food was edible, but that was about it; nevertheless it filled his belly and kept him reasonably healthy. Twice a day, he'd be let out into a courtyard for daily exercises with other inmates, under close supervision. Now he was glad he'd behaved himself and was out in the world again. Ten years was more than enough time spent in that place for it was draughty when the wind blew across the moors, seeping through cracks in the walls. He couldn't remember ever having so many colds in his life. All he wanted now was to get away from the darkness and sparse conditions, leaving him free to get on with his life and roam the moors as he used to before he was incarcerated.

A noise in the distance stopped his daydreams. A black car rattled slowly along the road, drawing to an effortless halt in front of him. A thickset man in a brown woollen coat and hat, jumped out. He caught hold of Bernard's suitcase and ushered him into the passenger seat of the car.

"'Bout time!" Bernard grumbled, leaning back and closing his eyes.

"Sorry." His younger brother looked over at him, before returning his gaze to the road ahead. "I didn't realize until I reached Branton, that I didn't 'ave enough petrol to get 'ere."

"That was stupid of you, wasn't it? Why didn't you get some yesterday? You knew you'd 'ave to drive all the way 'ere." Bernard snarled at him, pushing the brim of his trilby further back on his head. He stared at his brother.

"I could 'ave, I suppose, but I didn't, so that's that. Anyway, yer safe now and I'm takin' you 'ome for a slap-up meal."

"Oh? And who's the cook? Not you, I 'ope!" Bernard's eyes widened dubiously, knowing that Ralph even had trouble boiling an egg!

Ralph laughed. "It's a surprise, so don't push me to tell you."

"Okay, brother, I'll wait, but it'd better be something better than your normal grub!"

Ralph didn't answer, just gazed ahead, a slight upward tilt to his thin lips. Bernard leaned against the back of the front seat and slept for most of the journey.

The moors were cold with a heavy mist enveloping them as they travelled north. A harsh wind was now buffeting the vehicle on the open stretches and Ralph had to slow down when they came to bends in the road. In the shelter of the valleys, he opened up the engine and surged ahead as best he could with the added hazards of winding roads, rolling hills and deeper than normal fords across the roads. Purple heather waved across open ground and as they neared the beautiful Exmoor forest, a dozen or so wild ponies looked up from their positions to watch the strange sight pass them by. Not one animal seemed concerned.

It was almost two o'clock by the time they pulled up outside Ralph's small house in the centre of a row of cottages on a narrow cobbled street on the outskirts of the sleepy little town of Branton. The cold wind had eased by now as the merciless moors of Dartmoor were behind them.

Bernard picked up his suitcase and hurried in through the slightly open door. Ralph followed behind. A woman stood silhouetted before them, her arms extended in greeting. Before Bernard had time to speak, she drew him to her and kissed him fully on the lips.

"Oh, Bernard . . . oh, 'ow I've missed you, my love."

"May?" He said, extricating himself almost immediately. "What the 'Ell are you doing 'ere? I'd 'ave thought you'd have married some poor sod and 'ave a brood of screaming brats by now."

"Oh," May said. "I 'ad a few offers and some I don't mind admittin' were very temptin', but I told you I'd wait for you, Bernie—you know I wouldn't 'ave gone back on me word." She paused, pouting a little. "'Ave I changed too much for you now—I ain't as young and pretty as you remember any more."

"You ain't any younger, that's fer sure, May, but I've aged too, so I guess it goes without sayin' that I'm 'appy you waited fer me, and," he tweaked her nose affectionately, "yer still pretty good lookin' as far as I'm concerned. You waited a long while—I still can't believe you did. But, May, the best years of yer life 'ave passed you by, like it 'as me, so if we were to wed, we'd not be able to 'ave kids now would we?"

"I'm only thirty nine, Bernie; I *could* still 'ave a kid . . . if you'd like one. But, you'd 'ave to marry me—I'm not going to 'ave a bastard, even for you, darlin'! I 'ave sense enough for that!"

"Well, I'd 'ave to think about it, May. Not that I'd ever consider marryin' anyone else—'cos you're definitely the girl for me. But . . . I just got out of prison and marriage ain't part of my plan right now." He glanced passed her to where Ralph was watching them with an amused look on his face. "Anyway, like I said before, what are you doin' 'ere?"

"Ralph told me 'e was going to fetch you from that place . . . and I decided to make you a fine dinner for yer return. I can only imagine what kind of food you've bin eating all these years, as I can see you've lost even more weight . . . you didn't need to do that, you were skinny enough before you went in!"

Bernard pushed passed her roughly. "So, what 'ave you dished up for my timely arrival?"

"Roast pork, per'aps that'll 'elp fatten you up a bit." She pushed open the Kitchen door and allowed him to step inside before her. "See, I even bought candles and a bottle of wine."

"Where'd you get the money for wine?" Bernard said.

"Never you mind where I got it—just be glad I did. I bet you 'aven't 'ad even a snifter of the stuff since you left." May grinned at him and moved towards the stove, where she bent down and took a roasting pan out of the oven.

"True enough." Bernard tweaked her bottom lightly. "I 'aven't 'ad a snifter much of anythin' while in there, May. Perhaps you can remedy that for me later?"

She moved away quickly to place the hot pan on top of the stove. Turning, she threw her arms around his neck again and hugged him close.

"Well, we'll 'ave to see about that won't we. Fer now, enjoy the meal. Let 'later' take care of itself!"

After supper, the three settled down in Ralph's small parlour, beer in hands and smoke from thin, home-rolled cigarettes curling upwards towards a murky soot-grey ceiling.

"I've got somethin' to tell you." Ralph suddenly said, at one point.

Bernard lazily glanced across the worn carpet to where his brother was sitting expectantly forward. "Well, what?" He said.

"Remember when you told me about findin' someone who may have an axe to grind with those people?" Ralph stared at his older brother.

Bernard frowned, vaguely remembering, but hoping suddenly not to have to become involved with the scheme he'd planned years ago. He flicked ash into a black ashtray in front of him. "Well, spit it out!"

"Well, I think I may 'ave found someone." Ralph looked pleased with himself. "It took a lot of lookin' about, if you know what I mean, but I just came about 'im by accident."

Bernard sat forward. "If it's one of your 'arebrained schemes, Ralph, then I'm not interested. Of course, if you 'ave somethin' worthwhile to say to me, that's different."

"Okay, okay!" Ralph then relayed news to his brother that Bernard knew he'd have to act upon.

Once away from Dartmoor, Bernard Webb relaxed and enjoyed what little remained of the autumn. October had proven to be one of the warmest in British history and Bernard was not about to ignore that fact. With the pleasant temperatures and gentle breezes, the Badgworthy Waterway that ran under the packhorse bridge near Malmsmead brought people out to enjoy the last remnants of good weather before winter finally set in.

Taking advantage of both the weather and his brother's revelation of a few days ago, Bernard swung his lithe body into the saddle and nudged his mount forward. He trotted lazily down the slope towards the bridge, which would, in turn, lead him directly to the Silver Falcon Inn. He'd ridden hard for the past half hour and had worked up quite a thirst, earning himself a visit to the local public house. Malmsmead was a typical west of England village nestled in the heart of the Doone Valley which lies deep in the mystical, magical forest of Exmoor that straddled the Somerset and Devonshire borders. This was Doone country, made famous by R.D Blackmore's sad fictional tale of 'Lorna Doone' and the love she had for John Ridd, son of the Doone's enemies that had caused anguish and bloodshed in the 1700's. The whole village had at the time fallen in love with the story and named the area after it. Consequently, the book's popularity brought newcomers and tourists to the area to see for themselves the little church nestled deep in the valley that was featured in the book.

Today was no exception. Shiny limousines brushed shoulders with a number of carriages. Bernard's sturdy roan seemed oddly out of place. He quickly jumped from the saddle and tethered his horse to a hitching post near the entrance. The Silver Falcon was jam-packed with smiling faces of people, most of which, Bernard was sure, were locals who had made it their watering hole. The sound of clinking glasses and rowdy laughter greeted him as he pushed his way through the smoky crowd and ordered a pint of their best ale.

Supping it quietly, he glanced around the pub. Of course, ten years was a long time to be away; he didn't recognize anyone. His brother had given him a skimpy description, saying only that the man was fairly old and wore dark clothes. Ralph had mentioned that the old man had had a younger man with him, but in trying to keep himself discreetly away, hadn't been able to take a lot of notice of him.

His eyes suddenly rested on the hunched shoulders of an elderly man sitting alone in shadow at the end of the bar. He recognized him. The old man had hardly changed at all; he still sported a long, reddish beard and his hair had now thinned considerably and what he had was straggly, hanging in disarray around his shoulders.

He walked over to him and pulled out a chair. The old man looked up and took a few sips of his drink.

"Good-day to you." Bernard said. "Mind if I join you? You are Silas Wiggins aren't you?"

With dull narrowed eyes and smelling of liquor, the man turned to his visitor.

Even after ten years, there seemed to be recognition in his red eyes. "Yep, Silas Wiggins at yer service. Need someone buried do ye?" The old man looked up into Bernard's face, screwing up his eyes. "'Aven't seen ye around these parts in quite some time." His voice was slurred, but his hands seemed steady enough when he set his pint onto the counter gently. "Bin away 'ave yer?"

"Indeed I 'ave, Silas—to Yorkshire." Bernard lied easily. "I've bin up there lookin' after the old folks. They be gone now, so thought I'd better return 'ome." Bernard wondered if the man had any concept of time as ten years was a long time to be caring for one's parents. "I don't like travelling by train and as I'm that much older, thought I'd retire in the area I know best."

"Why don't ye invest in one of them motor cars?" Silas Wiggins stared up at him, his rheumy brown eyes shielded under bushy grey eyebrows.

Bernard laughed. "Can't afford one—that's the truth. When I make my fortune, well . . . per'aps I'll do it, in the meantime, I'm quite 'appy with my trusty pony outside."

The man shrugged and took another gulp of the light brown liquid. "Can't say as I blame ye. They things are the most noisy, dirty contraptions, but I s'pose progress bein' what it is, they'll be 'ere to stay, I'd wager."

"I 'ave a question for ye, Silas. Now take yer time, but what I'd like to know is, if you've seen two strangers in the pub lately?"

The other man shrugged. "Times are a'changin'. There's always people 'ere that I don't know. Are ye lookin' for someone special?"

"Yeah. An elderly bloke. 'E was in 'ere with a younger one."

Silas shook his head. "That could 'ave bin anyone." He put his empty glass on the bar and slipped awkwardly from the stool as if he suffered some kind of muscular pain. "Why don't ye ask the barman? 'E serves everyone in the pub, 'e might be able to 'elp ye. I ain't stayin' no more. The missus'll be after me—I've bin 'ere too long now and well, you know women, they can get the best of you if yer let 'em." His mouth widened into the semblance of a smile, showing a wide expanse of yellowed teeth with a large gap in the middle. "Well, good to see ye again, but I'd best be off."

Bernard watched Silas Wiggins as he ambled none too steadily through the patrons and finally out of sight through the pub door. He went back to his pint and downed it quickly, beckoning to the young bartender for another. It was obvious Silas Wiggins had forgotten his name. Well, that was to be expected. He wasn't sure Wiggins would be so ready to talk to him at all if he'd realized that Bernard had been incarcerated in Dartmoor Prison for attempted murder!

"Can I get you another, Sir?" The fair haired young barman asked pleasantly, taking Bernard's empty glass.

"Yes, thanks. Same again." Bernard waited until the ale came. "I'm new to the area," he said, before the bartender moved away, "but was told to meet a gentleman 'ere. Unfortunately, I was not told 'is name. All I know is that 'e was elderly and 'ad a younger bloke with 'im. Do you remember seeing anyone like that in 'ere lately?"

The bartender shrugged. "We get a lot of elderly people in here, Sir. I'm not sayin' 'e wasn't but I can't remember everyone I serve, you understand, so I don't suppose I can 'elp you much." He said, turning back to polishing some wine glasses attentively.

"Do you know most of the patrons 'ere?" Bernard asked, glancing quickly around.

"All are locals, Sir," the young bartender looked at him oddly. "I know all of them."

"Would you check for me? If there's someone 'ere you don't recognize, per'aps 'e's the man I'm seekin'?"

The bartender looked around the room quickly then shook his head. "Sorry Sir, everyone 'ere are regulars." Then he paused. "No . . . wait, over there, by the window . . . that man in the black coat. Now you come to mention it, 'e did come in a couple of weeks ago with a younger bloke. I noticed them both particularly because they didn't fit in with the rest of the clientele here, if you know what I mean."

"By their dress?" Bernard ventured, feeling a quickening in his breast as his gaze took in the lone seated man, his face shielded behind a newspaper.

The bartender nodded. "Aye, and their speech. The older man especially 'ad a real posh accent and sounded like a . . . gentleman, if you know what I mean. Not the kind of folk we usually 'ave in 'ere."

"Well, I'll take a chance and talk to 'im, thanks. 'Opefully it's the man I'm looking for."

Bernard spread a few coins on the counter and slipped off the bar stool. Stepping over a few sprawled legs on his way towards the window, Bernard slowed to face the man, who, in turn, lowered his newspaper, an enquiring look on his thin angular face.

"Pardon me," Bernard began, "but were you in 'ere a little while ago with a younger man?"

"What if I was?" The man folded his newspaper and placed it on the table.

"It's important to know, as if you were, then I believe we have something in common to discuss. Something I'm sure would be to our mutual advantage!"

The man leaned back, his eyes brightening with curiosity. "And what could that possibly be?"

CHAPTER 12

JAMES was putting the finishing touches to a letter he was writing to the Keeley coal mine in the West Riding of Yorkshire. He'd had a phone call yesterday from one of the Plant Managers asking if James and Martin would be able to travel to the mine to discuss some major problems they were having with the workers. It appeared the miners were complaining about working conditions, including the lack of safety standards, as well as a requirement to increase their rates of pay. It would be a tricky situation as the Union was involved, something neither of the brothers enjoyed trying to placate.

In their opinion, the workers were paid the same as any other mining operation, but the working conditions perhaps needed some attention, so it seemed likely he and Martin would have to take a trip up there within the next few days to talk to the Plant Managers. Something had to be done quickly; it would be disastrous if the workers decided to strike.

He was just finishing off the last paragraph of the letter, when a knock came on the door.

"Come in." He murmured. He looked up to see Elspeth.

"Yes, Elspeth."

"Sorry to disturb you, Sir, but Mr. Rhodes is here to see you."

James frowned, wondering why he'd not heard Fletcher's car arrive. "Well, show him in."

"Yes sir."

A moment later, much to James' surprise, it wasn't Fletcher who walked into his office, but his son, William.

"Good morning, Captain Thorncroft, I apologize for disturbing you, but I wonder if you can spare a few brief minutes. I would like to talk to you."

James stood up, gesturing for William to take the chair opposite his desk. "Is something wrong, William?" He asked, frowning slightly. "Your father . . . has he taken a bad turn?"

"Oh no . . . nothing's wrong, Captain. I've come on a purely personal matter of my own that I wish to discuss." Obviously William, despite the smile in his eyes, was uncomfortable. "I may as well come straight to the point. I realize that now your daughter has reached her majority, this isn't technically necessary, but in deference to your family, I wanted to do it."

"Do what, William?" James prompted. He was sure he knew what the young man was about to relay to him.

"I would like to marry Rebecca, Sir." William paused, his face flushing slightly. "We would like yours and Mrs. Thorncroft's blessing."

James' eyebrows lifted as a smile crossed his handsome face. "You both, I hope, have thought about this very seriously. You know the ups and downs of marriage, m' boy. It isn't always as romantic as is first seemed."

"Yes, Sir. We know that we'll have our differences as we go on in life, but . . . I know we'll make it work. She and I are on the same wavelength; we like the same things, want to learn and grow together. We even want to make mistakes together—we feel that's the only way we can truly grow closer to one another. Once we're married, providing we have your blessing, Captain, we'll not burden you with living here or at Cavendish Hall—we'd like to find a place of our own, not too far away from everyone, you understand."

James leaned back, resting his arms on the edge of the desk, his fingers tapping lightly against his lower lip. "You and Rebecca have obviously thought this over very carefully; that is a very good sign." He paused. "Over the years, William, we have watched our children as they have enjoyed play times with you and your sister. There is a definite bond between all of you; that bond will give you the edge over others who perhaps do not truly know the backgrounds of their husbands or wives. For myself, I can only say that I'd be delighted for you and Rebecca to wed; I cannot speak for my wife, but I'm almost certain she'd endorse my comments." He stood up, holding out his hand. "Congratulations, William."

"Thank you, Captain." William smiled. "I believe Rebecca is at this moment saying the exact same things to your wife."

James grinned. "Now why doesn't that surprise me!" He said. "Why don't you make yourself comfortable in the Drawing Room, while I get my wife and Rebecca. This deserves a toast."

Not only did Catherine and Rebecca meet William in the Drawing Room, but Eden, Luke and Martin, who were in the vicinity, on hearing Rebecca's excited voice, joined them.

"Well," James surveyed the family. "I have an announcement to make which I don't think will be much of a revelation for any of you. William has just asked me for the hand of Rebecca in marriage. What is your word on that, dear?" He glanced at Catherine quickly.

"I heartily approve, James." Catherine slipped an arm around her daughter's waist to hold her close. "They'll make a wonderful couple and although I can't see into the future, I'm sure they'll be mature enough to handle the intricacies of married life as well as they handled their squabbles when they were children."

"Then," James said, "they have our blessing."

"Thank you, Mummy. Daddy." Rebecca said, flushing. "I love William so much . . ." she said, slightly embarrassed at revealing such an emotion to her family. "I have for many years. I didn't think he felt the same way about me, until about a year ago when I began to notice a change in his attitude towards me. He seemed to want to be with me; when we talked, it was . . ." she paused, her embarrassment rising even more, ". . . well, you know what I mean . . . I can't believe how lucky I am." She glanced over at William, smiling gently. "Being a married woman will be very challenging, I know that, but we want to build our home together as you and Daddy did. We don't wish to live at Ravenslea or at Cavendish Hall—not because we don't love it in both places, only that we want to live our own lives with our own set of ideals. Having said that," she added swiftly, "we wouldn't want to live far from Ravenslea or Cavendish Hall. I'm sure we'd be visiting often."

James moved to the cocktail cabinet where he poured some golden liquid into small wine glasses. Bringing them over on a small tray, he passed them around.

"There will always be ups and downs, Rebecca; no marriage runs straight and true all the time. So long as you understand the basics and respect each other's opinions, I really don't think you're going to have any major upsets." He raised his glass. "Here's to the happy couple; a toast for them to have nothing but glorious days, happiness and be able to overcome with composure the teething troubles that invariably come with even the best of marriages. To our darling daughter and her fiancé, William. God bless you both."

"To Rebecca and William." Everyone echoed.

"Have you set a date?" Catherine asked.

Rebecca shook her head. "Not yet . . ."

"Well, whenever you do, don't forget that your Aunt Penelope and I are here to help organize it, if you wish us to."

"I'd like that, Mummy." Rebecca said.

"We'll arrange an engagement party for you both." Catherine began.

"Oh, Mummy, William and I would prefer not to have a party."

"Why not dear?" James asked, puzzled, knowing how much Rebecca thrived at parties.

Rebecca glanced over at William. "We had planned to just go out for a nice dinner somewhere . . . perhaps with the two families . . ."

". . . where I would present Rebecca with a ring . . ." William jumped in quickly, pulling Rebecca gently away from her mother and holding her tight against him, " . . we don't really want a big fuss made of this."

"Well then," James said. "That's what we'll do."

Rebecca breathed easier. She'd thought her parents would be difficult at the suggestion of not having a social gathering for the occasion. "Aunt Penelope has offered her mother's engagement ring." She said, her eyes sparkling. "I think that's a wonderful idea—keeping it in the family and on show for the world to see. William said he wanted to purchase a new one, but I said I'd prefer his grandmother's ring; it would mean so much more to both of us, don't you agree, Daddy?"

"I do indeed, Rebecca." James glanced up at the mantle clock. "Now, much as I'd like to stay and discuss this further, dear, I really do have to finish off what I was doing. We can talk about this after dinner tonight, dear."

"Of course, Daddy." She kissed him lightly. "I realize this has been sprung on you without any kind of warning, so I'm sure you're going to want to know a little of our plans."

At that moment, Eden, Martin and Luke moved over to give her warm congratulations and kiss her. James took the moment to leave the room.

He walked into his office and closed the door gently behind him. This was good news indeed. He liked William Rhodes; he was a pleasant lad with a good head on his shoulders and he was sure William would make a respectable name for himself as he travelled through life.

James sat down at his desk suddenly not wishing to continue with the letter to the mining company. As he pondered the finishing sentence, the telephone rang.

"James Thorncroft here." He said.

"Captain Thorncroft." The voice sounded familiar, yet he couldn't place it. "This is Giles Mortimer. Remember we met at the Club a week or so back?"

"Ah yes, Giles. Good to hear from you." James said. How could he forget the man who'd monopolized him for much of that one and only evening he'd spent at the Tiverton Country Club recently. "Have you and your family settled in at your new place?"

"Pretty much so. I understand you are having a Guy Fawkes celebration next month?"

"Yes, as a matter of fact, we are. It's a tradition we have upheld over the years. You and your family, of course, will be there?"

"Indeed yes, thank you, Captain." Mortimer paused. "Well we are considering having a few people around for a house warming party a few days afterwards. We don't know many people in the area as yet, and thought this as good a way as any to get to know them. It'll mostly be one or two of our nearest neighbours plus a few from the Club. We'd very much like you, your wife and family to attend."

James leaned back in his chair. "Thank you. I'll certainly ask Catherine; she'll enjoy meeting your family. Give me your phone number and I'll call you back in a little while."

James wrote the number on a notepad. "We look forward to seeing you then, on November 5th?"

"Indeed yes, Captain Thorncroft. My daughter, Cynthia, is looking forward to meeting your children."

"We are all looking forward to seeing her; your wife as well, Giles?"

"Just Cynthia and myself, Captain."

"We look forward to seeing you then."

"Thanks, Captain. Goodbye." Giles Mortimer rang off and James replaced the receiver thoughtfully.

Giles Mortimer, a tall, thickset man in his fifties by James' reckoning, seemed more than a little out of place at the Country Club when they'd met a couple of weeks ago. From the look on his florid face, there was evidence he imbibed perhaps more than he should, but seemed a pleasant enough fellow and James liked his outgoing manner.

James seldom attended the Tiverton Country Club. It was a little out of his way and he rarely had the time these days. He had attended about a fortnight earlier, meeting Giles Mortimer for the first time then. Mortimer told everyone at the Club he'd come into some money. As he'd always wanted to live in the

West Country, he found out by chance that a piece of property had come on the market just at the right time, so he'd purchased it. Mortimer said he wanted to turn it into a Riding Stables with a Training Academy attached. As he'd already purchased three horses with which to start, his next aim was to secure the services of a well qualified riding instructor. It sounded a good proposition, especially through the summer months as the beautiful Exmoor Forest, Ilfracombe, Lynton and Lynmouth were favourite locations for tourists.

At least Mortimer was free to charge whatever he wanted for trail rides as there was no competition in the area; but James knew once the summer season was over there would be very few visitors around to pay for a bumpy horseback ride along narrow, difficult trails. Most people in the area were either already versed in the fine arts of horseback riding, or had no desire to learn.

James wondered about Giles Mortimer's wife. Obviously the woman was not going to attend the fireworks display and bonfire; perhaps Mortimer was a widower. In that case, he knew the Thorncrofts would go out of their way to make sure he and his daughter were made welcome.

Quickly finishing off the letter, he penned the Plant Manager's name and address on the front of the envelope. Stuffing it into his inside jacket pocket, he rose from his desk and walked out of the office, with the intention of going into Branton that afternoon to make sure it made the early post.

"I wonder what Giles Mortimer's wife is like." Catherine mentioned over dinner that evening. "If you only met Mr. Mortimer at the Club I don't suppose you've ever met her, dear?"

James shook his head. "No, I haven't and Mortimer didn't mention her once when we were talking. I thought it best not to pursue it. He spoke only of his daughter, Cynthia. I gather she's about seventeen and is hoping to make a career in accounting. This, he said, would assist him with the finances of the new business as he said he was useless with figures." He smiled, ladling some sprouts onto his plate. "She sounds a nice girl. I'm sure Rebecca would be willing to take her under her wing and show her some of the rudiments of the area, before her wedding day. Right Rebecca?" He grinned over at his daughter.

"Certainly, Daddy—you know how much I like to meet new people, but you must realize that from now on my life has taken a different turn. She will not be one of my priorities." Rebecca turned away to sip her wine, a thoughtful look appearing in her eyes. "Oh, by the way, we were going to discuss my engagement after dinner, remember Daddy? Could it wait until another time as I'd like William to be here. Since the refit of his ship, he has to be on board for sea trials. He has to leave later today and won't be home until tomorrow night. Perhaps we could arrange something after that."

"Of course, dear," James said, "we're not going anywhere and we'd love to have William here. In fact," he glanced at his wife, "why don't we have a dinner party for the whole Rhodes family, perhaps next week, how does that sound? As this only concerns the Rhodes and us, this will be in lieu of a proper engagement party."

Rebecca nodded happily, turning to her mother. "That would be wonderful,

CHAPTER 13

EDEN AND CHRISTIANA

Christiana couldn't sleep. She'd managed to doze off once or twice, but awakened in the early hours of the next morning with the image of Eden Thorncroft burning in her mind. His lean gait, mesmerising violet eyes and warm, all encompassing smile delighted her so much that she believed she'd almost burst if she didn't feel his arms around her; his lips against her soft hair; his mouth on hers. She sat up, turned and plumped the pillows into a bunch, then leaned back against them. Her attention veered towards the narrow slit between the drawn curtains to where a low full moon reflected onto the polished wooden floor. She looked away a frown creasing her attractive face.

In the short time she and Adam had been at Ravenslea Manor, the knowledge that Eden hadn't shown her any interest infuriated her. She'd always managed to entice other young men in her life with her seductive advances and smiling, sultry eyes, but Eden's indifference both annoyed and fascinated her. A smile suddenly curved her mouth upwards. She would use her femininity to win him over. It had worked before and Eden was a man wasn't he? Surely, he wouldn't be able to ignore her forever?

Christiana began to compare him with Cliff, the man she'd married when they were both only eighteen. He had been Captain of the football team in their High School days; the darling of so many of the girls at the school. Because of this, she'd challenged herself to snare him from the rest of the girls, so they could see he would only have eyes for her. He had been so easily captivated and for a while Christiana was in seventh Heaven realizing she'd done what none of her school friends had. However, as she'd found out after they'd married, Cliff was none of the things he portrayed. He was a complete innocent. Their romance waned drastically when she realized Cliff wasn't capable of acting the way a man should around an attractive young woman. Their lovemaking was awkward and even when she acknowledged his inexperience and tried to gently lead him to fulfilment, his inhibitions and inability to climax had come to serious arguments and eventual divorce.

She still liked Cliff and only wished him well, but hoped if he married again he had matured to manhood and would be able to satisfy his wife. She shrugged. Now, Cliff was slotted somewhere in her past; an episode in her life to forget now she had another man dominating her thoughts.

Christiana swung her long legs over the side of the bed and stretched her arms above her head. Yawning, she didn't feel like sleeping any more. She'd go down to the Dining Room and pour herself a Daiquiri and Coke, then perhaps search the library for a short story and curl back up in bed for a read.

As she opened the bedroom door and moved along the landing, she saw a light shining from James Thorncroft's Study. Intrigued and wondering why Eden's father would be up at that time of night, she decided to investigate. Now, she thought raising her eyebrows slightly, there was another fascinating man. If she'd been around when Catherine had been courting him, she'd have given Catherine a good run for her money; Christiana smiled knowing she probably would have won!

Creeping down the stairs, she glanced into the room. Her heart leapt . . . Eden was sitting behind his father's desk, his dark curly head bent. He was writing something in a book.

Quietly, Christiana crept back upstairs and donned her most revealing nightgown with the matching negligee. She ran a brush through her shining blonde hair. For the final effect, she withdrew the stopper of her favourite French perfume, 'Bakanir', and dabbed a little on each wrist as well as behind her ears. She glanced quickly in the mirror, pleased with the image that smiled back at her. She then turned and crept back down the stairs. This time she would confront him; if he didn't notice her, then perhaps he was one of those men who really didn't like women. That would be a terrible shame, but this, surely, would clinch it for her, for surely no man could resist such a tempting sight as Christiana Whitney in a negligee.

Earlier, Eden awoke bathed in a hot sweat. Thin rivulets of warm, sticky moisture collected uncomfortably in the hollow where his throat and chest bone met. He sat up aware of a throbbing beneath his ribs. There seemed no reason for such a phenomena—it had to have been the roast pork he'd consumed for dinner that evening. Every so often it happened. He had eaten in a hurry and as a result was now feeling the effects of an upset stomach.

A full moon lay a shimmering shaft of light across the floor as Eden leaned back against the pillow contemplating his growing relationship with Christiana. His feelings were mixed. True, she delighted him with her sensual body, tantalizing smile, spontaneous exuberance and extraordinary American wit. Yet despite her obvious feelings for him, he knew his feelings were purely physical.

He raised himself up and leaned forward, perplexed suddenly at his reticence regarding Stephanie. Much against his will, he had to admit his feelings for her ran much deeper. He felt at ease with her; they shared the same pursuits; their companionship was one of warmth, stemming, he was sure, to the times he and his siblings along with Stephanie and William had played together as children. A smile creased his mouth as he recalled the wild spirit of the young Stephanie and realized that it hadn't changed much over the years. She, like his Aunt Fern, was a restless spirit. She couldn't sit still for long without getting up and pacing the room as she had no particular interest in sitting with other young women knitting, sewing or reading.

He switched on the light beside his bed and glanced over to the small clock. It was just 3:30! He'd never sleep now he was far too wide awake. He swung his legs out of bed, quickly covered his pyjamas with a brown robe, felt around for his slippers that had all but disappeared under the bed and left the room.

Eden meandered noiselessly down the stairs to his father's Study. Snapping on the switch beside the doorway, the electric light momentarily blinded him and he had difficulty focusing. He quietly closed the door. Once his eyes had adjusted, he moved to his father's ornate oak desk standing slightly off centre to the room. For some unaccountable reason, he wanted to be with Stephanie. He hadn't been able to talk to her since Rebecca's birthday, his time having been taken up with domestic chores; tenants' problems, like Enid and Ed Timmin's leaky roof and the broken spindle on Jack Frigg's plough. When he'd dealt with those and found some time spare, he'd been asked by Louise to take Christiana out somewhere. So he'd obliged. It was while they were on one of these short trips that his step cousin had told him she was more than a little bored with just wandering around the Ravenslea's gardens, even though they were beautiful. She needed some stimulation. From her manner, Eden determined that the only thing she found at all stimulating was to be in his company; a state of affairs with which Eden was not entirely comfortable.

He sighed. Tomorrow morning he decided to telephone Stephanie to see if they could go riding together. He wanted so much to see her again, so if she was agreeable, he would reserve a table at the Mayfield Arms near Exeter for a warm, candlelight dinner.

With his mind made up, he reached into the lower drawer of his father's desk and brought out a slim ledger. He'd heard about the problems with the Yorkshire mine and wanted to check for himself just how the finances were adding up. Last year, it hadn't looked good for the company, but this year he'd thought it was beginning to pick up again. Possibly not, if there were troubles up there. He'd not entered anything in the last week or so and knew that was a task he really ought to attend to. What better time than right now, when he was wide awake; it was quiet and he could think clearly. As he began turning a few pages, sifting through his spidery handwriting, he heard the Study door open—that annoying little squeak would have to be attended to one of these days. He glanced up.

Christiana stood there, looking delightfully feminine in a lilac negligee that reached to the floor in gentle folds, discreetly covering the soft rounded curves of her lovely body.

"Oh, Eden," she breathed, closing the door quietly behind her. "I heard a noise and couldn't sleep, so just had to investigate." She walked seductively towards him to perch on the corner of the desk. As the robe slipped from her knees, a fine expanse of shapely leg appeared which she began to tantalizingly swing to and fro before him.

Eden glanced at his step cousin, then stood up pushing the chair back.

"It's not prudent, Christiana, to have a tête-à-tête here in my father's Study, if that's what you're here for." Faced with that vision of loveliness, his friends would think he was completely mad, yet he had no desire to encourage the young American girl; all he wanted in life was the lovely Stephanie Rhodes. "You should go back to bed; there's nothing for you here and as you can see nothing is amiss in the house." He glanced at her, noting the slight pout of her quivering lower lip. "What would your mother think if she could see you down here with me . . . dressed like that?"

She laughed. "Oh, Mother would think it a hoot, Eden. She knows how honourable you are and would never believe you'd compromise me in any way—she likes and respects you too much to think otherwise."

"Humph." Eden gave a snort, quite believing that Uncle Martin's wife would be amused by their encounter. "Well, I'm going back upstairs myself. If you want to stay, I request you do not spend the rest of the night in this room. This is my father's private Study—not to be used by anyone except my parents or me, unless he expressly allows it. You do understand, don't you?"

"Oh, Eden, you really can be so . . . English . . . on times. Why can't you stay a while and talk to me? I wonder sometimes if you ever have any fun at all with such a prudish outlook on life!"

"You forget, Christiana, I *am* English. Our ways are sometimes much different to those of the New World." He paused. "Also, my life is a busy one; there are things I have to do to help run Ravenslea. In my quiet moments, my mind is full of decisions to make regarding the estate. This is one of those occasions when I feel our association here in the middle of the night in my father's Study, is inappropriate. If you believe I have a prudish outlook on life, then so be it." He moved quickly towards the door, opening it slowly. "You may spend the night in the library if you can't sleep; there are many books there you could browse through at your leisure. I'll see you in the morning at breakfast."

Suddenly, she jumped down from the side of the desk and swirled over to him. Before he could stop her, she'd thrown her arms around his neck, reached up and gave him a hard, lingering kiss on his lips. The impact caused him to lose his balance against the door, which went crashing backwards taking them both with it. Eden frantically tried to keep his balance, but with Christiana's added weight, his feet slipped. They both landed in a heap on the floor, just as the sight of a pair of familiar slippers came into the room.

"Eden! Great Scott! What's the meaning of this? Get that woman off you at once! Hardly appropriate conduct do you think?"

James stared down at his eldest son, his hands on his hips, as Eden began hurriedly to extricate himself from the lovely vision whose alluring lilac negligee had enveloped them both in a very provocative way. Eden hastily forced Christiana to one side and struggled to his feet. He ran a hand through his dishevelled hair, at the same time patting his pyjamas straight.

"Dad, it's not at all what you think. I slipped and accidentally knocked Christiana down. A pure accident, believe me." His face flooded with colour.

James raised an eyebrow. "Not a fitting response, Eden. I suggest the two of you return to your bedrooms immediately. We'll discuss this in the morning." He stood aside to let them pass. "I also suggest that next time you have a rendezvous in the middle of the night, you choose a less conspicuous place."

Christiana brushed passed Eden's father with a merry look in her eyes. To his surprise, she raised her perfectly formed eyebrows and proceeded to give him a saucy wink.

Watching them, James, far from being displeased with Eden's conduct, actually felt a trickle of envy course down his spine. The innocent, impudent wink brought to mind a past relationship with a feisty young woman who had been just as much fun as this young woman purported to be. It had been a brief encounter when he was in his early twenties; she had been a few years older than he and quite obviously unsuited to one another, yet he'd found her tantalizingly attractive, having never met anyone like her before in his life.

As James wandered slowly back up the stairs to his bedroom, he tried to recall her name. After a few minutes groping around in his brain, he came up with the name of Lily. Yes, he was sure that was her name. She'd been a dancer in some night club, as far as he could remember and he'd met her in London when he was around twenty-two or -three. He was naïve as far as women were concerned and her alluring manner had bewitched him. He remembered she'd plied him with whiskey but James, who rarely touched liquor at all, managed to dupe her into thinking he'd drunk it by surreptitiously disposing of it when she occasionally turned away from him. He closed his eyes and remembrances of her came flooding back. Kissing, cuddling and laughing in her Dressing Room after one of her performances. Good Heavens!

He remembered going to London at that time to discuss some problem with their South African diamond mine while his father was up north discussing something rather disturbing with their Yorkshire coal mine. When the business had been concluded, he remembered returning to Devon, but not before he'd decided to take in some of the sights of England's capital City. During this time, he'd decided on the spur of the moment to visit a nightclub. He'd heard so much about them and had never ventured into one. It had been quite an eye-opener for him. It had been then that he'd met the alluring Lily. Though the incident with Lily had been purely platonic—after all what else could have taken place in the cramped quarters of a dressing room—he knew his father would be enraged to know that his son would even think of associating with 'that' kind of woman. So, although he hated deceiving his father, he knew that the half hour introduction to the playful advances of the delectable Lily had to be his secret. He didn't even tell Martin for fear it would somehow get back to his father. Up until now, the memory had remained hidden.

Sighing he closed the Study door.

Returning to the bedroom, he gazed down at his sleeping wife, discarded his robe and gently slipped between the sheets, snuggling up to the only woman in his life he'd truly loved.

CHAPTER 14

CHRISTIANA'S FRIGHT

Lunch at Ravenslea was a little later than usual the next day, owing to a slight disaster in the Kitchen. Edna had asked as she'd finished all her laundry chores, if she could help in the Kitchen. Agnes, being the kind-hearted woman she was, saw potential in the young woman, so asked her to make some tea, as well as boil some eggs for sandwiches. It was a simple request, but unfortunately Edna had decided to do something she rarely did—daydream. In doing so, she allowed the kettle to stay on the hob too long. It wasn't until she could smell acrid smoke that she came out of her reverie. To her horror she saw that the kettle on the hob was smouldering. She hurried over to it and was about to pick it up from the handle, when Agnes rushed over, pushed the girl to one side, and pulled the red-hot kettle from the hob with a thick cloth. Giving Edna an impatient glare, she promptly threw the blackened kettle into a nearby container.

"What on earth did you think you were doing, you silly girl?" Agnes said, harshly.

Edna's eyes watered and she pushed a hand against her mouth.

"I'm sorry, Agnes. . . it won't happen again, I promise."

"Well, if you want to spend time helping in the Kitchen in the future, young lady, or you'd better be sure not to doodle-ally between your jobs, or you'll be out the door as quickly as you came in!"

Luckily, as a cold lunch had been planned for today, it was decided to forego the tea in favour of fruit juices and cold milk.

Christiana was seated beside her mother, across the table from Eden and his mother. She looked coquettishly at him, smiling, trying to encourage him to smile back. His face was wooden; he wasn't even going to look at her!

She smothered a smile. So, despite his harsh words to her last night, she knew she'd awakened something in him. Something she intended to pursue, no matter how he tried to avoid her. Christiana mostly got what she wanted out of life and Eden Thorncroft was someone she wanted desperately. Not only because of his inheritance, but because he was so terribly attractive and obviously the most eligible bachelor in south west England.

She reached over for a piece of lemon pie. Still eying Eden, she lifted her fork, dug it into a small portion of the piece and slid it between her teeth provocatively. She knew he was uncomfortable.

"What are you doing today, Eden?" Unaware of Christiana's flirtations, Catherine glanced at her son.

"I . . . I was thinking of going into Branton. The library has a book I ordered."

"Oh," Christiana piped in quickly, "I would like to join you, Eden, if you have no objection. I want a library book; you don't have anything in your library that I find particularly stimulating. Would you mind?"

He fidgeted as she knew he would. "I . . . I . . ."

"I think that's a wonderful idea." Louise said, smiling widely. "It's a beautiful day; it would be a shame not to make the best of it."

"I agree," Catherine added. She glanced at Eden. "Why don't you ask Agnes to make up a flask of tea or coffee to take with you. I know it's not far, but it's a beautiful day and you might like to stop somewhere." She paused. "Don't spend such a lovely day in the library, Eden, you know how dreary it is in there."

He fidgeted again and looked down at his plate. Christiana tried to suppress a smile.

"Well, Mother, once I've picked up my book, I have no intention of staying any longer. I'm returning home, so don't see any need for a flask."

"Oh, Eden. I'm sure Christiana would like to have a tour around this part of the world. She hasn't been far since first arriving here, you know. How do you feel about that, dear?" Catherine looked over at the girl across the table from her.

"Indeed I would love to see the area that is going to be my home for a while, Aunt Catherine." Christiana's eyes were warm.

"Well, then, Eden, you just do as I say. It's about time Christiana had a look at something other than Ravenslea." Catherine took a sip of orange juice and pushed her chair back.

He glanced at the girl across the table from him. "You really want to come?" She nodded and he shrugged. "Well, it's up to you, of course, but you'll be quite bored at the library."

"I won't, Eden. If you don't mind waiting while I find something to read, I think it would be a super idea." Her eyes were twinkling with merriment and she could see his obvious reluctance, knowing there was no possible way he could refuse her.

"Well . . . if you're sure, Christiana? I'll do as Mother says and get Agnes to make us something to take with us." He pushed his chair back. "I'll be leaving in about half an hour."

"I'll be there. You haven't taken me for a drive in that wonderful car for ages. It'll be great to see the beautiful countryside around Devonshire."

Going back to her bedroom there was a spring in her step. Her reflection in the mirror was wreathed in smiles. She didn't know why she was so smitten with Eden. She'd met many men in her life; most of whom she'd had brief passionate affairs before she'd married Cliff. None of them even came remotely close to her feelings for the handsome Eden Thorncroft.

She stood up and moved towards the wardrobe. She ran her hands over the only clothes she'd brought from the States, finally settling on a primrose knee-length dress that clung to her shapely body very satisfactorily. One day she and her mother would take a trip into one of the towns to get some clothes. She was bored with the ones she wore day after day. A new country should demand a new set of clothes, in her opinion.

After adorning her ears with golden earrings and matching necklace, she went back to the mirror. Here she applied warm, brown-toned lipstick and brushed her hair into an elegant chignon, moving backwards, happily surveying the overall result.

The last thing she did was drape a gold and white trimmed shawl over her shoulders that she could, if she wished, cover her hair if the weather turned windy.

Downstairs, Elspeth informed her that the car was waiting outside, intimating that Master Eden seemed more than a little impatient.

"Thanks, Elspeth." Christiana grinned as she flounced out through the front door into the sunshine.

Louise was standing on the top step. She turned and gave her daughter a kiss.

"Enjoy yourself dear. Don't worry about time. I'm sure Branton has some sights for you to see as well."

"I will, Mother." Christiana skipped down the steps, waved to her mother and stepped into the waiting Lagonda. Today, Eden had turned the car into a convertible, so Christiana quickly tied the shawl over her shining blonde hair.

The ride was perfect. The sun was high; birds were going about their business and singing to the tops of their voices. There was a light breeze which rustled through the trees overhead and she was riding in a beautiful car with Eden Thorncroft. What more could she ask?

She was glad she'd remembered to bring her camera. Bulky as it was, she had it safely strapped around her body crosswise not to get in her way. She had every intention of taking as many pictures as she could while out with him today. In fact, she was hoping he'd stay still long enough for her to capture him as well!

As she glanced now and again at Eden, she felt sure he wasn't too happy about her being with him, but really, what mattered? She was enjoying it and that was what she wished. Just to be seen with this eligible man was enough to boost her morale as actually living at Ravenslea was boring her to tears!

"What's the book you're picking up?" She asked after about five minutes of no conversation at all. She had to break the silence somehow.

"Nothing you'd be interested in." He said. He didn't proffer any more information, just sat behind the steering wheel staring ahead as he manoeuvred the vehicle along the narrow winding road with its high hedges. Occasionally, a farmer's gate would appear behind which sheep or cows grazed contentedly.

"Aren't you wondering what I would like in the way of a book?" She coaxed, wishing he'd relax and talk to her.

"Not in the least, Christiana. I have no wish to know or particularly care what kind of material you enjoy."

"Oh, Eden!" She exclaimed, her mouth drooping in a scowl. "How mean!

How can you say such a thing? That's most impolite!"

He shrugged. "It probably goes with the 'English' side of me!"

She laughed delightedly. "I guess I asked for that, though I really didn't think English people were impolite."

"Well some are, so if you're going to live here, you'd better get used to it." Eden turned to her. She wouldn't be ruffled by his rudeness—instead she slipped her hand through his left arm, even though he was steering with it.

"You must bring me out in this beautiful vehicle again, Eden. It's a gloriously smooth ride and I love it." She said, leaning closer to him. She felt his resistance, but clung even tighter to his arm.

They travelled slowly for about ten minutes. He turned a corner moving swiftly up a rise that was flanked on either side by blackberry bushes. As they crested the brow of a hill, Eden slowed the Lagonda. He pulled up beside another farmer's gate.

"We can stop here for a bit if you like." He said. "I've put a blanket on the back seat which we can spread out on the grass. The family often picnic here. The field belongs to Joe Brackett a very good-natured farmer who has no objection to anyone using it for picnics so long as they clean up afterwards."

"Sounds great!" Christiana stepped from the car, wandered over to the closed wooden gate and rested her arms along the top. "It smells so earthy, Eden. I love it! I've always imagined the English countryside to smell like this; don't ask me why as I've never set foot in the country before. We do have similar fields in Connecticut, you know, but these seem somehow different to ours."

Complete with a tartan blanket and small canvas bag, he joined her. Putting everything onto the ground, he unlatched the gate and allowed her through.

A few minutes later, he'd laid the blanket on a slight rise beneath a tree and Christiana availed herself of a comfortable portion of it.

Instead of tea or coffee as they thought Agnes would have supplied, they found the flask to be full of apple juice.

"How wonderful!" Christiana cried, taking a couple of sips and holding the glass up to the light to see the juice's clearness. "Of all the juices, I think I like apple best.

"Glad you do." Was his rather terse reply.

For a while they sat looking over the area. Buttercups and daisies were sprinkled over the ground and when Eden stole a quick look at her, he could tell she was enthralled by it all.

After a while, she sat up, leaning her elbows on her knees. She pointed ahead. "What's that over there?" She asked.

"Where?" He narrowed his gaze to where she was pointing. "Oh . . . looks like a Romany gypsy encampment. We get a lot of them around here, you know."

"Are they from Britain?" Christiana asked, genuinely interested.

Eden shrugged. "There's a lot of contention about their roots. It's mostly believed they originated somewhere in Scandinavia, but further back in history, there's documentation that they could have come from India. There's even some thought that the Vikings had something to do with them being in Britain in the first place. I don't think anyone really knows from where they originated. I was always under the impression they were Hungarian, but I'm not sure."

"How interesting. Have you spoken to any?"

He shook his head. "Not really—only the ones that have come to the door selling things like clothes-pins, flowers or children's wooden toys that the gypsy men make. That's the only way, to my knowledge, that they can make any money. They are loners; don't mix that well with the British folk. They keep themselves to themselves and don't really seem to want to make any trouble."

She smiled. "I did hear something a long time ago, that gypsies kidnapped little children."

For the first time that day, Eden laughed. "Well, perhaps some do, I can't speak for all of them, but I think that's a myth. It probably started when children misbehaved, so to give them a bit of a fright, their parents would tell them things like that."

She stopped her questioning and looked across the field. The bushes at the edge of the field obliterated much of what lay beyond, but at certain points in the hedge, gaily coloured caravans could be seen. She stood up, brushing down her dress.

"I want to have a look at their camp, Eden."

He shielded his eyes against the glare of the sun to look up at her. "I'll come with you."

She shook her head. "No, that's all right, I just want to see what it looks like. I'll be right back."

"Well, if you've never come across them before, I must warn you they're usually not receptive to strangers entering their encampments; they're very private people, so be careful how you approach them."

"I will. Don't worry, I won't be long!" She picked up her sunglasses and walked quickly down through the meadow grass until she disappeared from his view.

Eden leaned back. What a quixotic character she was. She appeared unafraid to venture into unknown territory; tended to wander where perhaps she shouldn't. She wasn't his type that was certain, but she had a certain allure that he found fascinating. There was a lot of Stephanie's character in her, yet they were eons apart in everything else.

A bee buzzed around him; the warm sunshine lulled him and before long, Eden drifted off into a dreamy snooze, all thoughts of his library book forgotten.

Christiana reached the small stile that led to a narrow, picturesque lane. Hitching up her dress immodestly, she climbed over. There they were. Three caravans gaily painted in various shades of reds, blues and greens with shining copper pots hanging on the sides, net curtains at the small windows and olive-skinned children playing. Dogs were running around, some yapping excitedly while men hitched up ponies to each caravan. A small foal was being petted by a little girl in a bright yellow dress, her dark, curly hair tied back from her face with a light blue ribbon. Christiana was quite taken with the domestic scene.

She pulled out her camera intending to take a photograph as it was obvious they were moving on. Just as she was about to click the photo a boy of about ten spied her and stopped what he was doing. He ran towards a woman and clutched her long, bell-liked skirt.

"What is it, Elijah?" The rather stout woman asked, her voice melodious with an unusual accent.

The boy pointed to where Christiana was standing, but didn't say anything. The woman looked over at her.

"You want something?" She didn't smile.

"May I come and talk to you?" Christiana took the camera away from her eye.

"No! We don't want strangers around 'ere! And we don't want anyone taking photographs! Get along with you." Her accent was hardly recognizable as English, but Christiana understood the gist of what she was saying.

"Oh." She caught her lip, but walked towards the woman slowly. "I don't mean any harm. I'm from America and have never seen anything so beautiful as these . . ." She indicated the caravans.

The woman frowned. "Then take a look and be off with you!"

A tall, lean, dark-haired swarthy man joined her. "We don't want strangers here." He said harshly. "Do as my woman tells you; go back where you come from!"

Christiana ignored him. "Are you packing up to leave?"

"We are!" The man said, coldly. "So, you'd better go as there's nothing here to see." He made to come forward. Suddenly Christiana felt a spasm of fear and stepped backwards.

"I'll go. I hope you don't mind if I just watch you get yourselves together before you go. I think your caravans are so fascinating; they're nothing like the ones we have in the United States and I'd so much like to see them before you leave. I may never get the chance again."

"Go!" The man demanded, this time coming forward faster. "Leave us alone!"

Christiana knew she could not stay, so raised her arms in capitulation, moving towards the stile. She nodded. Stepping over the stile into the field, she made a pretence of moving away. However, she didn't. She stayed behind the hedge, out of sight until the caravans had hitched up their three ponies; two piebalds and a non-descript horse that looked as if it was ready to be put to pasture. She then stepped back into the lane and watched them distance themselves from her. She drew the camera out, quickly snapped a photo and tucked it back into the pouch attached to the strap around her neck.

Once the rowdy scene was gone, she was left with an almost silent world of chirping birds and the sound of the wind in the trees. She didn't want to go back to Eden immediately. He was no fun, really. He didn't seem too interested in having her with him, so why didn't she take this moment alone to explore the area? She wouldn't be long as she really wanted to spend as much time as she could with Eden. He had now become a challenge—she had to get him to talk to her!

At the crossroads a few yards away there was a small signpost with an arrow pointing to her left. It read that half a mile down that road lay the ruins of a 13th Century monastery. Now that would be so fascinating! She decided to go and check it out before returning to Eden.

Lifting her face to the warming sunshine she walked briskly along the uneven road. It was so beautiful. The path took her passed tall trees on each side of her, meeting as a canopy over top. Small, beautifully coloured songbirds trilled in hedgerows and cattle lowing in a field gave her heart a lift.

After a while she came across a tree encircled copse that housed a derelict building in the centre. It was now a ruin, but as she viewed it, she could imagine how glorious the monastery must have looked when it was first built. A placard that was hardly legible announced that this, indeed, was a ruined monastery. She moved quickly through an overgrown opening into the field and walked towards the remains of what must have been a stone building at one time. She again pulled out her camera. Taking pictures was now something she enjoyed. She had found her niche. Perhaps she'd learn some new techniques from Eden's brother, because the photographs around Ravenslea were beautifully arranged and uniquely original.

Christiana moved closer to the building, walked up some rickety, broken steps in between cracked, chipped stone pillars until she was inside. Well, 'inside' was not quite accurate as the roof was the sky; clear and blue. She felt good; glad she'd decided to come. She felt an aura about the place; as if monks still roamed. She strolled ahead, feeling as if she were walking the same route they had; only she was quiet, while they were undoubtedly chanting as they went about their ecclesiastical chores! That was one thing she had always loved about England and, in fact, Europe in general—their dedicated respect for their country's history.

She put the camera away to walk further into the ruined monastery between the chipped pillars, under domed archaic arches and small flagstone floored rooms.

Now she wished she'd agreed to have Eden come with her. She wondered if he knew about the place; whether he'd have liked to have experienced it with her? Well, too late now as she had no intention of returning to bring him here. Perhaps another day; there was still plenty of time to go touring and investigating this and other areas. She moved ahead until she reached the last of the stone pillars, pausing only fractionally to look out onto the grassy area.

She wandered around, touching the sun-warmed stones, brushing away the odd insect or two that seemed to have a fascination for her perfume. After a while, she realized she had to get back as despite his apparent indifference towards her, she was sure Eden would be worrying where she had gone. After all, she said she wouldn't be long and he would surely have noticed that the gypsies had moved on. She turned and walked around to a side of the ruin she hadn't seen. Walking into a sunlit patch of ground, she noticed a spectacular view through one of the low stone pillars. She crouched down with her camera to capture the scene. As she moved to find a perfect angle, she suddenly felt the plinth she was standing on give way. To her horror, she heard a terrific splitting sound and before she could move away, the ground disintegrated beneath her. She suddenly lost her balance to plummet down a large hole.

Screaming in terror, she flailed on her way down until she landed in a dis-oriented heap on the ground. Debris from her journey fell all around her, in her hair, in her mouth and over her body. The force of the impact knocked the breath from her, just as her head slammed against the side of the chute.

A few moments passed before Christiana managed to regain her composure. Looking up the shaft, the sky seemed so far away; she was covered in broken timber, stones and earth. Her heart pounded in fear as she realized the predica-ment she was now in. She wondered if she could climb up, but as there didn't appear to be any footholds she had to acknowledge that she was trapped! Tears formed. Tears of fear; of frustration and of shock! What was she to do now?

She screamed to the top of her lungs, but knew no-one could hear unless they were in the copse. There had been no-one around when she'd entered the area; why would there be anyone there now?

She had a deep fear of mice, rats and insects. In fact, all night creatures alarmed her. The taste of earth in her mouth did nothing to dispel her fears.

Christiana had a horrible feeling she wasn't going to get out of this dreadful place! That no-one would ever find her! Eden had no idea where she'd gone! She was going to die down here! She had visions of someone in the future find-ing her bones—eaten away by the insects she abhorred!

CHAPTER 15

E DEN awoke with a start. He thought he'd been daydreaming, but it appeared he'd actually fallen asleep. Groggily, rubbing his eyes, he sat up and leaned on one elbow. He glanced at his wrist watch and a frown crossed his face. Christiana hadn't returned. Where on earth had she got to? He stared ahead to where the gypsies had camped, but there were no caravans there. They'd obviously moved on. He knew they didn't stay long in one place.

He got to his feet, shielding his eyes against the glare of the sun.

"Christiana!" He called. "Come on! Wherever you are, we have to get going!"

There was no response. Pursing his mouth, he crossly bundled up the blanket and flask, hopped over the closed gate and stowed them into the boot of the car.

Back over the gate, he ran down the slight incline, over a small rise in the field until he reached the gate where he'd last seen her. He glanced up and down the road, but there was no sign of her.

At first he was annoyed. Then he began to think about those gypsies and a cold feeling washed over him. Could he have been wrong about them? Could it be that they'd kidnapped her? He shook himself. That was impossible. For one thing Christiana would kick and scream if they'd manhandled her and he knew he'd have heard her. He called her name again and again, but still received no answering call.

Now what was he to do? He would firstly search for her and if that came up fruitless, then get the car and go into Branton police station. Once there he'd relay what had happened to them and then telephone his father.

After fifteen more minutes of wandering up and down the road, over the crossroad as well as down each of the other roads, it was obvious Christiana was nowhere around. Puzzled, he realized he'd have to do as he'd planned. He felt his heart pumping unnaturally. It wasn't as if he was all that fond of her, but he was responsible for her welfare while she was with him. He had to find her!

Running back up the road, he turned right to where the Lagonda stood. Jumping nimbly in, he started the vehicle and sped down the twisty lane towards the little town of Branton.

Once there, he pulled up and rushed into the constabulary. He told the constable behind the desk what had happened.

At first he had been nonchalant. "How old is this young woman, Mr. Thorncroft?" He said, licking the end of his pencil and writing on a pad of paper in front of him.

"What difference does that make?" Eden began. The constable frowned and

Eden pursed his mouth in frustration. "If you have to know, she's in her twenties, but really that's not the point. She's from America and doesn't know the area. She said she wouldn't be long so I felt she'd return within a reasonable time. It's not like her to just disappear like that." Eden paused. "I'm concerned that she may have come to some harm."

"What kind of harm, Sir?"

"Well," Eden paused. He didn't honestly think the gypsies had anything to do with her disappearance, but at the moment that was all he could think of. "There was a Romany gypsy camp across the field from where we were. Christiana wanted to go to see them as she'd never seen them before. So she went, promising to be back in a short while."

The constable perked up, raising a greying eyebrow, his dark eyes questioning. "A Romany gypsy camp? Well, if you knew there was one there, why didn't you go with her?" The constable frowned at him, scribbling something more on the pad.

"She said she didn't want me to come. She's usually quite capable of looking after herself in circumstances like these, constable, that's why I'm so concerned about her now."

The constable slipped the pencil in the top pocket of his uniform.

"Wait here, Mr. Thorncroft. I'll talk to the Superintendent." He moved towards the back of the room and disappeared through a doorway.

"May I use the telephone? I want to call my family." Eden asked.

The constable waved a hand to the black phone on the desk. "Go ahead."

James was beside himself when he phoned, but though Eden was sure his father wanted desperately to censure him for allowing Christiana to wander off alone, he did not. Instead he told Eden he'd round up Martin, Luke and Adam and meet him at the bottom end of Joe Brackett's field in half an hour.

As he slipped the telephone back onto its rest, Eden began to fret. What if Christiana had returned? She would surely panic when she saw he'd left without her. Normally, Eden was under the impression that Christiana wasn't a person to quickly panic about anything, but something seemed to be telling him that she could be panicking right now.

He began to pace the floor, anxiety tying knots in his stomach.

"We can see your distress, Mr. Thorncroft." A large policeman looked at him over the counter; another younger policeman stood slightly to one side of him. "I'm Superintendent Campbell. Perhaps you could go with Officer Gibbs to the area. I suggest you start the search by trying to find the gypsies you mentioned."

"Thank you, Superintendent."

Police Officer Gibbs, astride his motor-cycle, followed the Lagonda back the way Eden had come. To Eden's relief, the gypsy entourage hadn't travelled far. Their caravans could be seen quite clearly; their bright colours clashing against the natural greens of the countryside. They had travelled about two miles from where they'd been camped.

P.C. Gibbs stepped from the motor-cycle. He approached a thickset man with shoulder length curly black hair who on seeing them, began to gently rein a hefty piebald to a stop.

"Is something the matter?" The man asked, in broken English.

"Have you seen a young woman around these parts within the last hour?" Officer Gibbs asked.

The gypsy shrugged. "Well, we saw a woman back there a while ago." He turned and pointed back the way they'd come. "We were leaving and she wanted to talk to us. I don't know where she went after we'd pulled away." His accent was odd, but at least he was understandable.

Gibbs nodded. "We'll take a quick look around your caravans."

The gypsy stood to one side. "I don't know what you're going to find. She's not with us."

The search proved fruitless so Officer Gibbs allowed the gypsies to continue their journey.

"Well, Mr. Thorncroft, that didn't serve any purpose. Perhaps we should search further afield from the point where you last saw her."

"Yes, I think that's about all we can really do." Eden commented. "I have telephoned my father. He will be joining us. I thought some extra help in the search would be prudent."

P.C. Gibbs nodded, smiling slightly. "Good thinking, Mr. Thorncroft. There are a lot of twists and turns in the roads around here; the lady could have gone in any direction. The more help we have, the more chance we'll have of finding her."

By the time they'd reached the spot where Eden had last seen Christiana, the Rolls Sedanca was waiting. James, Martin, Luke and Adam were either leaning against the vehicle, or pacing up and down the roadway, their patience obviously wearing thin.

James moved forward as Eden pulled the Lagonda to a stop just behind the Rolls.

Eden introduced the family to the constable quickly. "Well, it doesn't appear the gypsies have anything to do with her disappearance." He said

"Well that's good to know, but what's the next step?" James demanded, his brow furrowed, his voice worried.

"We must search the area. Hopefully we'll be able to find the young lady before the daylight completely disappears, or we'll have to abandon the search . . ." Police Constable Gibbs said.

"We'll not abandon the search, Officer." Adam said, moving forward. His worry was evident in the unusual harshness of his tone and the thin line of his lips. "We must find her! If I have to stay here on my own all night, I will find her!" He reached into his pocket. "I have a flashlight with me; I could see the daylight fading and brought it along in case we may need it."

"Very astute of you, Sir." Police Constable Gibbs said, dryly. "Well, if we're lucky, we may not need it. We can't stand here discussing this, we must get on with the search immediately."

They split up into sets of two, moving in different directions and agreeing to meet back at the gate within the half hour. By then the sun would have sunk between the distant hills quite noticeably. James and Luke moved quickly into a field opposite the gate; Martin and Adam walked to the crossroads taking the left turn, while Eden and Constable Gibbs took the right road.

Shadows appeared as night clouds began to suffuse the sky. The six men desperately continued their search; each couple shouting Christiana's name as they slowly walked down the narrow lanes. It was almost twenty minutes later when suddenly Eden heard a shout from a distance away to their left. They were thankful the night clouds had created an echoing effect, as it served well to bring the voice clear to them.

He glanced at the constable, who nodded in understanding. Quickly, both men turned to run back the way they'd come, over the crossroads and beneath the overhead trees.

Back at Ravenslea, Louise was beside herself with worry. Fluttering her hands around in front of her face, she couldn't keep still for one moment.

"If anything's happened to her, Catherine, I . . . I don't know what I'd do." She said, over and over again.

"Nothing's going to happen to her, dear." Catherine slipped an arm across Louise's shoulders. "There are enough people there searching the area; I'm certain they'll find her before long. After all, there's nothing much around there, except fields and hedges as far as I can remember, so she probably decided to take the time alone to investigate the area. You know how venturesome she is." She smiled at the older woman gently, desperately trying to ease her anguish. "There are only lanes criss-crossing one another, some leading to farmer's cottages, or just plain dead-ends. She's probably just gone a little off-course and now can't find her way back. Don't worry, Louise, please. It won't help."

Louise looked up at her, pressing her lips together, then nodded. "You're right of course, as you invariably are, Catherine. It's ridiculous me carrying on like this." She glanced out the window. "Night's coming . . . oh dear, I should have gone with them."

Catherine shook her head. "That wouldn't have been wise, dear. You couldn't have done any more than what they are doing right now." She pulled Louise's arm gently, steering her towards the Drawing Room, thinking that if her sister-in-law had gone with them, the men would have had the added burden of watching her as well. Louise had a tendency to wander off on her own, to do her 'own thing'. That would have been a severe handicap in the search process. "Look, why don't we all sit down and relax. I'm sure Christiana will be home before long in her usual buoyant, carefree manner, thinking it all a wonderful escapade!"

Louise reluctantly allowed herself to be led into the Drawing Room, while Catherine rang the bell-pull. Doris hurried into the room.

"Bring us some tea please, Doris; we may have a long night ahead of us, so we may as well be comfortable."

"Here!" It was Adam; he was running towards them from a nearby field. "She's fallen! There's a ruined building here. Come! She can't get out! We have to get more help!" His voice was full of fear and even in the twilight, Eden could see his stark, staring eyes.

By this time, James and Luke had joined them. All jumped the gate to follow Christiana's almost hysterical brother.

Adam pulled out the torch and shone it down the hole. Christiana's pale, frightened face peered up from them from a great distance below.

"Adam! Adam! Get me out of here!" She cried. Her voice was scratchy as if she'd been screaming and crying at the same time. Adam knew she was terrified, obviously thinking she'd never be found.

"It's okay, Chris!" He cried down at her. "We'll get you out. Just hang tight; we have to get some help."

"Don't leave me!"

"I won't!" He cried back at her.

"We'll get some help." Constable Gibbs said, his voice sombre, his expression grim. "Come with me, Mr. Thorncroft." He addressed Eden. "We don't have time to get back to the station, so we'll solicit the help from one of the farmers around here."

"Joe Brackett will help—I know he will." Eden said quickly. "He has all kinds of equipment in his barns that I'm sure will be all we need. All I hope is that he's home."

"If he's not, Mr. Thorncroft, we'll commandeer the equipment."

"Yes! Yes! I know he would not object!"

Joe Brackett was cleaning out one of the stables when Constable Gibbs and Eden arrived. On hearing of Christiana's predicament, he was full of concern. Quickly, he told his wife what he was going to be doing over the next while, then ran back to the stable where he pulled down a long rope, twisting a loop in one end.

"We'll 'ave 'er outta there in no time at all, Mr. Eden." Joe said, throwing them both an encouraging smile.

Adam insisted on climbing down the rope once it had been lowered into the hole. He drew the loop over his sister's shivering body, then shouted for them to bring her to the top slowly. They did, then lowered the rope again for him.

On the ground, Christiana was crying with relief, the cold, fear and pain. In

Adam's torchlight, they saw the deep cuts on her arms and legs; the gash on her forehead with dried blood that had run down the side of her face. Fortunately, when Adam helped her to stand up, she was a little unsteady, but it appeared she hadn't suffered any broken bones.

"I'll return to the station, Mr. Thorncroft." Constable Gibbs said, once astride his motor-cycle. "I'll have to make out a report and will also inform the County to get that hole secured. I don't think we'll need to trouble you any more."

As they motored back to Ravenslea, Christiana couldn't stop thanking everyone. "I . . . thought I was going to be there forever. I had visions of my body being found in a couple of years . . . eaten away by maggots . . . rats!" She buried her head in her hands. "Oh, you don't know how welcome it was to hear everyone up there . . ." she began to babble, obviously a form of delirium had set in.

Adam was sitting in the back of the Sedanca with Christiana, while Martin sat beside James who was driving; Eden and Luke were travelling slowly behind in the Lagonda.

A subdued, but thankful sextet arrived at Ravenslea almost an hour after James had left.

Because of the traumatic episode that Christiana had experienced, the County checked the hole. On inspection of the shaft, there was evidence it had been used as a wine cellar at the time the monks used it back in the 13th Century. The hole where Christiana had fallen had subsequently been filled with dirt, stones and other debris. The thick rotted wooden trap door was replaced by level paving stones. The County couldn't afford to have a lawsuit on their hands should such an unfortunate mishap occur again.

CHAPTER 16

THE INVITATION

Noon sunlight streamed in through the small oval window above Cavendish Hall's front door onto the figure standing by the side of the stairway. It was a Saturday and William had gone over to Ravenslea to call on Rebecca. Stephanie was thrilled to think that one day, she and her best friend would be sisters-in-law. She remembered the days, long ago, when the Thorncroft children played together in either one of the houses; fun days, adventurous days, exhilarating days. Neither household had provided their children with governesses or tutors as both families felt they should experience the fellowship of other children. So Stephanie and William had attended Branton Elementary school with Rebecca and her brothers; later, the girls to High School; Eden and William to Grammar School in Barnstable. The fact that they were mixing with other children from different classes, had not deflected their friendship in the least.

The whole of the Rhodes household were overjoyed when William announced he and Rebecca wanted to be married. Still thinking of William's future plans, Stephanie walked dreamily towards the small pile of packages on the hall table absently. As she began sorting through them, she caught sight of a scribbled note to her in her mother's handwriting.

Puzzled, she unfolded it and on reading the gently curved words her mother had written, an excited cry escaped her lips. Eden had telephoned earlier and asked her mother if Stephanie would be available next Wednesday to go riding with him. Her mother told him she wasn't sure what her daughter was doing, so mentioned on the note for Stephanie to call him back. Well, she'd certainly do that.

She glanced up at the clock on the mantelpiece and moved towards the telephone on the small table near the bottom of the stairs. She put the receiver to her ear, turned the handle and asked the post office operator to call the number she gave him. A few moments later, she heard it ring. After a while the receiver at the other end was picked up and a feminine voice answered. A feminine voice with a decidedly American accent.

"Hello." Stephanie said. "Is that you Miss Whitney?"

"Yes. You are?"

"Stephanie Rhodes. Are you feeling better since that dreadful mishap you had a little while ago?"

"Much thank you, Miss Rhodes. What can I do for you?"

"Could I speak to Eden, please?"

The woman hesitated. "He's not here at the moment. Can I give him a message or get him to call you back?"

"He called earlier and spoke to my mother asking if I'd be able to go riding with him next Wednesday. Would you mind giving him a message to say I'll be at Ravenslea on Wednesday afternoon around two o'clock."

"Of course, Miss Rhodes. Goodbye."

Christiana replaced the receiver thoughtfully, then with a sly smile creasing her mouth she walked stiffly into the Music Room. Should Eden ask if Miss Rhodes had phoned, Christiana would tell him that it wasn't convenient for this Wednesday, but perhaps one day next week. It was a blatant lie, but she'd work her way around it, if ever it surfaced.

Stephanie awoke, stretched and jumped nimbly out of bed. It was Wednesday at last. The days since Saturday seemed to take forever. She had mentioned her meeting with Eden to her parents who'd obviously been pleased for they smiled a lot. For once in her life, her day suggested excitement which, in turn, spurred her into quickly bathing and changing into light tan pants with a purple shirt. She'd change after lunch into the new riding habit she'd bought a couple of weeks ago. It was stylish; the rich mahogany colour bringing out the sparkling reds in her hair.

She strolled into the Dining Room where her mother was busy sorting through some mail while at the same time eating some toast with a steaming cup of tea beside her. Penelope looked up and smiled as her daughter leaned over to give her a kiss before sitting across the table from her.

"So you're meeting Eden today, dear." She said, laying some envelopes on the table beside her.

Stephanie nodded. She buttered some toast and filled a delicate china cup beside her plate with tea. "I don't know where we're going, but it'll be good, I'm sure of it. I haven't been to Ravenslea for a while, so it'll be nice to spend some time with him. Maybe even Rebecca will join us at some point."

Penelope smiled knowingly. "I'm not sure she'd do that, dear, she's got a lot on her mind right now. Anyway, she probably thinks you'd prefer to be spending the day just with Eden." She paused. "You're very fond of him aren't you?"

The direct question startled Stephanie for a moment and she almost choked on her toast. "Of course I am. I've always liked him—the same as I like Rebecca and Luke, of course . . ."

"I think, my dear, that you are showing signs of becoming more than just a little fond of him. Whenever his name is mentioned, or he comes into a room, you take on a completely different air."

Stephanie laughed. "That's nonsense, Mummy. Like I said, I'm fond of him—

he's good company and we have a lot of the same interests, so we get along really well. It's nothing more than that." Stephanie didn't like deceiving her mother and felt uncomfortable talking to her in this manner. She knew, however, her mother was perceptive and would eventually see through her deception. Penelope was an astute, intelligent woman—she had this amazing ability sometimes to read into people's minds. An attribute Stephanie found most annoying. It was almost impossible to keep a secret at Cavendish Hall for long without somehow her mother finding out.

"Anything interesting in the post?" She said, peering over her mother's shoulder. Anything to get the conversation off Eden Thorncroft.

"A few bills—that's about all." Penelope said.

After Stephanie had left to go to Ravenslea later that day, Fletcher appeared in the Morning Room. He'd just awoken from a nap as he'd been having headaches lately that had worried him, though did not disclose this to his wife. He just told her he was feeling especially tired today and wished for a rest before getting up. Luckily, she'd believed him. So when he arrived downstairs an hour or so after Stephanie had left that same afternoon, he found his wife reading a book with her feet up on the couch in the Sitting Room. He leaned over to kiss her fondly on the forehead.

"And what have you been up to, my love?" He limped over to join her on the couch, laying his cane against the arm. He'd also been finding walking tremulous, so had resorted to using the cane once more.

"Not much, dear. I sat outside for a while because the weather was so warm—it was so nice out there and so stuffy in here, I had to experience it. By the way, Fletcher, are you feeling better since your nap?"

Fletcher nodded. "Much, dear. Surprising what a little bit of sleep can do to clear that tired, groggy feeling." Fletcher drew a pipe from his jacket pocket and stuck the stem between his lips. "Where's Stephanie? I was expecting her home."

Penelope smiled. "She's at Ravenslea, probably with Eden. She and Eden are going riding this afternoon and I expect she's stayed over for a while. You know, she's getting quite enamoured by that young man. I can see why. He's extremely presentable and has much the same temperament as she. Neither appear to take offence at the ribbing they give each other. They seem an ideal match, don't you think?"

Fletched nodded. "It would really cement our relationship with the Thorncrofts if Stephanie and Eden were to marry, Penelope, but I think they're both a little too young at the moment to understand their true feelings as yet." He smiled over at his wife. "It would be best not to speculate on something like that; we'll just have to wait and see what happens."

Stephanie slipped off the back of her quivering mare, lightly pulling the reins over the animal's head. A young man of about nineteen walked up to her, a warm smile lighting up his brown eyes. She'd met him once, before he came to Ravenslea. He used to work in the village blacksmith's shop with his father, but when he perished in a fire that took Mike's whole family a few months ago, Mike found himself out of work. When the Thorncrofts advertised for a stable-boy, Mike jumped at the chance. He secured the job, proving his worth ever since.

"Hello Mike, would you mind rubbing her down for me please and slip a blanket over her back. I rode her hard to get here as I'm a little late."

"Yes Miss." He grinned and led the mare away.

Straightening her jacket, she adjusted her riding hat. Smiling happily she ran up the steps that led to Ravenslea Manor's high oak door. She pulled the bell-rope hanging at the side and waited. Her heart raced with anticipation. Where would they go that afternoon? She felt a shiver of happiness trickle through her body at the sudden thought of them together. It wouldn't matter where they went so long as she was with him. Eden had done something to her; something that thrilled and excited her, yet he'd never actually ever touched her except to hand her down from the back of her horse. She'd tried to look at other men, but none of them appealed to her or gave her the glorious feelings she had for the good looking heir to Ravenslea Manor.

Suddenly, her daydream was shattered when the huge oak door swung slowly open. Elspeth, the housekeeper stood there, looking down her long nose at the girl standing before her.

"Yes," she enquired, brusquely.

"Oh, Elspeth, is Eden around?" Stephanie gave her a quick smile, which was not reciprocated.

"Come inside, Miss Rhodes. Wait in the Drawing Room—I'll see if Mr. Eden is in residence." Elspeth said primly, standing aside as Stephanie swept passed her, into the foyer and through to the Drawing Room. Closing the front door firmly behind her, the dour housekeeper disappeared quietly through one of the other rooms, leaving Stephanie to ponder in the huge, delightful Drawing Room that she considered was one of the most beautiful rooms at Ravenslea Manor.

Stephanie slipped her arms behind her back, entwining her fingers thoughtfully. She walked around the room exhilarating in the scent of musty tobacco smoke, obviously from Martin Thorncroft's pipe, which mingled oddly with another aroma that she did not recognize. The plush multi-coloured Turkish Carpet beneath her feet felt soft and warm. As well, the unlit fireplace recessed into the north wall, seemed somehow fitting. The whole room suggested boundless affluence, yet the Thorncrofts were anything but arrogant with their position in life. She'd never met any family in her travels that were more down to earth and friendly as were these lifelong friends of her parents.

A noise at the door made her turn, a smile on her face for Eden. The smile, however, slowly faded. The American girl was leaning against the doorpost watching her critically.

"Oh, Miss Whitney," Stephanie said, coming forward in greeting, "how are you settling in at Ravenslea?"

"Very well, Miss Rhodes." Christiana's sultry voice had no warmth in it. "And what do we owe the pleasure of this visit?"

"As mentioned on the phone, I've come to go riding with Eden this afternoon."

Christiana surveyed her cannily and raised an eyebrow. "Oh, but Hon, you must be mistaken. Eden and I are exploring the moors this afternoon." She laughed. "It was quite an impromptu arrangement, but as it's such a wonderful day, we decided it would be good to take advantage of it."

Stephanie's face fell. "But . . . but . . . I asked you to let Eden know I'd telephoned. I was concerned that he didn't return my call as he asked that I meet him today, Wednesday and we'd go riding together."

The American girl thought for a long moment, shrugged and shook her head. "I remember your call, Miss Rhodes, but I think Eden wished to go riding with you next Wednesday. He knew he'd be busy today. You must be mistaken in your date." She said. "I saw Eden this morning; he didn't mention anything about meeting you today."

"But . . ." Stephanie's colour heightened. "Miss Whitney—how could you not have given Eden my message."

"I did, dear." She said, a trifle condescendingly. "I was under the impression that your arrangement with Eden was for next Wednesday, not today." Christiana's eyes narrowed slyly, which only served to render Stephanie with fury. She'd deliberately manipulated the situation to her own advantage. Christiana pulled away from the doorpost decisively. "He can't come now anyway, because he promised to take me on a tour of the area this afternoon. Now, if you don't mind, I must go upstairs to change into my riding gear, I can't have the most handsome man in the whole county waiting for me to join him on what sounds to me like a wonderful riding experience." She almost glided towards the stairs, turning with her hand on the newel post. "Please let yourself out, Miss Rhodes. I will mention your visit to Eden when I see him; I'm sure there must be a very simple explanation for this."

Stephanie stared at her. She wondered, vaguely, if her mother had made a mistake in the day, but dismissed it. Penelope Rhodes was the most meticulous person she knew and would make certain she'd have the day correct before writing that note to Stephanie. No, obviously Christiana had decided that only she should be allowed Eden's company. Stephanie slowly retreated towards the front door, opened it and walked with remarkably steady steps towards the pathway. Perhaps she should seek Eden out and find out for sure if she'd made a mistake. Forthrightly, she turned her direction towards the stables, but Eden wasn't around. She wandered over towards Mike, who was busy rubbing down Eden's stallion just outside the stable door.

"Hello Mike." She said, "I presume as you're preparing his horse, Eden is going riding today?"

"I believe he and Miss Christiana are taking to the moors for most of the day. Master Eden asked me about ten minutes ago to saddle the two horses."

Stephanie bit her lip, clearly agitated. The fact that Mike had confirmed what Christiana had said, didn't make her feel any better. She wondered why Eden hadn't called her again. What could Christiana have said for his silence? Suddenly she stamped her foot, a habit she used when a child. She would not let this go unchallenged. She had no desire to allow Christiana Whitney license to take her place with Eden that afternoon. If it came to a confrontation, then let it be—she was in the right and she intended to let them both know!

Walking resolutely up the steps to the front door, she gave the old bell-rope a tug and waited impatiently for Elspeth to answer the door. When the housekeeper did, she pushed her way inside none-too-gently and demanded to speak to Eden immediately.

"I'll see if I can locate him, Miss Rhodes—if you wouldn't mind waiting in the Drawing Room again." Elspeth said, woodenly, closing the door behind the irate young woman.

Stephanie walked into the Drawing Room, her head spinning, her mind reeling and her heart pounding. She would have it out with him!

Elspeth walked through the open doorway a few moments later to announce that she had no idea where Master Thorncroft was.

"Would you like to wait . . .?" She began, when a noise from outside stopped her.

Stephanie hurried to the window. Through the criss-crossed latticed panes, she saw to her dismay and anger, two horses thunder out of the courtyard. One she recognized as Eden on Jake; the other was Christiana astride another animal that could only have belonged to Luke.

CHAPTER 17

THE MAYFIELD ARMS

Earlier that same day, Eden sat on the side of the bed and pulled up his knee socks. Standing up, he glanced at himself in the mirror. Somehow showing Christiana the moors on this day, was not something he wished to do, but as Stephanie obviously had other plans, he had no other option but to reluctantly give in to Christiana's plea to take her riding over the moors. He'd promised her, so it may as well be now as later.

Eden was extremely disappointed at not sharing the day with Stephanie, as he had been looking forward to seeing her again. He'd missed her jovial company. So sure was he that she'd have accepted his invitation, he'd taken it upon himself to arrange for them to have a candlelit dinner at the Mayfield Arms overlooking the meandering River Exe. Now, as he would be bereft of Stephanie's delightful company, he'd agreed to take Christiana there instead.

Running down the stairs out into the warm sunlight, he strode towards the stables where Mike was deftly adjusting the saddle on Jake's broad back. Eden was glad they'd hired this young man. Mike had been alone for almost six months. The tragic house fire that had taken his family had left a huge hole in Mike's young life. Now he'd recovered sufficiently to be able to face the world again. Luckily, Mike had been at the cinema with a girl that evening, otherwise he too would have been a statistic. When he'd arrived home nearing midnight, the house was nothing but a black cinder. His parents, sister and baby brother had perished.

Alone, Mike had gone to stay with an elderly aunt, but had been miserable with her and wanted desperately to get away. Eden, like his father before him with Abraham and Joshua Higgins, had taken pity on him. His circumstances had struck a compassionate chord in Eden's heart. He'd hired him on the spot without even mentioning it to his father. He knew James would not object. Mike was hard-working, loyal and friendly.

"Is Miss Christiana around?" Eden asked, pulling on his riding gloves.

Mike glanced up at him before standing. "I saw her earlier, Master Eden. I think she's probably changing for your trip. By the way," he added, "a young lady called about half an hour ago. She was looking for you. When I mentioned that you'd arranged to go riding with Miss Christiana she seemed very upset and left. Perhaps I should have asked her to wait, but I wasn't sure how long you'd be. I hope I didn't do anything wrong, Master Eden, it was not intentional."

Eden's heart suddenly lifted. "No, Mike, you did nothing wrong. Did you recognize her by any chance?"

The boy frowned and rubbed his forehead, pushing a dark tress of hair out of his eyes. "Well, I think it was Mr. and Mrs. Rhodes daughter, but as I don't know her very well, I can't really be sure."

"Damn!" Eden exclaimed, banging his riding crop against his thigh angrily. "So she did receive my phone call—I wonder why she didn't call me back?" He murmured, a deep frown etched between his dark eyes.

"Both of the horses are ready when you are, Master Eden."

Eden turned, absently. "Thanks, Mike. I'll see if Miss Christiana is ready."

As Eden grasped the reins from the stable-boy, he saw Christiana running down the front steps towards him, smiling happily. He noticed that her blue and white riding habit didn't include a long calf-length skirt, but a pair of matching trousers. Despite her slight lack of modesty, Eden had to admit she was a stunning looking woman especially with the matching riding hat sitting atop neatly coiled blonde hair.

"Oh Eden." She cried. "We couldn't have picked a nicer day for a gallop over the moors."

He shrugged. "You're right. You look very nice."

"Thank you." She cooed, suddenly leaning up to kiss his cheek gently. She glanced across the paddock where another animal was pawing the ground impatiently. "This is Marie? She's adorable."

"Have you ridden side-saddle before, Christiana?" Eden asked as Mike opened the gate to allow Rebecca's mare into the yard.

"Side-saddle? Good Heavens no! In the States I always ride Western style the way a horse should be ridden!" She laughed.

Eden glanced at her, then at Mike. "We don't have Western style saddles at Ravenslea, Christiana. Rebecca rides side-saddle, so Marie is familiar with only that kind of saddle. I'll have Mike saddle up Luke's horse, Hudson." She nodded and he turned to Mike. "Take Marie back, Mike and saddle up Hudson for us."

Mike nodded and disappeared into the stable.

Both unaware of Stephanie standing horrified at the Drawing Room window, the two of them thundered out of the grounds towards the steep incline of the Devonshire moors, skirting beautiful purple heather and yellow gorse bushes.

The air was sweet with summer scent with not a single cloud in the azure sky. Eden took a deep breath and smiled at his companion, pleased to see that the American girl was as capable as any he'd met in handling Hudson.

"We'll go to Piper's Head, Christiana." He said at one point. "It's a popular spot; I'm certain we'll be undisturbed this afternoon. The view from there is spectacular. I'm sure you'd enjoy it."

"Sounds great." Christiana murmured, gazing into the distance. She felt so alive and privileged riding alongside the handsome Eden Thorncroft. His presence sent shivers through her body. When she tried to compare him with Cliff, she knew there was no comparison at all. They thundered up a long steep incline, both animals labouring with the effort.

Within fifteen minutes, they'd arrived at Piper's Head. Both jumped from their horses and tied them up to the back of the solitary seat overlooking the Bristol Channel. Christiana neared the edge, drawing in the lush warm breeze, marvelling at the vision before her.

"It's beautiful, Eden." She breathed, closing her eyes as the gentle wind blew in her face. "I must bring mother here—she'd adore it."

Eden stood beside her. "Piper's Head has had its fair share of tragedies though." He said, after a while.

"Really?" She turned to face him.

"Umm. Way back in the last century, one of my ancestors, the young woman whose picture is in the Music Room, fell from the cliff and perished. It was a terrible accident and one we've never forgotten. I don't think any member of my family have ever ventured up here without wondering how such a tragedy could have occurred."

"Gee, that must have been horrible." She moved closer to the edge peering anxiously over. "It's one helluva long way down there. Did she commit suicide? Or perhaps someone pushed her? At just the right moment, anyone could slip over the edge if given a slight push!"

Eden shrugged. "There was an inquest, and no-one could be faulted for the fall. No, it was definitely classed as an accident we're all very sure about that. I understand the woman was quite fiery by nature, so could have been in a strange mood and wasn't aware of what she was doing. Anyway, I thought I'd just mention it to you—now you can look on that young woman in a different light."

"I sure will, Eden. If it's the young woman I think it is, she's a rare beauty and I'm sure could turn many a young man's head if she so wished."

He glanced at his wrist watch. "Would you care to take a trip to Exeter, Christiana? Unless, of course, you have something else planned for this evening?"

"I'd love to. Take me anywhere; I love being in your company."

He gave a slight smile and caught her elbow. "Come then, we'll take a gentle canter to the River Exe—I know a beautiful public house that does excellent meals. By the time we get there, I'm sure we'll be famished."

It was a long trip to the River Exe and the Mayfield Arms and both of them were indeed ready for food. After cleaning up at the Inn, they settled outside just as the sun was beginning to set. Lanterns had been placed on the deck, hanging from rafters; a small wood-burning fire crackled in a bricked pit to keep the patrons warm.

Eden, sitting beside Christiana, instantly regretted agreeing to bring her to the Mayfield Arms. He could, after all, have cancelled as he wished only to share this delightful moment with Stephanie. Well, the deed had been done, so he might as well enjoy it.

When Stephanie arrived home later that afternoon from her disappointing visit to Ravenslea, she was surprised to see Nigel Whitfield waiting for her in the Drawing Room.

"What on earth are you doing here, Nigel?" She asked. "I thought you'd gone up north to be with your ailing father?"

"It wasn't as bad as first thought, so stayed for a while. As he improved it was obvious I really wasn't needed, so decided to take some holidays due to me." Nigel said, helping her off with her riding jacket. "Did you enjoy your ride?"

"No, as a matter of fact. It was a complete waste of time . . . but . . ." when she could see he was about to ask her about it, ". . . I don't wish to discuss it now."

"I was thinking that you and I could spend the rest of the day together somewhere, unless, of course, you have something else you have to do." Nigel said, sensing her reticence.

"Yes, why don't we? I have nothing planned. Why don't you wait here while I go up and change."

He nodded, settling into a comfortable armchair, picked up a magazine.

Stephanie ran up the stairs, her mouth a thin, determined line of disappointment. If Eden wanted to spend 'their' riding day with that American girl, then she would play him at his own game. She liked Nigel. It would be good to be with someone to take her mind off her irritation, so made up her mind to enjoy the rest of the day with him. Slipping into a brown calf-length skirt and apricot blouse, she ran fingers through her dark hair, applied a little make-up and went lightly back downstairs.

"Where would you like to go?" She asked as she entered the room.

He shrugged, laying down the magazine. "You decide, dear. I know nowhere around here. Just not to Branton. I've wandered around it a few times and consider there doesn't seem to be much going on there, especially in the evenings."

"You're right about that! It doesn't even have a museum or art gallery for anyone who wants to visit!" She smiled. "Let's take a tour in the car. We don't need Barnaby—I'm a good driver and can show you some historic sights. There are some pretty villages stretching from the Somerset border down through Devon to Cornwall. There's still some light left, so why don't we do that? We could stop off somewhere for a bite to eat on the way. What do you say?"

Nigel was happy to go anywhere with her, but Barnaby wasn't happy at allowing the shiny limousine to be driven by the young mistress of Cavendish Hall. Stephanie strongly assured him that she'd take good care of it, promising not to grind the gears, something he disliked intensely.

"Well, if you're sure, Miss." He ceded, grudgingly, "then have a good time."

He watched as the two young people stepped into the vehicle and drive out of the grounds to disappear down the road. He lifted his cap and scratched his head apprehensively. Young women were into everything nowadays. It wasn't like this when he was young; he wondered as he walked back to the garage, what the world was coming to with young women donning trousers, of all things, and driving cars! The next thing they'll be piloting aircraft—he shuddered—perish the thought!

Stephanie drove carefully. She knew better than to try racing it along the narrow winding roads. She wouldn't want to bear witness to the ranting she'd receive from her father if she so much as scratched the paintwork!

Stephanie knew her way around this part of southwest England and enjoyed showing Nigel as many interesting places as she could before the sun began to dip. First, at his insistence, she took him to see the ruins of Glastonbury Abbey in Somerset. Enthralled by the ancient stones he spent a lot of time wandering through the long grass between the huge pillars. A plaque told that it was here that the legendary King Arthur was purported to be buried. Nigel, a keen historian, was captivated by it. He wanted to linger in this place where he said he could almost feel the aura of Glastonbury's monks as they went about their business, but Stephanie insisted there were other sights to see that would interest him too.

Once they'd crossed the Somerset boundary back into Devon, Stephanie motored up to Piper's Head. Stopping at the top, Nigel insisted they sit on the bench holding hands for a while. She was content to do that. She wished Eden could see her with Nigel in this way. Perhaps it would thrust a point home to him. She shook herself. She mustn't let Ravenslea's heir intrude on her thoughts at the moment. All she wanted to do was enjoy herself with the attentions Nigel was happy to give her, but before long they both acknowledged they were hungry.

"We'll go into Exeter, Nigel." She said, as they stepped back into the car. "It's a little way from here, but I know a pretty little Inn there that do really good food and I could do with a meal right now, what do you say?"

He grinned and squeezed her hand before she put the car in gear. "Anywhere with you, my love, would be paradise to me."

She laughed. "Oh, don't be silly, Nigel. You do say the most outrageous things."

"True, true, I suppose I do, but I mean every word of it!"

It took them a little longer than they thought to get to the little Inn. First, Stephanie took a wrong turn, after which she noticed the petrol gauge was registering low and had to stand in line at the petrol station. By the time they reached the Inn, the sun had dipped well below the horizon, leaving the earth in a gradually darkening twilight. However, it didn't detract from the beauty of the area. Small lanterns hanging from hooks placed at strategic points on the outside walls and trellises of the Inn's Tudor façade, swayed in the gentle breeze that wafted across the patrons from the river. Inside, warm soft orange lighting encompassed secluded booths.

Stephanie would have liked to have gone onto the terrace which overlooked the River Exe, but the waiter told them all the seats were taken. Disappointed, they chose the next best thing, a booth near a window overlooking the patio deck and beyond that the glittering water from the River Exe. It was a beautiful warm night and from their table, the pleasant scent of the burning coals in receptacles on the patio deck and the heady aroma of long trailing honeysuckle emanated through the slightly open window. Night insects buzzed around the lanterns.

Stephanie glanced over at her escort. She had to acknowledge as they ate in companionable silence, she enjoyed Nigel's company. He was a gentle person who obviously adored her. The knowledge gave her comfort, yet she knew where his mind was heading. That niggled at her conscience; the only thing marring the otherwise perfect evening.

Further along into the evening, Stephanie laid her cutlery onto the plate and glanced up. A woman drew near obviously making her way to the washroom. Stephanie felt her jaw drop in surprise. It was Christiana Whitney, dressed in a pair of exquisite blue slacks and a tight fitting blue and white shirt. She did not see Stephanie as she swept passed. A couple of minutes later, the American girl reappeared; this time their eyes caught.

"Oh hi, Miss Rhodes." Christiana said, smiling brightly through flashing white teeth. "What a delightful surprise at finding you here with," she glanced at Nigel with interest, "your young man, I presume?" She held out a long fingered hand. "I'm Christiana Whitney—Martin Thorncroft's stepdaughter. I don't believe we've met?"

Nigel, oblivious of the slight hostility between the two young women, rose, smiled and grasped Christiana's hand warmly.

"How nice to meet you, Miss Whitney? I'm Nigel Whitfield. Are you staying at Ravenslea?"

"Oh yes, indeed. It is my home now, Nigel" she said with a familiarity Stephanie found offensive. "Wherever Martin and my mother goes, then I and my brother, Adam, will go too. It's a wonderful place and I love living there. You are from this area…?"

He shook his head. "No, I'm from northern England, just here for a few days to be with Stephanie. We are good friends…"

"I can see that," Christiana said. Stephanie detected smug intonations in her speech. "I am here at the express request of Eden Thorncroft. We had a delightful romp over the moors and he'd already arranged for a table for two for us here. It's a great tavern; we have nothing like it in the States—and the food is fabulous."

"I agree." Nigel said amiably. "Would you and Mr. Thorncroft like to join us?" He glanced quickly at Stephanie as an afterthought. "You would have no objection would you, my dear?"

She felt a bristling of resentment, but knew she could not disagree and nodded. "Of course not, Miss Whitney." She said, though her lips thinned at the thought of spending even a moment in Eden's company under these circumstances.

Luckily, Christiana shook her blonde head. "Thank you, but no. We have a wonderful seat with a perfect view of the River Exe. Unfortunately, there isn't room there to add another two places, otherwise I would definitely have you join us." She smiled sweetly. "Perhaps another time."

"Yes." Stephanie said hurriedly. "Another time."

They sat back in their seats. For an instant, Stephanie curbed the desire to look onto the patio, though she wanted desperately to catch a glimpse of Eden. However, her resolve faltered and she knew she'd have to see for herself. While Nigel was occupied by finishing off his dinner, she strained to see if she could see them and she did! Christiana's blonde head was very close to Eden's dark one and to Stephanie's dismay she noticed their hands were touching. They appeared to be talking intimately and a flurry of anger pulsed through her body.

"She seems a nice person, doesn't she, dear?" She heard Nigel say as he placed the napkin back in his lap.

"Yes . . ." She spluttered. "If you are partial to forward, flamboyant women! I would like to leave now, Nigel, if you don't mind. I have the start of a headache and would really like to go home." She looked over at him. "Do you mind?"

Nigel stared at her first of all with surprise at this sudden change in her attitude, to one of concern for her welfare.

"Of course not, dear. I'll just get the bill and we'll return. If you like, I'll drive back if you show me the direction; that way you can relax and try to get rid of your headache."

"Thanks, Nigel." She stood up. "I just want to freshen up. I'll meet you by the car in a few minutes."

He stood up and gestured to their waiter, requesting their bill, while she hurried into the ladies washroom room to tidy up and compose herself for the trip back to Cavendish Hall.

CHAPTER 18

THE NEXT MORNING

A COOL breeze rippled through the long grass at the back side of Cavendish Hall's stables as Eden reigned in Jake, jumped down and tied him to a railing beside the open door. Inside the rather run-down structure, he heard someone whistling and a lot of scurrying about. Intrigued he wandered inside to see tousled fiery red hair bobbing up and down behind a stall fence. A young man in his early twenties looked up from cleaning out one of the stalls and stopped what he was doing.

"Hello." Eden said, nearing him. "I don't think I've met you before. I'm Eden Thorncroft from Ravenslea Manor. You must be new here?"

The young man pushed a hand across his forehead; his whistling stopped and he gave Eden a grin. "Aye, me name's 'Arry Bixton. I've bin 'ere about two weeks." Harry Bixton had a very strong West Country brogue that Eden always considered amusing, yet was pleasing to the ear. "I'm that pleased to meet you, Mr. Thorncroft. I've 'eard nothin' but good things about your family."

"That's very nice to hear. Do you happen to know if Miss Rhodes is at home?"

"Oh, I'm sorry, Sir." Harry Bixton shook his head. "She's gone out with 'er young man."

"Really?" Eden frowned. "Does her 'young man' come here often?"

Harry shook his head. "I've only seen 'im once before and then only for a short while." He moved back, picked up a rake and began to steadily level out the straw in one of the stables. "They took the master's car, then I noticed it was returned looking pretty dirty, so I gave it a quick wash. It was then that I noticed Miss Stephanie's mare was not in 'er stable, so I expect she's gone off somewhere on 'er own as 'er 'orse is the only one missing from the stable."

"Oh . . ." Eden felt a trickle of concern bubble inside of him. "Well, is Mrs. Rhodes at home?"

"I think she be in the back garden, Sir." Harry said.

With a quick farewell, Eden left Jake tethered. He moved lethargically across the gravel yard. For some reason he had no desire to return to Ravenslea without talking to Stephanie about last night. He had to put right the wrong he'd obviously done her. He knew he had things to attend to at Ravenslea, but the compulsion to wait overrode that. Perhaps her mother might give him some idea as to where she'd gone.

As he crossed a small crazy-paved pathway which led to the lawns in front of Cavendish Hall, his thoughts turned again to Stephanie, blaming himself for this turn in their friendship, yet he was annoyed to think she'd just go off with someone else without phoning him.

Deep in thought wondering how he was going to approach Stephanie, he sauntered across the lawn that definitely needed mowing. Glancing up, he noticed Stephanie's mother on her hands and knees at the border tackling some well-needed weeding, a large rather battered straw hat shielding her from the sun.

"Hello, Mrs. Rhodes." Eden walked leisurely towards her as she sat back on her heels, brushing a soiled hand across her brow, leaving a smudge. She turned, but there was no welcoming smile on her usually friendly face.

"Eden? What are you doing here?"

"I was looking for Stephanie. We were going to go riding yesterday, but there seems to have been some kind of mix-up. I understand that she came to Ravenslea yesterday but we unfortunately missed each other. She must be upset with me for not being there, especially at my invitation. I really would like to find her and talk about it. Do you know where she is?"

Penelope shook her head. "No idea. She came back here yesterday quite disturbed. She wouldn't discuss anything with me, so I surmised you and she had had some kind of argument. At breakfast this morning she was quiet and uncommunicative." She paused, glancing up at him. "A friend of hers came to the house earlier today, which I thought was quite convenient. He would help, I'm sure, to take her out of her doldrums. They went somewhere in Fletcher's vehicle. I heard the car return, then noticed Stephanie riding off on her own immediately after. I have no idea where she's gone, or where her friend is. She didn't even stop to speak to me before she left so hurriedly. I must say, I was both annoyed and concerned; it really was too bad of her!" She looked up at him.

"Well, I'll try to find her, Mrs. Rhodes. I have an idea she may have gone to Piper's Head. I remember her telling me years ago, when she was upset about something, she often went there to mull things over. I'll ride up there—if I can't find her, I'll return and let you know." Eden didn't care if she was with her 'young man' as Harry so eloquently mentioned. If it was Nigel, then it might be good to meet him again anyway.

"That's good of you, Eden, as both her father and I will be worrying if she doesn't return before sundown." Penelope returned to her gardening.

"Goodbye for the moment then, Mrs. Rhodes. I hope I'll find her. I'm concerned at the way she left Ravenslea yesterday and wish to discuss it with her."

"I understand." Penelope said, turning slightly with the small trowel in her hand.

Eden went back to the stable, mounted Jake and rode swiftly out of the grounds. Whether Stephanie was there or not, he needed to give Jake a good run and the invigorating gallop to Piper's Head was one very good way of doing it. Piper's Head situated on a picturesque promontory a few miles from Cavendish Hall, comprised a pristine piece of land that overlooked the Bristol Channel. This beautiful part of the Devonshire coastline had long been heralded as a special place for lovers, hikers as well as the occasional tourist. It was also an inspirational area for painters and authors. He knew Luke had taken photographs from different angles quite a few times. One of those photographs was now hanging over the mantlepiece in the Dining Room.

Thundering over the moors kicking up turf and mud towards Piper's Head, Eden couldn't get Stephanie out of his head. He had never known a young woman quite like her. He was enamoured of her in every way. He didn't know if it was love . . . perhaps it was. He only knew that he liked being with her, sharing things with her. When she went away to Finishing School, he'd not realized just how much he missed her. Now she was home, he wanted her back in his life.

As he neared the flat top of the peninsula, he breathed a sigh of relief. There she was, sitting on the wooden bench that had seated so many people over the years. She was alone and his heart lifted. Her honey coloured mare was munching on the lush grass a few yards behind her.

"Stephanie?" He called, shuddering to a stop just behind the bench. He jumped down from Jake's back, tossing the reins over the back of the bench. "What happened to you yesterday? I thought you and I were going riding?"

She turned sharply, her thoughts abruptly interrupted. "Oh . . . Eden . . . I thought so too, but it seemed you had other plans." She looked away.

"What's the matter?" He urged, moving beside her, touching her shoulder gently.

She shook his hand free. "Nothing, Eden. Nothing with which to concern yourself."

He persisted, moving forward quicker now, catching her arm. He roughly swung her around to face him. "Don't pretend to me." He said, lifting her chin so their eyes met. "Tell me what's upsetting you—maybe I can help!"

"I think . . ." she said, slowly, hardly audible, "I think you've done enough already! I saw you . . . and Christiana! I don't think I need to say anything further!"

He stared at her guardedly. "What did you see?"

"You were at the Mayfield Arms; sitting really close—intimately it seemed. You and she . . . you can't deny that, can you?"

He pulled away, a heavy sigh escaping from his firm mouth. "If you didn't hear us, you had no idea what we were discussing. You have it all wrong—it was completely innocent." He caught her to him, aware of her stubborn resistance. He maintained his hold, his fingers cruelly biting through her warm woollen jacket into the tender flesh of her upper arms.

"But, you were . . ." she spluttered.

"You just stay quiet long enough to hear me out." He paused. "At first, I didn't see you, Stephanie. But," he turned her head to search her face. "I did see you leave the restaurant with the man I met at your house."

"Nigel—yes. We went for dinner the day you and I were supposed to have gone riding. When I went to Ravenslea, I was told you were going with Christiana, I was very hurt that you didn't wait for me . . .'"

"Whoa, Stephanie! I didn't know you had agreed to go riding with me."

Stephanie stared at him, puzzled. "I did phone. I spoke to Christiana and asked her to give you the message that I'd be happy to go riding with you. She said she'd tell you as soon as she saw you again."

He frowned, a deep furrow appearing between his dark eyebrows. "Christiana did say you'd phoned, but only to say you'd had other plans—that you'd arrange to see me next week."

Stephanie looked up at him.. "I didn't say that, Eden. I told her that I'd be over to meet you at the given time on Wednesday. Why would she tell you something different? I can't believe it!"

Eden's dark eyes narrowed, his mouth pressed in a firm line. "She lied, Steph! She deliberately lied—but for what reason? I know she wanted to go riding with me at some time as she'd shown an interest in seeing the moors, but to lie about that sounds completely irresponsible and cruel." He touched her face gently. "I'll have it out with her when we return, my dear. She must have misheard what you said. I'm so sorry."

"Oh, Eden, I can't believe just how trusting you are sometimes. If a woman like Christiana sets her sights on a man, she'll go as far as she can go to get him and . . ." she laid her finger against his lips as he was about to protest, ". . . no, Eden, think about it. She's young, slightly brazen in my opinion, and lonely. She saw in you a handsome escort; someone with whom she wished to be seen. What better opportunity for her to accomplish that, than to have you take her over the moors on horseback? She didn't give my feelings a single thought."

He shook his head slightly. "I can't believe she'd think like that, Steph." Yet, as he said it he believed it could well be true. Her flirtatious encounter with him in his father's Study should have warned him, but his ego had got in the way. "I'll talk to her and find out why she lied to me."

Stephanie leaned over, drawing him to her. "Leave it alone, Eden. Let her believe her ruse worked. You and I know different. Let's not make waves—who knows what kind of things Christiana could do to upset your household, even mine for that matter, if you and she became embroiled in conflict."

He didn't answer for a moment. "I did so want to take just you to the Mayfield Arms, Stephanie. I had already arranged it before any of this happened, with you in mind. Christiana had obviously seen the perfect opportunity to take your place." He slammed his hand against his thigh. "I can't believe I was so blind! You have to forgive me, my love . . ."

"I do, now that you've explained." She said.

"If I'd only given it more thought; I should not have taken Christiana until I'd spoken to you, but to be perfectly honest, I was extremely cross with you. It was somehow my way of punishing you." He paused and closed his hand over hers. "I'm so sorry, my dear, it was only because I felt you really didn't care; that Nigel meant more to you than I did."

She looked into his dark eyes searchingly. "I thought you knew me better after all this time. Oh Eden, surely you must have realized something was wrong when you didn't hear anything from me? Why didn't you phone or ride over to find out for yourself? When I came to Ravenslea and couldn't find you, I wondered what had happened. I was in your Drawing Room when I saw you and Christiana thunder out of the grounds. You both seemed quite happy. What was I supposed to think?"

He stared at her for a moment. "It was a dreadful misunderstanding, Stephanie. What a cad you must think me! I feel wretched to have caused you hurt, my dear; it wasn't intentional I can assure you." He paused. "I had difficulty sleeping last night and when I came down to breakfast this morning Christiana told me that she had seen you at The Mayfield Arms. You were having an intimate dinner with Nigel, so I naturally thought you preferred to be with him. Then, when I arrived at Cavendish Hall, your mother informed me you'd gone out with Nigel in your father's car, came home again, then took your horse out. She was quite upset that you didn't say anything to her."

"Eden. I was angry with you and I did the first thing that came into my head. I hoped that by taking Nigel around the district, it would dispel the hurt I was feeling. My friendship with him is purely that—friendship—there is nothing more to it than that we are good friends. This morning, I took him into Branton. He wanted to get something for his mother's birthday. I left him there as he also had some telephoning to do. So I brought the car back and decided to go riding on my own." Stephanie said. "Yesterday, Nigel turned up at Cavendish Hall on an impromptu visit. He wanted to spend some time with me before he returned north. He's very nice; I didn't want to let him down, so as I wasn't going riding with you, decided to spend the time with him. The fact that we ended up at the same Inn as you and Christiana was a coincidence. I was most upset to see you with Christiana, when we were supposed to be together. Oh, Eden . . . I'm so mixed up." She stared up into his warm violet eyes. "You must have known I wanted to be with you. I felt so . . . betrayed when I saw you with her."

"I'm so sorry, my dear." He said, leaning back against the seat, his arm resting lightly around her shoulders, "You must remember that Christiana is lonely in England. I believed she just snatched at the chance to go riding. She gets pretty bored at Ravenslea some days, so I quite understand why she did it."

"So she should go exploring with her brother, or find some friends." Stephanie pursed her mouth, surprised to hear the venom in her voice. Normally, she was not a vindictive person, but whenever she thought of Christiana Whitney, she couldn't help feeling somewhat spiteful towards her. "I suppose I'm a little envious, Eden, to think she's living in the same house as you and can be with you more often than I. She's beautiful, you must admit that."

He shrugged. "She's attractive, I suppose, but it's mostly paint, Stephanie. You are the most natural beauty of all; any make-up you wear is always tasteful and never overdone." He drew her to him. "Would you be terribly embarrassed if I told you that I want to make violent love to you . . . here . . . now . . . on the moors . . .! That would tell you just how much you mean to me."

Ever practical, Stephanie looked up at him. "Not only would it be highly uncomfortable, but what would Christiana say?" A smile lit up her face, erasing the downcast expression almost immediately.

"I don't care a fig what she'd say." He laughed. "Please say you'll forgive me, my dear; that you and Nigel really are only friends, nothing more. I'll tell you in all honesty there is nothing at all between Christiana and myself. In fact, my love," he paused, fidgeting slightly. "I've been wanting to say this for a very long time—despite all that has happened over the last day or so, would you consider having me as your husband?"

She stared at him, her eyes smouldering, then reached up and kissed his lips warmly. "I've always loved you, Eden; even when we were kids playing together, I was drawn to you." She paused, adding shyly. "And yes, I'd be truly honoured to be your wife."

"You will? You don't know how happy that makes me, my love." He paused, drawing her close and pressing his warm lips against hers gently. "I wrestled with this misunderstanding with Christiana all last night. Sleep was almost unattainable for me. I thought that if you found out I'd gone riding with her, you'd think my feelings had changed towards you; that I was in love with her. I wish I could erase the whole blessed business. Let's go back to Cavendish Hall and tell your mother. I'd like to see her reaction." He pulled her to her feet. The violet eyes that so bewitched her, glistened and Stephanie knew without a doubt, that the love she felt for Eden, was reciprocated.

"I don't need to go back to see mother, Eden, I know exactly how she'll feel, as will father. They'll welcome you into our family with open arms and their sincere blessings."

Later that evening, holding Stephanie's hand, Eden informed his family that Stephanie had agreed to marry him. They suffered the love and kisses bestowed upon them as had occurred when Penelope and Fletcher had been told.

Two days later, Christiana, on hearing Eden's news, informed the family that she was going to phone the shipping lines to book a passage back to the States. Her real reason was because she now knew that pursuing Eden was not going to bear any fruit. The reason she told the family was that although she loved Ravenslea and England, she found her existence too quiet. It was best if she returned to where she could forge a more meaningful life.

Two weeks later, Martin and Louise motored to Southampton to see her off to the States and a new life.

CHAPTER 19

OCTOBER 1930

THE REUNION

Fern brushed a hand over her eyes and twisted around to sit on the side of the unfamiliar bed. After a while, she stood up and moved towards the windows to draw the curtains. It was a misty morning, but even though it was October, the air seemed mild. As the summer had been warm, Fern hoped it would signal a shorter winter—one could always hope.

Excitement had at first made rest difficult especially in such unfamiliar surroundings. She'd arrived late last night, tired from the journey and ready for a good night's sleep. Fortunately, she was able to attain this, despite the pillow being less comfortable than the one she was used to at Ravenslea.

She gazed out over the busy street that led down towards the docks, then moved towards the small wooden dressing table. Critically looking at herself in the mirror, she noticed her eyes were bright. The thought of being with her adored husband after such a long while away from each other, seemed to have turned her from a middle-aged woman, to the young, playful woman she'd been when they'd first met. Her body throbbed with excited anticipation as she counted down from hours to minutes before her beloved Simon would be with her again. Bathing and carefully dressing in the brown and white suit she knew Simon liked, Fern arranged her hair, applied a little make-up then went downstairs to breakfast.

She'd arrived the day before Simon's ship was due to dock, having previously arranged for them to stay at The Finchbury Hotel for a couple of days before returning to Ravenslea. By choice, she'd decided to travel by train, even though Martin had offered to take her in the car. She wanted to be alone with the man she'd married and who had been away from her for so many months. This time, so Simon had told her in his last letter, he was going to be home for good. He'd taken an early retirement with full status as Captain Simon Danby; Fern was extremely proud of this achievement. She had no idea just what Simon was going to be doing once he'd settled back into civilian life, but that was something to discuss at a later date. For now, she'd just have him back with her and together they'd create a new, exciting life together. Fern knew Simon would be eager to join her and James as a part of the Desdemona's crew; something they'd discussed many times in earlier years.

She smiled as she recalled how Emily and Constance had pleaded to accompany her, after all, they'd not seen their father in as much time, but soon understood their mother's desire to be on her own with him. Once back at Ravenslea there would be little time, except in the bedroom, when they could be sure of being alone.

The Finchbury Hotel's Dining Room was quaintly laid out with six tables seating four people each, covered with maroon square tablecloths on the bottom with delicate lace ones placed diagonally over them. The maroon matched the burgundy Regency wallpaper and elegant white trimmed woodwork and doorways. Even in October, each table sported an elegant red rose with a small spray of fern to enhance it.

Two gentlemen were sitting at different tables when she entered. The oldest, with a receding hairline sported a wonderfully bushy grey handlebar moustache. He was reading a newspaper while sipping a delicate bone china cup of tea; noticeably so by the elegant white teapot standing in front of him. The other was a younger man who appeared hurried as he was gobbling his food down as if the Devil was after him. He glanced up as she sat down at her allotted seat, smiling abstractedly.

The older man turned and folded his newspaper. "Good morning, my dear, it looks like it's going to be a lovely day, despite the clouds, don't you think?"

She nodded. "Indeed yes, I feel the sun will soon make a welcome appearance."

"I'm Lt. Colonel John Wickham." The older man continued. "I'm a resident here. I don't mean I live here all the time, but come down at the end of summer and most of the autumn months. The owners of the hotel afford me the same accommodation each time I come. It is very restful though having been in the Army many years ago, for some reason I find it very comforting to be near the sea."

"I can quite understand that, Lt. Colonel Wickham." Fern said.

"You are staying here for a while?" He asked conversationally.

"Just for a couple of days. My husband is arriving by ship from India this morning and we'll be staying here for a few days before returning home."

"Ah," Lt. Colonel Wickham's eyes lit up. "Your husband is in the Army, perhaps?"

She nodded. "Yes. He's been away quite a while—stationed in Karachi."

"I finished my stint in the Army at the beginning of the dreaded War. Karachi! Hmmph! Dreadful place, full of wogs!"

Fern felt her face infuse with colour. Glancing quickly across the room to the young man, she noticed him stare at John Wickham accusingly. The derogatory statement always annoyed her and she turned away, thankful to see a waiter approaching.

"Please excuse me," she said to the elderly man turning her attention to her breakfast.

A few minutes later, Lt. Colonel Wickham pushed back his chair. He moved awkwardly towards her as if he was suffering some kind of leg wound. "Perhaps," he said, touching her shoulder gently. "Perhaps when your husband arrives, we could get together for a chat. I do know a little about Karachi and he might like to talk about it."

She smiled up at him. "I doubt it, actually, Lt. Colonel Wickham, I think he'll just want to discuss things that would not remind him of things that happened over there. But thank you anyway; I'll certainly mention it to him."

Satisfied and understanding, Lt. Colonel Wickham brushed passed her with a quick nod to disappear through the Dining Room door.

A few minutes later, the other man left the Dining Room, leaving Fern to eat her cereal and toast in the quiet atmosphere with a gentle Mozart piece playing on a phonograph somewhere out of sight.

Simon's ship was due to arrive close to noon that day. Fern asked the receptionist how far the dock area was for meeting disembarking travellers. The kindly woman in her late fifties said if she felt fit enough, she could definitely walk it.

"Just down the road to the next turning, about six houses down, then turn left for about a quarter of a mile. You'll see all the signs after that." She smiled at Fern. "You meeting your young man?"

Fern laughed. "I suppose you could say that," she said, "I'm meeting my husband."

"Oh, I'm sorry dear, I didn't mean to . . ."

"That's quite all right—in fact, it's nice to think you believe I'm young enough to have a 'young' man." Fern grinned amiably.

"You certainly do, my dear." The phone rang then and the woman turned away.

Fern walked out of the building and into the street, her back straight, her heart pumping. She'd be with Simon very soon . . . how she'd longed for this day since the moment she'd heard his date and time of arrival.

That evening was the most wonderful evening Fern ever remembered sharing with Simon. He'd showered her with gifts from India; gifts that, to her, seemed so expensive and unique. He bought her a very special gift for her birthday coming up towards the end of the month. Despite his protestations that she should wait until her birthday, she couldn't resist untying the little pink ribbon, pulling off the paper and opening the box. Inside, laying nestled against black velvet, was a beautiful gold brooch in the shape of a scarab.

Fern looked up at her husband, quickly pinned the scarab on the side of her blouse, then wrapped him in her arms.

"Darling," she murmured, kissing his lips warmly, "it's so beautiful. It looks as if it could have cost you a fortune."

He scowled, but smiled. "Don't spoil the moment, beloved, by speaking of the cost . . . anything I purchase for you is priceless. I love you so much, I'd give you the whole World, if I could, to do with as your happy heart desires!"

That night Simon and Fern joined together in the large, comfortable bed, making love over and over again; each exploring, kissing, fondling and murmuring words of love, trying to catch up on all they'd lost over the past few years.

When morning arrived, the sun had come out, the mist had lifted. They knew it was going to be a wonderful day to spend together roaming and seeing the sights the old town had to offer at their leisure, before taking the train back to Ravenslea.

CHAPTER 20

LILLIAN - OCTOBER 1930

L ILLIAN moved with the lethargy normally associated with drug over-induce-ment. Her manner was disoriented; her speech slurred; yet somewhere in the farthest reaches of her brain, something was registering. Flashes of cognition fought to penetrate the fog that was clouding her senses. A face here; a place there; a voice.

She felt a hand at her elbow. "Come back to your room, dear." A nurse—always the same nurse. Kindly, efficient, friendly—yet her voice irritated Lillian. She was tired of hearing patronization by people around her. Always cooing and saying things that made her feel like a child just learning the rudiments of life.

She shrugged off the hand impatiently, but offered no resistance when the nurse led her back to the room she shared with three other women.

The nurse helped her into bed, tucking the bedclothes tightly around her thin, almost emaciated, body.

"I'll be back in a minute, dear." She said.

Lillian watched her out of the corner of her eye. In a couple of minutes, the tall, white coated nurse appeared again, this time laden with a glass of water in one hand and a small white paper cup holding a single pill in the other.

"Here, now take this, dear—it'll help you relax and get a good night's sleep. You'll feel so much better in the morning."

"I feel all right now." Lillian moaned, turning her face in the pillow defiantly. "I don't want it!"

"Oh come now, you must—doctor's orders. You wouldn't want me to get into trouble by not administering the medication I've been ordered to give you?"

"I don't care— I feel better without it."

"Sit up and take the pill this minute, or I'll have to call the Duty Nurse. You know what she's like."

Lillian did know; she was a cow of a woman with a big mouth and as much compassion as a cat when it tortured a mouse. She felt suddenly trapped. Hesitating briefly, she gave in and struggled to a half-sitting position.

"All right," she said dispassionately. "But I refuse to take any more." Her voice rose significantly as she realized the nurse had got her way.

"Now, put the pill on your tongue, dear and wash it down with the water. You'll be so happy you did." Lillian wished the silly nurse wouldn't keep on calling her 'dear' like she was some little child or a geriatric patient. She'd always hated that expression when it was used by anybody other than family—it seemed so patronizing.

She picked up the pill from the little cup and placed it on top of her tongue. Lowering her head slightly, she quickly tucked it between her back teeth and the side of her cheek. Taking a sip of water she swallowed some and put the glass on the bedside table. The nurse seemed satisfied and told her to lie down again.

"Sleep well, dear." She cooed as she drew the thin cream cotton curtains along the rail around her.

When the nurse had left, Lillian spat the still almost intact pill into what was left of the water. By morning, it would have melted and no-one would be the wiser! She needed her wits about her for the next while; the pills just made her drowsy and uncoordinated.

Outside the window, a light setting sun glowed over the four occupants in the hospital room. Inside, the slightly camphor smell of the oil lamps being lit wafted over the hospital. Everyone was refreshed after their evening meal before bedtime and half an hour or so later the patients in her room began to settle down for the night. Lillian waited until everyone was breathing gently, then slowly lifted herself from the bed and froze as one of the bedsprings squeaked noisily. A moment's pause and she put her feet to the floor.

The idea to escape had come earlier that afternoon. The woman in the bed opposite had been admitted to her ward on a one-night stay for observation; her clothes had been placed in a large linen bag with handles and hanging on a hook at the side of her bed. Lillian had no idea if the woman was her size, but if possible she'd use those clothes to make her escape. No-one would recognize her—after all, she was supposed to have been given a sleeping pill and wasn't due to awaken until the morning staff arrived. She quickly stuffed her pillows under the sheets hoping it would resemble a sleeping person. When the staff made their periodic rounds, the humped up pillow under the bedclothes would be a sign that this patient should not be disturbed.

Slowly, she crossed from her bed to the one opposite, aware vaguely that her feet were dragging on the cold floor. The woman was sleeping soundly, even giving a little snore now and then. Glancing quickly around, Lillian lifted the bag from the hook and hurried back to her bed. She promptly divested herself of the unbecoming hospital gown and slipped easily into the other woman's clothes. A few minutes later, Lillian shrugged on a black gabardine raincoat which smelled damp. She then put her used hospital gown in the bag and returned it to the hook beside the woman's bed.

Now came the difficult part; to find the stairs to the main floor without being detected. She crept into the corridor. The Nursing Station was directly ahead and the Duty Nurse was facing away from her. Keeping close to the side, Lillian moved forward. Somehow she had to get passed the Nursing Station to the narrow passageway that housed the elevator and the stairs. This was going to be tricky.

At that moment, two nurses turned the corner towards the Nursing Station. One was holding a sheaf of papers, while conducting an animated conversation with the other. Lillian ducked into a semi-darkened ward and waited until the two had passed. She stayed for a few seconds then glanced back into the corridor just as the two nurses turned another corner and disappeared. Lillian took a deep breath, crossed her fingers and uttered a little prayer that she'd be able to escape without arousing suspicion.

She was luckier than she'd first thought, as the Duty Nurse stood up from her desk, stuck a pen in the top of her pocket, picked up a board with papers clipped to it and left the area. Good! She would make her escape now.

She hurried passed the empty Nursing Station and turned slowly into the narrow passageway. No-one appeared in the corridor and the doors to the stairs were within sight. With a swiftness that amazed her, Lillian reached the door, pushed it open and after closing it, leaned back to catch her breath.

So far so good! She couldn't believe her luck. She descended the stairs from the fourth floor to the ground floor and encountered nobody on her journey down. The ground floor door opened into the large Emergency Admittance area where a few sleepy people were seated. More activity here; but everyone was in street clothes—she'd blend in perfectly.

Straightening her shoulders, she walked steadily towards the main doors to the outside world. No-one spoke to her; no-one stopped her; all at once Lillian was outside and free! The sky had darkened considerably and light rain was falling. Now, where could she go? She had no money, so had no way of hiring a taxi or catching a bus. All she could do was walk.

She pushed her hands into the pocket of the raincoat and touched a leather pouch. A wallet! This would never do. If caught with it in her possession, she'd definitely be arrested as a thief! But needs must and she had to have some money.

Finding a damp park bench near some trees and an overhead gaslight, she sat down and opened the wallet. A picture of a smiling woman of about forty wearing a large white-brimmed hat and holding a poodle close to her ample breast, was tucked in a see-through part of the wallet. The woman in the ward! Under the gaslight, Lillian could just make out the woman's name—Flo Turner; but that meant nothing.

Lillian opened the money section and found two five pound notes along with some pennies, sixpences and three half-crowns. Not much, but it was certainly better than what she had before! Though it was against everything she believed in, she slipped the wallet back into the raincoat pocket, knowing she'd have to use it.

She reached the railway station a little before eight o'clock that evening. Arriving at the ticket counter she delved into the pocket of the gabardine raincoat and threw some coins under the metal netting. The ticket officer handed her a stub and told her which platform she needed.

"You're going to have to wait awhile, Madam," he said, kindly, obviously wondering about this rather unkempt woman who seemed tired and slightly disoriented. "Your train is already running about half an hour late. Why don't you rest and have a cup of tea in the waiting room next door while you wait? There's a small concession desk where you can get some biscuits or sandwiches just to tied you over—nothing too elaborate." He smiled at her

Lillian nodded and said she would. She realized she was hungry and the railway ticket only cost her 1/3d, so she had more than enough to purchase some refreshments.

Moving into the waiting room, she chose a sandwich and a cup of tea. Finding a reasonably clean vacant bench seat, she settled down to leisurely enjoy the food. After a few minutes, she felt more refreshed having consumed the sandwich and cup of strong tea, so struggling up from the bench seat, she wandered back onto the platform. Glancing around she looked for the sign that would lead her to the required platform. On seeing the arrow, she walked slowly across a footbridge to the other side of the railway tracks. Platform 4 was full of people. She sighed. She'd hoped she'd be able to get a compartment to herself, but with this many people waiting, she had her doubts.

Seating herself on the edge of a bench that was occupied at one end by an elderly couple, she leaned back suddenly feeling the familiar wave of fatigue wash over her again. Leaving the hospital had been a risky business, as she'd not had any exercise and the little meal she'd just eaten was obviously not enough to sustain her for long. Once again she began to tire. Of course, the walk from the hospital had been interminably long and unusually heavy mists made her feel bone-chillingly cold. She shivered. All she wanted now was to sit down on a dry comfortable seat and close her eyes. She knew a nap would do her the world of good right now.

Before long, she felt herself drooping, her head falling onto her chest; the noises around her becoming muffled and unreal as if she had entered some kind of netherworld. It lasted only a short while, because she was suddenly awakened by the sound of a whistle and the chug of an engine. She struggled into wakefulness and looked down the platform to see the big, black iron monster belching grey and black smoke into the air, its wheels scraping against the rails as it drew to a halt at the edge of the platform. She winced as a pain suddenly shot down her right side.

As soon as the train had stopped, doors opened, people on the platform rushed to find seats. She trudged as quickly as her weary body would allow and soon found a carriage with two women inside. She gave them a brief smile and sank back against the rather grubby upholstery, a feeling of relief washing over her.

"Are you all right, dearie?" One of the women asked when the train began to steam out of the station.

"Oh ... yes," she said, "I ... I've had a long day and am feeling a little tired. I'll be fine in a little while."

"Oh well, that's all right then. Luckily it's just the three of us in here, so you should have a peaceful journey."

"Thank you." Lillian smiled at the portly woman with the friendly face who leaned back, brought out a ball of pink wool and began knitting quickly.

Lillian was thankful the two women were quiet, only talking intermittently in low voices. She slept for the whole of the journey, eventually being drawn awake by the kindly woman tapping her gently on the shoulder.

"We're at the end of the line, dearie. You'll have to get off."

Lillian looked up at her and blinked a couple of times to clear her vision. She managed a smile.

"Thank you." She murmured.

"Yes—are you sure you're all right?" The other woman asked, looking anxiously at her.

Lillian nodded. "I'll be fine. Thank you." Although these two women were kind to her, she really didn't want to talk to them or anyone else.

She watched them walk tittering away and sighed, trying to drum up some energy to leave the station and find the bus that would take her to her destination. To her relief, the heavy mists that were abound in Bristol, had gone and though the air was cool, at least there was no precipitation. She located and boarded the bus, bought a ticket and asked the Conductor to let her know when they'd reached her destination.

She found a seat near the front of the bus. This time she didn't close her eyes. She had to think clearer now.

She fidgeted in the seat as the bus stopped a few times before the Conductor turned to her.

"Your stop is next, Ma'am." He said.

She alighted quickly and drew the gabardine raincoat closer around her thin body. It was windy here and light rain began to fall. She felt a sneeze tickle her nose and expelled it loudly as she walked along the road. In the dark, cloudy night, she walked steadily along unfamiliar territory. When the moon showed itself briefly, she took the moment to glance down at a piece of paper in her hand to read the address. Soon she stopped before a small cottage, silhouetted against the night sky. She checked the number and pressing her mouth firmly together unlatched the gate. Walking up the path, she felt her heart bumping in her throat nervously. Once at the door, she hesitated before ringing the doorbell.

The door opened. "Good Heavens!" A woman's voice cried. "Lillian? Oh, my goodness, what . . . do come inside you'll catch your death out there."

The familiar woman who had been with the family since her mother had died some years ago, opened the door wider. She ushered Lillian into a room that immediately warmed her. Faint earthy smells of her father's briar pipe wafted sweetly across at her and for a moment the years slipped away. She suddenly recalled the vivid and often volatile memories of life with her parents.

"Mary." She murmured, shrugging off the gabardine raincoat and moving quickly towards a roaring fire. "Oh Mary . . . it's so good to see you again. How have you been?"

"I've been fine dear, but what are you doing here . . ? I thought you . . ." Mary stopped, a flush of red tingeing her round cheeks.

"What, Mary? What did you think?"

"Well, it's just that your father said something about you'd had an accident and had . . . died!"

"Died?" Lillian frowned, her head spinning. "Why on earth would he tell you that? I've just been away for a while that's all. I had every intention of returning one of these days." This was not entirely true—she didn't know how long she would have been staying in hospital, but she certainly didn't want to tell Mary that.

Mary looked puzzled. "Well I never . . . I wonder why he told me that?" She turned to go into the Kitchen. "Perhaps I misunderstood . . . I really thought . . ." She straightened her shoulders, embarrassed. "Well, for whatever reason, I'm really happy that it isn't true, Lillian dear. I obviously must have completely misunderstood what your father said. I'm so glad I was wrong. So . . . did you visit exotic places?"

Lillian shrugged. "Not really. I went here and there, but now I just need to see father again." She looked up at the woman. "Is he home?"

"No. He left a while ago." She smiled warmly at Lillian. "Your father tries to get out as often as he can. He takes the car out some days as he seems to like travelling around on his own. Well, that's all right, he's a good driver and never seems to come to any harm. Occasionally he'll get Tom to take him into Bristol." She steered Lillian towards a comfortable chair in the parlour. "You sit there, dear and I'll bring you a nice cup of cocoa. If I remember rightly, you always liked one before you retired for the night. While you're relaxing with that, I'll make up your bedroom for you. Nothing's changed since you left so suddenly a while ago."

Lillian turned and smiled up at her. "Yes, Mary, I'd like the cocoa—it's a tradition that I've never stopped. And thanks for making up the room for me."

Mary grinned. "Your father should be home shortly and you can have a good chat over old times. I know he'll be surprised to see you. You and he will have a lot to catch up on since you last saw each other."

Lillian smiled. Oh, yes, she thought, he'll be very surprised to see her; she had no doubt about that!

Close to midnight, Lillian awoke to the sound of the front door shutting. She sat up in bed and rubbed her eyes for a moment disoriented. Then she remembered where she was. This cottage held no particular memories for her—her mother had died eight years earlier. By now Lillian had retired from show business and had returned to the house in Kensington. It wasn't long after that the three of them had moved to Watersfield. It was small, and the only reason it was neat and tidy was because of Mary. She was a good housekeeper, but this house lacked the feminine touch more in keeping with Lillian's mother, Margaret. She had been a wonderful interior designer and decorator, making all the curtains in the townhouse where they'd lived in London; keeping the house clean and no matter what her mood, Lillian's mother would never be seen without sprinkling a little perfume over herself. Those perfumes seemed always to permeate the air in the townhouse. It was noticeably missing here.

Lillian stopped her musing when she heard voices below. She scrambled out of bed, into her slippers and the robe hanging behind the door. Quietly, she opened the door. From the landing, she could see Mary's back. She was talking, obviously, to her father. Feeling unusually nervous, Lillian crept down the stairs, just as she heard Mary announce that she had arrived. Lillian was taken aback by his reaction.

She saw him turn towards Mary and there was a look of shock and . . . what was it? . . . dismay? on his face.

"What!" He cried. "But . . . she's dead, Mary. We must have an impostor in our midst!"

Mary shook her head. "No Sir. It's Lillian all right. She arrived earlier this evening and seemed exhausted, so I made up her room where she is right now. If you wish, I could ask her to come downstairs . . . but I think it would be best for her to get a good night's sleep. As I said, she's exhausted and doesn't actually look too well."

Lillian's father didn't answer. His shoulders drooped as he turned towards the chair that Lillian had so recently vacated. His head dropped to his hands and for a moment she felt a confused mingle of emotions coursing through her. To all outward appearances, he seemed to be showing some kind of compassion, but she knew she mustn't be fooled by it. She remembered that he'd insisted she be hospitalized. How could he feel any kind of compassion for her now? No, there had to be something else to explain that dejected droop of his shoulders. She decided to confront him and get the matter into the open. She didn't care that Mary was there; that she would be witness to her accusations; suddenly she didn't care at all what anyone thought.

She straightened up and made a noise going down the stairs, her eyes fixed on her father's hunched back until he looked up and saw her.

"You!" He exclaimed, struggling to his feet. By the time he was standing, she'd reached him. He glanced over at Mary. "Please leave us, Mary. This is between my daughter and me."

"Yes Sir." Mary said, obediently leaving the room, glancing with puzzlement at Lillian as she closed the door.

"I'll come straight to the point, father. Why did you have me admitted to the Bristol Royal Infirmary? I wasn't sick in any way." Lillian accused, her blue eyes looking thunder into his.

"Because you were showing signs of becoming unstable." He answered plainly. "I thought it in your best interest to go somewhere where you could get treatment and someday, maybe, you could return and lead a normal life again."

"That's complete nonsense and you know it, father!" She said, bitterly. "You told everyone I was dead. Why did you do that?"

"Would you have liked it any better had I told them you were . . . insane?"

She recoiled. "Insane! I am no more insane than you are, father! You had me put there for a reason known only to you. I can only think it was done for some devious purpose. There is no other reason for doing it."

"Think what you like, Lillian." He said. "For now, you should get yourself off the bed; we'll talk about this in the morning."

"No! I'm not just going to bed and fume about this. I want an explanation. I am perfectly sound of mind and body and you had no right whatsoever to take me there."

Her father gave her an odd smile. "I had a doctor examine you . . ."

"Yes, one of your old cronies. He would do anything you asked. What did you offer him to lie for you?" She looked steely-eyed at him. "You have to tell me why you did it. I demand to know."

"You can demand all you like, young woman, I will not divulge things that will frustrate and worry you any more than you already are. Suffice it to say that I decided your future would be jeopardized if you didn't get the medication you needed to calm your nerves."

She suddenly stamped her foot, frustration making her feel an irrational desire to strike him.

"You are talking absolute nonsense, father! Is this what my mother had to contend with all the years she was married to you? Was this what eventually killed her? I believe it is you who has some kind of mental disorder, not me . . . not mother . . . you, father!"

He moved quickly across the floor, giving her a resounding slap on her left cheek, which sent her reeling back against a high backed leather chair.

"You are going back to the hospital in the morning, my girl! I don't ever want to see you or know anything about you from now on! You are a disgrace and I'll be glad to be rid of you." He turned away. "Now, get back up to your room. In the morning I'll take you personally to the Bristol Royal Infirmary where you will be staying, probably for the rest of your life!"

He glared at her harshly, before walking straight-backed from the room, closing the door behind him while Lillian looked at his retreating figure with a feeling almost of hate in her heart for the man who'd sired her. How could a father do this to his only daughter?

After a moment, she quickly ran up the stairs to her bedroom, shutting the door firmly behind her. She decided she would leave this dreadful place. Where she would go, she had no idea, but anywhere had to be better than here! She would not be admitted to that place again!

However, before she left she suddenly wanted to have some recollections of James Thorncroft. Why he'd come into her head at that moment was quite beyond her, but something seemed to be compelling her. She hurried over to the small writing desk near the window, switched on the light and pulled open a drawer. After rummaging through some papers, she found what she was looking for, quickly tucked it into the pocket of Flo Turner's raincoat and slipped into the bed.

Lillian had always managed to program her body to awaken at a certain time when she really wished to. She hoped that this would work for her again tonight. It did! The following morning Lillian awoke at close to five o'clock. She stretched and glanced out the window to see the moon suspended in a dark cloudy sky. She hurriedly slipped into Flo Turner's clothes and crept downstairs. To her horror, she saw her father dozing in a chair beside the front door. Despite his age, there was nothing at all wrong with his hearing and when one of the stair treads creaked, his eyes sprang open. He turned and even though Lillian couldn't see his features, she knew he had a sickly smile on his face. He'd anticipated her reaction to his threat last night and although she tried to skip passed him he barred her way, catching her cruelly by her left arm. He didn't speak—his intentions required no conversation. He dragged her out into the dark night towards the waiting car. Thomas had obviously been told of the plan, as he opened the rear door dutifully, as Rutledge pushed Lillian into the seat before getting in beside her.

Without a word to his daughter, Edgar Rutledge ordered Thomas to drive them both immediately to Bristol where he proceeded to have her once more committed to the Psychiatric Ward.

CHAPTER 21

PAST ALLIANCE

I T was one of those odd mornings when it felt more like early spring. A cool breeze blew around the grounds and one could not venture outside without first slipping on a warm jacket or pullover, but it was so pleasant that Catherine just had to take in the unusually mild air before the really cold winter weather set in.

Joshua was busy raking leaves and waved to her as she neared the entrance to the greenhouse. She waved back and smiled.

"Is your brother around, Joshua?" She asked.

"'E's gone into Branton, Missus." Joshua took off his rather battered cap and rubbed the back of his wrist across his sweating forehead. "I think 'e's gone to get some fertilizer for the veggies out back. 'E should be back soon. Can I be of any 'elp?"

"Only if you have time. Abraham did mention that he would get around to pruning the roses soon and if you've seen the ones at the side of the summer-house, I think you'll agree they're looking extremely bedraggled. We pride our-selves in our display of roses each year and to ensure a good show, I do think they need some attention."

"Say no more, Mrs. Thorncroft," Joshua said, "I'm nearly done 'ere. I'll get on with it in a jiffy."

"That'll be splendid, Joshua. Thank you."

She turned slowly back towards the house when Phoebe came hurtling around the corner, carrying something in her mouth and wagging her little white tail excitedly. Catherine smiled at the little dog, leaning down to see what she'd found. It was a squirming little mouse.

"Oh, Phoebe. What a naughty girl. You let him go this instant!" She repri-manded, horrified. As if the little dog understood, she made a funny little noise in her throat and promptly dropped the terrified rodent, who scampered away, happy to be still in one piece!

Catherine was very much aware that lately the little West Highland terrier had been bringing mice, birds and voles into the house, causing quite a stir with the Kitchen staff. She wondered, vaguely, why she was doing this, as Phoebe had never shown any desire to terrorize wildlife in the past. Oh well, she was grow-ing older now so perhaps she'd found these pursuits much more challenging to her rather humdrum existence at Ravenslea. Sometimes Catherine wondered if they shouldn't have taken two puppies for Rebecca at the same time as they'd got Phoebe—they'd have been such company for each other. She shrugged. Well, she hadn't and had no intention of getting another now.

As she began to slowly climb the steps towards the front door, the sound of a rather noisy engine came to her ears and she turned. It was the postman. Black smoke billowed in plumes from behind his vehicle and the still air was suddenly pierced with the unnatural sound of gears grinding as he neared the house. She groaned. It was about time Mr. Jennings talked to the post office about purchasing another van—she was sure this one was going to give up before much longer.

The small, wiry little man in a neat blue and red uniform, pulled up at the bottom of the steps. He gave her a slight incline of his thinning grey hair.

"Good morning, Mrs. Thorncroft. I do believe it's going to be a fine day. Glad to see you're taking the air while it's still warm enough to do so." He reached into his bag and pulled out a wad of letters. "Here's your post, Ma'am. Do you have anything you want taken back?"

She shook her head and took the letters from his outstretched hand. "No, not today. How's your wife? I heard last week that she'd been feeling quite poorly."

"Much better. Thank you for asking, Mrs. Thorncroft. Just a bit of lumbago bothering her. The doctor's given her some medicine and it seems to be doing the trick." He turned and climbed back inside the van. "Good-day, Mrs. Thorncroft, I do have one or two more deliveries before finishing for the day. The missus and I are taking our grandkids to Bristol Zoo later. The two year old, hasn't been there yet."

"Oh, that'll be so nice, Mr. Jennings. Do have a wonderful time."

He touched his cap and climbed back into his vehicle. She smiled and waved as he turned the vehicle around, puffed out some more rather black evil smelling smoke and trundled back down the pathway to the road.

Catherine glanced through the letters and hurried inside the house. Shuffling through them, she suddenly saw one addressed to herself with writing she didn't recognize. Puzzled, she slit open the envelope and drew out a single sheet of plain white paper with the Bristol Royal Infirmary letterhead stamped on the top. Frowning, she unravelled the note and read the signature on the bottom. 'Lily Starr'. How odd?

Leaving the rest of the letters on the hall table, she moved quickly into the Sitting Room and shut the door behind her. Picking up her spectacles from a nearby table, as the room was unusually dark, she switched on the side light and began to read.

'Dear Mrs. Thorncroft,

You do not know me, but I have some information to relay to you that is of dire importance. Would you please consider visiting me as quickly as possible. It is of the utmost urgency that I talk to you. I am in Ward 8 of the Bristol Royal Infirmary Psychiatric Ward. I implore you not to divulge the contents of this letter or the fact that you have received it to anyone; and do not inform anyone if you decide to visit me.

I do hope to see you soon,

Your obedient servant,

Lily Starr.'

Catherine re-read the letter and frowned. She'd never heard of a Lily Starr before and was extremely mystified as to why this complete stranger would wish to talk to her.

Glancing quickly through the words again, Catherine felt a twinge of apprehension. Not having had the occasion to visit a hospital's psychiatric ward in her life before, plus the fact that she had no knowledge of this woman, she wondered if, in fact, she should disregard the letter. Yet, if Lily Starr had been astute enough to search and find out where Catherine lived, perhaps there would be some advantage to meeting with her.

It was a sudden intriguing situation that Catherine's adventurous nature considered would be worth investigating. The only way Catherine was going to have any light shed on this mysterious letter, was to go to see this Lily Starr as soon as possible.

She pushed the letter back in its envelope. Despite Lily's insistence that she tell no-one, she had every intention of informing James of this new development.

James was dozing in an armchair by the fire in the Drawing Room, a newspaper placed over his face in his normal way. She hated to awaken him as he'd been complaining of tiredness all morning, but wake him she must because she had every intention of arranging to go into Bristol that very afternoon and didn't wish to leave it too late.

She nudged him gently. He snorted and pulled the paper away, rubbing his eyes.

"Catherine? Is anything the matter? You don't usually disturb me when I'm resting." He said, sitting upright in the chair.

She wasted no time, but thrust the short note in front of him. "Do you know this woman, James? It came in the morning mail and it has me entirely perplexed. I thought you might have heard of her?"

He pulled his spectacles from the inside of his jacket pocket and placed them on the bridge of his nose, focusing on the letter in front of him. As he read it, Catherine heard his sudden intake of breath.

"Do you know who she is?" She repeated, watching him closely.

"Well, my dear, I did know a Lily Starr many years before I even set eyes on you, but if it's the same woman, she has to be in her late fifties at best. I wonder what she wants."

"That was my thought. I want to go into Bristol to see her this afternoon, James, but if you could give me a little information on her, it might help me understand whatever it is she's going to tell me."

He sighed, folded the letter and placed it in the envelope. Handing it to her, he took off his spectacles.

"I'm against you doing that, Catherine." He said, looking up at her. "Whatever she wants, you can be sure it won't be something good. I suggest you ignore it."

"I can't do that. She took the trouble to find our address and send us the letter. If she hasn't seen you for a number of years, perhaps what she has to say is important."

"She's given you that impression, of course." He said, cautiously, "but I'd not approach her, especially if she's in a psychiatric ward."

Catherine sat on a pouffe in front of him, her hand resting on his knee. "Who is she, James? At least tell me that."

"I met her very briefly when I was in London, dear. I was on my own, went to a nightclub where Lily did a dance and singing routine on the small stage. She was very good and I enjoyed watching her. However, as I was alone at a single table, she seemed to take more notice of me than anyone else in the nightclub and later called me to her dressing room where we talked for a while." James stopped, watching the anxiety creep over his wife's face. He caught her hand gently in his own. "It ended there, Catherine. After about twenty minutes or so, Lily had to do her last number and I went home. I have never seen her again."

Catherine was silent for a moment, digesting this information. "Then what on earth would she want with us now?"

He shrugged. "Who knows? I don't think you should see her. I believe she's possibly living in the past, remembering the short time we spent together or she's fallen on hard times and is looking for some kind of hand-out. You may be getting us into a lot of unhappiness if you go to see her."

"I want to see her, James. I'll be careful. I'm quite resourceful you know and usually can tell if someone's trying to trick me in some way." She stood up, squeezed his hand gently and moved towards the door. "I promise I'll not be swayed by what she has to say, unless I feel she is genuinely concerned about something."

"Go with Martin, dear." James said, knowing that nothing he said would stop her. "You may need some moral support."

"She asked that I speak to no-one about this and I will honour that. She may have something really important to tell just me; if Martin were there she might just clam up!"

He shook his head. "Well, don't say I didn't warn you, Catherine. You'll be going against my wishes, but that's entirely your decision."

"I needn't have told you, James." She said a trifle irritably. "I could have made some plausible excuse to be going into Bristol and you'd be none the wiser. Instead, I decided to tell you – now I wish I hadn't, for I don't want you to worry about me when I'm there."

"I hope you find her well, Catherine." He paused. "She was beautiful once, graceful and elegant. I found her fascinating, but my feelings for her went no further."

She gave him a smile, kissed him lightly and moved quickly out of the room. The very fact that James had known this woman in his past was motivation enough for her to see her. She hurried into the bedroom, dressed and within half an hour was climbing into the Sedanca with Percy behind the wheel. He would take her to the station, where she'd board a train to Bristol.

Catherine stepped down from the trolley car outside the imposing hospital, drew her coat closer around her and walked steadily towards the main entrance.

At the Admitting Desk she asked directions to the Psychiatric Ward.

"Which part, Madam? It stretches almost a whole wing." The nurse behind the desk asked, pushing a strand of dark hair from where it had landed across her right eye.

"Ward 8."

"Ah, yes . . ." the nurse showed her the way and Catherine thanked her.

Walking down the route she'd been told, the smell of disinfectant and other unrecognizable odours was overpowering; the white spotless walls, nurses and doctors in white uniforms and phones, buzzers and bells ringing at work stations, left Catherine feeling as if she were in a completely different world. She'd never visited a hospital before; even when her children were born, she was lucky enough to have had easy births at home. She grimaced. Much as she admired all these wonderful people who cared for the sick, she knew it wasn't something she could do.

Within a few minutes, she'd reached Ward 8. A buxom nurse was sitting behind a square enclosure surrounded by the usual material associated with hospital files. She was talking on the telephone. Catherine glanced at her. The woman looked up, indicating to take a seat until she was free.

At length the nurse put the phone down and asked if she could help. Catherine told her she wished to see Lily Starr.

The nurse glanced through a list on her desk and glanced up at her. "We don't have a Lily Starr here, Madam; we have a Lillian Rutledge registered. Are you sure you have the right name?"

Catherine frowned. "It could be—I was told her name was Starr, but I could be mistaken."

"Well, I'll have to phone the Administrator, who'll contact Miss Rutledge's doctor before I can let you see her. What's your name?"

Catherine told her.

"Are you a relative?"

"No, but it's imperative I speak with her."

The nurse looked cagily at her. "You should have made an appointment, Mrs. Thorncroft. This is highly irregular, but if you'd please take a seat while I get an authorization for your visit. It may take a while."

Catherine settled herself in a wooden-armed chair and picked up a woman's magazine.

After almost half an hour, a tall middle-aged doctor approached her. She looked up at him and laid the magazine down on the table beside her.

"Mrs. Thorncroft?" He asked. "I'm Dr. Paul Morgan. I understand you wish to see Lillian Rutledge? May I ask what this is about?"

Catherine caught her lip, but after a short pause reached into her handbag and handed him Lily's letter.

"This is why I'm here, Dr. Morgan. As you can see, Lily seems anxious to speak to me about something that she's obviously not willing to disclose in the letter."

He glanced through the words, frowned and handed the letter back.

"I'll take you there myself, Mrs. Thorncroft, if you'll just follow me."

Catherine stood up and walked alongside him.

"Lillian isn't violent," Dr. Morgan said as they turned a sharp corner, "but I want to be certain that when she sees you, she won't become distressed."

"Of course. I certainly wouldn't want to upset her, but I have a feeling I won't because it was she who asked to see me, not the other way around."

He smiled as they reached a closed door with the number 31 stamped on the outside.

"It's just a precaution, Mrs. Thorncroft. Let's go in and see how she's doing."

Dr. Morgan pushed open the door to reveal a single bed with rails placed at either side. A woman was laying on her back, staring up at the ceiling. She moved her head slightly as the doctor approached.

"Hello, Lillian," he said softly, "how are you feeling today?" As she didn't answer, he continued. "I have a visitor for you. A Mrs. Thorncroft, do you wish to see her?"

Lillian's eyes flickered and she slowly nodded.

"Yes . . . I do . . . I must talk to her." She moved awkwardly to a sitting position.

"Then I'll leave you to talk. If you need anything, just remember the little bell by your bed." Dr. Morgan said kindly, almost as if he speaking to a child. He turned to leave. "Try not to agitate her, Mrs. Thorncroft. She can become most distressed quite quickly if riled in any way."

"I'll be careful. Thank you, Dr. Morgan." Catherine smiled at him as he moved out of the single room, back into the corridor.

Catherine moved towards the bed, laid a hand on the rail and looked down at the woman in the bed. Could this emaciated woman be the same as the one from James' past? She felt a sudden surge of compassion for her. The sallow complexion; the slightly sunken eyes revealed she'd suffered much through her life.

"Hello Lily." Catherine said softly.

The woman looked intently at her. She had the most exquisite light blue-green eyes Catherine had ever seen. Obviously in her youth she had been very beautiful and if this was, indeed, the woman James had known all those years ago, she could quite see how he could have become bewitched by her.

"Hello." Catherine repeated, leaning against the rail. "I'm Catherine Thorncroft—am I talking to Lily Starr?"

"Yes, I'm Lily Starr. That was once my stage name." The woman smiled up at her, transforming her dull, lifeless eyes to something resembling spirit. "Thank you so much, Mrs. Thorncroft, for agreeing to see me. I hope you had a good trip."

"I did indeed. Now I'd like to hear what is so important that you'd write me that letter."

"Then I'll not waste your time. I am grateful that you came, especially when I mentioned I was in this ward." She took a deep breath. "First of all, my father decided a few months ago, to have me committed on the grounds that I was mentally unstable. I can assure you Mrs. Thorncroft that is a complete falsehood." Catherine watched her animated face, thinking that all people committed to such a ward, would say something to that effect but decided to dismiss it. "I am as mentally stable as you. Anyway, I have no idea why my father would do such a thing, but something seems to be telling me that he wishes harm to your husband." She paused, plucking idly at the white blanket covering her knees. "You see, at one time my father was a successful dentist working from Harley Street in London. When my mother passed away a few years ago, he went to pieces. He lost most of his patients due to botched appointments, incorrect fees, and general inferior workmanship. This resulted in him losing the practice altogether. He'd accumulated a large amount of debt, so eventually had to sell. After settling his creditors, he bought a small cottage in Devon, a place he had always wanted to retire to. By that time, I was much older and finding it more and more difficult to get work on the stage, so decided to retire, hoping to find some other work in Devon. My son and I moved with father to Watersfield. Father's an old man now, Mrs. Thorncroft, but where he doesn't seem to have much time for me, he idolizes my son. It didn't work very well; father and I were constantly bickering—he seemed to find fault with whatever I did." She paused, breathing heavily. "I believe he wants to use my brief association with your husband to somehow acquire money for my son's future." She leaned over and caught Catherine's hand, squeezing it gently. "I have no idea how he'd go about such a thing, but even though he's old, Mrs. Thorncroft, he's surprisingly fit and very crafty; I'd not put anything past him if he sets his mind on something."

"I still don't understand what your son would possibly have to do with my husband?"

"I don't know either, but whatever it is, my dear, he'll not succeed. If I remember James correctly, he's a strong-willed man who'd easily see through a hoax." She paused. "Has James ever mentioned me to you?"

"If you are the Lily Starr he met when he was a young man—yes, James did discuss your association. But, Lily, please go on."

She leaned against the pillow. "When Mother passed away, father became belligerent and I found it almost impossible to live with him, so I took an apartment and began night-club singing." She smiled. "I did have a good voice once,

Mrs. Thorncroft, and it got me through a lot of difficult times. Anyway, it was at one of these performances that I met James. It couldn't be classed as an affair because nothing at all happened, but a few weeks later, I went home and stupidly mentioned to my father about meeting this wealthy young man. I believe my father has remembered this and is scheming in some way to use this information to his own advantage." She leaned over and took a few sips of water. "One day, my father and I had an almighty row and the next thing I knew, he'd arranged with one of his medical friends to examine me. Between them they had me placed here. My own doctor doesn't even know I'm here, Mrs. Thorncroft. There is no way I can get in touch with him—whenever I mention his name to the nurse, they disregard it." She sighed. "Anyway, I don't know the reason behind any of this, only that I think my father feels I'm some kind of threat to his future plans." She paused again, glanced quickly out the window, then back at Catherine. Her lower lip trembled slightly and Catherine could see she was fighting back tears. "It all came back to me when we were having the altercation. My father and mother had constant fights when I was young. Father's temper was appalling; I know he hit her more than once." She stopped.

Catherine looked at the woman compassionately, then leaned over and covered the woman's small, frail hand with her own.

"Thank you for telling me this, Lily. What is your own doctor's name?"

"Dr. William Bradshaw. He lives in London—I have his telephone number here." Lily turned to her bedside cabinet, opened the drawer and handed Catherine a folded piece of paper. "You think you may be able to do something?"

"I don't know. You have mentioned things that only the Lily that James told me about, would know. I have a feeling you should not be here so I'll do a little checking of my own and if what you tell me is confirmed, I'll do my best to see you get out of here as soon as possible."

Lily looked up at her, the dormant tears now visible under the long black lashes. "Oh, Mrs. Thorncroft, would you do that for me? I can't believe that you'd take a chance on me like that. You must have a wonderful marriage, my dear, for James to have told you about me."

"James and I . . . well, we do everything together." Catherine said, smiling down at the woman in the bed.

"You are very lucky, Mrs. Thorncroft—would that I could have had such a wonderful, lasting relationship."

Catherine stood up. "Don't mention a word to anyone that I've been here, I'll keep in touch and come to see you again shortly. Don't give up, Lily—you have a powerful ally in me."

Catherine meant every word as she walked away from the ward. For some unaccountable reason, Catherine had a feeling of misgiving. If Lily's father was so unscrupulous, it was imperative that she keep an eye on things around Ravenslea from now on. She had an idea something was going to happen that would not be in the best interests of the family. The knowledge worried her intensely.

She was now approaching the Nursing Station. Once again the woman was on the phone, but when she'd finished, Catherine asked if she could talk to Dr. Morgan again.

"As a matter of fact, Dr. Morgan specifically said he wanted to talk to you before you leave." She turned and pointed down one of the corridors. "His office is the third door on the right. He is expecting you."

"Thank you." Catherine said.

Dr. Morgan rose when she walked into his office. He smiled and indicated for her to be seated. Catherine was relieved that he was quite prepared to discuss Lily's case with her.

Catherine told him as briefly as she could all that she and Lily had discussed. "Miss Rutledge did mention that her own doctor is not even aware of her being here. She gave me his telephone number. I wonder if you could check with him. Perhaps that way, we'll all be certain whether or not she should be in here."

He took the paper she handed him, turned and picked up the receiver on his desk. He spoke into it briefly.

"I've put a call in to him, Mrs. Thorncroft. If you'd like to wait, we can find out here and now about this disturbing matter."

A few moments later, the phone rang and when the doctor replaced the receiver, he pursed his mouth.

"Dr. Bradshaw is out of town for a while, Mrs. Thorncroft. Why don't you give me your number and I'll call you as soon as I hear what he has to say."

She nodded. "Thank you, Dr. Morgan. For the moment, I would like to keep this as quiet as possible."

"It sounds positively intriguing." The middle-aged doctor smiled at her, raising a dark eyebrow. "I have always felt that Lillian was telling me the truth when she said she had no business being in the psychiatric ward, but I would have to discuss this with the doctor who admitted her, then it would have to go before our psychiatric panel for their recommendations as to whether or not she could be released."

He stood up, tucked a pencil into the top pocket of his clean white overall and smiled at her. "We'll get to the bottom of this one way or the other. I'll certainly give you a call as soon as I hear the result of my discussions with Dr. Bradshaw and the psychiatric panel. Good day, Mrs. Thorncroft."

When Catherine arrived home later that day, she found James in the stables on his knees with Luke beside him, closely looking at Hudson's right fetlock. They both turned as she moved quickly towards them.

"Trouble?" She asked, a look of concern crossing her face.

"We've called the vet." James said, turning his attention back to the horse.

"Hudson's limping badly and we believe he's pulled a tendon. Won't know for sure until it's been examined."

"Oh dear." She said. She glanced at Luke. "What happened?

Luke shrugged. "He caught his foot awkwardly near the old abbey where Christiana had her accident. He fell, throwing me. I'm not hurt, but I had to walk him home as I didn't wish to make the matter worse."

James stood up and brushed straw from his clothes. "Well, the vet shouldn't be long, Luke. You can tell him all he needs to know." He caught Catherine's arm and together they strode out of the stable, where he steered her towards the summerhouse. "I'm eager to learn what you and Lily discussed, dear. Let's go in here and you can tell me all that transpired."

She nodded and once they were settled, she relayed to him everything she'd learned at the hospital.

"I firmly believe, James," she said after she'd finished, "that Lillian should not be there, but, of course, it's not for me to say. Dr. Morgan is going to contact Lillian's own doctor and I suppose there will have to be some kind of meeting before a verdict is reached. We'll just have to wait until I receive a call from Dr. Morgan before I can do any more."

"How did she look, dear?" James asked, leaning back against the wooden bench.

Catherine hesitated. "To be honest, I don't think she looked very well. She's thin, seems undernourished and has that lack-lustre appearance that often goes with people who have been hospitalized for a while." She paused. "She has the most beautiful eyes though and I could tell she was once a lovely looking woman."

He sighed, pursing his mouth. "Lily was indeed attractive and very talented." He paused. "I didn't want you to go, Catherine, but now that you have I'm rather glad you did. It's now out in the open for me. I swear I have no other secrets from you!"

She smiled. "I believe you James. Now lets go back indoors. I'm in need of one of Agnes' lovely cups of tea."

CHAPTER 22

GUY FAWKES NIGHT – 5TH NOVEMBER 1930

I N regions spanning England's West Country, members of the aristocracy, military and even Royalty, used to frequent stately homes in the summer or early autumn months each year to take part in a gala gathering called The Landowners' Ball. This practice was abandoned during the 1914-18 War and never rekindled. Instead, the Thorncroft family joined together with friends and family in a rowdy gathering to celebrate Guy Fawkes Night at the beginning of November. A huge bonfire was always erected at a large spare unused area at the edge of the Ravenslea grounds far enough away from trees and tenants' homes not to cause any problems from sparks or smoke. This bonfire was fashioned from twigs, old fencing, broken wooden furniture and anything else that was considered good for burning.

In London in 1605, Guy Fawkes along with twelve others, decided to rid themselves of King James I and possibly the Prince of Wales, by blowing up the famous Houses of Parliament. This was foiled by a traitor in Fawkes' group; but the threat still remained to this day that someone with a similar idea, would re-enact the deadly affair. From then on, Guy Fawkes Day was an annual event practiced throughout the British Isles when bonfires would be staged; an effigy of Guy Fawkes placed on top of it and lit. Fireworks were later added to round off the celebration. Ravenslea's festivities were always well attended and each year Catherine arranged an exquisite array of food. This was usually catered by her good friends in Branton, Maria and Herbert Donetti. A medium sized Ballroom had been added to Ravenslea shortly after the fire of 1904 and this was where the lavish banquet was held after the outside festivities were concluded.

This year, Mike, Abraham and Joshua set up the bonfire and firework display. This was something entirely different to their normal duties and they were obviously elated to be given the responsibility. Added to this, colourful lanterns were weaved around the perimeter of the house and in some nearby trees. During the daylight hours in the days preceding the event, often the agile and energetic Mike could be seen diligently climbing ladders to wire them. He received a few cuts and bruises, none of which appeared to bother him.

James hired a company to set up a display that would show the illuminated head of King George V and Queen Mary at the end of the firework display. Everyone at Ravenslea would then lift up their voices in a resounding rendition of the National Anthem that could be heard for miles. As a dance had been arranged for later, the beautiful grand piano was polished and tuned to make sure the sound was just right. Always, the revelry would last well into the night.

Fern and Simon helped with the festivities along with their daughters, sons-in-law and grandchildren. Their family unit was now complete and nothing, in their opinion, could be finer than to be together at last. Simon grew to know and love his grandchildren; Emily's little boy, Richard just seven months old and Constance's son, Alan who turned four years old on May 3rd this year. Simon also found his daughter's husbands very amiable and easy-going men. Emily's husband, Gary Edgecombe, an architect, was a keen fisherman who also loved sailing; and Simon knew that Constance's husband, Paul Saunders, along with James, had taught Fern everything she knew about sailing.

Before the guests were due to arrive, James and Martin were relaxing in the Drawing Room watching the last minute preparations drinking sherry, when the door opened and Louise came in, followed by Adam. As always, she was effervescent and bubbly.

"This sounds like it's going to be so exciting, James dear." She said reaching up to give him a peck on the cheek. "We don't celebrate this in the States; but I know we are going to be thrilled to bits with it all; I just wish Christiana had stayed long enough to experience it with us."

"Well, it's all part of English heritage, Louise." James said. "I'm surprised you've not heard of it in Connecticut?"

"Oh, we've heard of it, but thought nothing more, because it didn't have any connection with us. But now, if I'm going to stay over here and that's my intention, then I'm going to have to learn all about Guy Fawkes and anything else that is historically British!"

"Well," Adam piped in as he sat down beside his stepfather. "If we're going to learn all about British history, mother dear, it's going to take us until we're in our dotage! Then what on earth would you do with the knowledge you'd gained!" He laughed and everyone laughed with him.

"I didn't say 'everything' Adam; just enough to show we have an interest, that's all. I know I have always wanted to see the Tower of London, go for a river trip on the Thames (she pronounced it literally as 'Thames') and other places where the regular tourist doesn't go."

"There will be plenty of time for that, dear," Martin said, rising from his seat and going over to her. He caught her hand in his, squeezing it gently. "I want to be able to take you everywhere you want to go."

Just before sundown, people began to show up at the manor. Various designs and styles of motor vehicles swept through the open iron gates; walkers, some with children on their shoulders, or just carrying walking sticks strode purposefully along the gravel path towards the beautiful lawns. Some people arrived on horseback; bicyclists and one or two horses with buggies, all convened at the grand front entrance to Ravenslea.

The rather corpulent Mayor of Branton with his wife, daughter and grandson arrived in the County's Rolls Royce while neighbouring farmers and their families, came by whatever means they could. Barnaby drew the Rhodes' Armstrong Siddley in through the gates and the family alighted, keen to enjoy the festivities.

James and Catherine watched happily, glad to see so many of the invitations had been honoured. Unlike the Landowners' Ball of years ago, there was no delegate from Royalty, but the festivities would not suffer from the loss.

The evening wore on with no problems, except one when the Mayor's grandson wandered off and found it necessary to play in Joshua's neatly stacked compost heap. Even in the semi-dark, the four year old had no fears. When the exuberant little boy meandered unconcernedly back to his family, after spreading the compost heap all over the place, the stench caused much screwed up noses and distancing from him. The Mayor's daughter, Beatrice, and Ravenslea's maid, Doris, promptly grabbed the child and marched him into the house where they stripped him of his smelly clothes, and put him, protesting strongly and struggling against their iron grips, into a warm hip bath to wash him off. The clothes were washed hurriedly and dried before the roaring fire in the Kitchen, while Doris found some old clothes of Luke's in a storage room. Beatrice, with Edna's help, promptly dressed the squirming little boy in extra warm clothing so that he could finally rejoin the festivities, half an hour later.

Musicians hired by Catherine two weeks previously, wandered throughout the guests, before the bonfire was lit, strumming guitars or playing violins, giving the scene a festive spirit. Two hired waiters mingled with trays of glasses of half-full wine, cocktails and juices for the children. All in all, it was a carefree, relaxing atmosphere and when the sun disappeared, the children, especially, began to show their excitement by jumping about excitedly. All wanting to see the bonfire lit when they could then set off their sparklers and firecrackers—the highlight of the evening!

James Thorncroft stood at the top of the steps, a satisfied smile crossing his face as he watched the happy crowd below. The Thorncroft family had organized the Guy Fawkes Day get-togethers now for the past ten years and each time more people had attended. The bonfire seemed higher; the fireworks seemed more spectacular and it was only last year that they'd decided to include well sculptured fiery portraits of the King and Queen, which went over very well with all attendees.

James didn't miss the original Landowners' Ball and was actually relieved it had been discontinued as he'd never really enjoyed those gatherings. All those stiff speeches and hot, clammy rooms hadn't ever appealed to him, and his proficiency as a dancer was questionable. Dancing the waltz once with Rebecca and twice with Catherine at Rebecca's party had been quite enough for him. He hoped he wouldn't be called upon to dance any more.

Catherine came over to him, linking her arm through his affectionately.

"It's going all right, dear, isn't it?" She said. She glanced towards the happy throngs of people, then nodded towards a lone couple standing nearby. "James? Who are those two? I don't remember seeing them before—do you know them?"

James screwed up his eyes, then relaxed and grinned. "That's Giles Mortimer and I presume his daughter, Cynthia. You remember, I told you about how he's going to invite us to his home for a house-warming party."

"Oh yes, I remember. Is his wife with him? I'd like to meet her and draw her into my activities if she'd like to."

"I don't think she is, dear." James said. "Like I mentioned before, Giles Mortimer has never mentioned her—just his daughter, who I can tell he is devoted to."

"How odd that he doesn't even mention a wife."

He nodded. "Well, if he'd wanted to, I'm sure he would have. I'm not going to press him about it. Let's go down and talk to them for a while."

"You go, dear. I have to see Agnes for a few moments."

Nodding, James moved towards the two newcomers. It was then that James noticed Rebecca standing close to William and a smile touched the corners of his mouth. He remembered those wonderful days with Catherine when they had first become engaged. He knew how they were feeling. He was glad they'd decided to take that often bumpy road through married life; he enjoyed William's company and knew the two of them were quite compatible – it would be a good match.

Giles Mortimer and his daughter turned as James approached.

"Good evening, Giles. Nice to see you again; this must be your lovely daughter. I'm James Thorncroft, dear."

"Good evening, Captain Thorncroft." She murmured shyly, as James took her hand warmly in his. "It looks as if it's going to be a wonderful evening."

"Thank you, Cynthia. It does seem that way." He released his grip and extended the hand to the man at her side.

"Hello James." Giles Mortimer grinned. "Cynthia was looking forward to coming to Ravenslea today. She has it in mind to meet your wife and children when the opportunity presents itself."

"Which it certainly will." James said, looking directly into the young woman's burnished gold eyes, thinking what a picture she made. He glanced around meaningfully. "Where is your wife, Giles?"

Giles Mortimer hedged, ill-at-ease. "She passed away a few years ago."

"I'm sorry." James commiserated warmly. "Well, when you feel like it, you could partake in some light snacks and refreshments over there by that tree. It's just to keep people happy until we can all convene inside the house after the fireworks."

While his father was talking easily with the two newcomers, Luke, who was standing a few yards away, found it almost impossible to take his eyes off the young woman standing between the two men. Her petite frame and flyaway light brown curls captivated him. Once she laughed, infectiously; by that laugh alone he could tell she was a fun-loving girl, full of energy and pep. He just had to meet her. Moving away from his position, he meandered nonchalantly towards them, stopping every now and then to speak to some of the other guests. As he approached, she became aware of his presence and turned. He felt a quickening in his breast as she smiled at him.

James turned as Luke approached. "Ah, Luke." He grinned. "Have you met our new neighbours. Well, actually, they're hardly neighbours but they *are* new to the area." He turned to the thickset man. "Giles, meet my youngest son, Luke. Luke, this is Mr. Giles Mortimer, who has purchased some property a few miles from here." The two men shook hands. "This is his lovely daughter, Cynthia."

Cynthia turned and held out a small hand, which Luke clasped easily around his larger one.

"Pleased to meet you, Luke." Her voice was smooth, gentle and slightly musical.

"Likewise." He said, trying desperately not to blush or behave like an infatuated schoolboy.

"I'm so glad we were invited, James." Giles said, as a fiery rocket whooshed overhead to end in a shower of brightly coloured stars. "You do this every year?"

James nodded. "Mostly. There have been one or two occasions when one or other of the gentry around here have done it. We enjoy opening our grounds to visitors." James caught the man's elbow gently. "You will have to come and meet my wife, Catherine. I know she would like to meet you before attending your house warming next month. You too, Cynthia. Rebecca, my daughter, is dying to meet you and bring you into her circle of friends."

Earlier that evening, tucked out of sight at the edge of Exmoor Forest, Bernard Webb leaned nonchalantly against a thick oak tree, shivering slightly. It may have been to do with the coolness in the shade of the forest, but it was more likely due to his reason for being there in the first place. The time had now come to carry out the deed he'd intended before he'd been sent to prison. This time, he had some help. He patted the pocket of his jacket with reassurance. The man at the Silver Falcon had provided him with the weapon. Bernard was puzzled about him, wondering if perhaps he was a well-known person and didn't wish his identity known, for he'd never mentioned his name, only told Bernard to call him 'Ed'. Between the time of their meeting and now, 'Ed' had taught him how to use it. Bernard had mentioned that he'd suffered a lot of indignities in Dartmoor Prison and had no desire to spend any more time in there. This time, he said emphatically, he'd do the job properly.

As he watched the proceedings, he wondered as he'd done a dozen times since meeting 'Ed' why he wished James Thorncroft's death. Of course, it couldn't be nearly as crucial as Bernard's own reason. His was a personal one—one of revenge, yet Bernard's courage in the past had failed on so many occasions. His stint in prison had hardened him to the point where he had no qualms now about carrying out the task; this time he promised himself it wouldn't fail!

Guy Fawkes Night had been the best choice. With all the firecrackers exploding everywhere, along with the shouts from the crowds of people, his plan would succeed if he played his cards right. It had been a long time coming, drawing close to thirty years ago that his sister had perished in the fire at Ravenslea, but now his thoughts were centred on justice; once the deed was done, she would be able to rest in peace knowing he'd done all he could to avenge her death.

He'd been 31 years old at the time of Amelia's death—the eldest of five siblings—and his love for her had been constant. She'd provided for them after she'd married Martin Thorncroft, bringing them out of the poverty that had plagued them since their parents had died. He owed her a lot and for her to die in such a manner filled him with loathing for the entire Thorncroft family. If there was any way he could make them pay for her loss, he would go the extra mile to do it.

When he'd met 'Ed' at the Silver Falcon that day, his elation at finding someone who also had an axe to grind with the Thorncroft family became an obsession with him. He suddenly had an ally, though Bernard wasn't sure he actually liked or particularly trusted the man. 'Ed' had to be close to eighty years of age from the signs on his wrinkled face. He had a full head of greying hair and he spoke impeccable English, proving to Bernard at least, that he'd come from a good background. He was slim in build with slightly foxy features and observant eyes that didn't appear to miss a thing.

Bernard shrugged, leaning forward while cupping his hand over his eyes against the glare of a sudden piercing shaft of a brilliant sunset through a gap in the leaves. He turned his attention to the grounds before him, dimming now as dark night clouds were closing in. The vast lawns were almost obliterated by people enjoying the upcoming Guy Fawkes extravaganza. People were moving around from group to group, laughing and generally enjoying themselves.

Watching them, Bernard hated them even more. Why should they have such affluence? Why couldn't their wealth be shared amongst those less fortunate? Yet, even as he thought it, he remembered hearing how every Master of Ravenslea had been more than generous with charitable donations as well as charging decent, low rents to his working tenants. Under other circumstances, it might have been a good vocation for him to have become one of their tenants. However, it was no use thinking along those lines. He had a job to do and this was the perfect day to do it. With all this activity going on, suspicion would likely fall on one of them as it appeared practically everyone from the village of Branton and outlying villages had convened at Ravenslea tonight.

He glanced across at the lower window nearest the front door of the large manor house. It had been arranged beforehand that sometime during the firework display, his contact would lure the Captain into the house at a particular time when the house was still. He'd said that the phone had to be off the hook when the signal had been given him, but had not explained any further. He was relieved when his contact had not asked why. Bernard mentioned only that he wished to speak to Captain Thorncroft in private—no-one should be aware that he'd even come to the house.

He'd wait now until the lantern would swing right and left at the window, then Bernard would slip into the house through a side door that had been previously opened. Quickly, he'd do as he'd planned, quietly leave the way he'd entered, disappear into the woods, pick up the money 'Ed' had promised and make a hasty retreat by way of a tethered horse at the perimeter of the forest. No-one would be any the wiser and he knew his collaborator would not give him away. It had been lucky someone who lived in the house could give him access to Ravenslea Manor for this plan to work successfully. A feeling of contentment surged through him as so far he could not see any glitch in this plan. He returned his gaze to the groups below, the trace of a smile on his lips.

In the increasing darkness, he suddenly saw James Thorncroft appear at the top of the steps. A circle of yellow light from the open door illuminated his slim, upright body. A young woman ran up the steps and caught his arm.

Bernard slipped his hand into the pocket of his tweed jacket, curling his fingers around the handle and trigger guard of the .38 Smith and Wesson. Oddly, Bernard had no fear for his own safety, only a burning desire to see the Thorncrofts suffer in any way possible. He also desperately needed the money for completing the job. The firework display would be his moment to act; no-one would hear a shot as he'd time it to coincide with the moment the firecrackers were discharged.

He had it all planned. Once the job was done, he'd change his name and move up north where no-one would find him. He'd cut and change the colour of his hair, as well as try to fine-tune his accent.

He knew May would be upset, but as she had no idea what was going on at this moment, he would find some plausible excuse for this sudden move. He would lie to her saying he'd send for her later, knowing he never would as she would not be able to fit in with his new, conservative image. With the money, he'd buy a decent set of clothes to give the impression he was a well-to-do gentleman and hope he'd be able to pull it off. He'd be a different man in every respect. It would take a very astute, talented copper to locate him!

He pulled his jacket closer around his shoulders, waiting for the signal. Trees stood majestic and dark behind him, giving him confidence that no-one in the grounds would be able to see him in the darkness. Luckily, Bernard had learned patience when he was in prison and was content to spend a while priming his pistol, fixing the silencer and running an experienced eye along the barrel of the gun to check his aim. He felt a trickle of excitement course through his body, as well as a slight thumping in the region of his ribs, but a smile creased his face as he slipped to a crouching position on the ground to wait. Once he'd carried out the deed, he'd been instructed to leave the pistol in a special place on the outskirts of the wood, where he'd pick up the money. He wondered why 'Ed' would trust him not to just pick up the money and flee without carrying out the deed. He shrugged. Well, as Bernard also wanted vengeance on the Thorncrofts, he had every intention of doing what was required, leave the gun and disappear as planned. He had no desire to be found in possession of the gun that was the instrument of a murder!

"Why would you want to go to Ravenslea Manor tonight, Grandfather?" The young man said as he stepped into the vehicle. "There are fireworks on the green we could see."

Edgar Rutledge looked at his grandson. "I've heard they are a far more superior extravaganza than they ever have here, Gideon. It's a clear, crisp night and I thought a drive there would round off the evening nicely."

Gideon Rutledge shrugged. "Perhaps, but I really didn't think you were into this kind of thing."

"Just something different to do." Was all his Grandfather said.

Gideon leaned back against the plush seat as Edgar Rutledge drove north towards the small town of Branton. It was, as his grandfather had said, a clear, beautiful night and as neither of them had anything planned, perhaps it was a nice change.

They reached the impressive manor about half an hour later. Many vehicles of every shape and description were parked in various parts of the driveway and outside in the lane around the perimeter of the grounds. Edgar parked a few yards from the front entrance and the two of them alighted and joined the throngs of people already filling up the grounds. The bonfire had been lit and children with sparklers, along with delightful showers of overhead fireworks lit up the area.

They chose a large tree with overhanging low branches to watch the display continue before them, their warm winter coats pulled up around them to shield the bitingly cold wind that was tainting their cheeks with a red glow.

Edgar Rutledge occasionally glanced towards the dense tree formation at the west side of the house wondering if Webb would be there as had been arranged. Despite the avidness of Webb at the time they'd talked at The Silver Falcon, Rutledge had given the man the gun with some reservation. After all, the man may decide not to chance being caught again; it was a thought that troubled him. Perhaps it hadn't been a good idea to allow a known criminal free reign with a gun that originally belonged to Edgar Rutledge; anything could happen that would most certainly be connected with him. Well, it was no use worrying about it. He only hoped that Webb would use it the way Rutledge wished him to.

He glanced over at his grandson. He had not told Gideon his real reasons for being here tonight. He sighed. He hated deceiving his grandson, but knew that once the deed had been carried out, Gideon would understand. Edgar sighed, thinking suddenly of Lillian. It had been necessary to have her admitted to the hospital; not because there was anything mentally wrong with her, quite the opposite. If she had any idea what he was planning, she would do everything in her power to stop him. With her out of the way, that was one hurdle Edgar didn't have to cross.

Gideon, unaware of the thoughts that were running through his grandfather's head, was enjoying the show. It was years since he'd seen anything so lavish as this. He wished his mother were there to share it with him. A cloud washed over him as he thought of the mother he adored. He had no idea she'd been so sick. He'd been in Paris when he had received the letter from his grandfather to say that she'd passed away. He wished desperately he could have been with her and was sick with grief. They had a terrific bond; he could talk to her so much better than he could ever do with his grandfather.

"Glad you came, Gideon?" His Grandfather said, trying to sound as normal as he could, when his heart was racing with speculation that at any moment the proceedings would come crashing to a halt.

Gideon nodded. "A good idea—the firework show on the green would certainly not compare with this."

They continued watching, one with speculation, the other with pleasure.

CHAPTER 23

ANXIOUS MOMENTS

Half an hour earlier, Rebecca ran lightly up the steps, a martini in her hand. She looked up at her father. "Oh, Daddy," she said, "where've you been? Aunt Penelope and Uncle Fletcher have been looking for you." She glanced back towards the flock of people craning their necks and smiling with anticipation standing around the unlit bonfire. The mayor's grandson, his hand in his mother's protectively, was sucking on a sticky lollipop as were some of the other children. Even from where she was standing, she could see the look of wonder on his small face.

Pointing over the tops of some heads, she said to her father. "Over there. I don't know what they want, but they seem anxious to talk to you about something."

He kissed her on her brow gently. "I'll see what's troubling them; in the meantime, dear, go and see your Gran in the Sitting Room. She's upset about something and I can't get any sense out of her. You usually manage to talk to her all right."

Rebecca said she would and ran lightly up the steps in through the open doorway.

James pushed his way passed little groups, reached over at one point to take a glass of white wine off the tray of a passing waiter then waved to Penelope's husband who was standing with his back against the bark of a stout elm tree.

"Oh, there you are." Fletcher grinned. "We were wondering when the bonfire's going to be lit and the fireworks begin. Penelope's getting a little tired for some reason. We don't want to leave until we've seen them, because you never disappoint us."

James glanced up at the clear sky. "It's not really dark enough yet. Perhaps another half hour or so." He frowned. "Is Penelope sick?"

Fletcher shook his head. "I don't think so. She arose really early this morning and did a lot of work at the house before coming here. Sometimes she gets these whims where she can't sleep any more and has to do housework. Heaven knows why—she has no reason to. We have staff who attend to everything." He shrugged. "I just think she's a bit overtired. I'm sure it's nothing to worry about." He paused. "If it continues, of course, I'll try to get her to see the doc. As you know, she has an aversion to seeing anyone about medical problems. Though," he grimaced, "she doesn't seem to have the same problem when it comes to one of the children or me."

James grinned. "I know how Penelope feels about such things." He touched his friend's arm gently. "Well, if you're sure she's going to be all right?"

"Yes. She'll be fine. You'll have to excuse me, James, I can see her beckoning to me. I'll talk to you later." Fletcher downed his wine, placing it on a nearby garden table before moving towards his wife.

James strode leisurely around the grounds between the guests making easy conversation. As he'd stipulated, half an hour later, the sun had almost completely disappeared, leaving just enough light to see shadowy people on the lawns. It was time for the festivities to begin!

James by now had mounted the steps to stand at the top between a low ornate stone wall. He raised his arms to silence his guests. Everyone turned, stopping their conversations, eager to hear what the likeable Master of Ravenslea had to say to them.

"Good evening everyone. I'm not going to make a long, dull speech, however, I would like to say a few words to thank each and every one of you for your attendance here today. So far, it's been a delightful experience and luckily, the weather has held for lighting of the bonfire. The 'guy' was made by five of our tenants' children and to whom we offer our grateful thanks. They've done a wonderful job—it hardly seems right that we're going to see him burn. However, they all realize that and don't seem to have any objections." He smiled at the five youngsters, standing with happy expressions on their faces at the bottom of the steps. "Now, without any further ado, let's get on with lighting the bonfire with fireworks to follow." He turned to where the two gardeners were waiting patiently for the cue. "Okay, Abraham; Joshua, set it off!"

Everyone let out a great cheer when the two gardeners set light to the bonfire and while it gained momentum, they hurried across the grounds to begin lighting the roman candles and firecrackers. Within a few seconds, the first Roman candle was lit, sending brilliant stars raining down on them. After two or three more displays in the same vein, James ran back down the steps to view the show for himself. It was then that he saw his housekeeper treading a hasty path towards him.

"Sorry to disturb you, Captain Thorncroft," Elspeth said. "But there's a phone call for you."

"Oh? Who is it, Elspeth? Can't you take a message?" He asked distractedly, his gaze still centred on the bonfire and the children with their sparklers.

She shrugged. "I don't know—he wouldn't give his name, but he sounded quite upset. I really think you ought to come."

"I'll be right there, just ask him to hold the line for a moment or two."

"Yes, Sir."

James turned to Martin who'd joined him. "I'll be back in a few minutes, Martin, there's a phone call for me. I can't imagine who it could be." He shrugged. "Oh well, I should check it out, I suppose. Won't be a minute." He finished the last dregs of the wine, slipped it on a nearby table and walked across the lawns to the peace and quiet of the house. Whoever could be calling him now? He'd invited almost everyone he knew to the party, so it had to be a stranger. He felt a twinge of misgiving as he walked through the front door into the quiet Hallway towards the telephone.

With the flickering light from the bonfire's flames reflecting in the Hallway, James noticed the receiver dangling from its rest. He picked it up. "James Thorncroft here." Whoever had been at the other end, obviously had no patience as there wasn't a sound coming from it. He replaced the receiver thoughtfully.

As he turned to go back into the garden, he felt an uneasy presence. Turning slightly, thinking it was Elspeth, he was about to say something, when a tall shadow appeared in the doorway from the Kitchen directly behind him. In the scanty light given out by a nearby candle in a sconce, James saw something shining in the person's hand. His quest for survival kicked in as he recognized the object as being a pistol. He veered to one side. As he did so, he heard a noise like a dull thud and immediately felt an excruciating pain pierce through the left side of his upper body. Within seconds, his legs suddenly lost their strength; the next moment, he blacked out and fell to the floor.

At the moment James' body hit the floor, Rebecca appeared through the Sitting Room door, her grandmother a few steps behind her. She'd noticed someone hurrying away towards the Kitchen just seconds before and paused for only an instant, before falling down beside her prostrate father.

"Daddy!" She cried. "Daddy! Speak to me!" He was laying awkwardly half on his back, half on his side and as she reached over to touch him, her hand suddenly felt sticky. Horror struck her as she saw a huge dark red stain oozing from a hole in his shirt. She swung her head around to Elizabeth. "Gran! Call the police! I think Daddy's been shot!"

Elizabeth looked terrified; her eyes suddenly welling up with tears. "James! Oh Rebecca, I . . . can't! I've never . . . used the phone. I'll get someone from outside."

Reluctant to leave her beloved father, Rebecca stood up, picked up the receiver and asked the operator to contact the Branton Constabulary urgently. They said they'd get onto it immediately and also send for an ambulance. It only took a couple of moments before she was again beside her father. He'd not moved and her heart sank.

Elizabeth, leaning heavily on her walking cane, hurried as best she could to the front door out into the clear night. The fireworks were in full force, lighting the skies and shooting stars in all directions; flames from the bonfire, too, reached high into the night sky. With all the noise, no one could possibly have heard a gunshot.

She stood at the top of the steps, shouting as loud as she could, but no-one was looking her way. Mumbling to herself she moved cautiously down the steps, but half way down suddenly missed her footing, toppling down to land in a heap at the bottom. The fall winded her for a few seconds. By the time she'd regained her composure and managed to sit up, Catherine had noticed her mother-in-law's predicament and ran up the steps to kneel beside her. Elizabeth's mouth didn't want to work. Her voice had no sound and she felt numb everywhere.

"What is it, Mother?" Catherine said, leaning over trying to coax her into speaking. "What on earth were you thinking of, coming out here, dear, without someone to help you, in the dark like this. That was most unwise of you. Here, let me help you up." Catherine turned and seeing Martin beckoned him over. "Mother's fallen, Martin. Give me a hand to get her back indoors."

Elizabeth shook her head and began pointing back up towards the patio doors. "James . . ." she gasped. "James . . ." then collapsed in a heap in Martin's arms.

Distressed at the panic in his stepmother's voice Martin, with Catherine's help managed to half-carry Elizabeth back up the steps into the Hallway. It was then he saw Rebecca bending over her father's body on the floor.

"Oh no!" Catherine cried, leaving Elizabeth with Martin. She rushed over. "What's happened? Get the light switch, Martin; we need more light in here."

Rebecca had tears in her eyes. "Daddy's been shot!"

Catherine's face paled and dropping on her knees beside her husband, felt for a pulse. "Oh, dear Heaven! Did you call the police, Rebecca?"

Rebecca nodded. "I called the operator. He said he'd get on to it immediately." She glanced at her mother quickly. "Is Dr. Ashton outside?"

Catherine nodded. "I believe so. I'll ask Doris or Edna to find him and bring him here, dear."

"I'm here, Mrs. Thorncroft. I could tell something was amiss and followed you both up the steps." Dr. Ashton hurried towards them, knelt on the floor and immediately checked for a pulse. "He has a pulse. It's weak, but there's a chance." He glanced at Rebecca standing trembling beside him. "Could you fetch me some thick towels, my dear, your father's bleeding badly. We must try and stem the blood as best we can until the ambulance gets here."

Rebecca ran into one of the lower bathrooms, reappearing seconds later complete with an armful of white, fluffy bath towels. Dr. Ashton took them from her and began to tie them around James' injured body. The blood was oozing into the towels, saturating them within seconds. Reaching up to her cream blouse, Catherine extracted a diamond brooch which she handed to the doctor. He quickly pinned the towel in place.

Catherine glanced over at her white-faced daughter. "Did you see what happened, Rebecca?" She asked, gently.

Rebecca shook her head violently from side to side, tears flowing down her cheeks. "No. I heard a noise in the Hallway that sounded like a loud pop just as Gran and I came out of the Sitting Room. Someone rushed passed us into the Kitchen. I didn't recognize him, but it was dark, so it could have been anyone."

Catherine looked down at James, her heart hammering. "What do you think, Doctor?"

He shrugged, sitting back on his heels. He brushed a hand through his hair and glanced up at her. "Until we get him to the hospital and find out if the bullet is still lodged in his body, it's difficult to say. However, I know your husband has a strong constitution; whenever he comes into my office for a check-up his heart is strong. I believe he'll survive this . . . but until we do some tests and remove that bullet, we can't be entirely sure. You understand?"

"I do, doctor." Catherine had a sinking sensation in the region of her stomach. The chance of losing her beloved James was more than she felt she could endure. Yet she knew she had to be strong, for her children's sakes, but at this moment, seeing him laying there still and bleeding, she felt so helplessly inadequate. Hot tears were beginning to form behind her eyes.

Her thoughts were scrambled as Eden and Luke rushed into the Hallway. Both young men fell down beside their injured father with wide disbelieving looks on their faces, shock registering in their bright eyes.

"Dad! Dad!" Eden cried. "What happened? Is he all right?"

Catherine told them everything she could, trying desperately not to show her own emotional distress. She felt she was dying a little along with James.

Martin knelt beside Catherine, his face ashen. "Who in Hell would want to harm James?" He murmured, unable to apologize to his sister-in-law for his profanity. "He's the best of men and I believe one of the most generous Masters this great house has ever had."

"I echo that, Mr. Thorncroft." Dr. Ashton said, looking at Captain Thorncroft's twin brother compassionately. "I've yet to hear anyone say anything derogative about him."

Catherine suddenly couldn't help herself. She began to sob; unstoppable tears flowed down her face. Martin caught her to him. Lifting her to her feet, he steered her to a dark area of the Hallway. He kissed her gently on the forehead and she clung to him; thankful to have his gentle arms around her. "Oh Martin," She cried into the collar of his jacket. "Why would anyone do this! What could he have done to promote such . . . evil!"

Martin frowned. "I don't know, dear. We will find out in due course and I believe Dr. Ashton is right about him. James will come through this—you mustn't upset yourself, Catherine. It won't do him any good, you know." He leaned back. "Umm. I wonder if Elspeth saw the culprit?"

"Why would she?" Catherine glanced up at him, pushing tears from her eyes.

"Because Elspeth came to find James to tell him there was a phone call. Perhaps she could throw some light on it. She surely must have seen the person who ran from here!" He looked down at his distraught sister-in-law. "Will you be all right, dear, if I go and find her."

Catherine nodded, rubbed her eyes once more and returned to James.

Elspeth wasn't in the Kitchen when Martin opened the door. Instead, he found Agnes, Doris and Edna sniffling, their eyes red from weeping.

"How . . . is the Captain, Mr. Martin?" Agnes found her voice and faced him, blowing her nose loudly in her apron.

"I can't tell until the doctor's been able to check him over, which can't be done in the Hallway." He glanced passed her quickly. "I'm looking for Elspeth—have you seen her?"

"A few minutes ago," this came from Doris, who sighed loudly, then stood straight before him, trying desperately to accomplish some kind of dignity. "She came into the Kitchen, muttered something about the Master being hurt, then hurried passed us out into the garden. She seemed very upset—but that's to be expected."

"Did she say anything to you at all that was intelligible?" Martin asked a trifle impatiently.

"No. She was very distressed, as is quite understandable." Agnes answered, straightening her apron and trying to sound in control of her emotions. Her red face and swollen eyes told a different story.

"Umm." Martin strode through the door that led to the vegetable garden. "Which way did she go, did either of you notice?"

All shook their heads regretfully. Martin turned on his heel and disappeared into the night air. It had darkened considerably by now. A crescent moon gave out limited light but it was enough to enable him to find his way along the little path that ran beside the vegetable patch. It was useless. Too much time had elapsed since the person had fired the pistol. Whoever it was had to be far away by now. Martin stopped. The police would wish to check the grounds when it was light so he shouldn't go any further in case he obliterated any footprints.

He returned to the Kitchen and closed the door.

Back in the Hallway, a larger crowd had gathered. At Dr. Ashton's request, Eden was trying desperately to tell people not to enter the house. The doctor needed space to watch over his patient and the police would need easy access once they arrived.

A few minutes later, a clanging of bells was heard. A police vehicle, as well as an ambulance screamed to a stop at the bottom of the steps. Horrified guests stood to one side to allow them entrance.

"What has happened here?" A tall thin man approached them quickly. "I'm Detective Inspector Stanley Wilkins from the Barnstable Constabulary. I was led to understand there's an emergency here?"

Martin moved towards him. "Yes, Detective Inspector. My brother has been shot. The Doctor is with him right now, but my brother has lost of lot of blood."

"Then we'll waste no more time." The Detective Inspector turned back to the crowd of people who'd climbed the steps eager to see what was going on in the big house. "Please clear a path." He boomed. "We need to have immediate access to the ambulance."

Two white-coated men ran up the stairs with a stretcher between them, as people obligingly moved aside.

Within half an hour James was carefully taken down the steps, into the ambulance.

Dr. Ashton's face showed anxiety for his patient and as Catherine approached he caught her arm, giving it a gentle, encouraging squeeze.

"He's very strong and healthy, Mrs. Thorncroft. I know you must be extremely worried about him, that's to be expected, but he has everything to live for. From what I have determined from the short examination in the Hallway, I believe the bullet is lodged somewhere near one of his left ribs. Unfortunately, I don't have the instruments to take out the bullet, so I won't be able to give a correct diagnosis until that is done." He glanced up at the distraught woman, a kindly smile for her distress tempering his words. "Your husband, Mrs. Thorncroft, has always been an extremely positive man and I know he'll pull out all the stops to make sure he stays with us. All we can do now is to offer prayers for him."

"Oh, I'm doing that already, Dr. Ashton." Catherine said, haltingly. "I . . ."

"That's all right, my dear," the kindly doctor said. "I know exactly what you're thinking and I can only ask you to be patient and think as positive about all of this as Captain James would want you to do." He almost said that he hoped the gunshot hadn't pierced a lung, but refrained in time. Catherine was worried enough as it was. He smiled at her warmly. "I'm optimistic that he'll pull through this, but it's going to take time."

"Thank you, Doctor." Catherine gave him an unhappy smile as he helped her into the waiting ambulance. She had to be with James all the time he was experiencing this. She would stay with him through this, if it took forever!

When she'd realized Bernard had shot Captain Thorncroft, Elspeth was horrified. As soon as he rushed passed her in the Kitchen, she hesitated only briefly before following him along the narrow pathway that led around the house towards the northwest side of the dark forest. He'd been swift, but she knew Bernard would have gone in that direction. She had to catch up with him and ask him what he thought he was doing.

Her mind was working feverishly. If she'd only forced him to tell her what he was planning to do, she knew she'd not have gone along with it. She'd wondered, of course, what was so desperate to say to Captain James that couldn't be said during the daytime. She'd never given a thought to the fact that Bernard had such an evil plan in mind. If she had, she'd not have co-operated with him and she probably would have done everything she could to discourage his action. Bernard had only said that he had something desperate to relay to him and it was for his ears only. It was best, he'd told her, that he speak to him at a quiet moment in the house, when everyone else was outside the building.

Elspeth had always liked the good-natured Captain James. She admired him for his resilience, the caring concern he had for his tenants, staff and family and his elegance. She couldn't remember a time when he wasn't civil with her or any of the Kitchen staff. He would joke with them, as he would with others. No, if she'd have known Bernard's atrocious plan, she would somehow have stopped him and definitely would never have collaborated. Now she was afraid. If the gallant Captain had, indeed, passed into the next world, it would mean Bernard was a murderer. Her own brother! If he was caught, he'd most probably end up once more in Dartmoor Prison. She couldn't believe he'd take another chance. Surely ten years in that place would have deterred him from ever entering it again. Who knows, if Captain James didn't survive his cowardly attack and Bernard was convicted, he could receive the death penalty. She shivered. Stupid man!

She swung around the corner of the house, screwing up her eyes to see if she could detect any movement in the bushes at the edge of the garden, but nothing moved. Steadfastly sure she'd eventually meet up with him, Elspeth hurried onwards, passed the rose-bushes, the newly painted summer-house, the shed where the gardeners kept their tools, skirted the rather offensive smelling compost heap that was at that moment spread all over the place, until she reached the edge of the estate. Trees loomed up tall and unyielding and she took a deep breath. Going into the woods at night wasn't something she liked to do. At this moment, she would have been much happier curled up in her warm bed reading the mystery story she'd picked up at the library a few days ago, but instead she'd chosen to search for her wayward brother. She needed an explanation—desperately! It must have been something of dire importance for Bernard to even contemplate such a foolhardy act.

There he was! He was bending down on his hands apparently searching around an area behind a huge rock. In the darkness, it was difficult to see exactly what he was doing, but Elspeth had an idea it wasn't something good. She frowned. Moving slowly forward she accidentally stepped on a twig snapping it and froze. Too late, Bernard had swung around and in his hand was the gun he'd obviously used to shoot Captain Thorncroft. She gasped, then gradually moved into a small patch of moonlight until he recognized her. He stood up, thrusting the gun in his pocket, then caught her arm, hissing something unintelligible and dragged her into the bushes.

"What the 'Ell do you think yer doin' creeping up on me like that? I could 'ave shot you, you damned fool!" He snarled.

"You ask me that, Bernard? I think you know why I'm here—I want to know why you shot the Captain. You'd better be honest, because I'm having a hard job believing that a brother of mine would do such a terrible thing!" Elspeth's dark eyes were blazing with accusation.

"You don't think I go around killing people unless it's for a very good reason do you? You silly woman!" He said brusquely, cruelly digging his fingers into her arm.

"No, I don't think that—but why Captain James? What has he ever done to you? You must be mad to think you could ever get away with this?"

He laughed softly. "'E's done nothing to me, personally, I'll give you that, but 'ave you ever given our dead sister a thought? You know it was 'is fault she died, don't you? Our sister—the one person 'oo'd done everything to give us the life we managed to 'ave after our parents died. We owed 'er a lot, Elspeth. If it weren't for the Thorncrofts, she'd be alive now!"

Elspeth frowned. "You're talking absolute rubbish, Bernard! Amelia was a menace to herself. She was obsessed with owning Ravenslea Manor for herself, Mr. Martin and Allison. She'd go to any lengths to get it. Did you ever discuss the circumstances of the fire with Eric? He knew what happened. He could tell you exactly why Amelia did what she did."

"I 'aven't seen Eric in months, Elspeth, because he's a fool. 'E's always been a fool. I'd never believe a single thing 'e said."

"You're wrong about that. Eric was not a fool. Eric is consistent and very shrewd, obviously a lot smarter than you." Elspeth said stoutly, taking a chance that Bernard might strike her for her insult. "He told us that Amelia tried to have him destroy that lovely ship of theirs, the Desdemona. She had flown into a murderous rage when Eric spilled the beans to Captain James. Not being able to carry out her intended plan, she decided, instead, to hit them even closer—by setting fire to their beautiful home. Unfortunately, Amelia felt she was going to lose the only thing in her life that she loved—her little girl. When she thought that Allison was still inside the burning house, she ran into the building and unfortunately, perished, not knowing that Allison had been saved from a terrifying death herself, by the future Mrs. Catherine Thorncroft."

Bernard looked at her, suddenly unsure. How could be believe that Amelia set that fire herself? He'd been under the impression she'd been trapped inside Ravenslea while the fire had been started unexpectedly in the cellar and travelled upwards. No-one had bothered to try and save her. No, Elspeth must be wrong, but his resolve seemed suddenly to falter.

"I can't believe our sister would be capable of such a thing, Elspeth. Are you telling me the truth? The absolute truth?"

"Of course it's the truth—when have I ever lied to you! Obviously, the only way you're going to believe me, is to have Eric substantiate it. You must go to see him quickly. I know you two haven't exactly been close, because of certain differences between you, but you'd better shelve those differences now and get the truth from him. He was there, remember. He knows exactly what occurred. He'll definitely remember what happened; I don't think a day goes by when he doesn't think of how his sister behaved at that time." She paused. "Despite what you feel about our younger brother, Bernard, he is far from a fool, only a gentle man who'd never wish to harm anything or anyone."

"If what you say is true . . . !" Bernard fell against the bark of the tree opposite her, and slithered to the floor. "What 'ave I done? All because I wanted to 'ave Amelia avenged, not to mention the money . . ."

"Money! What are you talking about?" She said sharply. "You're not in this alone, are you? There's someone else involved. Tell me who it is. I must tell the authorities."

"No!" He hissed harshly. "You mustn't tell anyone. If you mention it, they'll know you 'ave some knowledge and will eventually connect it with me. No, Elspeth, you must keep well out of this. If what you say is proved true, I will make amends some'ow and 'ope Captain Thorncroft isn't dead. I . . . I . . ."

Suddenly Elspeth felt a sliver of compassion for her gullible, slightly dimwitted brother and reached over to touch his arm gently.

"I'll not tell them anything, Bernard. If you have somehow got yourself in a mess, you're going to have a find a way out of it yourself. The less I know of your source, the better. Now you go and talk to Eric as soon as you can." As he stood up, she gave him a gentle push. "Go on, get out of here. I've got to get back to the house unseen, which may be a little awkward with all those people milling around everywhere."

"Thanks, Elsp." Bernard said, using his nickname for her. "Can you get word to me on Captain Thorncroft's condition?"

"I'll try, but it may be a while."

She watched him quickly disappear deeper into the woods and as quietly as she could, retraced her steps back to the house.

Bernard hurried along the forest path towards the narrow road, then remembered. The money! 'Ed' said he'd place the money near the rock if the gun was there. He'd forgotten. Damn! Turning around, he retraced his steps, found the rock and was about to place the gun there when he heard a sound behind him.

Twisting around, a figure blotted out the shadowy moonlight.

"Webb." A man's voice said. "You've done it?"

Bernard straightened and stared at the silhouette, suddenly feeling uncomfortable. "Yes . . . is that you, Ed?"

"You have the gun?"

"I do—I was about to place it where you said . . ."

"No need to now, Webb. Give it to me and I'll hand over the money."

Bernard hesitated for a moment, then reached over and handed the gun to the man. "I've done it; now if you'll just give me the money, I'll be away and you'll 'ear no more from me. Your secret is safe with me and, I would assume, my secret is safe with you."

The man grabbed the gun, but ignored Bernard's outstretched hand. "Oh, I don't need to worry about my secret, Webb, no-one will ever know I was even involved in this."

"But . . ." Bernard began to splutter as he noticed the gun was aimed directly at him. A terrified look crossed his pale face. "What are you doing? You . . . you don't 'ave to do this. I'm not going to be living 'ere . . . there'll be no connection between us . . . if you pull the trigger, it'll be 'eard at the 'ouse and in the grounds. There be no fireworks going now . . ."

"Ah, you're quite right, Webb, but there's so much confusion going on down there, I doubt if anyone would hear a gunshot. You are also right when you say that you're not going to be living here . . . in fact, you're not going to be living anywhere. I don't need you to become a nuisance to me . . . and for you to live, you definitely would be. Sorry, but it's imperative that you not be around to complicate my affairs." With that, he aimed the gun at the terrified Bernard and pulled the trigger. Bernard stumbled and fell backwards with a scream of pain. After a few twitches, he lay still.

The man moved forward, looked at Bernard's motionless body and prodded him gently. Satisfied, he knelt down. With a great deal of exertion for a man of his years, he dragged the dead man's body off the path into the bushes. After curling Bernard's fingers around the gun handle, he crouched with his hands on his knees before straightening. Catching his breath for a moment, he turned back along the path towards the narrow lane where Gideon and the car stood with engine running. He'd promised Bernard Webb £1,000 for killing Captain James Thorncroft, but as he hadn't seen that amount of money in a number of years, there had been no money waiting for Bernard's greedy little hands. The man scowled. Even if he'd had the money, he had no intention of wasting it on someone like Bernard Webb.

CHAPTER 24

AN UNEXPECTED DILEMMA

James' condition improved. The bullet had been successfully removed from an area close to his heart and he now had to stay quiet for the large open wound to heal. At this time, the Police cautioned Catherine and Martin to keep the fact that James had not succumbed to the shooting, a secret at least for now. So, once he was able to be moved he was put into a private room in the Isolation Ward at Branton Hospital. If at any time anyone wondered and asked why there was no funeral planned, Catherine and Martin had been informed to say that James had slipped into a coma and wasn't expected to live more than a few weeks. Against her honest upbringing, Catherine felt a lump in her throat at having to tell this to her children and the staff at Ravenslea. All were devastated to hear the news; Rebecca sobbed hysterically at the thought of losing the father she loved so desperately; Eden and Luke walked around the house disoriented and troubled. Catherine had never seen such long faces and red-rimmed eyes.

With the knowledge that her husband was, in fact, recovering nicely, Catherine tried taking on the role of a woman facing impending widowhood. This was very difficult for her. Yet, she managed it. She went around the house in dark clothes, quietly attending to her duties at the same time sympathizing with her children in their tearful moments. The apparent impending loss of their father was hard for them to bear and Catherine's heart went out to them. She wanted to take them in her arms and tell them the truth, but respected the reasons for the deception. So the days went by in this manner with her visiting James at Branton Hospital as regularly as she could to 'see how he was faring'. Each time she returned, she'd put on a sad face and shake her head but would not utter a word to anyone as to his progress. She didn't want to intensify the lie, yet knew she had to continue with it—at least for the next little while. The children wanted to visit him, but Catherine told them the hospital would only allow her to see him at this time. If, she said, he did manage to pull out of the coma, they could definitely see him. Her reasons seemed to suffice, at least for now.

A few days later, the weather turned particularly nasty. High winds and cold temperatures, violent rains and a few mud slides around the Branton, Barnstable and nearby areas caught everyone unawares. Bitter winds whipped across the Devonshire Moors and light snow suddenly fell around Ravenslea Manor.

One afternoon after Catherine had returned from her usual morning hospital visit, Phoebe ran out into the snow romping with enthusiasm, yapping happily, her little nose white, her eyes sparkling. Catherine walking a few paces behind her, couldn't help but laugh at the antics of the West Highland Terrier as she tried to jump over snow drifts, consistently landing somewhere in the middle of them.

"Phoebe, don't you go too far." Catherine called at one point when the dog ran towards the outer limits of the grounds. "Keep away from the woods, there's a good dog." But of course, Phoebe not understanding did what she wanted, disappearing into the woods as was her right. Nothing was more fun than dodging through the trees, giving a human a run for her money!

Catherine grumbled as the snow was somewhat deeper at the perimeter of the grounds and she had no real desire to go trudging through the woods to find the dog; yet she knew she'd have to as Phoebe didn't have much sense of direction and could easily become lost.

Climbing over the small bank to the snow layered trail, she called the dog while following her little footprints. That was one good thing about snow, footprints gave the game away!

Then the footprints moved away from the path and Catherine stopped. It was brambly and difficult to negotiate off the beaten track. She called Phoebe again, and heard some snuffling and a little whine.

"Oh, you bad dog!" She cried. "I suppose you've got yourself stuck." Catherine crossly pushed her way through the bracken. Skirting protruding tree limbs, she saw the dog whining and digging at something. What the dickens had she found now?

Gingerly stepping towards Phoebe, Catherine pushed the animal to one side. Suddenly she stopped in horror as she saw what the dog had uncovered. A body! A man's body, face down in the earth, partially covered with a smattering of snow. She felt herself go limp, but managed to keep her equilibrium. She grabbed Phoebe's collar, then knelt down beside the prone form on the snowy woodland floor. Grimacing, she brushed some of the snow away from the side of the face, but she had no idea who he was. Feeling slightly sick, Catherine tucked Phoebe under her arm, turned and hurried back to the house. Inside, she sought out Martin and Eden, telling them what Phoebe had uncovered. They quickly abandoned their tasks to hurry off in the direction she'd given them.

Catherine went into the Kitchen. She needed a drink, so poured herself a cup of clear, cool water. After sipping the cool, refreshing liquid, she splattered a little over her forehead; she needed to keep her balance as she was dangerously close to crumpling to a heap on the floor. Agnes walked into the Kitchen and seeing Catherine hunched over the sink, hurried over to her, rubbing damp hands down her apron worriedly.

"Mrs. Thorncroft? Whatever is the matter?" She caught hold of Catherine's arm and gently guided her to a wooden stool. "You sit here, Mrs. Thorncroft while I get you a cup of tea."

"I'll be all right thank you, Agnes."

"I don't think so, Ma'am. I don't know where you've been, but the only time I've ever seen you look so . . . upset, was when the Master was . . ." she paused awkwardly, "well, you know . . ."

Catherine swallowed a little more of the water. "I'll be all right in a minute thank you, Agnes. I would like that cup of tea though . . ."

"Of course. Now why don't you go into the Sitting Room; I'll bring one right in for you. Just relax and whatever gave you that scare will recede in the background."

Catherine managed a small smile, stood up and carefully made her way into the Sitting Room.

Martin and Eden returned half an hour later, grim expressions on both their faces. Catherine turned when they came into the room.

"Well," she said, "do either of you know who he was?"

They both shook their heads.

"Not a clue, dear." Martin said, "but of course the Police must be informed. I wonder what he was doing in that part of the woods at this time of year."

"Perhaps a poacher?" Catherine suggested, but immediately dismissed that as unlikely. There was no game at Ravenslea at the moment for anyone to poach.

"No, I don't think so." This came from Eden, who began pacing the room. "I'm wondering if he had anything to do with . . . the shooting." He caught his lip and glanced at his uncle.

"That's a possibility, but as I said before, the Police must be called." He moved towards the door to go into the Hallway. "I'll give Branton Constabulary a call and get someone out here right away."

Within the hour, Detective Inspector Stanley Wilkins arrived. Catherine remembered him very well, as even in the dim light that had been given out in the Hallway that dreadful day when James had been shot, he had an almost military bearing which commanded respect.

He listened intently as she explained how she'd come upon the body.

"Thank you for acting so promptly, Mrs. Thorncroft. Of course, we'll have to investigate this new incident, so don't be alarmed as we want to spend as much of the day as we can in the woods before we lose the light. We must check the area for evidence, you understand, so the body can't be moved until we feel we have covered everything."

True to his word, the Detective and his constable could be seen from some of the windows as they made their thorough investigation at the edge of Exmoor Forest beside Ravenslea's grounds. Just before the sun began to sink, an ambulance arrived and took the body to the morgue. After that, the Detective Inspector joined the family in the Drawing Room, explaining to them that he'd been assigned to the investigation of Captain Thorncroft's shooting. As he happened to be in Branton at the time Martin had phoned, he considered as it may have some bearing on the case, decided to check it out. The dead man, he said, was known to the police as having just recently been released from Dartmoor Prison after serving a ten year sentence for attempted murder. He didn't go into any more details, but it was plain to see the family were on edge knowing that the dead man could have been involved with James' assault, yet it seemed the Detective Inspector didn't wish to reveal any more information at that moment.

The next day, Catherine was called to the phone. It was the Detective Inspector, who had been told at the hospital about James' condition. Being the astute man he was, Catherine knew he'd never reveal his secret to anyone but herself and Martin. He told her that the bullet taken from the dead man was of the same calibre as the one taken from James. This was a relief as now at least he had only one gun to locate which, once found, would most likely identify James' assailant as well as the killer of the dead man in the woods.

As the average citizen would not own a gun of the calibre that was used in the shootings, it was now necessary to concentrate on the sale of hand guns as opposed to shotguns and rifles normally used in the pursuit of game and in the disposal of vermin.

"We will search the area until we locate the gun and it won't be long after that before we find the killer, mark my words." The Detective Inspector told them with a degree of confidence. "Villains are quite notorious for making mistakes and when this one does, we'll have him. Don't worry—he'll be behind bars I'd say, before Christmas."

By the end of the next week, Catherine was happy to see that James was beginning to show signs of improvement. This was noticeable mainly because of his restlessness in the Isolation Ward. He wanted to come home, there was no doubt about that, but she told him in no uncertain terms that he would have to remain until his assailant had been caught. Only then would it be safe to resume his normal life again. He grudgingly understood and she arranged for him to have a radio placed in his room, as well as books and magazines to read to occupy his time.

CHAPTER 25

AN ALARMING REVELATION

Next Tuesday morning, a vehicle pulled up in front of Ravenslea's open gates. The lone occupant inside stared at the beautiful house, bereft now of much colour, but the gardener still maintained exquisitely manicured lawns. The slim, dark-haired man looked towards the front edifice. His eyes drifted to the left of the building where a white and blue painted gazebo stood in watery sunlight. How different everything looked today, in the cold, stark sunlight, to the rowdy Guy Fawkes extravaganza of a few weeks ago. He'd wanted to enter the grand home at that time, but had heard that the Master of Ravenslea had sunk into a coma since arriving at the hospital.

Since the night he and his grandfather had visited Ravenslea Manor to view the firework display, he'd been having odd feelings about it. It had been uncharacteristic of his grandfather to wish to see such a display, but Gideon had not given any thought to the Captain's assailant. Grandfather had just said how sad it was that Captain Thorncroft had been shot, but if he passed away from his wounds, it would lead to bigger and better things for him, Gideon. At first he'd not understood what his Grandfather had meant, but now with the incriminating letter in his pocket, he realized that if everything turned out as his grandfather had planned, this beautiful property would soon belong to Gideon.

Once he'd learned this, being an architect, he began to envisage how he'd like Ravenslea Manor to look once he was in control of it. He'd keep all the hired help exactly as they were. No need to go to the expense of hiring new employees when these would at least be familiar with the Manor and the grounds.

On his way over this morning, he'd thought a great deal on what he would do with the property once it was legally his to do with as he wished. He had an idea the interior would be old fashioned and possibly in need of repair. It didn't matter anyway, as he intended to tear down much of it. The plans that were fermenting in his active mind would turn Ravenslea Manor into a country club catering to only Society's rich and famous.

First of all, he'd change the name from 'Ravenslea Manor' to 'Rutledge Court'. That way it would cease to be known as a property that was owned by the Thorncroft family. In time, everyone would be happy with the wealth that 'Rutledge Court' would generate to the West Country. That would give his ego a good boost, resulting in his and his grandfather's name eventually being known as the place to go for a fun, easy going time.

He wanted to bring influential people into the establishment. Celebrities like

Hollywood film stars. He shivered with excitement at perhaps being able to entice someone as wonderful as Jean Harlow or Carole Lombard to the manor! He couldn't get enough of watching those two beauties on the silver screen! Also, what a great advertisement that would make! Gideon almost rubbed his hands together with the prospect.

He had it all planned. Extensions to the property would be made to incorporate suites of rooms for those who wished to stay for a while. An indoor swimming pool complete with palm trees, wrought iron tables and chairs; tennis and squash courts would also be part of his plan. Riding stables with the very best of horses. In season, he'd introduce pheasant, grouse, partridge and other game for the elite to shoot. Perhaps, if everything went as smoothly as he envisaged, he'd apply for a gaming license; as well he had it in mind to install a beauty parlour to pamper to the vanity of the wealthy women guests.

In his mind's eye, he could see people laughing happily, drinking cocktails beside the shimmering blue pool; the sound of hooves as riders galloped out of the grounds to explore the vast Devonshire moors and later, if it were granted, the tinkling sound of the little white ball as it bounced around the grooves of the roulette wheel.

He wasn't so naïve that he didn't know that it would take a lot of money and time to get to the point where he could sit back, relax and let his empire soar. The renovations and new furnishings alone would be very costly, but he had an idea the finances would be easily obtained once the bank knew their intentions. He would make sure he'd get a good advertising company to promote the casino all over Britain, then when it became more popular, he'd contact travel agencies to bring people in from all over the world.

It was a high dream, but with foresight and good marketing, he felt the day would come when he'd be able to sit back and rest on his laurels. His grandfather's financial worries would be over and they'd be living free.

However, that was far in the future. It was the here and now that he had to contend with and he pressed his lips together wondering how the family would react when faced with the bombshell he was about to give them. It would be a terrible shock, but he felt his need was greater than theirs at the moment. The Thorncrofts were wealthy people; the only drawback for them would be that the property had been in their family since the mid 18th century and they would obviously not be readily conducive to his startling announcement.

He lifted his brown trilby and pushed a hand through his hair, then slipping the vehicle into gear, moved slowly down the driveway towards the front entrance where he stopped and switched off the quiet engine. He waited a moment, mostly to catch his breath and think quickly on how he was going to relay the information to Mrs. Thorncroft.

Finally, he stepped from the vehicle and walked with confidence towards the heavy door. Pursing his lips, he pulled the antiquated bell-rope and waited for someone to allow him entrance.

A moment passed and it was opened by a rather austere woman wearing a dark dress that reached just below her knees.

"Yes?" She asked, a trifle curtly, as if she'd already had a bad start to her day.

"Good morning." He smiled. "I would very much like to talk to Mrs. Catherine Thorncroft, if that is possible?"

Elspeth stared at him, unsmiling. "Is she expecting you?"

"No, as a matter of fact, she isn't, but once she knows the nature of my visit, I'm sure she'll be interested in seeing me."

Elspeth hesitated before opening the door a little wider. "Take a seat over there, Mr. . . . .?"

"Rutledge, Gideon Rutledge." He said, moving towards an ornately carved chair, covered with plush red velvet.

"I'll see if Madam is free."

Gideon Rutledge sat down, placing his hat beside him. He glanced around the Hall. It was, as he'd imagined, warmly welcoming. Thick rich carpeting graced the wide stairway. A large circular Indian rug resplendent in blues, greens and reds rested luxuriously on the highly polished oak floor beneath his feet. The aroma of beeswax and lemon tickled his nose and he absently pressed his lips together, nodding in speculative admiration. The walls, also as he'd imagined, were adorned with exquisite oil paintings in large fancy frames and an overhead candelabra winked in the morning sunlight shafting down through a small circular window above the doorway. Perhaps at least this part of the house may not need too much renovating, thereby saving him money.

Elspeth appeared. "Mrs. Thorncroft will see you in the Drawing Room, Mr. Rutledge, if you'll just follow me." The woman looked at him through slate grey eyes. He picked up his hat and fell in step behind her.

The Drawing Room door was open and a slim woman moved forward, her hand outstretched.

"I am Catherine Thorncroft." She said, smiling a welcome. "What can I do for you?"

"Thank you for seeing me, Mrs. Thorncroft. I do hope I haven't come at an awkward time; I realize I should have telephoned first, but as I was in the area, it seemed opportune to talk with you immediately. Gideon Rutledge is my name." He paused. "First of all, I'd like to offer my sincere sympathy on hearing the dreadful news about your husband."

Catherine nodded her head graciously and indicated a seat for him. "Thank you." She said. "Please have a seat, Mr. Rutledge and state your business."

He made himself comfortable on a chair near a cosy fire burning in a large mahogany mantled fireplace.

Catherine watched, aware of his discomfort. She had no idea why he would wish to speak with her, but whatever it was, it was causing him quite a lot of unrest. He picked up his hat and began twisting it around in his hands; looking away, unable to bring himself to make eye contact with this elegant woman who had received him so graciously. She sat in a wing-backed chair opposite him and leaned back, folding her hands neatly together in her lap.

"What I have come to see you about will do nothing to ease your pain, I'm afraid, Mrs. Thorncroft. In fact, it will most probably add to it and for this you have my apologies." He said, straightening and breathing heavily. "It is in relation to the heritage of Ravenslea." He noticed her sudden intake of breath, but continued as if he hadn't. "My story, I feel sure you will not believe, but it is, indeed, the truth. I have proof . . ."

"Please get on with it, Mr. Rutledge." Catherine's voice showed growing anxiety.

"Your husband is in a coma, I believe and not expected to live more than a few weeks?" She nodded. He caught his lower lip with his top teeth and looked away. "You have a son, Eden, correct?" She nodded. "Well, should your husband . . . pass away and his Will read, it will undoubtedly state that your son is heir to Ravenslea. You see . . ." he paused as if for effect, "my dear Mrs. Thorncroft, I am here to dispute your son's legal claim to this beautiful house. I have evidence here that clearly states it is I who is heir to Ravenslea Manor."

There was a pregnant silence and for a moment, he wondered if she'd actually understood what he'd said. "Do you understand . . . ?" He began.

"This is outlandish, Mr. Rutledge! You speak as if my husband has all ready passed into the next World. He is in a coma and although it appears he may not survive, where there is life, there is also hope." She stood up. Despite the knowledge that James had almost recovered, she felt a sense of vulnerability build up in her. "This is nothing but pure fiction and I resent you coming here at this time with such a disgraceful story." Her voice had become cold, unyielding. "My son is the only heir to Ravenslea Manor there is absolutely no doubt about that."

"Don't be so sure, Mrs. Thorncroft. I have proof with me here . . ." he reached inside his black jacket and pulled out the letter. He handed it to her. "This is a letter my mother received from your husband many years ago. It clearly states that James Thorncroft is my biological father."

She turned the sheet of paper to face her, reaching at the same time to pick up a pair of spectacles. There written on a worn sheet of notepaper was the familiar scrawl that could only belong to James. She caught her lip, unable to bring herself to look at the young man smugly sitting before her.

"This is all nonsense, Mr. Rutledge! Though I admit the writing is familiar, I know this cannot be possible. My husband would never do anything as underhand as this." She took off her spectacles trying desperately not to let him see her hands shaking. She faced him squarely.

"You only have to look here, Mrs. Thorncroft." He leaned over to point at the wording that Catherine had seen with sinking heart. "It clearly states that my mother was engaged to James Thorncroft; that she would be joined in marriage to him in a few months. What other proof do you need?"

"I see it, Mr. Rutledge, but I do not believe it." She stood up. "You will allow me to keep it for the time being."

"No, Mrs. Thorncroft, I cannot allow you to keep the letter; you may destroy it . . ."

"I'm not in the habit of wilful acts." She said harshly. "You can trust me to keep the letter intact as you have shown me."

"All the same, Mrs. Thorncroft, I do not wish to let it out of my hands."

"Then I will make a note of all that is written on it. I will need to talk to my lawyer about this. If what you say is true, which is extremely doubtful, then we most definitely have to discuss this in more detail." She paused. "If at some later date, my lawyer wishes to see the original, you must be prepared to relinquish it. When you realize the mistake you've made and the trouble you'll obviously cause for yourself, not to mention us, you might think again about proceeding with this ridiculous idea."

He hesitated. He had no desire to give the letter to her. His grandfather had warned him not to allow her to keep it; it was the only proof they had that Gideon was the sole beneficiary of Ravenslea Manor, yet he had no reason to stop her writing down the details.

"If you decide to take me to Court, Mrs. Thorncroft, I am confident I will win the case. It wouldn't matter whether Captain Thorncroft passed away now, or at some later date, I have the evidence right here that Ravenslea Manor will become mine to do with as I wish." He gave her a candid look. "You may, of course, record what you see on the letter, Mrs. Thorncroft, but I must insist I keep the original document with me at all times."

She quickly wrote down every word and handed the original back to him. She could feel herself shivering inside at the mere suggestion that Eden would be unable to claim his birth-right should anything happen to James. She would fight this man as much as she could to deny his allegation.

"As a matter of interest, Mr. Rutledge, what is your date of birth?"

He looked surprised, but answered quite openly. "August 18th, 1897."

"Thank you." Catherine looked at him hard and critical. No longer was she smiling; she foresaw danger here with this man and wasn't sure she could handle it alone. She would go to the hospital the very next day to talk to James. She also thought it might be prudent to bring his cousin Stephen into the secret. There were deciding factors here that upset and unnerved her. The letter was dated November 28th, 1896. James had been 22 years old at that time. She'd not known him, but still felt she knew him well now enough to believe he'd never have left a woman with child, especially if he'd promised her marriage.

Her heart thudded unnaturally and she turned away, unwilling to let Gideon Rutledge see her discomfort. There could have been a moment when James had transgressed, if the woman had been beautiful and persuasive, but even as the thought entered her head, she dismissed it as she was certain he would never have done anything of that nature to sully the Thorncroft reputation. Yet what could explain his writing that letter to this man's mother all those years ago?

She faced him. "I cannot let this matter rest here, Mr. Rutledge. I will need to get in touch with you in a few days, when I've discussed this with our lawyer."

He shrugged. "As you wish. No lawyer will be able to deny my claim—you can have him check as much as he likes. It is here, clearly written by your husband." He stood up. "If you wish to discuss this further, I will gladly give you some time to mull over the letter at your convenience. Now, if you'll be kind enough to give me your telephone number, I'll be on my way. I'll call you on

Saturday evening next to make another appointment to see you. By that time, you should have found out the truth and will cede to my inheritance."

"Not without a fight, young man." Catherine's voice held rancour. "Call as you suggest. In the meantime, I'll have my lawyer thoroughly check this out." She straightened her back and threw him a hard, calculating look. "I have no doubt, Mr. Rutledge, that your claim will be classed as nothing more than pure invention!"

She scribbled the telephone number onto a piece of paper and handed it to him. "Good-day. My housekeeper will let you out."

She turned her back on him; her head spinning. She prayed this man was just an opportunist and not as he'd intimated; yet how could that letter be explained. It was definitely James' handwriting. Gideon Rutledge appeared to be right, there was no other explanation. Yet, there had to be . . . there had to be!

Tears of humiliation, concern and a sudden feeling of betrayal filled her eyes as she watched Gideon Rutledge swing his shiny automobile around in the courtyard and speed back down the driveway towards the road. Only then did she draw the curtains together and lean against the side of the window frame.

A moment later, she moved out of the Drawing Room deep in thought. Surely James would have said something to his family at the time. There had to be some misunderstanding—some dreadful mistake. James would never commit himself in such a manner without making everything legal and above board.

As she walked across the Hallway, she suddenly remembered Lillian Rutledge's warning! Her heart lifted slightly. Although Lillian may not have known what her father had been plotting, she'd obviously had some foresight that something was about to happen as she'd made every effort to inform Catherine of her apprehension as regards James. It all now depended on the prognosis of her mental condition given by the hospital review board as to whether Lillian, in fact, was wrongly committed and would now be eligible for release.

Despite that moment of hope, Catherine recognized that an unwanted cloud was beginning to form over Ravenslea Manor. A cloud that could, if not handled carefully, change their lives forever!

CHAPTER 26

THE CONFRONTATION

Her mood felt disconnected; her step heavy as she climbed the wide steps to Branton Hospital, along the sterile corridor to her husband's room. Despite remembering the discussion she'd had with both Lillian Rutledge and James, she couldn't help but feel they were not telling her the truth. The letter that Gideon Rutledge had shown her looked too genuine to be a fake! She knew her husband's handwriting very well. After all they'd been married 25 years! Yet, how could she face him with this accusation after he'd told her nothing had happened between him and Lillian all those years ago? He would think she believed this Gideon Rutledge over him. But what else could she think? The letter was there, plain to see; James had been engaged to Lillian Rutledge sometime in 1896, with a promise of marriage in the near future. If this was, indeed, true, then Gideon Rutledge could well be the legal heir to Ravenslea Manor. Her eyes were smoky with tears as she turned the corner at the top of the stairs her breath laboured.

When she entered James' private room, she found him propped up with pillows, glasses perched on his nose, reading a mystery novel, something he'd cultivated since being relegated to the hospital. He looked up, took off the glasses and closed the book. He threw her a warm, lazy smile that always managed to make her heart beat just that little bit faster.

"Hello darling." He smiled and drew her to him.

"Hello, James. How are you feeling?" Catherine sounded cheerful as she leaned over to kiss him.

"Medically speaking, surprisingly well, however, I'm so bored. I want to be home with you and the family. I do miss you, you know." He paused and frowned, a puzzled expression appearing in his eyes. "What's the matter, Catherine? Are you ill?"

"No, James, but I have to talk to you about something." She caught his hand in hers. "You must listen to me and don't interrupt." She took a deep breath. "Before I tell you what's troubling me, I want to ask you a question. It's probably going to be difficult for you to answer, but it's something that must be one way or another."

"Go ahead, darling." He looked at her, his mouth a grim line, a frown settling between his dark eyebrows.

"Can you cast your memory back to the year 1896 when you may have visited London?"

"Good grief! 1896? Now that's really asking something."

"I know it is, dear, but please try and remember something you did; or where you were at that time." She paused, feeling a little better with her husband's hand in hers. "You really don't know just how important it is to know."

He leaned back, closed his eyes, a wrinkle appearing on his brow. After a while, he shook his head.

"I'm sorry, Catherine, it's too far back to have an accurate picture. All I can tell you is that sometime in the '90's, Father and I went up north, but the actual year completely escapes me." He remembered going to London all too well; that was where he'd met the alluring Lily Starr, but couldn't be sure of the date. "As Dad's not here any more, you could ask Martin. He didn't come with us, as I remember correctly, but he may remember something and . . ." He lifted a finger as if an idea had just occurred to him. "I've just thought of something; have him check the old filing cabinet in the Study. Dad kept every little thing in there, from grocery receipts to major purchases. We always joked about him being a squirrel—that filing cabinet was almost bursting at the seams! After he passed away none of us had the heart to discard the contents in that cabinet. Heaven knows why—we made enough fuss about it before. Perhaps it was for this very reason. Who knows? I know we haven't had to look in there for years, but if you're saying it is imperative we find out what we were doing then, perhaps it'll turn to our advantage."

She leaned over and kissed him, jumping up from the bed, her spirits suddenly soaring. "Thank you James. I'll keep my fingers crossed that Martin can find something to tell us that you were somewhere other than London during that time."

He caught her arm as she was about to leave. "Now, my dear, don't you think you ought to tell me what all this mystery is about?"

She hesitated. "Let me talk to Martin first. If we find what we're looking for, then we'll tell you the whole story."

"Please, Catherine . . . don't leave me in suspense like this." James' handsome face showed a crease of concern.

"If it's something you have to worry about dear, then you'll know soon enough. For now, don't worry—Martin and I will get to the bottom of it. Now go back to your novel and don't worry about a thing!" She stood up and kissed him quickly. "Now I really have to go. Percy's waiting patiently for me in the parking area to take me home. I'll come in again tomorrow. By then I may have some information for you."

"I'll count the hours, my sweet." He blew her a kiss as she smiled and left him.

When Catherine returned to Ravenslea that afternoon, she sought out Martin. Not seeing him anywhere in the grounds, she walked into the Hallway as Doris approached from the Kitchen.

"Oh, Doris. Have you seen Mr. Martin?"

"He's outside, Madam, talking to Joshua round the side of the house." Doris said.

Catherine hurried into the sunny morning air and stopped at the top of the steps. There was her brother-in-law talking to the younger gardener, both leaning against the terrace balustrade.

"Martin." She called. "I must talk with you, it's very important."

Martin turned, said something to Joshua who touched his cap respectfully and moved away.

"Of course, Catherine. Is James all right?" He added softly for her ears only.

She nodded. "James is coming along well, but something's happened and I'm hoping you'll be able to help."

Leaving nothing out, Catherine told Martin the whole story and when she'd finished, his face turned pale.

"This is ludicrous, Catherine!" He said, harshly. "This can't possibly be true. It has to be some sort of hoax to get at the Thorncroft family wealth. You said this Gideon character will be contacting you this coming Saturday evening?"

She nodded. "And if I know anything about him, he's going to be a difficult man to bend. James mentioned something about an old cabinet in the Study. Can we go and look now to see if something's there to see if James was in London in 1896."

"You're right, dear." He said, as he ran lightly back up the steps and in through the open front door. "You know, I do remember James going to London, but that's about it, I don't know the actual date." As they slipped into the Study, Martin stopped. "There was something. I think there was trouble at our mine up North which coincided with an important meeting with our foreign investment firm in London. If I remember correctly James went to London on his own." He shrugged ". . . it could, of course, have occurred at a different time, Catherine, but I do remember James going there at the end of the last century sometime."

"Well, we have to find out, Martin and hope we come up with something positive. We have the added incentive of fighting to keep our beautiful home out of the hands of fortune hunters or usurpers!"

Martin, Eden, Catherine, Rebecca and Luke spent the next four hours searching for some clues as to where James was at the time Gideon's Rutledge's mother conceived him. To their disappointment, the years from 1895 to 1897 were missing from the cabinet in James' Study. The situation looked grim because this loss seemed to confirm that Gideon Rutledge had told the truth. James had gone to London, married this man's mother and eventually became the father of Gideon Rutledge, thereby acknowledging him to be the rightful heir to Ravenslea Manor. Perhaps, Martin said, James had mentioned it to Father, who had decided not to keep the record, preferring to destroy all evidence of his eldest son's infidelity and allow life at Ravenslea to continue as per normal.

It all sounded so unbelievable. Why would James offer marriage, then return to Ravenslea Manor without his bride? That very fact alone gave Catherine and Martin hope that the whole accusation was false.

Martin leaned back in James' desk chair, "I know my brother very well. One can't have a twin without knowing how the other one thinks and I'm pretty sure I know James' character better than anyone." He banged his fist against the desk in frustration. "I honestly don't believe any of this. If James had promised marriage to someone, he'd not have reneged on it. He'd have brought the woman home to meet the family; that didn't happen, as we all can contest to. Something's obviously not adding up at all here."

"I agree," Rebecca said. "I'm sure Grandpa would have mentioned something somewhere about going to London at that time. But, I wonder why those records from the old cabinet have disappeared."

Eden nodded. "That in itself is a mystery. If there were investment problems in South Africa which the visit to London seems to suggest, surely Grandpa would have kept a record somewhere, knowing how fastidious he was about such things. Well," he said glancing at them shrewdly, "we'll have to solicit the help of Stephen. With his knowledge of the law, he may be able to give us some guidance."

The door opened as Eden uttered the last words. They turned to see Elizabeth standing there, leaning heavily on a cane.

"What's all the huddling about?" She demanded, closing the door and walking slowly towards them. The fall down the steps on Guy Fawkes Night had left her with a painful hip for which Dr. Ashton had given her some painkillers. When the weather was wet or humid, the pain increased considerably and she always had difficulty walking. However, today she appeared to be able to cope much better as she walked into the room. "If there is any trouble, I want to know about it."

They all glanced at one another. Martin stood up to help his stepmother to a comfortable chair near the dying embers in the fireplace. He placed a couple of coals on it quickly and returned to James' chair.

"It may be nothing at all, Mama." He said with a smile. "So, I shouldn't concern yourself with it."

"On the contrary," Elizabeth argued, "anything to do with life here concerns me. So . . . out with it!"

Eden bit back a smile at her bluntness. "Actually, Uncle Martin, perhaps Gran could help." He paused and turned his attention to Elizabeth, a flicker of hope in his eyes. "How good is your memory, Gran?"

She was a little taken aback and didn't speak for a moment. "It rather depends, Eden, on how long ago you wish me to remember?"

"Say to November, 1896?"

"Good gracious," she exclaimed, "that's over thirty years ago. Well, let me see, give me a little space to think." She was quiet while everyone waited expectantly for some words of optimism from her, but after a while she shook her head. "I seem to remember something about a disaster at the coal mine up north. I can vaguely remember what it was about. I think that my Jonathon with your father went up there as there was some kind of mine disaster. Some men were killed, as far as I can recollect and I believe they stayed for almost a fortnight, but when it took place completely eludes me." She paused, a light appearing in her eyes. "But, there is a way of finding out when it happened. When your father and I were married, Martin, I began to keep a journal. It wasn't for every day, I only noted things I considered important, like the birth and development of my darling Fern." She smiled at her attentive audience. "So, if you'd like to go through those journals it may just help. But before you do, would you please explain to me, now . . . just what you want to know?"

Martin nodded. "Of course, Mama. We want to know if James ever went to London during 1896. It's very important to have accurate information on this, as someone is claiming to take over Eden's inheritance of Ravenslea. It has been challenged that Eden is not the legal heir to the estate."

"What utter nonsense!" Elizabeth exclaimed, leaning forward indignantly. "Of course Eden's heir to Ravenslea—what on earth is this person talking about?"

"Well, until we find out from your journals or from some other source, we can't be absolutely certain!"

"I'm certain!" She flared, her eyes dark with fury. "How dare anyone think such a thing? Is he saying that James was . . . indiscreet during those years? If he is, then I know him to be wrong. James would never lower himself in such a way . . ."

Martin raised an eyebrow. "I agree, but it was a long time ago, Mama, James was much younger and probably vulnerable. It could have happened—it's not impossible. However, I do believe we should check out those journals before passing judgment."

Elizabeth paused before nodding her head in agreement. "Of course, Martin dear, you're right. I must not get myself all worked up over something I know could never happen. You'll have to go up into the attic. There's a padlocked black lacquered box. It's probably a bit heavy, so be careful bringing it down from the attic." Elizabeth warned. "I have the key to it in my bedroom, so when you bring it down you can get it."

"We'll be careful." Eden said. "Come on, Luke, between us we should be able to manage."

The two young men sprang to their feet and hurried from the Study. While they were gone, Martin rang a little bell on James' desk and a few moments later, Doris came into the room. He asked for some tea; she nodded and left closing the door gently behind her.

"Well, Mama," he said, leaning back in the chair, "let's hope this bears some fruit, for we were at our wits end when we found nothing in the cabinet for those years." He paused. "If Papa had been so diligent in keeping records, it does seem a little odd that there was no reference to going to London during those years."

"Could be," Rebecca suggested, "that was because Daddy didn't **go** to London—nobody from Ravenslea did and that this Gideon person is just a fortune hunter and a liar!"

"But the letter, dear," Catherine said, "there's no denying it exists, I saw it clearly."

"Some people are clever, Catherine," Martin said. "Who knows what lengths people will go to try and prove they have come into money by false accusations or even blackmail."

"It's all so unsettling." Rebecca murmured and moved towards the door. She opened it and peered upstairs anxiously. A lot of bumping and banging was audible and she shuddered. Her brothers were not always the most careful and the trapdoor into the attic was situated right outside her bedroom, the door of which she knew she'd left open. If one of them fell and landed in her room with a heavy box in his arms, he could not only hurt himself but also damage her beautiful antique writing desk located close to the door.

"Oh dear," Elizabeth said, suddenly leaning forward in her chair anxiously. "I do hope they're not damaging that box. My brother Robert and his wife Amy brought that back from a trip they made to Singapore a couple of years after they were married. To me it's one of my greatest treasures; I only wish I had room to keep it in my bedroom, but it's so large there's nowhere to really put it. I do hope they'll be extra careful."

"Don't worry, Mama," Martin said, tapping her hand gently, "I'm sure they'll bring it down without a scratch. They know quality when they see it."

"Well, I hope you're right; boys being boys, you know. I've kept that box in spotless condition all the years it's been in my care; it would be a crime if they were to drop it." Elizabeth said anxiously, not too convinced with her stepson's response.

They needn't have worried. Eden and Luke entered the Study a couple of minutes later. Although a thick layer of dust covered the lid and had collected at the hinges and metal clasp, the box itself was actually in extremely good shape. Gently, the two young men laid it on the floor beside their father's desk and at his grandmother's directions, Luke ran upstairs to bring the key.

There were so many journals of every size and description in that box and Rebecca, especially, was enthralled with all of them. She picked one up—it was for 1882 and thumbed gently through it. She was surprised to see her grandmother had once upon a time had a knack for description. The wording was clearly written and made for good reading. Rebecca considered the old lady would have been a great novelist had she taken up that career in her youth. If Gran would let her, she would love to take them all up to her room and read them. However, reading a journal dated 1882 wasn't the reason the box was now sitting on the floor in her father's Study.

"Here it is. It's the one for 1896." Luke said, raising a brown and white trimmed book that was neatly closed with a faded brown ribbon.

"Let me open it, dear." Elizabeth said. Luke handed it to her and sat on the side of her chair expectantly. She opened it at the first month and glanced quickly through it. She did this with each month until reaching September. Then she stopped. She glanced at everyone, a smile on her lips and a light coming into her eyes. Everyone sat quivering, watchful, wondering what it was she'd discovered. "Now I remember exactly what happened in 1896, though it wasn't in November!" She cried, laying the book in her lap. "It was as I said. I have it all written down here in quite a bit of detail. I can't believe I documented it so precisely. Your grandfather and a man named Charles Keeley jointly owned The Keeley Mine in Yorkshire. Your grandfather governed from Ravenslea, leaving the actual operation to Charles Keeley. Apparently, Keeley was cutting corners by keeping shoddy safety practices. One night two carts of coal, amounting to somewhere in the region of five tons, was being drawn up the steep ramp to the 5th Level when suddenly one of the pulleys snapped sending the two carts hurtling back down. Both carts jumped the rails knocking out three or four thick wooden posts that held up the tunnel. This resulted in the tunnel collapsing on about thirty miners all of whom, unfortunately, died." She glanced back at the book. "When your grandfather and James arrived at the Keeley mine, it was to find that Charles Keeley was dead. On realizing the seriousness of his lack of safety procedures at the Mill, he couldn't face the charges that would eventually be laid upon him that he would have to live with for the rest of his life, so he committed suicide. The mine still belongs jointly to the Keeleys and us, but James and Martin are now regarded as silent partners. The actually running of the mine is now under the management of Robert Keeley who, learning from his father's deadly error is making sure safety in the mine is of prime importance." She paused. "It seems that James left earlier at that time, to honour an important appointment at Lloyds in London, returning almost immediately to Ravenslea. All this occurred at the end of September, so," she snapped the book shut and placed it on her knee, "there you are . . . James was not in London in November of 1896—he was here at Ravenslea!"

"Oh, Gran!" Rebecca came over and hugged her, kissing her lightly on the brow. "You're a marvel. How fortunate you took the trouble to keep a journal. Then that letter has to be a fake." She looked triumphantly at Catherine, ran over and hugged her.

"We hope so, dear." Catherine said, her spirits rising. Not just because the inheritance will remain with Eden, but also because her beloved husband had not lied to her about his relationship with Lillian Rutledge.

Elizabeth grinned and patted her granddaughter's hand affectionately. "Well," she said, "perhaps now we have something concrete to tell this man when he comes to erroneously claim his rights to this wonderful house."

"We do indeed, Mama." Catherine said, laying an arm along the back of Elizabeth's seat. "We do indeed. If he causes any more problems, then we'll get Stephen to deal with it." Catherine didn't mention the fact that Gideon Rutledge could contest the journal as a falsehood, after all, it wasn't a legal document. She lay back in bed that night thinking that if what her mother-in-law had written was correct, there had to be documentation at the Keeley offices as well as the lawyers who handled the tragedy at that time, not to mention the appointment with Lloyds of London in September of that year.

Turning over in her bed and plumping up her pillows, she suddenly felt a wave of relief wash over her.

CHAPTER 27

BARNSTABLE

RAIN dappled against the grimy office window, paving a thin line from top to bottom clearing the dirt on its way down to the window ledge while a pale sliver of sunshine pushed its way into a light, airy office. A phone jangled imperiously on a desk that housed a disorganized clutter of papers, some of which fell to the floor as Detective Inspector Stanley Wilkins picked up the receiver. Pushing a hand through his thinning sandy hair, he spoke abruptly into it, not welcoming the intrusion.

"Stan," someone said, excitedly, at the other end of the line. "Tom Storm here. I've found the address of a man who owns a gun similar to the one you're searching for. It's registered to a Mr. Edgar Rutledge. Got a pencil handy?"

"Good morning, Sir. Go ahead." Stanley picked up a pencil stub from a well-worn, chipped coffee cup standing at the side of the phone, licked the small piece of lead at the end and poised it on a scrap of paper in front of him. Tom Storm was Stanley's Chief, a few years his senior, whose manner was always brisk; rarely showing emotion, so Stanley was quite taken aback by the upbeat tone of voice. Obviously it had been an ordeal trying to find this information, but it was a break-through and Stanley was looking forward to questioning this man.

Once he'd noted the address, he told the Chief he'd be on his way to interview him promptly that afternoon.

"Good man. I would have sent someone myself, but we're really shorthanded at the moment. Keep me posted." The Chief Inspector said.

"I'll certainly do that." Stanley said, lowering the phone back into its cradle thoughtfully. He leaned back in his chair. He wondered what this Edgar Rutledge was like; he could be a rough and ready man, just ripe for a fight, so to be on the safe side as he wasn't partial to fisticuffs, he'd take Sergeant Frank Owens with him knowing the hefty Welshman could pack a punch if one was required. He pressed the buzzer on his desk and asked one of the girls in the office to send Owens in immediately.

Sergeant Owens was a tall, husky man in his mid twenties. Born and raised in Cardiff, Frank Owens had lost his parents in a boating accident off the coast of Swansea when he was only three years old. Being pushed from one family member to another, then finally to an orphanage, he was a man who'd had to fight his way through his young life. A keen rugby player, Owens also dabbled in boxing, so a villain only had to take one look at him to know he was a formidable adversary—one perhaps they shouldn't provoke. Perceptive and intelligent, Stanley knew he would make a solid, sound thinking detective one of these days. He was pleased that he had him as a partner.

Frank Owens walked into the room and stood cautiously before Stanley. "Yes, Sir?"

"Sit down, Frank." Stanley waved to the chair in front of his desk. "We've got an assignment in . . ." He glanced down at the pad in front of him, "a small town called Watersfield. It's a few miles north of here. Do you know it?"

Owens shook his dark head. "No Sir. But I really don't know much of the terrain around that area. What's the scoop?"

"We have to question a man named Edgar Rutledge in relation to a gun he owns. It appears this gun was similar to the one used in the assault on James Thorncroft at the beginning of November."

Only the Detective Inspector knew that James had survived the attempted murder. He had told his staff that Captain Thorncroft was in a coma and it looked likely it would be terminal. It was better that way; the less who knew the truth, the more likely the perpetrator would slip up. He looked over at Owens who was studying him intently. "I'm hoping a good talk with Rutledge will close the case and we can go home and enjoy a good, quiet Christmas." He said this lightly, not really believing that the case could end so easily.

Owens lifted his wide shoulders. "So, what's the next move, Sir?"

"You and I are going to Watersfield to talk to this man Rutledge this afternoon. Find out what he knows."

"But, you remember, you asked me to search for records of missing persons . . . in relation to the young woman who went missing last week."

"I'll give that assignment to someone else. This is far more important now."

"Yes, Sir." Sergeant Frank Owens stood up. "Perhaps Miller could do it, he's helping me and knows how far I've got. What time are you leaving?"

"After a bit of lunch then we'll be on our way; so be ready."

A little after one thirty that afternoon, the two plain clothed men climbed into an unmarked police vehicle and headed north. By now the rain had worsened. The slow windscreen wipers were having a tough job clearing the way for Stanley to see the road ahead, making visibility difficult at best, so their timing was slow. They didn't arrive in Watersfield until close to four and as neither knew their way to the address given them, they decided to register somewhere for the night before going any further.

It had obviously been market day in the main street that day. Some of the stalls were gone while others were being dismantled and sweepers were busy tidying up the remains of fruit, vegetables and other debris littered around the area.

They watched for a little while, then began searching for a place to stay. It took them no time at all to find a small picturesque Inn at the edge of the village. They went inside. It was warm and cosy and the first thing they did was order two beers from the bar.

The following morning after a light breakfast, the Detective and his sergeant searched the map to find the address the Chief Inspector had given them. Frenchay Road was a few miles to the east of Watersfield. Traffic was fairly light, so by ten thirty the two men had located the address—a small thatched cottage surrounded by a paint-peeled white wooden fence, complete with matching gate with a broken latch that slipped at an odd angle as they pushed it open. The gardens were overgrown with weeds and the cultivated flowers were having a hard job surviving. Moving quickly up the narrow pathway, Stanley lifted the brass lion's head knocker and rapped on the door.

A shuffling of feet and the door was opened by a woman of about fifty.

"I am Detective Inspector Stanley Wilkins of the Barnstable constabulary." Stanley explained pulling out his identity wallet. "Would it be possible to speak to Mr. Edgar Rutledge?"

She frowned. "If you'd care to wait, I'll see if he's available." She said, begrudgingly.

"This is an official visit, Madam. We need to speak to him immediately on a matter of some urgency. Would you please let him know we're here."

Hesitating slightly, she finally opened the door wider, allowing them entrance into a small parlour where a cat was sitting on the window ledge licking itself nonchalantly.

"Wait here for a moment, please."

Frank Owens moved over to the cat, having a fondness for the animals, and stroked its fur gently. He could feel the throbbing purr beneath his fingers and smiled. At least it didn't hiss at him as some other cats had done on occasion.

After a few moments, the door opened again and an elderly man walked into the room. "Good day, gentlemen. I am Edgar Rutledge." He said, his voice guarded, but pleasant. "My housekeeper says you wish to speak to me?"

"Good morning, Mr. Rutledge." Stanley studied him quickly. He was a good judge of character and this man seemed edgy, despite his friendly greeting.

"Please sit down, both of you." Edgar Rutledge indicated a couple of seats at a round wooden table near the window and sat opposite.

"I'll get straight to the point, Mr. Rutledge. We are here on official business and need to know your whereabouts on the night of November 5th."

The man frowned as if in deep thought. "Well, let me think. There was a firework display on the village green which I attended. From there I came home and as far as I can remember, I went straight to bed as it was quite late. I tire easily now, you see. I am eighty years old and rarely stay up at night much past nine o'clock. What is this about?"

"Were you in the vicinity of Ravenslea Manor near Branton that night?"

"Ravenslea Manor? I've never heard of the place—why on earth would I go all the way up to Branton at that time of night. No, Detective Inspector, as I just told you, I went to the village green to watch the fireworks, then returned home where I stayed for the rest of the evening."

"Hmm." Stanley paused. "Do you have anyone to substantiate your story?"

He shrugged. "I live here with my grandson, who was away that night, Detective Inspector, and my housekeeper left early. So, no. I don't have anyone to verify I was, indeed, here."

Sergeant Owens scribbled the information into a notebook and looked guardedly at the man.

"I see," Stanley said. "On another tack, Mr. Rutledge. Do you own a gun?"

"A gun? Well, yes I do; quite a few as a matter of fact. Are you interested in purchasing one, Detective Inspector? I have some here that I could certainly recommend."

"No, Sir, I'm not in the market for a gun." Stanley said, dryly. "However, we are interested in one particular kind of gun and we're under the impression that you own a .38 Smith and Wesson. Is that true?"

"I did, Detector Inspector, but it was stolen."

"Did you report the theft to the Police?"

The man shrugged, but once again Stanley's keen eyes detected that Rutledge seemed edgy.

"Well, no, I actually didn't. I realize that's quite remiss of me, but the thing is, someone broke into my home. It wasn't until I came down the next morning that I noticed the gun was missing. I was naturally upset to think that someone had the audacity to break into my home. It's such these days that law abiding citizens aren't safe even in their own homes."

"Quite." Stanley said. "When did this happen?"

"I'm not entirely sure. It was definitely before Guy Fawkes night, but how long before I really couldn't say."

Sergeant Owens quickly scribbled something in his notepad. "Having a gun stolen, Mr. Rutledge, should alert you that the reason someone wants a gun is usually for mischief." He said

"I realize that, but there's nothing I could have done about it. I'm sorry I didn't report it, but you see, I do suffer lapses of memory once in a while—it goes with the territory of getting older, young man. One of these days, you'll find out for yourself how awkward it is to be a little forgetful."

"Yes," Stanley said, feeling a surge of impatience with this man. He had the uncanny feeling he knew a lot more than he was telling them and this 'forgetfulness' was possibly a deception. An elderly man can always fall back on lapses of memory when a situation becomes too difficult for him to handle.

"Would you like to see my collection, Detective Inspector?" Rutledge asked. Not waiting for a reply he stood up and walked towards a cabinet set into a nearby wall. He opened it to display a large collection of pistols. "As you see I am a collector. Most of these guns have never been used, at least not in the last forty odd years. I doubt, in fact, if any of them would work."

"Do you have ammunition?" Stanley asked with genuine interest. He'd never seen such a large display, except in a museum.

"Indeed I do, Sir." Rutledge said, opening a drawer and bringing out some cartridges and single bullets from open-ended boxes. "I've kept these pistols along with the bullets for most of my life. If you wish to check them yourself, you'll see they've not been fired in years."

"Umm." Stanley said. "You certainly have a good selection, but our main concern right now is the whereabouts of the gun you had stolen."

"The Smith and Wesson. Well, I used it once about six months ago, to kill some rats in my garden shed. I didn't have any rat poison at the time and thought this might just do the trick. It did, but it's an expensive and noisy way to get rid of vermin, so I purchased some poison which also does the job extremely well."

"Where did you get a Smith and Wesson?"

"It belonged to my father. He told me that he went over to America some years ago and purchased it while there." Rutledge closed the cupboard and faced him. "Look, Detective Inspector, where is this all leading. You're asking me a lot of questions, which I'm answering as best I can, but now I think you owe me some kind of explanation."

"You take the newspaper, I gather?" Rutledge nodded. "Then you must have read about the attempted murder of Captain James Thorncroft of Ravenslea Manor on the night of November 5th."

"I did indeed, Sir. A dreadful thing! I didn't know the man personally, but now that you mention his name, I have heard of him. I wasn't aware he had a home near Branton." He paused and Stanley noticed him catch his lower lip slightly anxiously. "Have you any clues as to who would do such a terrible thing, Sir? I don't think I've seen anything in the newspapers since reading about it when it occurred."

Ignoring the request for information on clues, Stanley forged ahead with his reason for meeting with Rutledge in the first place. "Our investigation is ongoing, Mr. Rutledge. As a .38 Smith and Wesson gun was involved, we ascertained that as you own such a weapon, we naturally are curious to have it analyzed in case the bullet fired from it came from your gun."

Rutledge shrugged, shaking his grey head. "Well, I'm sorry, but as I told you before, it is no longer in my possession. If some maniac used my weapon to harm Captain Thorncroft, I certainly hope you wouldn't incriminate me in any way, after all, I imagine there are many guns of that calibre around Devon and Cornwall."

"Unless other similar weapons have not been registered, it appears yours is the only one accounted for in this area. It is most urgent that we locate it and by doing so, perhaps eliminate your involvement in this crime." Stanley made to leave the room, when he suddenly turned. "Just one more thing. Do you have a copy of the registration? If you do, I'd very much like to see it."

Rutledge hesitated. "I do have a registration—I keep a record of all my weapons. If you'd like to wait a moment, I'll see if I can find it." He shuffled slowly out of the room, carefully closing the door behind him.

Stanley and his sergeant waited a couple of minutes then stared at each other. Both had the same thought. Rutledge was an elderly man, but they felt he was fitter than he at first appeared. Quickly, they moved through the door to see him moving quickly along a passageway, through a door and into the morning sunlight.

Edgar Rutledge stumbled hurriedly towards the side of the house.

"You go that way, we'll head him off behind his shed, as that seems to be the way he's going." Stanley said, his voice low. "Try not to let him hear you. Surprise is what we need right now."

Owens nodded and skirted across the damp scraggy lawn while Detective Inspector Wilkins moved in the opposite direction. By the time Stanley had turned the corner of the house, he saw Rutledge getting into a black vehicle.

"Here Owens!" He yelled and Frank came running. "Stop!" Stanley cried. "You'll not get far, Mr. Rutledge. You'd better get out and tell us what's going on!"

Edgar Rutledge pulled the starter button, but the vehicle only spluttered and stopped.

"Mr. Rutledge, you'd better get out; you're only making matters worse for yourself."

Giving a sigh of defeat, Edgar Rutledge climbed from the driver's seat and closed the door resolutely behind him.

"All right, Detective Inspector. I should have told you before, but I didn't want to become involved. Come back into the house and I'll tell you what you wish to know."

Mary the housekeeper was aghast to see the pallor on her employer's face as they all returned to the parlour. The cat sent them a cautious look, turned to lick its paw and returned to the sleep mode.

"What are you trying to do to this old man?" Mary said, irritably. "He's not been well over the past few months and doesn't need people like you hounding him like this?"

"We weren't hounding him, Madam," Stanley said, "we merely wished to ask him some questions. He obviously has some reason not to come clean with us, hence the reason he ran to the vehicle. We had no intention of upsetting him."

"Get us some tea, Mary." Rutledge said, wearily.

The woman made some grumbling noises, but did as she was bid, moving quickly in through the door which obviously led to the kitchen area of the little house.

"Well, now perhaps, Mr. Rutledge, you'll explain a little more truthfully about the gun and its whereabouts?" Stanley Wilkins sat back in the chair he'd vacated only moments before.

Gideon Rutledge telephoned promptly on Saturday evening as planned. An arrangement was made for him to come to Ravenslea Manor the following Tuesday evening. Catherine was not looking forward to the altercation, as she knew that was what it would be, yet the conflict had to be faced. It was odd that Gideon Rutledge had divulged this fantastic disclosure to them, for surely he'd know they'd check and recheck it before agreeing to relinquish their hold on Ravenslea Manor. Catherine knew they'd never do that without a formidable fight!

Martin had finally been able to contact his cousin, Stephen Hallett who was horrified to think that someone was so cunning as to come up with such a ruse. He told Martin he had every intention of thwarting Gideon Rutledge's claim.

The following day when Catherine went to the hospital, she gave James an update on what had been happening and he was furious; she'd never seen him so upset and for a moment she was troubled by his attitude. Why would he be so irate when it seemed the episode would mean nothing; Ravenslea would remain in the Thorncroft's hands for Eden when the time came.

"I think, James," she said at one point, "you're going to have to tell me what's causing this dreadful anxiety on your part. Is there something that you've not told me that perhaps you feel you should?"

He looked at her. He loved her with all his heart—he didn't want to lose her, yet he knew that eventually it would all come out. He had been with Lily in those far-off days of his youth and Catherine, as his wife, had to know the truth. He calmed down, laid back against the pillows and tapped the side of the bed. She joined him, and he clutched her cool hand in his.

"My love," he began, "no-one at Ravenslea knows anything about what I'm about to tell you. I'd like to keep it that way. I have deceived you long enough. I thought that by not mentioning it, it would die a natural death. Obviously, that is not the case." He sighed. "You mentioned earlier if I could remember anything about 1896? Well, as a matter of fact, I do. My father and I had to go up to Yorkshire. There was some trouble at our mine. At the same time, or thereabouts, we had been having problems with one of our overseas investments. To cut a rather long story short, I left Yorkshire alone halfway through our visit to keep an appointment with one of our financial advisors at Lloyds in London. After this, I decided to stay for a day or two. I'd never been to London except when I was a schoolboy with my parents, so this was an opportunity to see the City without encumbrances. I was free to do as I wished." He sighed. "I went to see a number of the usual tourist sights and then one night I decided, as I was at a loose end, I'd take in a nightclub. There I met the lead singer at the show, her name was Lily. She was a few years older than I and I was flattered to think that she'd look twice at me. In fact, she looked more than twice at me. She singled me out at the end of her performance and invited me backstage to her dressing room for a drink. I remember she stepped behind a screen to change her stage costume. I thought, 'this isn't so bad—she seems decent enough to a chap like me.'" James paused and coughed. "At first I was nervous having never encountered such a woman before in my life. At one point she plied me with all kinds of drinks, but when she wasn't looking, I managed to tip some drinks into a nearby potted plant. I don't know if that poor plant ever survived the amount of different kinds of liquor with which I doused it, but it most certainly saved me. You see, dear, I felt she was getting a little too amorous and, to be honest, I found it very difficult trying to act gentlemanly around her."

Catherine felt her pulse quicken. "Go on, dear—this is most fascinating." She said, her voice low.

James shrugged; "There's nothing more to say. Nothing sordid happened as I only stayed in her dressing room. So we didn't end up in bed together. When she suddenly asked if I would like to return to her flat after her performance, I realized this was something I might not be able to get out of, so I made an excuse to leave." He suddenly laughed. "If any other chap of my age had been there, I'm sure he'd think I was completely mad but I remember thinking of Ravenslea and envisioned risks of a scandal hovering over my head. I couldn't do that to my family. So, you see, everything was really quite innocent."

"Did you ever write a letter to this . . . Lily Starr?" She had to ask, eager to see his response.

He thought for a moment. "Well, I don't know if you could actually call it a letter, dear. I just scribbled a little note to her telling her that I was returning to Ravenslea and wouldn't be able to see her again. That's all, why?"

"I'll tell you later, dear, once I've discussed this with Martin."

"When is this chap visiting you?" He asked as she pulled away from the bed. "I'll not rest easy until I know the charlatan has been told in no uncertain terms that he cannot intimidate the Thorncrofts in such a flimsy manner."

"On Tuesday evening next at seven thirty."

"You must come to the hospital promptly on Wednesday morning, then. I have to know what went on."

"I will, darling." She leaned over to kiss him. "Now I must go. I'll see you again tomorrow, same time."

CHAPTER 28

A THIN sliver of light shone around the partially open door. The old building smelled musty as Stanley entered through the wooden, paint-peeled door. Shutting it behind him, he slowly climbed well-worn steps with the chipped wooden banister beneath his hand, wincing and wrinkling his nose with distaste. 'I'll never complain about my office again,' he thought, 'at least I have a good sized window to look out of.' How anyone can do a decent days work surrounded by such decaying odours and paint peeled woodwork, was beyond him. It was about time the County came up with another location for the Criminology Department.

He stopped before a door with a frosted half window and pushed it open. The room was as expected, dimly lit from a couple of single bulbs hanging from frayed cords below a questionably painted ceiling. Cabinets lined the walls with various quantities of papers, books, old dried up inkwells and other office equipment overloaded on top. A few slips of paper were on the floor with footprints on them indicating that as they were of no use, why bother picking them up. In the centre of the room, a thin, balding man in his late fifties looked up from a table and waved for him to enter.

"Good to see you, Stan." He said, looking over his wire-rimmed spectacles. "I have some interesting findings for you."

"What Vincent?" Stanley peered over the older man's shoulders to where a gun rested on a stained white cloth. "That the gun that was found in Webb's hand?"

Vincent Barrow nodded. "Yes and if you look here . . ." he leaned forward to the handle of the gun, "see, there's one set of prints, very well defined. There's another print on the trigger, matching the one on the handle; when we checked the files, we could tell without a doubt it was Webb's index finger. He had a deep scar across the top of all his fingers on his right hand, probably due to an accident earlier in his life. Fortunately, the imprint is quite deep, which shows without any doubt that Webb did fire the gun . . . but only once. However, if you look through the microscope, you can see another print slightly off centre on the trigger to one side but partly over the top of Webb's. The newer one, luckily, is fairly pronounced. I had my staff check the known offenders and we've come up empty. So we can only presume the second print must belong to the person who shot Bernard Webb." Barrow looked up meaningfully. "From this evidence, we can't rule out murder, Stan. To all intents and purposes, by the way the gun was in Webb's hand when we found him, it all pointed to the fact that he'd committed suicide. The other print obviously has to rule that idea out."

Stanley took a deep breath and nodded grimly. "I thought as much. I just couldn't find a reason why Webb, who'd not long been released from prison, would shoot someone then take his own life like that." Stanley looked at Vincent Barrow with admiration. "I don't know what the force would do without you; you always manage to come through for us." He moved away thoughtfully. "It now remains for us to locate the owner of the second finger print."

"You have a suspect?" Barrow said, standing up from the table and laying a hand on his lower back from the effort.

Stanley nodded. "Quite possibly. Tomorrow I'm hoping to get a sample that matches the top print—if I do, then I think we'll have our man!"

The rain of yesterday had dissipated and a watery sun shone on the little cottage at Watersfield as Stanley Wilkins and Frank Owens arrived. It had been raining earlier for certain, as although the path was dry, the foliage that leaned over the pathway dripped water on them as they passed. A fresh smell of damp earth greeted them. As if they were expected, the front door opened as they approached. Mary, the housekeeper, stood there frowning in apprehension.

"Good morning, Detective Inspector. If you're looking for Mr. Rutledge, he's relaxing in the parlour." She paused and opened the door wider. "If you wish to speak to him, I'd like to offer you both a cup of tea?"

"That would be kind, thank you." Stanley smiled at her, slipping off his trilby. Frank Owens did the same as they stepped inside the warm entranceway. She didn't return the smile, but Stanley was used to that. He was always amused by the way he was greeted by people. Some, reluctant to say anything; some wary and unapproachable; others, more congenial, though those were not common.

Edgar Rutledge turned as the door opened and from the light from the window, Stanley was sure he registered fear, but it could have been a trick of the light.

"No, don't get up." Stanley motioned for the old man to return to his seat as he was half-way out of the chair.

"Thank you. Do take a seat, Detective Inspector." Rutledge said. "How is the investigation going?"

Stanley shrugged. "Slowly, I'm afraid. But . . . we haven't come here to discuss the case. I was thinking about the guns you have here, Mr. Rutledge and was wondering if you're still game for me to purchase one?" He paused. "It's not for me, actually, it's for my nephew. He's taken up target shooting and is in the market for a gun. As you seemed keen to sell me one on my first visit here, I would like to see what you have that my nephew might be able to purchase." Stanley wasn't used to lying, but had to get some fingerprints somehow and felt in this case it was warranted.

"Oh, couldn't your nephew have come with you?"

Stanley shook his head. "No, he lives in Milford Haven which is too far to come just to purchase a gun. He trusts my judgment to find just the right weapon for him. Not that I know too much about old pistols like these, but I remembered that you, being an expert, could perhaps point me towards the right one for him."

"Well, I do have quite a variety, as you know." Rutledge pushed back his chair, just as his housekeeper came in with a tray of tea for the visitors. His manner seemed less tense as he smiled at them. "Oh, Mary, thank you dear. Would you like tea before we look at the guns, Detective Inspector."

"Thank you, yes. It's a might cold outside and a warm cup of tea will definitely do something to warm us up? Don't you agree, Sergeant?"

"Oh, indeed, yes sir—I'm quite partial to the odd cup of tea." Owens mentioned dryly. If only the Detective Inspector knew how much he longed for a draft right now!

Mary was pleased and her eyes lit up, taking away the grim look of a while ago.

"Good, good." Rutledge said, reseating himself. "Do make yourself comfortable."

After twenty minutes of supping tea, eating home-baked biscuits and chatting informally, Stanley managed to put the man more at ease.

"What type of gun are you looking for?" Rutledge asked after a while.

"Not sure." Stanley replied. "What do you recommend?"

"Well," Rutledge pursed his mouth in thought. "If your nephew's into target practice, I have a good Colt .45 here that might be suitable." He suddenly turned and offered both men a slightly lop-sided grin. "Father brought back a Derringer too . . . though I don't think that would be what he's looking for, do you?"

Stanley smiled back. "Probably not. The Colt sounds alright to me."

When Rutledge handed him the gun from the barrel, Stanley was careful not to touch the area, duly accepting it from the handle. Turning it around in his hand, showing interest, he said he'd take it and gently placed it in his pocket. He had no desire to rub whatever prints he could with the lining of his pocket.

"What do I owe you, Mr. Rutledge?" Stanley asked, reaching into his inside jacket pocket and pulling out a wallet.

Rutledge shook his head and waved his hands. "For the moment, I'd rather you wait to see if your nephew is happy with your choice. If he's not, then you can just bring it back to me. If he is, then we can come to some agreement as regards price at a later date."

"Thank you, Mr. Rutledge, I will let you know later." Stanley turned to Frank Owens who was stroking the fur of the cat who had now decided to sit on the side of his chair. "Come along, Owens, it's time we left."

As Mary opened the door they both thanked her for the tea and walked from the cottage.

As he stepped into his vehicle, Stanley hoped they hadn't wasted their time with this man for if this fingerprint didn't work, it meant they were on the wrong track and the whole matter would have to be reinvestigated.

On the optimistic side, with Rutledge's more relaxed mood this time, he wouldn't have suspected the real reason for Stanley's interest in the gun.

That evening, the Thorncrofts received another phone call. This was from Detective Inspector Stanley Wilkins.

"Mrs. Thorncroft," he said. "Would it be an inconvenience if I dropped around to see you in about half an hour? I do have some rather interesting information for you."

Catherine's heart quickened. "Of course, Detective Inspector. We'll all be here. In half an hour then?"

She replaced the receiver and took a deep breath. The Detective Inspector had sounded excited. She hoped it was to their advantage.

"Detective Inspector Wilkins will be here shortly," she said to the family who'd convened in the Drawing Room. "He says he has something interesting to tell us."

Martin's brows lifted and he smiled, laying the book he was reading in his lap. "Well, perhaps this Gideon person has actually confessed and we don't have to worry any more."

"That would be a miracle, Uncle." Eden said, dryly. "Anyway, we can't speculate."

Detective Inspector Stanley Wilkins was prompt, arriving precisely half an hour later. He was shown into the Drawing Room

"You have us entirely mystified as to what you have to tell us, Detective Inspector." Martin said. "Would you like a sherry or port before you begin?"

"A sherry would be fine, thank you." Stanley Wilkins perched himself on an upright wing-backed chair and faced them, while Eden poured him a sherry, laying it gently beside him on a small table. "Now, as you know I've been on the lookout for a gun that would fire the kind of bullet that shot Captain Thorncroft. The bullet, apparently, came from a .38 Smith and Wesson revolver. We have since had constabularies searching this neighbourhood and others in this vicinity in an effort to locate gunsmiths with records of selling such a weapon. We came up with about ten, all of whom have been contacted." He paused to take a sip of the rich brown liquid, laying the glass back on the table. "Now to the interesting bit. One of the guns was registered to an Edgar Rutledge who lives in a little town called Watersfield near Barnstable. We have now contacted him and after a long while, he has told us some quite interesting facts."

"Rutledge?" Catherine asked. "It seems a coincidence that our recent visitor had the same name?" She also couldn't stop thinking of Lillian Rutledge!

"That's what we were thinking, Mrs. Thorncroft." Stanley commented.

"Then, perhaps that would mean that either this man or his son was the person responsible for shooting my brother." Martin shifted forward in his seat. This situation was appearing to be getting somewhere at last.

The Detective Inspector shook his head. "Not necessarily. At first, Rutledge told us he'd had the gun stolen and when we asked to see the registration of the gun, he tried to make a quick escape. By the way, the Gideon to whom you're referring, would probably be his grandson, as Edgar Rutledge is eighty years old. Anyway, on catching and bringing him back to his house, he finally told us he loaned the gun to another party, though said he didn't know why the man wanted it. That, in itself, sounded quite suspicious—not something a thinking man would do, in my opinion." Stanley said, shaking his head. "However, we managed to coax the man's name out of Rutledge—a Bernard Webb, whose body was found at the perimeter of Ravenslea Manor by you, Mrs. Thorncroft." She nodded, "Does anyone here know such a person?"

Everyone in the room stared at each other and all of them shook their heads, almost in unison.

"So," Stanley continued, "this man was not known to you. If that's the case, then there doesn't seem to be much of a reason for him to try to kill Captain Thorncroft? Unless it was for monetary gain; in other words he appears to have been a hired assassin!"

Martin frowned. "It sounds feasible, Detective, but from what you've told us so far, this Edgar Rutledge seems an intelligent, scheming individual despite his advancing years. Could it be that he and his grandson were trying to put you off the scent. It could have been him or Gideon who fired the gun and this Webb person was not involved at all. Perhaps Webb happened to be in the woods watching the fireworks and the killer saw a chance to exonerate himself."

"An interesting theory." Stanley said. "It could be as you say, but until we get some evidence to the contrary, we have to go with what we've learned so far for the time being." He suddenly sighed, running a hand through his sparse hair. "I was hoping it would be all over and done with by now, but it seems the mystery intends to continue."

"There could be someone who might throw some light on this." Rebecca piped up. She was sitting beside Luke on the arm of his chair. "Elspeth! Agnes and Doris said that she acted really oddly on that horrible night. I was wondering if, perhaps, she would have some knowledge of this Webb person?"

Martin raised his eyebrows. "Well, it's worth a try, I suppose." He glanced at Luke. "See if Elspeth's in the Kitchen, Luke. If she is, tell her she's wanted in the Drawing Room."

Luke nodded, returning a few minutes later. When she walked into the room, she seemed extremely nervous. She was having a hard time keeping from twisting her hands in front of her as she was faced with the family and the Detective Inspector.

"I . . . understand you wish to speak to me?" She said, trying desperately to steady her hands as everyone turned their attention towards her.

Stanley Wilkins moved forward. "We just want to ask you a few questions . . .

Elspeth?" She nodded, pressing her lips firmly together. "All we want to know is this. Did you recognize the man who shot Captain Thorncroft on Guy Fawkes Night?"

She faced him squarely, her shoulders back, her chin jutting out slightly. "I most certainly did not! The man ran passed me without a word and I didn't see his face. If I know him, I certainly didn't recognize him. If I had, Detective, I certainly wouldn't have kept that information to myself."

"When you received the phone call that night . . . what did the person say at the other end?"

"I . . . I really can't remember. It was noisy outside with all the fireworks, you see, and, well, he did seem quite in earnest. I just said I'd find Captain James and bring him to the phone immediately." Elspeth could feel her heart racing at the dreadful lies she was telling. There had been no call. She'd just taken the phone off the hook as her brother had asked but now she knew she had to be careful—this could snowball completely out of control if she didn't watch what she was saying in front of this obviously shrewd detective.

"Ah," the Detective Inspector said raising an eyebrow, "so it was a man on the other end of the line?"

"Yes," Elspeth said. She had to be careful here, because of course, there was no-one on the other end. "His voice was quite muffled, so it was difficult to hear him properly."

"Are you sure you didn't recognize the voice?" Stanley insisted.

"No, I didn't."

"Well, thank you, Elspeth. If you think of anything—anything at all, that might throw some light on this puzzle, please contact me." Stanley reached inside his jacket pocket and drew out a small card. "Here's my telephone number at Barnstable Constabulary. I can be reached at any time."

Hesitating slightly, she took the card from him and nodded. "Anything I can do to help will be topmost on my list, Detective Inspector. Now, if you don't need me any more, I must attend to some things in the Kitchen."

Once Elspeth had left the room and the door had been closed, Stanley Wilkins moved around the room, the back of one hand tapping gently against the palm of the other behind his back, his head stooped in concentration.

"Umm." He murmured. "I don't know if any of you noticed, but I had the distinct feeling the housekeeper was keeping something from us." He glanced around quickly. "Did anyone else get that impression?"

There was a general searching of faces, until Eden broke the silence. "As a matter of fact, I did, Detective Inspector. It was when you asked about the phone call she'd received. She seemed a little evasive. It wasn't really anything she said, just the manner she presented herself."

Stanley nodded. "My thoughts exactly, Mr. Thorncroft." He smiled. "You'd make a good detective, young man. Have you ever thought of joining the force?"

Eden grinned engagingly. "No. It's really not my vocation in life to be tramping around the streets, possibly getting attacked or even killed in the line of duty. I'm afraid I rather like the life I'm living here."

Stanley shrugged. "Just a thought. I too felt that Elspeth was hiding something. I think I'm going to have someone watch her, surreptitiously of course, until I can be certain it wasn't just nerves giving me that impression."

"I've never known Elspeth have a fit of nerves before, Detective Inspector." Catherine said. "She's always shown her mettle in everything she does. She watches the Kitchen staff like a hawk for any misdemeanours."

Martin agreed. "Yes. That's one of the reasons why we have kept her. Not only that but she's quite daunting to any vagrants who happen to come here for handouts or anything else."

Stanley moved towards the door. "Well, I may have some leads in this case. I'll keep in touch and . . . when you've talked with Gideon Rutledge on Tuesday, Mrs. Thorncroft, I'd like you to give me as much information as you can on the outcome." He picked up his trilby and opened the door. "In the meantime, keep your eyes and ears open for anything that you consider is in any way suspicious. If you do, I'd appreciate if you'd contact me." He reached into his jacket pocket again and handed Catherine one of his cards. "I'm in the office most of the day, but if I happen to be out, someone will get hold of me."

Catherine showed him the front entrance and after dispensing with the usual salutations, closed the door behind him.

As she entered the Drawing Room, she suddenly wondered if, in fact, Elspeth **was** hiding something. She remembered vividly the day she had seen her in Branton with that strange man and also the girl in the house earlier. Was it possible the same man was responsible for pulling the trigger that could have, so easily, caused James' death. She shuddered. He'd come so close . . . thank God James had moved when he did. Anything else would have been too dreadful to think about..

CHAPTER 29

Elspeth felt a wave of faintness engulf her and she clung tightly to the side of the Drawing Room door frame for fear of falling. She knew nothing good usually came from eavesdropping, but when the Detective Inspector had arrived and she'd shown him into the Drawing Room, she hid in a dark area beside the door. She could hear everything that was being said and when her brother's name had been mentioned she became alert. She knew her face registered shock at hearing that her brother had not only shot the Captain, but had been killed himself. It took a moment for her to gain her composure enough to move unsteadily away. She'd stumbled back towards the Kitchen but veered away. She had to go to her room for a moment to steady her nerves.

She hurried to the back of the house and once inside the safety of her quarters, she took some deep breaths to try to quell the rapid beating of her heart. Bernard dead! She shivered uneasily. She'd never been overly close to her older brother, but this turn in events had shaken her dramatically. She felt physically sick.

Going over to the wash basin she sprinkled some tepid water over her face and pulled a clean towel from the drawer beside it. It helped clear her head.

She knew now that she had to work to convince the Thorncrofts that Bernard's death meant nothing to her. She must not be found out as an accomplice, even though she had had no knowledge of his deadly plan.

Taking another deep breath, Elspeth straightened her shoulders, stared in the mirror at her wan colour and moved out of the room back to the Kitchen.

Agnes and Doris were busy clearing up after dinner. Both turned at her entrance.

"So, Elspeth, what happened in the Drawing Room?" Agnes looked up at her. "Did the Detective ask you a lot of questions?"

She caught her lip, desperately trying not to show any emotion. "Policeman are nosy devils; of course he asked questions. What copper doesn't? But I told him everything I could remember about that night. I believe he was satisfied."

Doris raised one dark eyebrow and glanced quickly at Agnes. "Just one thing we were wondering, Elspeth. What made you rush through the Kitchen in that way?"

Elspeth wasn't expecting that and for a moment became slightly agitated. "Did I? Well, I was extremely upset, of course, as we all were. I felt sick and just wanted some air—that's all. Nothing sinister in that, is there?"

Agnes shook her head. "Of course not. Don't think we're accusing you of anything; it was just odd that you didn't say anything and you also didn't come back for quite a while afterwards."

"What is this . . . an interrogation? Are you saying that I knew something that I'm not admitting to?"

"No," Agnes said, though deep down she felt that Elspeth was not telling the absolute truth. "We were just wondering . . ."

"Well, stop 'wondering', and start thinking about who could have done this terrible deed. Did either of you see the face of the person who ran through here?"

Agnes shook her head. "No, I was busy making pastry. It happened so quickly, I didn't see a thing."

"Well then, I don't suppose the Detective will want to talk to you."

Agnes didn't answer.

"What about you, Doris?" Elspeth asked.

"Well, there was just one thing." Doris said. "As he rushed passed, he stumbled against me in his haste and I smelled whisky on his person. At least I think it was whisky—it was certainly some kind of liquor. He certainly didn't smell very pleasant."

Elspeth frowned. "Well, I suppose that's a good point, Doris. Perhaps you should tell the police this little bit of information. Maybe they'll rush out and pick him up just on that point alone." She said it with a slight sneer in her voice. Elspeth was proud of herself. Thankfully, she began to feel calmer; her old character was returning. She had a feeling that now she'd be able to handle anything the police or anyone else asked her.

"Oh, I wouldn't say that," Doris was saying, the sneer going over her head, "I'm sure there are a lot of men who drink whisky and other spirits. It would be a very clever policeman indeed, who could find the gunman just by that one instance."

After Detective Inspector Wilkins left that evening, the family spent the rest of the time in speculative discussion of the day's events, especially on Elspeth's answers to the questions directed at her. By one o'clock, everyone, except Eden, had retired to their rooms. He had no desire to sleep; his thoughts strayed to his relationship with Stephanie. Nothing had been said to either family, mainly because it was so soon after Rebecca's engagement to William. He wanted his sister to be settled before he announced his and Stephanie's intentions.

Sighing, he moved leisurely towards the long latticed window in the Drawing Room and looked outside at the inky darkness, speckled with stars in a cloudless sky. Staring out into the night, he suddenly recalled his and Stephanie's meeting at Piper's Head the day after the disastrous misconception at Ravenslea. It was now resolved, of course, to his absolute satisfaction, but in retrospect, the confusion could have so easily been avoided if he'd thought to ride over to Cavendish Hall to meet with her. He'd not enjoyed Christiana's company that day and was annoyed with himself for not following up on his first phone call to Stephanie. He realized he shouldn't be thinking of this any longer as despite the mistake he made, his dream had come to fruition. Stephanie loved him as he adored her. That was all that mattered to him now.

He absently pushed a strand of hair out of line of vision as the Grandfather clock in the hall chimed two o'clock. Yawning, he decided he'd better go to bed. He poured himself a glass of whisky before leaving the room; that usually made him drowsy enough for him to sleep.

As he quietly opened the Drawing Room door, he noticed a figure standing at the bottom of the stairs. Someone was using the telephone. Feeling slightly uncomfortable as to cross the Hallway now would alert the person, he moved silently behind the door. Keeping it open as he was curious as to why anyone would be using the phone at such an hour in the morning, he decided to listen. He frowned when he recognized Elspeth's low toned voice speaking into the mouthpiece quietly.

"Hello." Her voice was hardly audible. "Sorry to wake you at such an hour." She paused as someone obviously was speaking at the other end. "I have to talk to you . . . now, if you can meet me. It's extremely important . . ." Pause, ". . . all right. I'll meet you there in about half an hour." She replaced the receiver and quietly disappeared towards the back of the house.

Eden stayed where he was for a moment, his heart pounding uneasily. He wondered if the housekeeper had some knowledge of his father's attack or something that had transpired while talking to the Detective had worried her. Now he had no reason to go to bed. Lightly running up the stairs to his room, Eden donned some warm outer clothes and moved partly back down the stairs. His intention was to see who Elspeth was meeting; perhaps this was the break everyone needed to find out who, indeed, was involved in his father's murderous assault.

Within a few minutes, Elspeth appeared again, dressed in the familiar heavy black coat and hat. She used a rolled umbrella as a walking stick and in her other hand she held a torch. When she disappeared through the front door, Eden moved quietly onto the top of the steps. She was hurrying along the path forgetting to exercise caution in case someone could have seen her; so imperative was her necessity to make her rendezvous. Eden's curiosity was aroused.

The night, as he suspected, was bitterly cold, but a half moon cast an iridescent sheen over the area. Eden would have to be extra careful in case Elspeth turned to look back. It would be very difficult to explain if he was spotted following her. He drew his warm coat closer around his body and, keeping a good distance away, followed her out of the grounds into the narrow lane. He paused, as she stopped for a moment and quickly turn in the opposite direction from the road that led to Branton. Eden kept up, still staying far enough away that she wouldn't see him.

At length, she stopped by the old oak tree that had been part of the landscape for centuries. A car was standing there, almost hidden in the shadows of the branches. The passenger door was pushed open from the inside and Elspeth entered. Eden ducked behind a tree, closing in to observe a little nearer.

He edged forward, still keeping hidden behind bushes, as the car slowly moved towards him. It only took a moment for Eden to recognize the driver—it was Giles Mortimer! Now he was completely at a loss to understand how Elspeth would have any connection with Giles Mortimer. How very interesting! They disappeared around a corner and out of sight.

Eden leaned against the bark of a tree, a puzzled expression in his dark eyes. He couldn't wait now to get back home, to inform his father. He could almost see the surprise and puzzlement cross his face, as it had for Eden.

That same day back in his office in Barnstable, Detective Inspector Stanley Wilkins was troubled. The man found in the woods last month had been formally identified as Bernard Webb—imprisoned for ten years for criminal assault. He leaned back in his chair, suddenly remembering those days when he'd been a regular policemen, pounding the pavements of Barnstable. He'd been eager to learn more about Bernard Webb's conviction as such crimes were scarce in the West Country in those days. For some reason, Stanley had found the case particularly fascinating. At the time he'd listened, read and followed up on the reasons why Webb had shot the child. Webb had been lucky the victim hadn't died and Stanley had often wondered why the judge had been so harsh as to give Bernard ten years for it. The child had survived with no apparent lasting injuries.

When the Detective Inspector in charge of the investigation at that time had taken Stanley to visit the prison shortly after Webb's conviction, they had talked with the prisoner. During this discussion, Stanley's acute senses were alerted to something devious about the manner in which Webb talked about the case.

Despite the numerous cases Stanley had been involved in since Webb's incarceration, at the back of his mind something still bothered him about this new incident. He was not entirely convinced that Bernard Webb was, in fact, guilty of assaulting Captain Thorncroft that night back in early November. He wanted desperately to find some similarities, but it would need re-opening up the first case in order to find something that might just shed some light on this one.

He was so wound up with it that he mentioned to Chief Inspector Tom Storm. Storm had turned his request down, explaining that opening up old cases was a waste of time; more important issues were imminent and other avenues had to be investigated before the truth would become known in this case.

However, when Stanley had seen Bernard Webb laying face down in the wood that day, with a gun in his hand, the one that had killed him, Stanley was puzzled. Why would he jeopardize his new-found freedom by shooting Captain Thorncroft in the first place? Obviously someone else was involved; that someone being the person who'd shot Webb. Stanley shook his head slightly. Something didn't add up here.

He'd been lucky when the Coroner had found a crumpled letter inside Webb's inside jacket pocket. It had been addressed to Webb, but the return address had been scrawled on the back of the envelope. Going on that evidence, Stanley had followed the lead to a small house just outside Branton. Here he located Ralph Webb, the dead man's brother. After the initial shock of hearing of his brother's death, Ralph had told him some interesting information about the man who Bernard Webb had met in a pub in Malmsmead. Ralph had no idea of the man's identity, but when Stanley checked the pub later, the description given by the young barman definitely fitted Edgar Rutledge. Stanley had then hurried back to Barnstable and solicited the help from his sergeant in finding out more about this man. It seemed his wife had passed away some years earlier from unknown causes.

The next morning Stanley, along with his sergeant, Frank Owens, arrived at the little cottage at Watersfield, armed with questions that the old man would have to answer honestly, or he'd be subpoenaed to the courts for further more in-depth questioning.

CHAPTER 30

GUEST AT RAVENSLEA

A couple of days later, Catherine was just about to go into the garden when the telephone rang. Frowning she suddenly had misgivings about James. Had he had a relapse? She picked up the receiver, her brain spinning.

"Catherine Thorncroft." She said, nervously.

"Oh, Mrs. Thorncroft. This is Dr. Morgan from the Bristol Royal Infirmary. I'm pleased to tell you that I have spoken to Lillian Rutledge's doctor who has since examined her. In his opinion, she should never have been committed to this hospital and after reviewing her case with our psychiatric panel, it has been decided she can be released immediately. Could you arrange to have her picked up as soon as possible?"

Catherine breathed easier. "Of course, Dr. Morgan. Thank you for telephoning. I can come in a little later this afternoon if you will be there?"

"I am here until 5:30 this afternoon, so would be happy to see you anytime between now and then. I will have her dressed and ready for your arrival."

"Thank you, doctor."

She lowered the receiver thoughtfully, then turned to find Elspeth.

The housekeeper was in the Kitchen talking to Agnes and they both turned at her entrance.

"Elspeth. Could you please have the sheets changed in the south east bedroom and give it a thorough airing immediately. We have a visitor arriving later today and will need that room for a while."

"Of course, Madam." Elspeth said. She turned as Doris came into view and relayed the message to her. "Get Edna to also vacuum and polish the room."

"Yes, Elspeth." Doris said.

"We'll be needing an extra setting for the table tonight, too, Agnes. Please arrange that for me."

"Indeed yes, Mrs. Thorncroft. We're having duck á l'orange tonight." Agnes smiled at Catherine, then turned back to her chores.

After lunch, Catherine set out for Bristol. The day had turned colder; dark clouds hovered overhead as Percy steered the vehicle through the Devonshire countryside into Somerset northwards towards Bristol. Spots of rain fell on the windscreen.

She rested against the warm, sweet smelling upholstery, her thoughts concentrating on how she could tell the family the reason why Lillian Rutledge would be staying with them. It would be awkward, but she felt the woman needed to have a place to relax, knowing her father would not be around to antagonize her. It was obvious she could not return to his house in Watersfield; from what Catherine could gather she had nowhere else to go. Well, she'd think of something, in the meantime she wanted to make sure Lillian would be comfortable at Ravenslea. When James returned, which she was sure he'd want to soon, that would be another problem she'd have to deal with.

With little traffic to hamper their journey, Percy pulled the vehicle up outside the hospital entrance at exactly four o'clock. Plenty of time for Catherine to talk to the doctor and get Lillian home again.

The doctor was in his office when she arrived. After greeting her amiably, he mentioned he wouldn't be able to discuss this in too much detail, as he had a meeting scheduled for four thirty that afternoon with the Hospital Administrator.

"The meeting is actually regarding Lillian, Mrs. Thorncroft. It is obvious that the doctor who admitted her in the first place was out of order. This cannot be tolerated and will be investigated thoroughly to make certain such a thing doesn't happen again."

"I'm glad to think that he won't be able to get away with such a scandalous action." She said.

He nodded. "It's quite possible he'll be stripped of his license, but that's what we're going to discuss. When we informed Lillian of the panel's decision she was told she'd have to return to her father's care. She adamantly refused saying, quite rightly, that it was he who had her brought here in the first place. So, Mrs. Thorncroft, if it's no inconvenience to you, we'd like her, in the interim, to be under your care until she is well enough to go back into Society. Would this be acceptable to you?"

"Of course, Doctor. Lillian appears delightful; I can't imagine her causing us any trouble." Catherine smiled at him as he stood up, tucking a pencil in his top pocket.

"I really must go now." He handed her some papers. "These are Lillian's release documents. Give them to the Duty Nurse as you leave. She'll have you sign a form, then you and Lillian will be free to go." He smiled at her and opened the door for her to precede him into the corridor. He shook her hand warmly. "It was nice to meet you, Mrs. Thorncroft. Good bye."

Lillian was dressed and ready to leave when she arrived at her room. Her face was a wreath of smiles; the wan expression now replaced by a little powder and lipstick to give her colour. She looked entirely different to the woman Catherine had seen earlier.

"Thank you so much, Mrs. Thorncroft. I really don't know what I would have done had you not offered your kindness."

"I wouldn't have known anything about you or your circumstances had you not sent that letter, Lillian." She smiled at her. "Anyway, we should leave. I'd like to get a goodly distance away from Bristol before it gets too dark."

Percy drove steadily home. The rain was drenching the land causing the windscreen wipers to have difficulty clearing Percy's vision. It was close to eight o'clock by the time they reached Ravenslea. Darkness had enveloped the area for the last few hours, but they all arrived safely.

Catherine and Lillian hurried inside, shaking their wet clothing on the floor while Elspeth took their coats.

"This is Lillian, Elspeth. She's a friend of mine who's going to be staying with us for a while. She's been ill and needs to have some rest to help her convalesce. For a few days, she'll probably stay in her room, but as I mentioned before she'll be able to take her meals with the family."

"Yes, Madam." Elspeth stared at Lillian searchingly.

Lillian returned her look, suddenly thinking how austere and unfriendly the housekeeper appeared.

Agnes appeared, brushing wisps of hair from off her forehead. "I've kept some dinner for you both, Mrs. Thorncroft. Once the lady has settled, perhaps you'd like to take her to the Dining Room where Doris will be happy to serve you both."

"Thank you, Agnes." Catherine acknowledged. She turned to Lillian, pushing her gently forward. "This is Lillian, Agnes. As I mentioned to Elspeth, she's going to be staying with us for a little while, so please include her in all the meals from now on."

Agnes smiled warmly at the newcomer and extended her hand. "Pleased to meet you, Miss Lillian. I hope you'll find Ravenslea accommodating."

"Oh, I'm sure I will, Agnes. Thank you." Lillian said, liking the kindly woman and smiling back at her.

Lillian settled in well at Ravenslea. Even when she'd lived with her parents in Kensington, she'd never had such a beautiful bedroom in such glorious, spacious surroundings. The lilac silk tapestries lining the four-poster bed matched perfectly the long curtains framing the lead latticed windows overlooking the virtually flawless front lawn and gardens. To her right she could see the gleaming blue and white summerhouse and longed for the moment when Catherine would consider it safe for her to roam the grounds. To feel the fresh country air would be a blessing right now.

As the days drew closer to the meeting with Gideon, Lillian kept very much to herself. She'd been introduced to the Thorncroft children, who accepted her as a friend that Catherine hadn't seen in many years. They didn't have any reason to suspect anything different.

Lillian up in her room folded her arms. Yesterday, she went outside for the first time, keeping a low profile near the shrubbery and rose gardens. It was delightful. Mrs. Thorncroft had loaned her a jacket and scarf to ward against the cutting wind and she'd enjoyed her brief walk. Today, as she gazed out her bedroom window to the cool sunshine, she again wished she could take a walk around the grounds. She wanted to be outside as much as she could— she'd been cooped up in that ward long enough with its sterile antiseptic aromas, surrounded by mentally unstable people. She needed to feel the gentle breeze caressing her face. However, Mrs. Thorncroft had cautioned her to limit her activities outside to be close enough away from the road not to be seen by any passing vehicle. While Lillian had been a little puzzled by this, she trusted Catherine's judgment and did as she was told.

Later, Catherine told her that something had been planned that would definitely startle her son and possibly jeopardize her father, but father or not, she really didn't care. She had no reason to care much for him any more after what he'd done to her.

She turned away from the window, her thoughts now moving to her son. She'd missed him terribly. The time she'd spent at the Bristol Royal Infirmary without seeing him was a long time to be away from a son she adored. She wondered what he was doing now. Her father had visited her only once in all the time she'd been in the hospital and never had he mentioned Gideon's wellbeing. Well, Mrs. Thorncroft told her that Gideon would be visiting on Tuesday evening next; it would be interesting to see him again.

Just then, she heard a vehicle drive down the pathway and draw to a stop outside the front entrance. From her vantage point, even though she craned her neck as far as she could, she couldn't see who was visiting. She sighed. How nice to be living a normal life again, to be able to receive guests, to entertain as she'd always loved in the past.

Lillian was now fifty-nine years of age knew the chances of her ever marrying again was gradually dwindling, but she continued to dream that one day she'd have a place of her own with a husband, a garden and Gideon with a wife and children coming to visit her. It was a bit of a pipe dream, but it made her smile and she felt a bubble of hope sparkle within her.

CHAPTER 31

MONDAY MORNING

PENELOPE was troubled that morning. Sleep had been almost non-existent as she continued to think and wonder why anyone would want to kill James. Although it had occurred a month earlier, the vicious act was still uppermost in her mind and remembering her previous feelings for the handsome James, she felt herself shudder knowing that someone had desired to harm him.

She thought, as she had on many occasions, about the days she had thought James wanted to marry her before she'd introduced her best friend Catherine Ellison to him. At the time, Penelope had been annoyed by James' obvious attraction for her friend, but in the meantime, Penelope had met and fallen in love with Fletcher Rhodes, so the new romance had taken over where her obvious girlish infatuation with James Thorncroft had finished.

She had to admit, James was vibrant, easy-going and although occasionally argumentative, really one of the nicest men she'd ever met, barring, of course, Fletcher. Looking back, she knew she would have loved to have been Mistress of Ravenslea—to own and be a part of the grand empire along with the wonderful house the Thorncrofts had nourished and protected over the years. Although her own family home of Cavendish Hall was a beautiful place in its own right, Ravenslea was known and revered throughout the area as a place for garden parties in the summer, Christmas gatherings and, until now, the celebrated Guy Fawkes night with the spectacular fireworks, wonderful food and a romantic dance to end off the evening. The last one ended in tragedy, so the food and candlelit dance had been abandoned.

She sighed and eased herself off the bed, not wishing to disturb her husband, who'd also had had a restless sleep. He was now turned away from her breathing rhythmically. Glancing at the clock beside her bed, she noticed it was almost six o'clock. Far too soon for her to be even contemplating getting up, but she couldn't settle, so it was good to arise before the family.

Sliding her feet into fluffy warm slippers, she drew on her dressing gown and moved towards the door. Once outside she hurried to the bathroom. After attending to her needs she felt a little better. It was so early, the sun hadn't even begun to show itself over the horizon, but she had no desire to return to bed. She'd only think of James and of Catherine's predicament knowing there was someone out there with death on his (or her) mind. The disquieting thought had often entered Penelope's head that the gunman just might not stop with James—there may be another person in his murderous sights!

She shivered. Thinking suddenly of James lying in a hospital bed in a coma, unaware of the events that had taken him there, she brought to mind the fate of her brother, Bertram. Always selfish, indolent, full of his own importance and fancying himself as a ladies man, Bertram had upset many people in his life. When he'd decided to go back to South Africa after the War with Germany, it had been a release for Penelope at the time. She'd been sick and tired of his continual complaining about England's politics, people and the environment that she was overtly pleased when he'd decided to leave them.

Once there, it wasn't long before he wrote telling them that he'd found an African woman by the name of Anu to be with. He'd sent a photograph. A good looking girl with a healthy looking chocolate brown body, braided black, shining hair and a bright, warm smile. Bertram said she was teaching him Swahili while he, in turn, was teaching her the rudiments of English. She'd been a good listener and Bertram told them she'd picked up the language well. At the time, Penelope and her father was pleased that at last Bertram was settling down. However, it didn't last as Anu had not told Bertram that she was married.

It was a few weeks after receiving the letter with the photograph that they received notification from Bertram's Commanding Officer that Bertram had been killed. A hand-written note by the C.O. himself had given them all the details, requesting that it be kept out of the papers. Apparently, Bertram had been caught in bed with Anu by her husband who had savagely attacked him. With two quick slashes of his long-handled knife, he'd killed Bertram, then took it upon himself to decapitate Anu.

Penelope shuddered, picturing the gruesome scene with horror. How could a man do that to another, even though Bertram had definitely been in the wrong, the murder was inexcusable.

The Commanding Officer had told them that Bertram's regiment had been informed that Bertram had become involved in a confrontation at a native village, resulting in his demise and he'd been buried in a military cemetery in Durban.

She now felt fully awake and moved out of the bathroom. Her thoughts returned to James later, wondering why someone could have such a powerfully evil force working within them that they could even consider taking another's life. It wasn't as if James had done anything so terribly wrong; his had been a full life of caring for his family and friends. He wouldn't hurt anyone—not as far as Penelope remembered him. Her heart hammered with the knowledge that she might never see James again; never touch him; never see his wonderful smile ...

With a little moan of despondency, she hurried down the stairs. On hearing noises in the Kitchen, she skirted in the other direction towards the door that led to the veranda. Penelope slipped outside into the crisp morning air, drawing her robe closer around her shoulders. The house felt slightly oppressive, mainly, she was sure, to her morbid, melancholy thoughts. Going outside would, she was sure, clear her head and enable her to think clearer.

She began to relive again, as she had a hundred times, the fatal Guy Fawkes night. She brought to mind the two men who'd been standing apart from everyone else, their heads close together obviously discussing something of importance. She'd never seen them before or since, but as she was sure she knew most of the Thorncroft's friends and acquaintances, she had the distinct feeling they had something to do with the shooting. At the time the shot had been fired, the men had been standing where they'd been all evening, close beside a tree at the back of the crowd. It was obvious they had nothing to do with James' death; yet why did she feel this prickle of unease.

She remembered quietly moving backwards, careful to keep herself hidden. It would not do for her to be found eavesdropping, but something seemed to be telling her to listen to their conversation if it was possible. When she used the shadows to creep closer to them, she was disappointed. The two men hardly spoke at all; both, it seemed, in awe of the grand fireworks show before them. Yet, she felt there was something . . . Penelope always managed to sense things that others, perhaps, did not and it was this acute 'sense' that was bothering her at this moment.

She shrugged and moved to a stone seat on the terrace that overlooked the grounds. It was sheltered here; the cool wind less penetrating. She knew she should, perhaps, mention her thoughts to Fletcher, but he'd probably say something like she was being over-imaginative as she usually was. Then he'd dismiss it as a quirky feminine peculiarity. Perhaps he was right, yet Penelope couldn't shake this feeling she was moving in the right direction.

As she sat there, she recalled the moment James had been shot. The two men had still been standing behind her, but even though it appeared they had nothing to do with it, she was puzzled about their reaction. They hadn't acted surprised, concerned or particularly interested, when everyone else was rushing around in horror and fear. A few moments later, they had walked quickly away from Ravenslea's grounds out of sight.

Feeling disappointed as she believed she'd discovered something that could have thrown some light on the shooting, she'd raced over the churned up lawns to where Fletcher and her family along with a multitude of people had convened at the bottom of the wide stone steps that led to the beautiful front door of the Manor, craning their necks to see what had happened.

She brought herself back to the present. The cackling caw-caw of a crow nearby broke the stillness of the early morning and she casually glanced its way. She loved to hear the night birds and the cool, raw smell of the upcoming dawn heralding a new winter's day. It wasn't until a sudden gust of wind blew strands of hair into her eyes, that she realized she was cold.

Later today, she told herself firmly, she would go over to Ravenslea. She couldn't keep this little bit of probably useless knowledge to herself—she wanted desperately to talk to Catherine. Turning around, she hurried back into the house, closed the veranda French doors and slipped back into her bedroom.

After Penelope returned to the bedroom, she slipped between the sheets beside her sleeping husband, her thoughts veering from one thing to another until she decided it was time to get up. She couldn't lay there a moment longer, dwelling on what might have been.

She gave Fletcher a friendly prod.

"I think it's time you got up, dear." She grinned down into his sleepy eyes and kissed him fondly on his slightly fuzzy chin.

He glanced up and reached over for her. "Not until we've . . ."

She laughed and pushed against him gently. "Not now, Fletcher, do you know what time it is?"

"Haven't the foggiest." He leaned up and glanced at the clock. "Good Lord— it's almost eight!"

"Precisely!" She jumped from the bed and slipped on her robe. "I'm going to freshen up; won't be long. You just get yourself together. I want to go over to see Catherine today— haven't seen her in a long time."

"All right, Darling." She heard him mumble. "Do you mind if I don't come? I have some letter writing to catch up on."

"That's fine dear. I can fill you in with any news of James or anything else when I return." She slipped on her robe and went out of the room towards the bathroom.

She could hear movement in the bathroom as she neared it.

"How long are you going to be?" She called through the closed door.

"Out in two minutes, Mother." Came William's chirpy voice.

Once she'd finished her ablutions, dressed and had partaken of breakfast, it was almost ten thirty. Donning a warm coat, she asked Barnaby to bring the car around the front as she wanted to go to Ravenslea for a short while this morning. He was always pleased to be of service to her and gladly did as she asked. The journey was short by vehicle, whereas if she'd had decided to walk, it would take close to an hour.

The gates were open when they arrived, so Barnaby drove slowly towards the manor house. Watery sunlight filtered through the trees and mirrored itself against the latticed windows as they approached the front entrance.

Eden, on seeing the car approaching had the door open for her. He threw her a broad smile and ushered her inside.

"Barnaby can go round the back, Aunt Penelope."

She swung around and motioned for Barnaby to go around to the Kitchen. He understood perfectly and gave her a little wave as he moved the car round to the side of the house.

"I've come to see your mother, Eden." For a moment, she detected a look of unease cross his face and she frowned. "Is something wrong?"

"Not really. Mother was complaining of a headache earlier so took a couple of aspirins and is resting."

"Oh dear . . . I've definitely come at the wrong time. I'll leave. Please tell her I'll drop by later, possibly this evening."

Eden laid a hand on her arm with a shake of his dark head. "No, don't do that. I'm sure my mother will want to see you. Why don't you wait in the Music Room and I'll talk to her."

"Only if you're sure, dear." Penelope said, doubtfully. "Please don't disturb her if she's not feeling any better."

He threw her the attractive smile that had smitten her daughter and reminded her so much of his father who she'd once loved desperately. "She's probably feeling better by now. I know she'll welcome your company." He moved up the stairs, "I won't be a jiffy."

In the Music Room, Penelope waited. She couldn't define her emotions at that moment, but there was something here at Ravenslea that troubled her. Something intangible that she just couldn't put her finger on. She'd never felt that way in this wonderful house before and it made her feel ill at ease. She walked around the room, unable to find comfort in an armchair or sofa. She moved restlessly towards the crackling fire and held out her hands to the inviting warmth. She stood above the ivory and black keys of the beautiful grand piano, then turned to look above the mantlepiece, to stare at the arresting portrait of Deanna Thorncroft. The lovely young woman who had died before she'd really had a chance at life. Penelope looked into the young woman's eyes aware of a sad expression lurking behind the smiling mouth. It was as if she knew something was wrong here.

The door opened suddenly and the Ravenslea's new maid, Edna walked in with a coal scuttle. She stopped startled on seeing Penelope and was about to retreat when Penelope smiled at her, motioning for her to continue.

"Please excuse me, Ma'am. I just wanted to put some more coal on the fire." Edna said. "It's gettin' that cold out and this room should always, in my opinion, be kept nice and warm. It's such a beautiful room."

Penelope smiled at the young woman with her curly fair hair and black coal smudge on her nose. She was a dainty little thing, keeping a low profile in the Ravenslea household. It was the first time Penelope had actually seen her.

"I agree. You go ahead." Penelope paused. "You must be Edna?"

"Yes, Ma'am."

"Do you like living here?"

"Oh, yes, Ma'am. I'm alone, you see. I don't 'ave any family. I'm an orphan and am that grateful to Doris who got me this job."

"Well, I'm sure that Doris is very glad you're here to help her."

A noise at the door heralded Catherine's appearance.

She hurried towards Penelope and hugged her warmly. "Oh, Pen, how nice of you to call. I'm so sorry I've not been able to be with you much since . . . that dreadful day. How are you?" She smiled at her closest friend. "Come along, sit beside me and tell me what's been going on in your life."

They waited until the young maid had placed some shiny black coals on the dying fire, discreetly leaving and closing the door quietly behind her.

Penelope shrugged. "She seems a nice little maid, Cath."

"Oh, she's fine. We just thought that as Doris is getting along in years a bit now, she needed someone to help her." She said. "But more to the point, what is the reason for your visit? Is something wrong at home?"

"Oh, nothing's wrong at home." Penelope shifted uneasily in her seat. "There's just something I wish to get out of my system. I'm hoping you can help." She paused.

"Go on, Pen. If there's something troubling you, I need to know." Catherine leaned back in the chair.

"Well, it's to do with that dreadful night that James was shot. A few minutes before that awful moment, I noticed two men talking quite in low tones near where I was standing. One of them mentioned Ravenslea and although the context of their discussion mostly escaped me, I had the distinct impression that by the tone of the older man's voice, it didn't sound very pleasant. The other, the younger, seemed at odds with the older one. They obviously had nothing to do with the actual shooting, because it happened while they were both standing there, but there seemed something . . . somehow shifty about their attitude that bothered me. I wanted to mention it to Fletcher, but I know he'd have thought I was imagining things, like I often do, so thought I'd mention it to you."

"Did you recognize either of them?" Catherine said, feeling an odd quirk of fear.

Penelope shook her head. "No, and I don't think you would have either. I know most of your friends and relatives, Cath and these two were definitely strangers to me."

"Perhaps you should mention it to the Police. We have a Detective Inspector Stanley Wilkins working on the case for us; he could look into it and perhaps put your mind at rest. It could, after all, have been just some passers-by who happened to be around for the firework display."

Penelope smiled. "You're probably right, Catherine, you usually are. I'm sorry to be bothering you with this, especially as Eden said you weren't well. I should have telephoned first."

"Oh, I'm feeling much better now. Just having you come to see me has cheered me up no end."

Penelope looked at her friend anxiously. "How is James? Do you think there's any improvement?"

Catherine caught her lip, looked away shaking her head slightly. "There's no change, Penelope. It's just a case of wait and see at the moment. I go to the hospital every day, but . . . well, I don't think I can help him much." She turned a sad face to Penelope, thinking how well she seemed to be covering up James' condition. "Could you perhaps stay for dinner tonight? Having you here has certainly cheered me up."

Penelope shook her head. "Thank you dear, but I must be getting back. I hope you don't mind me pestering you this way. I just had to talk to someone about those two men and now I do feel little better about it."

"You'd never be guilty of pestering me, Pen," Catherine caught her hands in hers and kissed her lightly on the cheek. "I am always concerned when you are concerned; so don't ever be afraid to come and talk to me about anything that bothers you, at any time."

"Thank you . . . you are such a good friend." Penelope squeezed her hand in friendship, picked up her small hat and moved towards the door. "If you ever feel like some company now that you're alone, don't hesitate to come on over. You know you are welcome at any time."

"Thanks, Pen. I'll be sure to do that."

Catherine opened the front door as Penelope drew her friend to her in a warm embrace.

"Why don't you come over tomorrow? Bring Rebecca; William will be here. I know those two have a mountain of things to discuss." She smiled at her friend. "It might just do you the world of good to get away from everything Ravenslea holds for you at the moment."

"Thank you, Pen. But I do have to go into the hospital tomorrow. Perhaps some other time. I'll mention your invitation to Rebecca; as you say, they have tons to arrange. I told them, by the way, that you and I would be more than de-lighted to share in the arrangements."

"You know I'll do anything. I love Rebecca; she's a fine girl and I know they're well suited. I don't know if you've noticed, but I've been detecting some simi-lar vibes coming from our Stephanie with regards to Eden." Penelope grinned. "Wouldn't that be wonderful if they too decided to get married?"

"I couldn't agree more." The two women embraced warmly as they stepped into the watery sunshine. "I'll talk to you tomorrow, Pen."

Penelope ran down the steps, turned and waved as she stepped into the vehicle.

As they travelled slowly towards the gates, Penelope suddenly wished to be able to see James in the hospital. She knew that Catherine had mentioned he not been allowed visitors except Catherine and Martin, but the burning desire to see him became almost compulsive. She leaned back against the seat thinking that if her prayers were answered, then James would pull out of the coma and it would be then she could see him. She sighed. It was obvious she would have to settle for that paltry solution.

Just before Barnaby turned the vehicle into the lane, Penelope suddenly asked him to slow down. Something made her turn and look back at the house. It was then she thought she saw a pale face at one of Ravenslea's upper windows. It couldn't have been Catherine—she'd never have made it up there so quickly. So who could it have been?

She felt an odd premonition, but signalled for Barnaby to continue. For an instant, she wondered if the Thorncrofts had a visitor, yet it seemed odd Catherine hadn't mentioned it. Other ideas came unwanted to her mind, but she dismissed them immediately as she knew the thoughts were treacher-ously untrue. As they increased speed away from the Manor, Penelope recalled Catherine telling her once that if anything were to happen to her husband, she would never become involved with another man.

She closed her eyes, frowning slightly. It must have been her imagination, a trick of the light, but as they neared Cavendish Hall, the image of the face at the window remained with her.

CHAPTER 32

REVELATIONS AT RAVENSLEA

WHEN Catherine awoke that Tuesday morning, it was to see a blanket of snow on the ground outside her window. The excited feeling she usually had on seeing snow, took a back seat this morning, replaced with unusual agitation. It was Penelope who had always had premonitions, but this time she had an odd sensation swirling around in her head that definitely troubled her. Perhaps this was also some kind of premonition and she had an idea it was because Gideon Rutledge was due to visit Ravenslea tonight.

Martin had finally managed to talk to his cousin, Stephen Hallett. Between them they'd planned an evening that would hopefully cut the young man down to size. Martin had told her that the astute, clever lawyer had additional documentation to help them.

She wondered about Lillian Rutledge. Catherine knew the woman was becoming bored in her room for most of the day, coming down just to share meals with the family, then returning shortly after it had all been finished. She wished she could chance allowing Lillian to venture outside, more often but felt nervous whenever she did. It might just be the moment someone would see and recognize her in some way and everything Catherine had worked toward would have come to nought.

It also could jeopardize an idea that had been materializing in Catherine's mind since Lillian's arrival. She told Lillian who was very excited to think that she could be a part of helping the Thorncrofts in their quest to keep Ravenslea; the fact that she would also see her son gave her the lift she so obviously needed and deserved.

Her thoughts turned to Gideon Rutledge. His almost inflexible insistence about his right to Ravenslea Manor was far from acceptable. She knew that Stephen Hallett, James' cousin, had been working zealously to find some loophole that would prove the incriminating letter as a hoax. She prayed that he'd come up with something concrete that could never be contested in a Court of Law.

She returned her thoughts to her premonition of this morning. Despite the fact that there would be unquestionable confrontation with Gideon later this evening, she was certain these uneasy feelings had nothing to do with him. There was something else and as she went about her duties that morning, she couldn't for the life of her think what it could possibly be.

Trying desperately to toss these dark thoughts behind her, she sat at her dressing table and ran a brush through her dark hair thinking absently that she needed her hair trimmed one of these days. It was getting far too long and unmanageable lately. She stared at herself in the mirror, suddenly wishing that James were here in this room with her. She could almost feel his warm breath on the back of her neck whenever she sat there brushing her hair. The feeling was so strong, she wondered if there was some way James could return to Ravenslea without it becoming general knowledge. It would undoubtedly be risky; there was always a chance the gunman would find out, but she hated deceiving their children. It was right they should know he had survived the bullet and wasn't in any kind of coma. It wasn't fair, in her opinion, they should be kept in the dark about their father's progress. She decided that whatever the outcome tonight, she'd broach it to her brother-in-law.

Downstairs, the family were indulging in gentle banter as they consumed the hearty breakfast always provided for them by Agnes and Doris. Lillian had returned to her room by the time Catherine walked through the Dining Room door.

"Good morning." She said, pulling out her chair and seating herself. "What's on the agenda today?"

"Well, as a matter of fact, Catherine," Louise began smiling widely at her. "Adam and I have decided to take a trip to London for about a week. Take in a show, do some sightseeing, go to the British Museum and take advantage of the wonderful shopping venues." She glanced at Adam mischievously. "I know Adam's not that keen on the shopping bit, but he'll be happy to accompany me to a few stores, so he told me. He might even look around for himself, won't you Adam?"

"Maybe, Mother. Who knows?" He gave her a dry smile.

"Have you decided on a date?" Catherine asked, picking up a piece of toast and buttering it generously.

Louise nodded. "Martin's taking us to Bristol where we can catch the train to London next Friday morning, to avoid the Saturday rush. I'm really looking forward to it. I wanted him to come with us, but I think he'd prefer to stay here and support you, Catherine. I do hope you don't mind if we leave you to settle this troublesome matter. I have a feeling everything's going to turn out fine once you've talked to this Gideon person and Adam and I don't wish to be in the way."

Catherine raised her eyebrows. That didn't sound a bit like Louise who, she thought, always liked to be around when situations heated up.

"Well, you certainly wouldn't be in the way, Louise, but if you want to take in the City, I really don't blame you. London during December is quite impressive—they have wonderful Christmas decorations and Trafalgar Square is home to one of the tallest Christmas trees I've ever seen."

Louise grinned. "So Martin said. It's why we want to go, dear, and also to purchase some different kinds of Christmas gifts for everyone."

There was a lull in the conversation after that, everyone intent on taking in the appetizing display of breakfast dishes.

"I'm meeting Stephanie later," Eden said after a while. "We're going into Barnstable to pick up tickets for a show that's playing at the new theatre there. We're going just before Christmas."

Catherine smiled. "Of course, I'd forgotten about that new playhouse. What are they showing?"

"It's a George Bernard Shaw play called Pygmalion. It's had a lot of favourable reviews. I asked Stephanie if she'd like to go and she said she would, so that's where we're off to this afternoon."

She smiled over at him. "I'm sure you'll enjoy it. Although I've never seen any of his plays, I did read one of his books some time ago and was quite impressed."

As she watched her son's animated face, she knew that one day she'd hear of his and Stephanie's forthcoming union. The knowledge lifted her spirits.

She glanced across at Luke who was watching his brother speculatively. Catherine had an idea that Luke was more than a little fond of Giles Mortimer's daughter, Cynthia. It was too early yet for either of them to really know their own minds, but since her youngest had met Cynthia, suddenly there had appeared in his studio a number of very pleasant photographs of the young woman. Things seemed to be pointing to his complete adoration of her.

After breakfast, she caught Martin before he went outside and asked him to join her in the Music Room.

"I'd like a word with you, Martin." She said, shutting the door behind her and sitting down on a comfortable chair.

"Anything wrong, dear?" He looked immediately solicitous and perched himself on the edge of the chair opposite her.

"Well, nothing wrong, as such," she said, carefully, "it's just that . . . do you think there is any way we could bring James back home? He's feeling so much better at the moment and is miserable living at the hospital."

Martin frowned and pursed his mouth. "I don't really see how we can, Catherine. He must not be seen . . ."

"I know . . . but perhaps we can talk to the Detective Inspector. Maybe he could come up with some way of doing it without causing too much attention."

Martin looked at her and shook his head. "No dear, tell him next time you see him, that it would be much wiser if he stayed in the hospital. We can't chance the servants, or even the children for that matter, letting it be known that James is well; that we deceived everyone into believing he was in a coma." He caught her hand squeezing it gently. "I know James isn't the most patient of people, but you must convince him. It shouldn't be more than a couple more days. Tonight might be the crux of the whole unfortunate affair."

She nodded, pursing her mouth unhappily. "You're right of course, Martin . . . how ridiculous to think of jeopardizing the situation."

"I understand completely your reasoning, Catherine, but we've waited this long, a few more days isn't going to make that much difference. I have a feeling that Detective Wilkins is getting some very positive results from his investigations."

She pouted. "How could I even think of risking James' life again." She stood up. "I'll not mention it any more. When I see James later today, I'll tell him to be patient—that something will be happening soon to finally bring him back to Ravenslea and . . . I hope that whatever comes out of this meeting, it'll be in our favour!" She moved towards her brother-in-law and dropped a light kiss on his forehead. "Thank you, Martin dear—I'm so happy that you and I are colleagues in this tricky issue."

He smiled and stood up beside her, drawing her close. "We're in this together, my dear, because we both love James. I know you and he would do exactly the same if the roles were reversed, right?"

She grinned. "Of course. I'm going to get ready to visit with James now and tell him what we've discussed. I know he'll understand and be patient, but as I said before, he's feeling better and wants to be out of there."

Early that same afternoon before Catherine left to visit James, Martin was in James' Study going through some Ledgers when there was a knock on the door. Elspeth came in at his command. Puzzled, he put down the fountain pen and leaned back in his leather chair.

"Hello, Elspeth. What can I do for you?"

"Oh, Mr. Martin. I was hoping Mrs. Thorncroft was with you. Would you mind if I found her and brought her here. I'd like to have a word with you both." She seemed very nervous, twisting her hands in front of her, exactly as she had been doing when Stanley Wilkins had talked to her a few days earlier.

"I'm busy at the moment—can't it wait?"

She pressed her lips together and shook her head. "No, Sir. I have something to say that is urgent and needs to be discussed now."

He sighed, pushed his chair back and stood up, then nodded. "I think I saw Mrs. Thorncroft in the Music Room about half an hour ago."

"Thank you Sir." Elspeth left as quickly as she'd come into the room.

Martin frowned. Elspeth was one of those people who kept themselves very much to themselves, never joining in much at Ravenslea and although she ruled the Kitchen staff with an iron hand, she never offered opinions or solutions on matters pertaining to the family. What could she possibly wish to discuss with Catherine and himself that was so imperative?

A few minutes later, the Study door was opened and Catherine entered with Elspeth close behind. The housekeeper firmly shut the door and faced Martin squarely.

"May I be seated?" She asked.

"Of course." Martin waved his hand to a nearby chair. "You too, Catherine. You have me quite curious, Elspeth. So do not keep us in suspense any longer."

Elspeth perched herself on the edge of an upright chair, facing her employers, an unyielding look on her face.

"I'll not beat about the bush." She said, stoutly. "What I'm about to tell you will come as a shock. I should have told you years ago, but didn't wish to jeopardize my position here. Once you've heard what I have to say, no doubt you will wish to dismiss me." She paused. "It will not be necessary to do that, because I will offer my resignation."

Catherine gasped. "Oh, Elspeth! Whatever are you talking about?" She was about to say something more, but caught Martin's eye. Reluctantly, she sat back in the chair, her emotions running rampant. Was this the premonition she'd experienced this morning?

Elspeth looked down at her hands and cleared her throat. She looked up, her face now calmer.

"When I was first engaged to be a part of the Ravenslea household, I told you very little about myself. I know it's a long time, but now, I feel I owe you some explanation of my circumstances before coming here." Elspeth took a deep breath. "You see, I was the middle child of a group of six siblings. Our parents were vaudeville entertainers and when they died, they left us bereft not only of parental guidance, but also of subsistence." She glanced over at Martin. "This information may come as more of a shock to you, Mr. Martin, as I am your sister-in-law. Amelia was my sister."

"What!" He exclaimed, leaning forward in his seat almost ready to jump out of it. "I don't believe it!"

"I came to Ravenslea for one purpose only," Elspeth continued, ignoring Martin's outburst, "to find out the truth about my sister's death. My brother, Eric, told me something about it at the time, but I needed to know for myself what exactly happened. Since I've been here, I learned the truth behind the burning of Ravenslea all those years ago. I have accepted that Amelia was the person responsible and that she was not persecuted by the Thorncrofts as we were led to believe."

"Persecuted!" Martin cried, again. "Good gracious, woman, of course she wasn't persecuted. She set that damned fire herself and unfortunately perished in it!"

"I know that now, Sir." Elspeth said, her voice breaking slightly. "We lost our sister. The one person who'd managed to keep us from starving. She'd found accommodation for all of us and when our youngest sister, Esther, married and moved away it became a lot easier for us to cope. When Amelia died, the situation changed dramatically. No longer were we receiving money from her. All our funds had been cut off. We suddenly had to fend for ourselves. It was difficult, but once I'd found myself a position here, I carried on where Amelia had left off. Everything was going well, until now." She took a deep sigh. "I have to tell you, in case you've forgotten from all those years ago when I first started here, that my name is Elspeth Webb. Bernard Webb was my brother."

A hushed sigh reverberated throughout the room and Catherine could feel her heart pounding uncomfortably. "Bernard Webb? The man who shot my husband?" She managed to say.

Elspeth nodded. "Yes, Mrs. Thorncroft. Bernard did shoot Captain Thorncroft. I can only hope and pray that the Captain recovers from the coma." She took a deep breath. "When I came to get the Captain on Guy Fawkes Day, I lied. There had been no-one at the other end of the phone line. It had been a ruse to get him into the house when everyone else was engaged elsewhere. Bernard had told me he wanted to discuss something of great importance with Captain James and didn't want any interruptions. He said that the Guy Fawkes celebration would be ideal for it." She paused licking her lips nervously. "I had no idea that Bernard had planned to shoot him. When the Captain fell, I was frantic and ran out of the house to catch my brother and ask him why he did it. I thought Captain James had died by his hand. When I caught up with him in the woods, I told him in no uncertain terms exactly what I thought of him. I also told him he was wrong to be harbouring such damaging thoughts against the Thorncroft family. I convinced him and he became quite emotional. He hadn't realized when this beautiful house was burned it was our sister who'd caused it. He was so sorry, Madam." This she addressed to Catherine. "He wanted to be kept informed on the Captain's condition, but I didn't get a chance to do that because that same night, someone killed him." She licked her lips, shivering a little. "Bernard was never a bad man, but he had an enormous lack of common sense. I feel sure he didn't do that terrible thing without some persuasion from someone else; someone he was too weak to face up to."

"Having told us that, Elspeth, could it be possible that you have some idea who could have killed your brother?" Martin said, quietly, leaning forward with interest.

She shook her head. "No, but it seems that whoever it was had something to gain by seeing Captain James dead. Bernard mentioned something about money—he'd obviously been offered a goodly sum of money to carry out the deed, but it seemed whoever was to give it to him, had no intention of honouring the agreement." She reached into her skirt pocket and drew out a handkerchief, into which she promptly wiped her eyes and blew her nose. Catherine was amazed to see Elspeth actually showing emotion. She had never seen her let her guard down in all the years she'd been at Ravenslea.

"Well, this is indeed an interesting story, Elspeth. I had no idea that you and my wife had been related. Amelia never mentioned much about her family, only saying that she had some siblings in London who needed some kind of income. I was only too happy to provide her with the extra money to send to them." Martin said, leaning back in the chair with his elbows on the arm, his fingers steepling against his lower lip. "But, even though this is bewildering and quite serious, I take it you had no involvement in your brother's scheme?"

"Oh no! I could never harm Captain James, Sir. I am very fond of him . . . and Mrs. Thorncroft. In fact, I am fond of the whole family. I wouldn't want anything bad to happen to any of the Thorncrofts. The only thing I did was smuggle him into the house when all was quiet. I certainly wouldn't have done that if I'd known Bernard's intention."

Martin nodded. "I believe you, Elspeth. As you've confessed all of this, I don't see any reason why you should desire to leave us. I think I can speak for Mrs. Thorncroft when I ask that you reconsider and continue in your position as usual."

She went quiet and caught her lip, once again twirling her fingers together in her lap. "There is one other thing. I may as well tell you this as well as everything else I've told you today. It is right to start the rest of one's life with a clean slate, don't you think?"

"Most definitely." Catherine said.

"Before the War, I met a soldier and we fell in love. Unfortunately, he was married. His wife developed polio a few years after they were married; as a result they were unable to have children." Elspeth managed a brief smile, and reached into the pocket of her gown. She gave a photograph to Catherine.

"Who is this?" Catherine asked, looking at the slim, attractive woman carrying a baby on her knee. "You?"

Elspeth nodded. "Despite what I have become over the years, Mrs. Thorncroft, at that time I was fairly attractive to the opposite sex. When we realized he was going to be sent overseas with his Unit, we engaged in a turbulent relationship. The result of which, was the birth of a child." She stopped as an invisible current seemed to permeate through the air at her words. "I was unmarried and had a child to care for. Her father was unable to marry me and was not even in England. I had at one time toyed with the idea of getting rid of the baby, but remembered that I loved the soldier; even if he didn't return, I would always have him with me, through the child. Anyway, after my baby was born, my sister Esther, who lives in Lincolnshire, cared for her through the War years. A little while later, I was lucky enough to find employment at Ravenslea Manor." She paused. "My baby's father is Giles Mortimer. Cynthia is my daughter." She stopped her face relaxing. The torrid secret was now out in the open. She realized she should have told the Thorncrofts this from the moment she'd started at Ravenslea, but had been loathe to mention it for fear of them turning her down for employment. By keeping her counsel, she'd managed to return Amelia's gifts to her family by sending money to her brothers, Bernard, Ralph and the youngest, Eric at every opportunity she could. She glanced at her employers, biting her lip self-consciously. Both were staring at her in astonishment.

"Well . . ." Martin breathed. "You really have had an interesting life, Elspeth. I would never have thought . . ."

"I probably seem to you to be a mousy, dull person with no significant life to be proud of." Elspeth interrupted with a shrug. "I hope you understand why I didn't tell you all of this earlier. I think it would have compromised my position here, especially when I see how much Master Luke seems to enjoy Cynthia's company." She stood up, brushed down her skirt and looked over at Catherine. "I must re-iterate my original statement, Mrs. Thorncroft. Under the circumstances, I have no other option but to relay this information to the Detective Inspector, then at an appropriate time will leave Ravenslea Manor. Once I know I'm cleared by the police, I've arranged with Giles to pick me up. We will be moving to Giles hometown in the Midlands. We won't be coming back. I would have liked, in some ways, to have stayed to see you nicely settled with another housekeeper, but feel this is the best way. I do hope you understand."

"I don't really understand why you are doing this, Elspeth." Catherine said, frowning. "You have spoken quite openly about your knowledge of my husband's shooting and we believe you. As far as you moving away, I find it puzzling why you'd leave Devon?"

"I want to marry Giles, Mrs. Thorncroft. He has found life extremely difficult here and wishes to return to an area with which he's familiar. I agreed and as soon as I can, I will be going with him."

"You are going to be leaving us with quite a task in engaging another to take your place, especially with everything else that's going on here at the moment. Could you not reconsider?"

"No, Madam. I'm very sorry to have to throw this at you at this difficult time, but it is right that I leave as soon as I've made a statement to the police, which I'm doing this afternoon." She moved slowly towards the door. "Providing it is acceptable to them, I intend to talk briefly to all Ravenslea's servants, before leaving. I have enjoyed this beautiful Manor, Mrs. Thorncroft, but I need Giles now . . . I've been without anyone for so long, you must understand and . . . please do not feel too badly about me . . ."

She opened the door, closing it gently behind her, leaving Martin and Catherine at a complete loss for words, staring wide-eyed at the closed door.

CHAPTER 33

Later that same morning Luke looped Hudson's rein over the protruding branch of a tree and ambled leisurely towards the small pond where he and Cynthia always met. He was early and eager to see the young woman who had quite taken his fancy since he'd seen her for the first time at the Guy Fawkes celebration last month. Life had certainly taken on a different hue since she'd come into his life. For one thing, his photography had suffered; he regretted this, but if Cynthia wanted to see him for whatever reason, at any time day or night, he'd dropped everything to be there for her.

Today, she'd called him and asked him to meet her at their usual spot. He'd been surprised as they had seen each other last night and didn't normally meet every day.

When Luke saw her come into view at the crest of the hill about fifty yards away on her honey coloured mare he felt his heart lift. He waved, watching her canter gently towards him. She jumped from her mare and looped the reins next to Hudson's. Nothing was spoken for the moment as Luke did what he always did, drew her into his arms to hold her close, but it was evident there was something different about the way she was holding herself. A stiffness that he'd never encountered before. He leaned down, gently turning her face to his and planting a kiss on her mouth. Her response was slightly impersonal; she pulled away, catching hold of his hand and guiding him to the wooden seat they always used. She stared out over the little pond, distractedly. Swans lazily swam by, but Luke knew she wasn't concentrating on them. He suddenly had misgivings.

"What's wrong, Cynthia?" He asked.

She glanced down first then, avoiding his eyes, stared vacantly at the pond. She was clearly agitated.

"Luke, I have something to tell you." She said.

"You've found someone else?" His heart plummeted.

"No . . . no, I have not found anybody else. It's just that . . . I'm going away."

"Going away? Why? I thought you and your father were happy here?"

"It . . . it's not working out for him, Luke. Father has decided that he and I should move from Devon. His business has fallen short of what he thought he could do and he can't seem to make much of a living here. I don't think he should have come here in the first place, but he had these aspirations of making some kind of fortune that have not materialized."

"But . . . you don't have to go, do you?"

She looked up at him, loving the way his mouth had slightly turned down. Even that was an attraction to her. She nodded. "I'm only seventeen, Luke; I'm under age and anyway. Father is insistent, my dear, so we have to go."

Luke stared at her, disappointment registering in his light eyes. He caught her to him, squeezing her arms tightly. "What about your vocation? The accounting? You could always find a job around here with that talent."

"I can't leave him, dear Luke. He relies on me too much."

He felt a surge of anger. "He can't be so selfish as to make you leave against your will."

She smiled at him. "Had I been older, this would never have arisen." She leaned up to touch his slim, smooth young face. "I have to go—I don't really have a choice."

"No, Cynthia . . . you can't do this. I thought we . . ."

She pulled away from his grasp and placed two fingers on his mouth, instantly stopping any more conversation. "It is as my father wishes. I'm too young to become as involved as we seem to be getting, Luke. I'm sure your parents too, have said we're not ready yet. You're not yet twenty years old and I won't be eighteen until the summer of next year."

"I'll never marry then. . ." Luke's voice took on a sullen tone.

She smiled sadly. "One day you will, Luke. I hope I'll always be a wonderful memory to you and that you'll forever think of me favourably, as I will you."

"You know I will, Cynthia." He paused, looking intently into her warm brown eyes. "So, this is it? You're just going leave me because your father has decided to go away . . . ? I hardly think that's fair warning, my dear. When . . . when is this going to happen?"

She pursed her mouth. "In a couple of days."

"How long have you known this, Cynthia? Why didn't you tell me before? At least I would have been a little more prepared—this is a little short notice, don't you think?"

She nodded. "I know and I'm sorry. Father didn't mention it to me until last night. I've been frantically packing since, worrying about explaining all this to you. I didn't want to leave and let you know by letter in a week or so."

He went quiet. "Thank you for that, anyway." He murmured, grudgingly.

Cynthia stood up and moved towards the mare grazing unconcernedly nearby. "I have to return, Luke dear. There are still a lot of things to attend to back at the house. I'm so sorry to have upset you in this way, but you will get over it." She paused. "Unfortunately, I doubt if I will return to Devon, but I want you to know that these last few weeks have been the best I've ever known, please believe me. You have meant everything to me." She slipped her foot into the stirrup and hoisted herself up onto the mare's back. "I wish you a happy and successful life, Luke. I will keep looking at pictures in the newspapers, on billboards, in shop windows . . . everywhere, knowing that one day your photographs will become famous." She leaned down and caught his hand in hers. He kissed it gently, held it for a moment then let it go.

"Despite what you say, Cynthia, I feel you and I are destined to be together. I will seek you out, perhaps when we're a little older and things may turn out differently."

"Perhaps," she said, twisting the mare's head around. "But for the moment at least, think of me often. Goodbye, dear Luke, you'll always hold a very special place in my heart."

She blew him a kiss and suddenly was gone. He stood, stunned, as the horse and rider galloped back the way they'd just come. How long he stood there he couldn't say, but she had long since disappeared from view when his reverie was shattered as Eden riding Jake came into view. His older brother slowed.

"Was that Cynthia thundering past me a few moments ago?" Luke nodded. "Is something wrong?"

"She's gone. I'll probably never see her again. Oh . . . I'm going to miss her terribly."

Eden jumped off Jake's sturdy back. "I'm so sorry." He said, simply. "Did you have an argument?"

Luke shook his head. "Not at all—Cynthia and I have never had any differences of opinion. We seemed to be in sync with pretty well everything. Apparently, her father has decided he can't cope with his new place and they're returning to his home town tomorrow."

"Good Grief! That's a bit short notice, isn't it?"

"I agree, but there's nothing I can do to prevent her from leaving. So, I'm going to resign myself to life without her."

"I'm sorry, Luke. I know how fond of her you are." Eden said. "She's a nice girl; I was fond of her. But, brother, you're still young; you'll look back on this as a very pleasant interlude in your life. I know how you feel, but it'll pass, believe me."

Luke turned back to Hudson who was standing munching grass at the base of the tree where he was tethered. "It is forgotten, Eden." He stated simply. "I do not wish to speak of her again. Let's go home."

Eden looked at his brother's unhappy expression and shook his head. The young man would remember his association with the lovely Cynthia for a short while, then, as time always fades, his love of photography would replace his love for her. He would once again wrap himself up in the artistic world that gave him so much peace and contentment.

"Right . . ." Eden grinned. "I'll race you back."

Luke managed a tight smile and the two young men galloped back to Ravenslea.

At 4:15 that afternoon, the bell rang at the front of Ravenslea Manor. Elspeth, glancing quickly in the hall mirror to flick a grey strand of hair back behind her ear, strode purposely towards the stout door and opened it. With her announcement to the family and staff, she had changed from the dowdy blacks

and greys, to a brighter coloured dress with a delicate yellow trim. With the change of clothes, so came a more acceptable appearance. She knew she looked better and the knowledge was reflected in the smile she flashed to her visitor.

"Good afternoon, Mr. Hallett." She said.

"Good afternoon, Elspeth." Stephen Hallett took off his tweed cap and stepped inside.

"Do come in. The family are waiting for you in the Sitting Room."

"Thank you." He grinned in response. "You are looking especially bright and cheerful, Elspeth, have you had some wonderful news to give you that rosy look?"

She coloured up a little. "Nothing of great importance, Sir." She stepped aside for him to pass into the Sitting Room.

Martin stood up and walked over to him, holding out his hand and smiling warmly.

"Stephen! You're early, but that's good, because now we can talk a little longer. Dinner won't be ready for another hour." He ushered him further into the room. "As you know, we're expecting Gideon Rutledge to arrive around 7:30 tonight. As a precaution, we've also asked Detective Inspector Stanley Wilkins and his sergeant to attend. They should be arriving sometime after Rutledge. I just thought it would be a good thing to have him close by so he can be aware of how the meeting is conducted, what is being said and if there needs to be some police action." He paused at Stephen's frown. "We're not expecting anything, of course, it's just a safeguard."

"Probably a good idea, but don't you think having the police here, could jeopardize our position?"

Martin shrugged. "I would just like him present, Stephen, just to keep a judicial eye on things. I know you're here for that, but it doesn't hurt to have back up, you understand."

Stephen raised an eyebrow. "It's probably a good thing, but we must be sure it doesn't put Rutledge on his guard—it might hamper his honesty if he knows the police are involved."

"I'm sure everything will work out well once the initial conversations become more relaxed." Martin gave him a confident smile knowing that Stephen had reservations on that.

For almost twenty minutes, everyone seemed to want to talk at once to the middle-aged lawyer who was such a favourite among them all. Elizabeth kissed him warmly and asked how his children were doing.

"We haven't seen Jerome, Julian or Josephine in years. You must tell us just what they've been doing with themselves since last we met them. It must have been just after the dreadful war when they came over for a short visit."

"Yes, I think it was now you mention it." Stephen said. "Well Jerome is just finishing University, he's going in for engineering. I was hoping he'd follow on the family business, but he has no head for law, so that was obviously out. Julian is in college in Edinburgh and Jo is now going to commercial school. She wants to become a secretary one of these days. She's got a good head on her shoulders and I know she'll do well." He paused. "They all say that they'd like to come to Ravenslea Manor one day to see you all."

"That would be wonderful." Catherine said, meaning every word. "When this dreadful business is over with, we'd be delighted to have all or any of them come to stay for a while."

Stephen smiled and thanked her. He was now fifty-one-years old and lived in a suburb of Barnstable along with his wife, Beth and their children. He'd taken over the law firm of Hallett, Cardew and Phillips after his parents, David and Deanna Hallett had drowned off the Desdemona. He was a perceptive, fair-minded man whose sharp wit and congenial manner warmed almost everyone to him. A gift, everyone agreed, handed down to him by his eloquent, sharp-witted father.

Over the past few days, Stephen had worked diligently day and night to find evidence on James' whereabouts and activities at the times and dates Catherine and Martin had given him. It had been a long process; a process that required his secretary to accompany him on a hasty trip up North; and the services of the people at Somerset House. He had, in fact, only returned from his trip to London that morning with evidence that he hoped was enough to stop further claims that Gideon Rutledge might have as regards his supposed inheritance.

He was tired, having tried to get a few winks of sleep on the trains from London to Bristol, and then the Branton-Barnstable connection this evening. It wasn't much, but he thought it was enough to sustain him through, perhaps, a gruelling evening. He envisaged questions thrown at him by the young man that might be difficult to answer, but he had methods with which to turn him and sway awkward questions away from uncertain answers. He hoped it would work.

"Dinner's ready." Catherine broke into his thoughts. "Come along, Stephen. I have you seated next to me. I hope you like roast venison?"

Stephen smiled. "I do indeed, but to be honest, I'm not terribly hungry."

"Did you eat on the train, dear? You are not ill are you?" Catherine asked.

Stephen laughed. "Not in the least. Just a little tired, but I did eat something at lunchtime that seems to have satisfied me."

"Lunchtime! That's hours ago. Anyway, it's all laid out in platters and dishes. You can take as much as you want." Martin ushered him into a nearby seat and pulled out the chair next to him. "Wine?"

"A little Merlot, please."

The dinner revived him and at the end when they all convened in the Drawing Room, he was happy to receive a cigar from Martin along with another glass of Merlot.

After dinner, Catherine asked to be excused from the table and moved out into the Hallway. Hurrying up the stairs, she tapped on Lillian's door. It was opened instantly. There were no words spoken. Lillian nodded, knowing exactly what was required of her and closed her door, following the lady of the house back down the stairs to disappear into the Kitchen.

While everyone was making themselves comfortable in the Drawing Room, they heard the sound of a vehicle moving slowly passed the front entrance towards the back of the house. Eden stood up and peered out into the darkness.

"Must be Percy moving one of the vehicles around." He said to no-one in particular.

When the front door bell jangled fifteen minutes later all conversation in the room stopped. All on edge. All uneasy.

The Drawing Room door opened and Elspeth stepped aside to show two gentlemen into the room. Martin held out his hand to the elder of the two men.

"Good evening." He said.

"Good evening." The older man repeated, stiffly, though did briefly grasp Martin's outstretched hand. "I am Edgar Rutledge, Gideon's grandfather. I thought I'd accompany my grandson in case he is faced with a huge delegation of people out to persecute him and steer him away from his rightful inheritance."

"Now, now, grandfather, that's hardly the way to greet people." Gideon glowered at him. He turned to show a fine row of teeth in a smile that encompassed everyone in the room. "I must apologize for my grandfather; he does tend to get a little irrational on times. You must excuse him; he is in his eighties you know."

"Of course." Martin said, biting back a retort. "I'm Martin Thorncroft, Captain James Thorncroft's brother. I don't think we've met." He paused and indicated a chair, then waved his arm to encompass everyone else in the room. "My family." He quickly introduced everyone, telling them only that Stephen was a visiting cousin. They'd find out soon enough that he was also their lawyer. "Would you like a glass of wine, or port?"

"I've not come here to spend a casual, friendly social evening." Edgar Rutledge said, curtly, plopping ungainly onto a plush red velvet chair nearby. "I also don't wish to spend all evening discussing something that, in my mind, is quite cut and dried. I have proof . . ."

"Ah," Stephen moved forward slightly. "That's just it, Mr. Rutledge. We've come together this evening to discuss this 'proof' to which you refer. We are here as a family to dispute your theory. Even though you have condescended to disallow us the original letter, I am certain that the one you have in your possession is nothing but a fake!"

"How dare you!" Rutledge exclaimed, making to get to his feet. His grandson touched his shoulder gently pushing him back down.

"Take it easy, Grandfather. We are, after all, here to discuss this matter as responsible adults. Losing one's temper, especially at the outset, is not prudent." He gave his grandfather a warning glance. "We are here to prove once and for all that should Captain Thorncroft die, Ravenslea Manor will belong to me. It's only natural the Thorncroft family would try to pull out all the stops to prevent that from happening." Gideon's eyes moved from his grandfather to Martin and quickly around the room. He was about to comment further when the metallic clanging of the front door bell could be heard. A few moments later, the door was pushed open and Detective Inspector Stanley Wilkins and his sergeant Frank Owens walked into the Drawing Room with an air of judicial confidence.

"Good evening, everyone. I hope we're not late." Stanley said.

"Good evening Detective Inspector; Sergeant. No, Mr. Rutledge and his grandson have only just arrived. So glad you could come. I don't think you know everyone here. Let me introduce them quickly to you." Martin said, smiling at them.

Once the introductions were made, Stanley immediately surveyed the situation noting how flushed Edgar Rutledge looked as he leaned forward in the plush seat he was sitting on.

"Please continue with your conversations, everyone. I'm just here as an interested observer for the moment."

There was an awkward silence as the two men found seats at the back of the room and sat stiff and formal to quietly watch the proceedings.

"Mrs. Thorncroft," Gideon coughed more nervous now in the presence of the law. He'd never met them, but from the almost paranoid look on his grandfather's face, it appeared he had. He wasn't sure he wanted to go along with any more of this; however, with everyone gathered in this gracious house to discuss his inheritance, he couldn't very well leave now. He sighed and looked back at Catherine. "Is there any change in your husband, Mrs. Thorncroft, that we should be concerned about?"

"No, everything is as it has been since that dreadful day." She replied, cautiously.

"It was mentioned that he was in a coma—although I'm not a doctor, I am quite surprised that a bullet wound would result in a coma. Perhaps you could enlighten me?" Gideon said, frowning.

"My brother had a terrific loss of blood, Mr. Rutledge. I don't know all the medical ins and outs of it; we were informed by the hospital that he'd sunk into a coma. All we can do is wait and hope he will soon pull out of it." Martin replied, glancing quickly at Catherine, noticing her waver. "I cannot tell you anything further than that."

"Oh," Gideon nodded, pursing his mouth. "I see. Well, the fact remains, that whether the Captain dies now or later, I have definite proof that Ravenslea will one day belong to me." He reached into the breast pocket of his jacket and drew out a crumpled piece of paper. "Despite the statement by Mr. Hallett that this is a fake, there is no denying that Captain James Thorncroft agreed to marry my mother all those years ago. Nothing . . . nothing, I say, can possibly fault that. It has the Captain's signature for everyone to see."

"Just a minute, Mr. Rutledge." Stephen stepped forward, carrying a buff folder which he laid on a table and opened. "I took the liberty of visiting Somerset House in London to investigate your birth certificate. It states here that your mother had no connection whatsoever with Captain James Thorncroft in November of 1896, which would be the approximate time of your conception. Your father is listed as 'unknown'. No marriage certificate could be located for your mother so it appears that you were an illegitimate child, Mr. Rutledge."

"This letter is no fake, Mr. . . . Hallett!" Edgar Rutledge had by now risen to his feet, his eyes blazing, blue veins protruding from his neck. "It is genuine!"

"Where did you get it, Sir?" This came from the Detective Inspector, who walked towards him purposefully.

"I . . . I . . ." Edgar Rutledge faltered. ". . . I found it among my daughter's possessions after her death. I had to go through her things, you understand, and there it was. I was horrified, of course, to think that she'd kept that information from me all these years, but I realized that an injustice had been done and my grandson was, in fact, heir to Ravenslea Manor. The rest you know."

Catherine had been standing near the doorway, sidling closer to it with every breath the Rutledges were uttering. Slowly she turned the handle, opening it to allow Lillian to come into the room.

"Father." She said quietly, theatrically, astonishing everyone in the room. "You know I didn't die! You know what you did to me! That piece of paper is as false as a wig!"

Edgar Rutledge swung around to the door, his face losing colour. He seemed to have lost the power to speak. Gideon stared first at the thin woman standing in the doorway, then turned to his grandfather.

"What the Hell is going on, Grandfather? Why did you let me believe that my mother was dead?" Gideon stammered.

Edgar Rutledge's knees seemed to sag and he mopped his brow with a plaid handkerchief he'd pulled from his pocket.

Lillian stepped towards the old man, her back straight, her head high.

"Because, Gideon," she said, staring belligerently at her father. "Your grandfather wanted riches for you. Riches that he knew neither he or I couldn't provide. He wanted the very best for his grandson."

Gideon frowned and moved towards her. "I . . . I can't believe this is really you, Mother?" His voice had softened as he touched her arm, almost as if he was afraid she'd vapourize. "You're telling me that your own father told everyone you were dead . . . for that?" His voice broke.

"You, like everyone else, thought I was dead. My father conveniently 'killed' me off so I would not be in the way of your inheritance. He knew I would disclaim the letter he has shown to everyone as worthless." She paused. "I did receive a letter from James Thorncroft around that time, but it was just a short note, mentioning that he had to return home unexpectedly—nothing resembling that!"

"How did you know about the letter, Lillian?" At last Edgar Rutledge had found his voice. He looked suddenly old and vulnerable.

"Because Mrs. Thorncroft came to see me a little while ago at the Bristol Royal Infirmary where you had me admitted. She'd written down exactly the wording in a letter that Gideon had shown her. I confirmed that it was complete nonsense." She pressed her lips together. "My father also arranged to have James killed, in order to claim the inheritance that he knew was no more his than it was the man in the moon's!"

"But . . . you mentioned the Bristol Royal Infirmary. Were you ill, Mother?"

Gideon was clearly in shock.

Lillian looked up at her son, her eyes melting with love for him. "No, dear. I was perfectly healthy." She turned her attention back to her father, with loathing. "You should ask your Grandfather the reason. Tell him, Father! Tell everyone what you did and how you arranged to have James murdered!"

"I . . . I . . ." Edgar Rutledge was now shaking violently and struggling to his feet.

Stanley stood up and moved beside Stephen. "Edgar Rutledge, you gave me some information pertaining to the gun that was used to shoot Captain Thorncroft. Now, as I have listened to the statement made by your daughter, I'm wondering if you know more about this matter than you're telling us. I have a feeling you know who assaulted Captain Thorncroft? A Bernard Webb, perhaps? He was hired by you to carry out the deed—isn't that what happened?" Stanley's voice was harsh with meaning.

Edgar Rutledge sank back in the seat, mopping his brow and wheezing noisily. Despite his horror at the altercation, Gideon obviously felt some compassion for his Grandfather's predicament. He leaned forward, caught hold of his hand, squeezing it gently in an attempt to calm him. He glanced up at the Detective Inspector coolly.

"Please, be a little gentler on him, Detective Inspector. He's an old man and anything could happen if you push him too far." He turned his attention to Edgar Rutledge whose breathing was laboured. "I think, Grandfather, you'd better tell them what you know. That you had nothing to do with shooting the Captain." Gideon looked down at him. His Grandfather's eyes searched Gideon's wildly and Gideon recoiled. He'd never seen him look so terrified before and for a moment he wasn't sure he recognized the man as he'd known him. "What's wrong?" He said, pulling away and getting slowly to his feet. "You can't know anything more about this . . . can you?"

"He knows far more than he's prepared to tell, Mr. Gideon." Stanley Wilkins said. "I'm going to backtrack here a little. First of all, was your Grandfather at Ravenslea Manor on the night the Captain was shot?"

Gideon raised his eyebrows and gave him a brief smile. "Yes, we both were. We were standing at the back watching the excellent show of fireworks."

"You heard the shot?" Gideon nodded. "Where was your Grandfather at the time?"

Gideon frowned for a moment. "He was standing right beside me. When it was known that Captain Thorncroft had been shot, Grandfather said he had to see what was happening. I was going to accompany him as I was as concerned as everyone else appeared to be, but he shook his head and told me to bring the car around to the front entrance where I would wait for his return. I waited for quite a while, but when he returned to the car, we turned around and went back to Watersfield."

"So, you didn't see which direction he went?" Stanley said, indicating for Owens to make a note of everything that was being said.

Gideon shrugged slightly. "I had no reason to believe he'd do anything different than what he'd said. At the time, I thought it a little odd as neither of us knew the Thorncroft family, but considered it could just be a case of normal curiosity on my Grandfather's part. Then I thought he, perhaps, wanted to convey his concern to the family on the shooting. Why else would he do that?"

"Why else, indeed, Sir. Did you actually see your Grandfather go towards the front of the house?"

Gideon's eyes narrowed. "No. I hurried to get the car."

"Then you don't really know that he went there? He could have gone anywhere? To the woods, perhaps?"

"Look, Detective Inspector," Gideon said, his voice hard, calculating. "I don't know where this is all leading, but if you think I'm going to stand here and answer all your questions at an informal meeting like this, you are sadly mistaken. If you have something you wish to say to my Grandfather and me that will bring this meeting to a close, I'd appreciate if you'd get on with it. After all, we are here simply to state our claim to Ravenslea."

Stanley shrugged. "As you wish." He glanced over to his sergeant. "We do have a reason for going through all of this—perhaps to kill two birds with one stone, if you'll pardon the pun! As you can see, Sergeant Owens has been noting everything that has been said here tonight, from everyone. This will assist us in determining if, in fact, anyone here had any knowledge as to why Bernard Webb was murdered. It may not yield anything, but if it does and we feel it requires further investigation after we leave, then we'll subpoena people to come before the courts. If you wish us to do that, then so be it!"

Stephen touched Wilkins' arm gently. "We should, Detective Inspector, just perhaps clarify one more point regarding the heir to Ravenslea. I have here documents on Captain Thorncroft's whereabouts at the end of 1896." He withdrew some papers and slipped on his spectacles. "At the beginning of September 1896, Jonathon Thorncroft, who was the Master of Ravenslea at the time, along with his son James went up north to deal with a serious dispute at one of the Yorkshire coal mines of which they are partners. They stayed up there for a short while. During this time, Jonathon Thorncroft asked his son, James to honour an appointment at Lloyds Bank in London. James was there only a few days. The document I have here was signed by Lloyds Bank and James Thorncroft, also witnessed by a bank employee; it was signed on . . ." he glanced down at the document in his hand, ". . . September 17th, 1896. He returned to Ravenslea on September 22nd as he had some work to attend to regarding the property. Jonathon Thorncroft was still in Yorkshire during this time." Stephen took off his spectacles and gazed unblinking at the two Rutledges. "I don't think you need to be a mathematician to determine that James was in London months before your daughter's indiscretion and therefore had no involvement whatsoever. I think that should make your claim null and void, Mr. Rutledge."

Lillian moved a little further into the room. "James Thorncroft is not your father, Gideon. I have never given that impression to your Grandfather in the time before or since your birth. I don't know how he managed to copy James' writing and signature on that piece of paper, but that's all it is—a copy. It has no worth at all." She paused, clearly uncomfortable. "You are the result of a brief affair I had with an Irish sailor named Shawn O'Casey in November. He was married at the time, living in Liverpool, I believe. He'd left to go back to sea long before I realized I was even with child, and as I had no way of contacting him, I left it that way. Your Grandmother was upset, naturally, but understood my predicament. She absolutely refused to allow me to abort my child, though Grandfather was ready to pay anything to have that done. I didn't want that and . . . I'm glad I didn't." Her voice softened again as she looked at her son. "Despite everything that's happened, Gideon, I'm proud of you. I don't believe you had any idea what your Grandfather had planned."

"This is ludicrous! Complete nonsense! The letter is genuine—!" Edgar Rutledge suddenly struggled to his feet, leaning heavily on his cane. "The letter was found in your drawer, Lillian. You can't deny it!"

She looked at him, venom in her eyes. She reached into the pocket of her dress and withdrew a crumpled piece of paper. "When I went back to Watersfield to see my father, I found this note crumpled up in a drawer in my bedroom. Something told me to keep it with me—almost like a premonition. This is the letter I'd received from James Thorncroft. It says nothing about him promising to marry me! He and I didn't have that kind of relationship." She thrust the letter into Stephen's hand. "I had asked James to come to my apartment for the evening for a drink after the performance. When I finished my act, the stage door manager handed me this letter. It was from James telling me that he had to return to Devon and couldn't keep the appointment. He was full of apologies as you'll see. I . . . haven't seen him since."

"Why did you keep the letter?" Stanley asked, taking it from her gently.

"Because . . . because I was very fond of James. If I wasn't likely to be seeing him again, I somehow wanted to have something of his to keep. All very sentimental I know, but underneath this rather straggly exterior, I am a sentimental person." She paused.

"How did you get hold of this letter, Mr. Rutledge?" Stanley turned to the old man who'd visibly sagged by now.

"I didn't lie about that! I did find a letter in one of the drawers in my daughter's bedroom years ago. I don't know why I felt it was necessary to keep it; I just did, that's all." He suddenly faltered, running a hand through his thinning hair, twisting his fingers together at the same time. "I . . . I . . . oh, I can't go on! Everyone's against me . . . I'm too old to fight any more. . ."

"That's because, Mr. Rutledge, you know you've been defeated! The letter I have here is the right one. You copied the style of handwriting, including Captain Thorncroft's signature, but made up the note yourself, didn't you?" Stanley shook his head, wondering at the twisted mind of the old man. "It was strange, however, Mr. Rutledge, that you didn't destroy the original. I would have thought you'd have made sure nobody ever found it."

"I . . . I . . . should have. I don't know why I didn't." Edgar Rutledge mumbled incoherently, his old body shaking. He was about to add more, when suddenly, the door opened. Everyone turned.

"I had to come, Catherine! I couldn't let something like this go by without being a part of something so enormously important as the future of my beloved Ravenslea." James walked in, leaning on the arm of a hospital orderly. His face was ashen—obviously the journey had been long and traumatic for him, but his eyes were sparkling with animation.

Startled, Catherine ran over to help the orderly get him to a chair. "Eden! Get him a glass of brandy, he looks frozen." She stared down at him anxiously. When she'd left him this morning, she had no idea he was going to attempt to get here, yet, was not entirely surprised. Knowing how involved and worried he was about this situation, it was exactly what he'd do. A small smile creased her mouth.

"But . . . but!" Edgar Rutledge cried. "You're . . . supposed to be . . ."

"In a coma?" James said, slowly. "Well, I'm sorry to disappoint you, as you can see I'm very much alive. For a while, it was touch and go. There was a real chance I wouldn't make it, because I did lose a lot of blood, plus the bullet was lodged close to my heart. However, I wasn't ready to go and once the bullet was removed, I recovered quite rapidly." He paused and took a sip of brandy that Eden had put onto a small table beside him. "I've also been listening outside the door. You are a depraved, devious man, Edgar Rutledge."

Gideon faced his Grandfather. No longer was he the young man concerned for the old man's welfare. His eyes held an odd expression—one of disbelief bordering on hate.

"Why, Grandfather? Why tell me my mother was dead? I can't honestly believe you did it to trick a bogus inheritance onto me! Can you imagine what kind of problems I would have faced if you had somehow managed to convince everyone you were right?" He took a breath, letting a puff of air escape. "I also can't believe you were responsible for shooting Captain Thorncroft."

"I didn't pull the trigger, Gideon . . ." Edgar Rutledge began.

"No, you didn't; I was testimony to that. However, but from what I've been hearing tonight, it appears that you did hire another man to carry out the assault for you and . . ."

"Gideon, oh Gideon." Edgar Rutledge's shoulders slumped in an attitude of defeat. "I did it for you. I had nothing to offer you and I'm getting old. I was beside myself wondering what to do for your future." He looked away. "Now it doesn't matter any more."

"The Hell it doesn't!" Gideon cried, letting go of his mother's hands. "Tell me why you'd go to such lengths! That's all I want to know—perhaps it'll make some sense if you do."

"Just a minute, Gideon." Lillian laid a restraining hand on her son's arm. "I think I will explain to everyone here—I know James will back me up at least on some of it." She turned to her father. "Sit down, Father. Pardon the cliché, but the game is up! Your plan hasn't worked—you've failed! I thank God you did!"

Everyone in the room returned to their seats, wondering about this agitated altercation, speculating on its outcome with interest. Catherine, clinging to her husband, was relieved as was James. The old man had some serious issues to face and from the look on his face, he knew he'd been beaten.

"First of all," Lillian began, "just to make things a little clearer for those who are probably wondering about what's going on here. I was once known as Lily Starr who worked in a London Nightclub many years ago. I am the daughter of Edgar and Margaret Rutledge and mother of Gideon. By now, I imagine you've all realized that." From there, Lillian recounted what she'd told Catherine the day at the hospital. James intervened here and there to clarify some minor points, but by the time she'd finished, the story had been told to her satisfaction.

"Well," exclaimed Elizabeth sitting at the front and who had been watching Lillian with unabashed interest, "I can't believe a father would resort to such a malicious act to further the future of his family."

Edgar Rutledge was silent.

Stanley stood up, facing everyone. "I think most of you know now that Captain Thorncroft's assailant was a man named Bernard Webb who was shot dead at the edge of Exmoor Forest where it abuts Ravenslea Manor's grounds." He turned to Edgar Rutledge. "The weapon was the same as had been used on Captain Thorncroft on Guy Fawkes night. You intimated to me, Mr. Rutledge, that someone had stolen the gun a few days before bonfire night, but I have since had it confirmed that the only prints found on the gun in Webb's hand, was Webb's and yours. This is enough to arrest you, Edgar Rutledge, for the murder of Bernard Webb."

The old man stumbled to his feet and began to pace the room. Suddenly, he lifted his head higher and walked a little unsteadily towards the Drawing Room door. Once there, he turned, slipped his hand into his jacket pocket and pulled out a gun. He waved it ominously around the group.

"You will not stop me, Detective Inspector. I'm going to leave here now and if anyone gets in my way, I will shoot! Believe me, I will shoot! If I'm guilty of killing Bernard Webb, then it won't make any difference if I shoot as many others as I wish!" He opened the door and backed out. "Don't try to follow me! It will do you no good!" He slammed the door behind him.

Eden opened the door gently just as a blast from the gun slammed into the doorpost. This elderly man obviously meant business. Eden closed it quickly.

"He's crazy!" Stephen leapt to the door and wrenched it open.

"No Stephen!" Catherine cried, running towards him earnestly. "Don't! He tried to have James killed and he'll try to kill you. Don't take any chances, my dear! Let him get away. He'll be found eventually."

At Stephen's hesitation, Gideon suddenly pushed him to one side.

"Grandfather! Grandfather! Stop this!" The young man rushed into the Hallway. Everyone saw Edgar Rutledge turn, a crazed look in his eyes. It was as if he didn't know where he was or what he was doing. He raised the gun and blindly squeezed the trigger three times.

Gideon clutched his chest with an agonized cry and fell to the floor. Rutledge, suddenly coming to his senses, dropped the gun, hesitated then rushed to his grandson's side. At the same time, Lillian screamed and ran over to her son, falling to the floor in a flood of tears.

"Gideon!" She cried, looking him over incredulously. "Oh my dearest, don't leave me! I love you as only a mother can! Please . . ." she collapsed beside Gideon, clutching his limp hand in hers.

Edgar Rutledge looked down at his grandson, his face full of guilt, remorse and defeat. "I did it for you! You have to live! You have to . . ."

With tears in his eyes, Edgar Rutledge slowly stood up, aware suddenly of his actions. "I am guilty . . . I am guilty . . . but you will not imprison me! I'm an old man . . . I intend to cheat the gallows, Mr. Hallett." His voice was suddenly normal; sane and in control.

As if he'd found extra strength, Rutledge turned, picked up the gun and hurried awkwardly out through the front door, slamming it forcibly behind him.

"Come back, Mr. Rutledge . . ." Detective Inspector Wilkins cried. He glanced at his sergeant. "Stop him, Owens. He won't get far!"

At the moment Sergeant Owens opened the front door, a gunshot was heard close by. For a moment everyone was rooted to the spot.

Detective Inspector Wilkins and his sergeant ran to the top of the steps. Halfway down lay Edgar Rutledge!

"Oh my Lord!" Elizabeth cried. "The foolish man has shot himself!"

It was as she'd said. When they found him, Edgar Rutledge lay sprawled on the steps, the gun barrel still warm, blood pouring from a wound in his temple. Stanley knelt down to feel for a pulse, then turned and shook his head. Edgar Rutledge was dead!

CHAPTER 34

APRIL 1931

THE drone of the aeroplane as it soared over the English Channel toward England's misty shores shuddered as temperature disturbances and air currents caused it to drop slightly. It had happened almost all the way across the water, but the two people sitting close together were hardly aware of any discomfort. They were happy just be to together. Stephanie snuggled contentedly against her new husband, her dishevelled reddish/brown hair laying in disarray against his shoulders.

She was drowsy, thinking of the wonderful two weeks she and Eden had spent on their honeymoon in Paris. In Montmarte, the little café with small lanterns overhead that they'd visited on the first night. She smiled as she recalled the middle-aged waiter, standing with head and shoulders slightly bowed, a white napkin draped over his left arm as he waited patiently for them to order. The slightly vinegary red wine Eden had chosen, which she didn't particularly like, but sipped some anyway. Then the romantic horse and carriage ride around the Place de la Concorde with the moon shining, it appeared, just on them, as if it knew they were so much in love and had only spent two married days together. The Louvre—how she loved the beautiful portrait of Mona Lisa with the gentle smile; the Arc de Triomphe; the beautiful Champs Elysees and the Paris Opera House where they'd heard a wonderful French version of La Traviata. Eden had even coaxed her into seeing the loud, happy Can Can performed at the Moulin Rouge. Then so completely different—the quietly reverent Sacre Couer Cathedral situated so close to their hotel. Her mind tumbled over with all the sights she'd seen and knew she'd never forget.

He turned his head a little to plant a kiss on top of the beautiful curls, a smile of love crossing his handsome face. Neither of them had ridden in an aeroplane before and they loved the experience, vowing that from now on, it was the only way they would ever travel overseas.

Stephanie stirred out of her daydreams, opened her eyes and stared out the tiny slightly distorted oval window. How fascinating, she thought, to be so high off the ground; above the clouds with a never-ending blue canopy of sky covering them. Instead of feeling afraid at the height, she smiled feeling safe in the arms of the man she loved so much. She sighed, shifting her position and disturbing the contented man at her side.

"You okay, my love?" He murmured.

"Umm." She said, looking up at him. "I'm in Heaven." She looked up at him and they both giggled. "Well, perhaps not literally, but being beside you and looking out that window does give me that impression!" She turned to kiss his lips gently.

"Paris was everything you imagined?" He asked, presently.

"I loved it, Eden. I want to go back on our anniversary every year!"

He grinned and tweaked her nose affectionately. "Some years we will, dear, but I'd like to see other places like Rome, Madrid, even take a trip to the New World and see America and Canada. But for now, we'll remember our wonderful honeymoon and the love we shared in Paris."

"It'll mean more to me than any other place we visit, Eden." She murmured.

The rest of the journey was uneventful and when they arrived in London, the rain had lessened to a drizzle on the runway. Once they'd passed through Customs and were out on the wet street, Stephanie saw Percy walking towards them quickly, a huge smile on his pleasant face. He welcomed them warmly and quickly taking hold of a carry-on bag that Stephanie had clutched in her hand, stowed it carefully in the boot of the Rolls Sedanca.

By the time they reached the outskirts of London, the rain descended upon them again, but it didn't mar their enjoyment. Percy drove slower than normal, trying to keep the ride smooth for the young lovers in the back. A couple of hours later, they decided to rest for a while before returning to Ravenslea. Near the town of Swindon, they registered at a small country Inn. The proprietor's experienced eyes could see these two young people were on their honeymoon and showed them to the best room in the house. Despite their devotion to one another, it was obvious the journey had been too tiring and before long Eden and Stephanie fell into contented sleeps, their arms around each other.

The next morning, Percy continued the journey, even though the rain cascaded over the car like a waterfall. A few hours later they arrived safely at Ravenslea.

As the Sedanca stopped at the bottom of the steps, the front door opened to reveal Catherine and James standing close together, smiling happily at their son and daughter-in-law. Almost immediately, they were joined by the rest of the family. Penelope and Fletcher stood alongside Catherine to greet their daughter and son-in-law.

Elizabeth watched from close by, her heart light. She'd been feeling so much better over the last few days. Having her beloved stepson back in the role of Master of Ravenslea had done much to ease her spirits and accelerate the healing process. The look of love between her grandson and his lovely new bride brought tears to her eyes as her memory became flooded with the wonderful feelings she had when she and Jonathon had first been married. She sighed as Eden began ascending the steps.

With Stephanie close beside him, Eden moved up the steps, oblivious to the rain soaking their hair and clothes. What did a little rain matter when one was so happy! As he neared his parents, Eden felt a sudden sense of pride and love for the wonderful family he'd been so lucky to have been born into.

Catherine slipped her arm around Stephanie's shoulders in a warm, comfortable embrace and James kissed his new daughter-in-law affectionately.

Rebecca and William, their arms interlocked professing their love, disengaged themselves long enough to give their respective siblings hugs and good-humoured teasing. Elizabeth drew them to her breast in a bear like hug as did Martin, Louise and Adam who was standing close to Allison.

As they all went into the house out of the rain, Lillian's petite figure dressed in a light grey and white gown, stood a little apart from the other staff, her face wreathed in smiles. She had been offered and accepted the job of housekeeper, taking over from Elspeth and she'd not regretted it. Now that Gideon was gone from her, she only wished to belong to a family; the Thorncrofts had made it very clear that she was more than welcome to become part of the Ravenslea household. Her warmth and generous nature became an instant success with Agnes, Doris and Edna as well as Abraham, Joshua, Mike and Percy.

Ravenslea Manor had returned its loving family to its bosom. Although no-one can see what will happen as time goes by, for the moment it looked as if nothing would mar the happiness of future Thorncroft generations. As the door shut behind them, the sun appeared, bathing the beautiful mansion in a rosy glow. Suddenly from one of the trees surrounding the grounds, a lone raven flew towards the house to settle itself at the bottom of the steps on top of one of the round stone posts. His perky bright black eyes stared up at the house, squawked and took flight, but only a short distance away. The ravens had returned. A symbol of peace and stability for all the occupants of the gracious mansion.

Even though in a few short years, life in Britain would be jeopardized, danger would not touch the beautiful mansion; there would no longer be clouds to threaten the Thorncrofts of Ravenslea Manor.

THE END